The Viper and
his Majesty

Written by Tiana Laveen
Edited by Natalie G. Owens
Cover layout by Travis Pennington

"Amor dey Rey!

To all outsiders... I'm not your friend. I'm not your enemy. I don't love you. I don't hate you. Simply put, I don't give a fuck about you. If by chance we should cross paths, and you decide to test me, see if the rumors are true about King Viper, then I'm going to pass your exam with flying colors of gold and black, and give you something to talk about. My name will be the last words you ever say, and they'll be written in your own blood..."

—Dominic 'Viper' Martinez

BLURB

Dominic 'Viper' Martinez knows nothing about walking the straight and narrow. As a notorious Miami-born Cuban gang member, his life has been rife with ups and downs, many of those years spent behind steel bars. Yet, he came out the other side dripping in gold and black, like his Latin King colors. Money and survival are all he has on his mind, until a sexy, headstrong woman moves into his neighborhood and causes ample distraction...

Majesty Wilson is tired. She's tired of lies. She's tired of the disrespect at her job. She's tired of no-good-men who see cheating as a way of life. Raising her nine-year-old son solo has been the most difficult job she's ever had, but her love for her child drives her to make a better life for the two of them. After moving into her new home, she comes face to face with King Viper. Repulsion and fear surface, yet sparks fly between them. Fangs out, he threatens to sink them deep into Majesty but perhaps, for her only, his bark is louder than his bite.

Dominic has never encountered a woman like Majesty, and her unexpected presence causes a storm to brew. He has one foot in Heaven and the other in Hell, but he can only serve one Master. Will that Master be love or hate?

Immense obstacles, shocking secrets from the past, and devastating blows lay at the feet of the couple, demanding their attention, and testing their resolve.

Majesty is tough, but Dominic melts the ice around

her heart. Can she trust a man who has spent his days mostly doing the Devil's work? Will he behave like his namesake, the snake that would strangle their love by winding his sins around it, thus snuffing it out, once and for all?

 Read "The Viper and his Majesty" to find out!

COPYRIGHT

<u>Please do not skip this section.</u>
The warning is here for your protection and to provide a heads up.

This book is intended for mature eyes ONLY. As the author, I never wish for my readers to be blindsided. If any of the below-mentioned topics offend you or may be a trigger, please proceed with caution:

1. Profanity

2. Graphic sexual encounters

3. Discussions and instances of racism, injustice, and prejudice, which include racial slurs

4. Plentiful graphic violence, including gang activity.

5. Discussions of abuse, mental illness, and neglect

6. Drug usage, drinking alcohol as well as smoking cigarettes and cigars.

7. Criminal behavior

8. Loss of loved ones

* <u>Please note:</u> This book goes into detail regarding the gang affiliation and related activities of the main character/hero: Dominic 'King Viper' Martinez. Creative license was exercised. However, extensive research was involved for the integrity and accuracy of this novel. That being said, it is merely a work of fiction, and any resemblance or likeness to any real-life person, place or thing, described or noted in this text, is purely coincidental.

This book does not condone nor encourage any criminal activity associated with the gang in question, or any other group or organization. Thank you.

Oh, one more thing: For those unfamiliar with my work, I purposefully write 'goddamn' as 'gotdamn.' It's an intentional spelling error. Just personal preference.

Let's continue…

DEDICATION

This book is dedicated to fresh air, great music, hot tea with honey, the art and science of falling in love, rainy days, stormy nights, burning candles, positive vibes, pretty potions, the excitement of a much-anticipated eBook, and the intoxicating scent of a new paperback book.

"A room without books is like a body without a soul." — Cicero

TABLE OF CONTENTS

Love Letter to my Readers

I want to first thank each and every person who purchased this book, "The Viper and his Majesty.' This is a new journey you've agreed to venture on and explore, and I am grateful that you chose one of my written babies to take such a trip. A lot has transpired in the last year and a half or so, and I had made the decision to write from the heart, which I always do, but also to bring more broken people to your doorstep, with no excuses or apologies. What that means is, the men featured in this book are for me, what civilization deems perhaps physically appealing, but internally, less desirable. Broken men have been the protagonists of tales since the beginning of time.

Broken means different things to different people. For some, it can mean someone not in tune with their feelings. For others, it can mean someone who is very much in tune with their feelings, but still chooses to express themselves in a socially unacceptable way. For others it can correlate with a sense of unrequited love, as in being heartbroken; and for many, it simply means a person who fell down and has not yet gotten back up.

I believe most adults would classify themselves as broken at some point in their life. We would not necessarily need to be drug addicted, incarcerated, or violent by nature to be deemed as such. It could be a case of losing a job and not knowing how we will pay our bills so panic sets in. Or perhaps, a painful divorce. There comes a time in all of our lives when we are dealt a blow. Sometimes, that blow is a consequence of our own behaviors; other times, it comes from something we had absolutely no control over. We accumulate these blows year after year, to varying degrees. The magic in being broken is the promise of being whole again. I want you to meet these shattered individuals and see them pull themselves together – one cracked piece at a time.

Being whole again is not initially on our hero's radar in his early years. The concept of mending himself is a foreign, abstract state of mind for the Viper. If we are not acknowledging that we're fractured in the first place, then there is no call to action to mend those cracks, correct? Why would we call a repairman for a HVAC unit we deem in perfect working condition? Or perhaps we do know it is broken, but we would rather pretend it is not in order to avoid the bill. There are consequences to ignoring our flaws and faults, especially when they negatively impact us, as well as those that we care about. Dealing with our issues always requires a payment of sorts. This can come in a sum of tears, it can come in disbursement of shame, but it must first be paid with admission of the truth. With that, oftentimes, comes pain.

Dominic has suffered a great deal of pain in his life due to his environment, life choices, wayward friends, and corrupt family members. These trials and tribulations were to be expected, and he must navigate them to the best of his ability. Sometimes, these routings take him circles, such as, entering the prison pipeline. Showing bravado and machismo is far more important than admitting a hard fact which requires self-analysis, honesty, and a plan of action for self-correction and healing. Ironically, Dominic AKA King Viper has attempted to begin that process—but he is a fledgling. However, at the moment that you meet him, he is ripe for intervention. He simply doesn't know it yet.

That 'yet' is a door to be opened. And that door is across the street.

Now in walks Majesty Wilson… Majesty is the type of woman who is quite aware of herself and calls things as she sees them. She's a single mother raising a son and trying to keep him safe and secure, while keeping herself together. Majesty is dealing with her own demons, but like Dominic, she avoids delving too deeply in past traumas that were out of her control.

Both are trying to get a new start on their lives, and at first, they fail to understand that their meeting at the right place and the right time was almost like divine intervention. This is not necessarily a case of opposites attract, for Viper and Majesty have obvious differences, one being that Viper is Cuban American and Majesty is

Black/African American. Still, they have a fair share in common. They're resourceful. Intelligent. Funny. Serious. And in need of more… More time. More understanding. More love.

So, without further ado, let's see what happens between these two people who meet one another and never knew what hit them. Get yourself something delicious to drink, perhaps a snack or two, curl up in your favorite chair or the comfort of your bed, and let's lie low in the grass, looking for the Viper slithering in the night.

Viper and his Majesty have been expecting you. Come right in…

CHAPTER ONE

Party Crasher

D OMINIC STOOD IN his long backyard as the Miami sun set behind wispy clouds. Sylvan Lacue's, 'Clam Chowda' blared from two towering speakers set on the cobblestone patio about twenty feet away, with lights flashing in tune with the cold, hard beat. The woofers pulsed and vibrated; he could feel the music crawl within and strangle the depths of his soul. Smoke eddied from his cigar and the lingering taste of Don Julio clung on his palette as he bobbed his head, enjoying the music, while the cool grass tickled his bare feet. He watched the people in the near distance, milling under a canopy of black and gold balloons and colorful flags and banners. Three of his

Pit Bulls, Chance, Sarge and Belleza, played in the yard and lazily rolled about around him, their glistening royal blue rhinestone and studded collars glinting in the light. Their wagging pink tongues lopped off to the sides of their wide-open mouths.

Chance's eyes were glossy as wet, onyx jewels. Bending down, he gave a good belly rub to the blue Pit Bull in a playful mood, then stood to continue surveying the scene. A breeze caught his hair, and it felt good massaging his skin and hitting his sweaty T-shirt. He felt the buzz of his iPhone in his pocket but didn't bother to check who was texting him. He'd been on the phone for most of the day, including an important call a few minutes earlier for which he'd needed the privacy of his backyard, so now he just wanted some peace.

His thoughts wandered like nomads. *Sometimes it's a good idea to step away, get a better perspective.* He was always watching. Always on the lookout. Even at home. Viper's guard was always up, like a teenage boy's cock in the wee hours of the morning. He figured his behavior bordered on paranoia, but one could never be too careful. Everyone was a suspect; everyone could be paid to turn their back and do the unthinkable.

The world around him was usually loud, in stereo. Music, laughter, cursing and fighting. But he'd gotten used to the quiet lately. Still, it felt just fine to have the Kings and Queens close by after such a long time away. It almost felt normal.

His phone buzzed again. He pulled it out of his pocket, hit the red decline call icon, and put it back. *I told her to stop calling me. I told her what the deal was when we met.* Janet was a strange woman. Cute, overly bubbly, far too idealistic and totally not his type personality wise, yet the bar waitress had an incredible set of tits he couldn't resist. He'd fucked her a couple of times a month ago and hadn't spoken to her since.

His phone vibrated a third time. Now she seemed to be leaving a voicemail. He'd delete that later without listening to it. He'd made himself clear. It wasn't his fault she didn't want to listen.

He sniffed the air and smiled. The pungent smells of gun smoke and residual firecrackers, grilled barbecue ribs, a whole pig on a drum, roasted corn, and tender chicken filled the air. He'd eaten a hamburger and a couple of hot sausages on warmed buns earlier, but now the feast was *really* about to begin. His Reye, Jose, also known as King Brick, was cooking. Jose was sometimes called Chef because he could really throw down on the grill. He was stout, solid, and bald. Dark, bushy eyebrows hovered above slanted dark brown eyes. A thick black mustache covered the guy's upper lip, making him appear perma nently frowning, and his signature diamond stud earring caught the sunlight and sparkled just right. As if knowing he was looking at him, Jose waved his fist in the air and laughed. He was the man on the grill. Viper offered a smile and chuckle, and waved right back.

Jose's prominent sun-braised gut was covered in pris on tattoos and the depressed and reddened scar of an old stab wound. Dominic took a drag of his cigar, watching as his amigo slowly turned the meat on one of two bulky grills, all while keeping a steady grip on a chilled bottle of beer and a cigarette dangling from his lips. The swine kept on cooking, flavoring the air, until it was soon falling off the bone. The boisterous crowd of friends was clearly enjoying the 'Welcome Home' party of their recently released brother, King Stacks—birth name: Pedro—one of Dominic's closest friends.

"Hey, Ashley. Relax. Chill," Stacks called out to one of the women that most of them in attendance barely knew. The lady was clearly intoxicated, picking fights with some of the other women over her man, Pedro. A short, scrappy woman with dark brows and a red skunk streak down the side of her hair, she didn't seem to realize she was playing with fire by getting mouthy with the queens. Stacks' ex-girl, Gia, was there, and was no stranger to slicing a throat or beating someone into their next lifetime. Gia had served five years for drug trafficking and aggravated assault, but the crimes she hadn't served time for were the ones that would make most strait-laced civilians' blood curdle. He smirked as he watched the show. Craziness. The strange woman kept going off, saying reckless things… things that would promise her an ass-kicking, if not a trip to the E.R. or perhaps the morgue.

She speaks like she's stupid. She's gotta be an idiot to let her jealousy make her speak to these women this way. She's not even that attractive. What the fuck is Pedro thinking bringing her here? She's going to get killed if she doesn't shut up.

"I saw you! And you pulled his elbow, trying to get him to kiss you!" the woman railed, her voice carrying louder and louder. The crowd had thickened around them, making it hard for him to make out what transpired from such a distance.

Stacks had been talking to Ashley while in prison, and now, she wanted to piss on her property and mark her territory – let everyone know that Stacks belonged to her, and her alone.

Things began to die down, and the crowd dispersed. The lady wrapped her arm possessively around Stacks' long, tattooed arm, her dark eyes darting back and forth, and held him close, as if on the lookout to beat up any woman who dared to even glance in his general direction.

Some of these women go crazy over my boy, Stacks. If a fight breaks out, I'll have to have Marie or Charlotte break it up.

The music grew a bit louder. He hadn't even noticed that someone had turned it down during the melee, as if to increase the tension. A lot of his brothers enjoyed a good cat fight. He imagined some may have even been instigating. All that was petty shit though, inconsequential. He looked past Ashley, and concentrated on the man of the hour. He'd barely had any time to speak to him. He'd bide his time and get with Stacks soon. Right then, Viper wasn't certain what to make of him.

Stacks looked almost like a completely different man from when he'd last seen him. He was heavier, more muscular. He used to be rail thin. So much so, jokes were made about how if a gust of wind blew or someone farted too hard close to him, they'd never see him again. He'd looked like a kid when he got locked up the last time. Now, he appeared beyond his earthly years. Though he'd beefed up and now looked like a formidable opponent, prison had beat up any shred of innocence he had left. Time and struggles were etched across his face like book chapters with footnotes and scribbled quotes, and he had a vacant expression, the light was gone from his amber eyes, now adorned with crow's feet and two teardrop tattoos. The man had just spent nine years in Union Correctional Institution. At one point, they'd been in together, along with several other Latin King brothers.

"Motherfucker, you can't beat me at dominoes! I'll take all of your money tonight. *Lo prometo.*" Nester chortled as he grabbed Pedro and hugged him tight.

"The cake is coming! We're going to bring it out. Make way," Marie called out from the open patio door of the kitchen. "Turn the music off." She yelled and snapped her thick fingers, a vexed expression on her wide, rosy-cheeked face as everyone barely paid her any attention. "We're going to sing to Pedro," she added when no one moved or did a thing.

"Why? It's not his birthday!" Javier smirked and shrugged. "Just cut the fuckin' cake, Marie."

"*¡Vete a casa!*"

"Go home? Why?" Ashley wasn't the only one lit. Javier had had too much to drink, too. He often said the wrong thing when smashed. Tonight was no exception.

Marie ignored the man, sucked her teeth, and turned away from the door. Her salt and pepper hair was pulled taut in a ponytail, and dark red rose tattoos that extended up the side and back of her neck stood out against her light, golden skin. Marie was a revered Latin Queen, one of the few that had survived the decades of violence that had stirred like the beginning flames of hell, then had exploded into an all-out inferno in the late 1990s. She was treated like a favorite aunt by all in Little Havana, and came across as if she wouldn't hurt a fly, but when the night fell, the whispers about her were true. She was dangerous when provoked, and would protect her own at all costs.

She'd paid her dues, had survived several bouts in prison, even took the rap for charges she hadn't committed, all to keep her ol' man safe. She was streetwise, and her tongue still curled with the heavy ethnic cream of a defiant Cuban accent that wouldn't dare let go. She'd come to America with her sisters and father at the age of seventeen, from her hometown of Santa Clara. Yes, everyone knew Marie. Three of her sons had been gunned down in the last several years, and her revered husband, Latin King Kilo, an elder, was serving a life sentence in Chicago for the murder of two rival gang members from The Satan's Disciples. She'd helped Viper several times, offering advice, letting him in on information that served him well, and treated him as well as her own children. At times, he needed that, regardless of his refusal to ever admit such.

People ignored Marie's request after she returned once again, demanding silence, so Dominic pulled himself away from his shady tree and the dogs lying at his feet, clapped loudly, then whistled. He had a whistle that was so loud, it rattled bones. The music immediately stopped. When *he* clapped and whistled, that meant everyone's attention was needed right away. Anyone who kept fucking around would suffer the consequences. Now things were so quiet, he could hear a lawn mower in the distance, and the revving of a motorcycle engine as it zoomed down the street.

"Javier, apologize to Marie for how you spoke to her earlier."

Everyone looked at the man, then at Marie.

"But I was just—"

"Motherfucker, don't argue with me. Apologize." Dominic crossed his arms and cocked his head to the side. Waiting. He was counting in his head. If he reached the three seconds mark, there was going to be a problem. A big one.

"Marie, I'm sorry." Seeming to sober up, Javier quickly lowered his gaze, first to the ground then at nothing in particular. The silence was deafening.

Dominic snapped his fingers, and the music began to play again, then the talking and partying resumed. The exhale from held breaths filled the world once more.

Viper suddenly felt out of place, despite the smile he kept on his face. Something didn't feel right. Something was missing. His home was beautiful, but he hated being away from Little Havana, where he still had family and friends. The people at the party weren't in their element. They all had traveled to *him*, just as it had been planned. He craved the familiar crowd of Little Havana, his King comrades, family and brothers, the familiar restaurants, shops and nightlife, but for now, this would simply have to do. Things had gotten hot, but he had business to attend to, and the last thing he needed was to go back to prison. He'd been out for three years and never wished to return, though he had to admit, some days it seemed easier wished for than done.

"Marie and Pedro, stand together," he ordered. People made way as the woman presented the big cake covered in layers of icing. She set it on the glass patio table, then wrapped her arms around Pedro who seemed to struggle to muster a sincere enough looking grin. He took a few photos of the two on his phone, then after Marie lit the flickering candles on the big white cake with black lettering and white and gold frosting, they all began to sing,

"Na, na, na, naaaaah! Na, na, na, naaaaah, Hey! Hey! Hey! Look who's ouuut! Na, na, na, naaaaah! Na, na, na, naaaaah, Hey! Hey! Hey! Look who's ouuut!" Pedro burst out laughing, showing a mouth full of gold before blowing out the candles. Everyone surrounded him now, holding and pulling him into vigorous hugs. When the man was finally able to come up for air, he raised his index, thumb and baby finger of both hands, overlapping them, forming a crown. The others followed suit to the rap tune of 'Shooter,' by Hector, which blasted through the speakers.

"Hey, we want to all officially welcome Pedro home," Dominic yelled over the music, which was immediately turned down again to allow him to speak. "It's been a long ass time. This, here is my brother." He pointed to the man with his tattooed hand. "When Marie asked if we could have the party here for Pedro, I didn't hesitate." Marie was smiling from ear to ear. "You're home now. I have your back. We have your back. Kings don't die. One crown. One nation!"

"*Amor dey Rey!*" many began to chant as the music was turned back up. "*Amor dey Rey!*"

After a while, a second wave of food covered plates began to pass back and forth. The eating, carousing, and dancing was nonstop. Liquor, wine coolers, and ice-cold beers were replenished and people indulged in the decadent cake, big bowls of fresh berries and mangos, and ice cream.

As the night drew on, and the setting sun was replaced with the glow of the fire pit, tiki torches, and half-moon, he found himself sitting back on a lawn chair, a celebratory cigar in hand. It wasn't long before Stacks approached him, puffing on a joint and donning his familiar tilted smile. This time, it didn't seem hard to come by. The guy stood there for a bit, as if not certain what to do with himself.

"Sit down, man," Dominic encouraged, pointing to the chair beside him. Chance barked at a passing car that was coming down the street. "Chance." He whistled then stomped his foot. "No. Silent." The dog immediately sat back down on his haunches, whimpering, then looked away sheepishly.

"How'd you train him like that, man?" Stacks took a drag of his joint and shook his head in disbelief.

"I learned the dog's language."

Pedro laughed. "I'm serious, Viper."

"I'm serious, too."

"Come on, man. Stop bullshittin'. I want you to teach me how you do it. I can't be out here sellin' anymore."

"Not just anyone can train dogs well, Stacks. They have to respect you. That's not something you teach. You either have it or you don't." Their eyes settled on one another. After a while, Stacks looked away and shrugged.

"You train these dogs like it isn't shit. Been doin' it for years. Glad you're able to make a business out of it now. Maybe I can get into it, too." The man reached down and ran his fingers along Sarge's head. "You're like the dog whisperer. Nothin' but a thing. I know you make nice cash doin' it, too."

Dominic nodded in agreement.

"Yeah, it's decent money. People come to me when they've got a dog no one else can break. That language thing though, sounds funny but yeah, I'm serious." He looked at his pets, then back at Pedro. "Everything and everyone has a language, my man. Even grasshoppers and fleas."

"So the dogs tell you how to talk to them?" Pedro burst out laughing before he could even finish getting the sentence out.

"Nah, that's stupid. That was a dumb thing to say." Pedro's smile immediately faded. "It's not up to anyone to teach someone else how to rule over them. Ya know, someone who wants to be their master will know their native tongue, and that's what I am. It's up to *me* to figure it out." He pointed at himself. "Trainers are a dime a dozen. If you learn and understand what drives a beast to act, to obey, to do everything you say, then you rule them. That's what makes me a master."

Stacks stared at him long and hard, then smirked.

Dominic mirrored the expression.

"I see you're on that Mr. Miyagi shit today." They both burst out laughing. "Thanks for havin' this party for me, man. I really appreciate this." They knocked fists together, then Stacks looked away, running his hand across the stubble on his cheek.

"Of course. *Tu eres mi hermano.*"

"Yeah, we'll always be brothers, man. No blood needed. No prison bars can keep us away from each other for long, either." Dominic nodded. "I got your birthday card."

Dominic gave him a quizzical look. "Birthday card? It's not my birthday."

"Nah, man. Not *that* birthday card." Stacks grinned as he dug in his jeans pocket and pulled out a folded piece of paper. After unfolding it, he handed it over. Dominic took it from him, and burst out laughing. It was his old mugshot and charges. The very first time he was sent to prison.

"Ahhh, man!" He chuckled. "Where'd you get this shit?"

"From Juvey." His chest filled with warmth. "He gave it to me last year before he got moved out of my cell. Told me to give it to you." King Juvey was dead. Good dude. He'd been killed in prison. The guards had found him in his bed, his neck slit. No one around. No snitches. No witnesses. No one was certain what had happened, but he had his suspicions. They'd all been close, grew up on the same street.

Dominic placed his cigar down in the black and green sugar skull ashtray he'd placed on the arm of the lounger, and read the prison intake information.

"Damn, this is so old… Let's see." He read the info.

Name: Dominic Martinez
Hair color: Black
Eye color: light hazel
Age: 22
Height: 6'3
Weight: 235 lbs.
Gang Affiliation – Latin Kings
Nickname – King Viper/Viper…

It was then that he noticed that it was not just his first charges listed, but everything was up to date. He continued to read the penal laundry list.

Rank in gang – Warlord – (LKs call this 3rd crown.)

Notable Tattoos – Cross on forehead, Crown on chest, 'Viper' on upper chest, Eagle wings on chest, Cuban black hawk on left side of chest, Christ crown on lower neck, Cuban flag on back of neck, 'L.K.' on side of neck, ADR on front of neck, Aztec structure on neck, Diamond on abdomen, large viper snake wearing crown on back – covers entirety of back, 'L.K' written beneath it, five black dots denoting five point crown on left shoulder, war symbol – Trojan with shield on left arm, large lion on right shoulder, skull with third socket for eye, three point and five point crown on hands, money signs on upper hands… and so it continued.

Prior incarcerations: 7

*Prior charges: Aggravated assault (13), resisting arrest (2),
2nd degree manslaughter (2), 3rd degree manslaughter (1),
larceny/theft (2), attempted bribery (2), breaking and
entering (1), 2nd degree murder (1), firearm use (13), motor
vehicle theft (2)*

Dominic continued reading the list of his transgressions, then turned the sheet over and checked out his old mugshot. He didn't feel anything when he looked into the eyes of a guy who'd been pretending to be tougher and harder than he was at the time, just to survive. But now, he truly was. He at times had to remind himself to smile. To feel. To simply *be*. The young man standing there in that creased, old photo had a look of death in his eyes, but on the inside, he'd been falling apart for years prior to that first incarceration. His first time going to prison had been a living nightmare. Viper had been afraid after sentencing, but he couldn't show it. He recalled so well how he knew he had to find his people in that institution once he got in there, or he'd be a target. He'd already been told what to expect from his brothers in the Nation. Prison wasn't a matter of *if* for his kind; it was *when?*

He had to find his niche, and if punked, he had to put in work. No insult or disrespect could go unpunished. He'd spent several initial days in the hole for fighting, and he'd made sure he won each and every combat. Later in life, after his third stint, things were more hectic, but he had a reputation to uphold. He'd climbed the ranks in the Nation by age twenty-seven. This brought a new set of problems behind bars. Most notably, he'd been jumped by three Crips all at once.

At one point he'd even temporarily lost his hearing in his left ear after being punched so hard on the side of his face. Once word spread that he was a Latin King Warlord, all bets were off. If you could take down a LK Warlord, that gave you big ass prison stripes. A badge of honor. You were considered the shit. After all, warlords were the ones that put in work. They were the enforcers. The muscle. The brawn. The best fighters. Fastest shooters. Quickest to stab. The tanks of the army. A one-man wrecking ball.

His enemies came unarmed that day, nothing but their fists. That was their first mistake. They knew his title, but not what he was about. He'd earned that shit, fair and square. You couldn't be a weak motherfucker, or stupid, to get the title of Warlord. One thing he was taught on the streets was to always know your opponent. Study him from a distance, bide your time, then strike like a viper. They'd done none of that. They also didn't understand him down to his black, rotten core. He didn't like to fight. Dominic *loved* it.

The pent-up energy residing inside him from years of emotional and mental torment had reached a head. He'd been prepared to unleash on anyone tempting fate. After all was said and done, he'd ended up with two minor scratches and a black eye, yet all three of his assailants got a trip to the infirmary. He fought three motherfuckers at once, with nothing but his knuckles, machismo, and strength, and that went down in history. He knew he couldn't keep at this shit forever, though. Unlike some of his comrades, he never got comfortable in the joint. That was no way to live. He needed his freedom. Vipers need room and space to roam. To hunt… and they preferred to work alone.

Dominic had to work hard to get out of that place, but also make his way up the Latin King levels. He was smart. He knew a hell of a lot about the law, so he imparted his knowledge to those in need. He knew the best Miami lawyers to hire, and which ones to avoid due to his mentor's affiliations. He knew about the judges, and how to impact, intimidate, and divide witnesses and juries should a case go to trial. He knew what prison guards from various slammers could be bribed or blackmailed. He knew all of this and more from his stints in jail, before he'd even served his first time in prison. He'd then perfected his knowledge once he'd entered the penitentiary.

Having murder charges definitely helped him establish a reputation, versus some of the guys in for petty drug charges or domestic violence. Over time, his enemies appreciated he wasn't afraid to kill. Regardless, that first second degree murder charge was bullshit. He'd killed far more before that, and certainly afterwards. That was just the charge the cops knew about. The one that had gotten messy. Snakes rattle, but never roll. Kissing and telling was for suckas. *Fucking jealous ass snitches…*

Dominic shoved the birthday card in his pocket. He casually picked up his cigar and took a long drag.

"How's that money? You good?" he asked Stacks, wanting to ensure his friend was okay.

"Oh yeah. I collected a lotta money tonight, too." Pedro jammed his hand in his pocket, pulled out a wad of crisp cash and flashed it proudly. "Should be enough for me to get my own spot if my parole officer lets me change my address from my mother's house anytime soon. I'm sure someone will take cash." The guy looked down, as if needing to work out the plan in his mind right then. "My girl tried to get me to come with 'er, but I don't think that's the right move. She's kinda possessive. Likes to yell and hit 'nd shit when she's drunk. If she hits me, it'll be a problem, man. I could fuck around and end up right back in prison so I think being on my own right now is the better option."

Dominic leaned forward and held his breath, but it was short-lived. He burst out laughing so hard that his chest burned with heat.

"Possessive, huh? Is that what they call that shit I saw tonight?" He laughed so much, his cheeks hurt. "That chick is crazy, man."

"Awww, come on, Viper." Stacks laughed lightly as he ran his hand along his knee.

"She's a fuckin' psycho. Real talk. You'll catch a case, just like you said. Drunk or sober, makes no difference. *Mujer loca!*"

"Yeah, she's a little crazy but she's aiight, Viper. She held me down when I was away."

Dominic understood that. He reached for his beer bottle and then realized his precious beasts had left him, seemingly all at the same time. He peered towards the patio, and could make out two of their forms. Then the third one came into view. The three Pit Bulls were lapping water and downing chunks of steak he'd bought for them the night before. *Marie must've filled their bowls.*

"I met her online," Stacks continued. "Always had money 'cause of her, and *you*… and she's been there since I got out. My family sure as fuck wasn't holdin' me down."

He got the double meaning behind the words…

Dominic shrugged, not wanting to discuss a woman that he knew would be gone in a matter of months, if that long. No one would ever remember her name or face once Stacks kicked her to the curb. Life was a revolving door of women who either stayed during a jail or prison term, left, and then were replaced by prisoner groupies, vulnerable ladies, or lonely women looking for love. They'd visit. Put money on their books and if the prison was set up right and the guards fraudulent enough, these girls would let them get in a quick fuck, fill them full of cum then send them on their way.

"That shouldn't be a problem. The whole change of address to your mother's…" He pulled on the cigar as he shook away the wayward thoughts. "If it is, let me know."

Stacks ran his hand over his spiky buzz cut.

"So how's it been livin' out this way, Viper? Out in Boca Raton? Jesus, man. You fancy now, huh?" he teased.

Dominic shook his head.

"Just tryna resist temptation, man." He sucked his teeth. "I'm less than 50 miles from Miami, but close enough to get there whenever I want. Same with Pequeña Habana."

"Little Havana has been changing a lot. I got out and was shocked... All the new construction. Too many fucking tourists now. It's not how it used to be."

"It's okay. Bound to happen," Dominic said. "Not just in Havana, but all over the city. More people from up north are movin' here lately. My boy up there in Yonkers said the jobs are sparse, some restructuring and urban flight did a lot of damage to smaller businesses. Didn't help that they had a rough winter." Stacks nodded. "Everybody wants to move to Miami now. We've got the nice weather, the jobs, the beaches, the nightclubs, the food, the sexy women... We've got it all." He leaned back and reflected on his own words, stroking his chin as a nice, sweet breeze bathed his face. "You know I've got a lot of family in Chicago, some in New York, Pennsylvania, and Jersey, too. Been all over the country. I will always come right back here, though. Miami. Where I was born and raised. This is home."

"I feel you on that, Viper. Miami is where it's at. I wish I could travel more though, like you did. Now that I'm on probation, I can't go any fuckin' where for a while."

"Just relax. It'll come your way. Opportunity always knocks, sooner or later."

Stacks seemed unconvinced. "So, how have you been doing here? One minute you're in Havana, then the next, King Torque tells me that you moved way out here, almost an hour away. Nobody is sayin' much. It's like you're under a protective order." The guy chuckled nervously.

"I'm tryna make moves, Pedro, this time more discreetly."

"You were always discreet."

Dominic tapped his cigar, letting ash fall into the tray.

"Apparently not enough. The FBI had been on my ass, right before my last stint in Coleman."

"Man, Sumterville can eat a dick!" They both laughed at that.

"Yeah... It was fuckin' ridiculous. Anyway, I'm always on top of my shit, makin' money. I don't have to report or anything, no tether. Ankles free. I decided that uh…" he ran his hand along his jaw, choosing his words wisely, "that I needed some different scenery. To get out of the element for a bit until things simmered down. I can't give the police or anyone else anything to make it easier. Just tryna get paid and laid without an FBI raid and being made."

"King Golden Boy just went in, Viper. They got him for bein' a lookout. Then he got tossed with tampering with evidence charges on top of that. Trumped up bullshit."

"Yeah, I heard. He got five, right?"

"Yeah. He got into it with a couple MS 13s, too. Lost a lotta blood and a tooth. Shit's been bad."

The dogs made their way back to him from the open patio door, roaming the yard before settling back down around them. Pedro reached down and rubbed Chance's head. They continued to talk about some of the fam that was locked up or dead. Everything from the corrupt prison guards who were bringing in cartons of cigarettes and selling them for three hundred bucks, the cellphones being bought and sold like candy, and the guys going crazy from living in a cage for so long, including the lifers. The kings pushing up daisies now lived on in their graffitied names gracing the back walls of abandoned buildings or inked along brokenhearted women's breasts and thighs. Such was life. The graffiti and ink would fade, regardless how everyone promised they'd never be forgotten.

"Ma told me she doesn't want me going back to prison, Viper. Said if I go back in, it'll kill her. Said she needs me. I gotta make some money though, man. This'll only last me so long." He patted his pocket.

Dominic got ready to respond, when he heard a sudden crash.

"Bitch!" someone screamed out.

"Awww, damn, man."

He and Stacks got to their feet and looked in the direction of the house. King Torpedo squeezed his head out the open patio doors, a look of frustration on his tattooed face. "Ashley is in here wildin' out. Control your bitch, Stacks." He flipped his thumb towards the back, then disappeared quickly out of view.

Dominic grabbed Chance, Sarge, and Belleza when they jumped to their feet barking and snarling, ready to tear inside and sink their jaws into someone fast. As he and Stacks entered, he heard Marie yelling at Ashley, as well as some of the other women, all clad in their gold and black attire, glossy lips and long dark hair in various styles.

"Take your woman home!" Aleja yelled. Aleja was like a little sister to him, and was known to pull a knife faster than lightning. Ashley was on the ground writhing about, moaning after the number she'd done to her. Her right eye was red, swelling fast and angry like pasta sauce bubbling from a pot. She'd been punched so hard, some of the vessels and capillaries were broken.

"Get 'er up and take her home. Let Pedro stay," Viper demanded.

"Oh naw, man. Viper, I'll take her home," Stacks offered, obviously feeling sorry for the lady who'd come in there drunk on courage. Now she was molly-whopped and brought back to reality. Aleja dog walked the fuck out of her. Viper shook his head.

"No. You stay here. It's your party." He turned back to the crowd.

"Aleja. Drive her straight home and don't do any silly shit." Two women, including Aleja, reluctantly dropped down on their knees, hoisted the woman up, and dragged her to the front door like they would soggy trash that had been left out in the rain.

"I should take her home, Viper." Anger and what Viper perceived as pure, unadulterated disappointment flashed in Stack's eyes.

"No, you shouldn't. She's drunk and that knockout will wear off, and then she'll be combative again. Aleja took it easy on her. What if she tries to provoke you? Worse yet, hits you with something, maybe shoots you because she's not thinkin' clearly. What if you get a DV charge, huh? You don't need that kind of problem."

"Aleja and I used to have a thing, though. This isn't going to be good. You know how women get, and I'm fresh out. Aleja and her guy broke up… She's been wanting to spend some time with me."

If Viper didn't know any better, he'd think Stacks was entertaining it.

"She'll be fine." He patted the man's shoulder. "Bianca and Marisa will make sure of it." Stacks nodded, and a few moments later, everyone was back to partying and drinking. Later in the evening as he caught up with some of his brothers and sisters he hadn't seen in months, he noticed the lights on in the house across the street. It had been dark for weeks.

What's going on over there? Is it up for rent again?

The house had been vacant twice during the ten months he'd been living there. A large white truck was parked in the driveway now, the kind used for storage and deliveries. He leaned in closer, trying to figure out what was going on. The last thing he needed was nosy neighbors, people in his business. After a few moments, he observed three Black men dressed in jeans and oversized white T-shirts getting out of the truck, two of them hoisting cumbersome furniture from the back of the vehicle into the sprawling ranch home while the other dawdled, a cell phone to his ear. A little boy sporting a bright red Transformers shirt appeared from the house's front door, bursting free, running down the slightly sloped front lawn, laughing and barreling back towards the guy on the phone.

I guess that old White guy rented it out again. Maybe he sold it this time. Who knows? I like to know who's around me... I'll get their names eventually. He turned away, walked over to the stereo, and turned it up. Trick Daddy feat. Lil Jon &

Twista's, 'Let's Go' boomed throughout the house, causing a ruckus as the crowd got hyped. Once the song ended and he'd gotten in on the action, dancing, drinking and yelling out the lyrics so loud, his throat burned, he made his way back into the kitchen to toss a beer bottle away. Marie was in there wrapping up a few pieces of leftover cake in cellophane. They'd eaten all the rest.

"Nice party for Pedro," she said with a proud smile.

"Yeah, besides his girlfriend, it's been good. You did a great job." Her cheeks plumped up and grew rosy. He made his way over to the kitchen window once again to dump some melted ice from one of the coolers into the sink. As he casually looked back out the frame, he paused. There in the yard, holding a cardboard box in her arms, was a gorgeous woman with long, wavy black hair parted down the middle, skin-tight mesh black leggings that hugged a ridiculously round and high ass, and a black crop top. Her silver and white sneakers practically glowed under the streetlight, as did her large silver and diamond hoop earrings. *Who the hell is that?* The stranger walked to the house after talking to one of the men. *Look at that ass… Mmmm, mmmm, good… Damn. Not too many Black people on this street. Hell, in the entire neighborhood. I bet the stuck up neighbors are gonna flip out when they see this shit.* He chuckled to himself. The woman came back out, bent down, and retrieved a box. She moved leisurely, as if in slow motion, and he found himself swallowing hard and enjoying the show…

He practically growled at the sight of her. Cleavage gleamed and shined like buttery biscuits. Her tits were practically leaping out, inviting him for a look. Women came in and out of Dominic's life as if he were a revolving door of a department store having a half-off everything twenty-four-hour sale. He'd had his share of gorgeous girlfriends since age thirteen, and had some decent relationships too along the way that just didn't work out for one reason or another. In a couple of rare cases it was because the fucking woman was wacky. He tried to steer clear of chicks like that. But surprisingly, the nutjobs were always the ones with the best pussy. A catch 22. Perhaps that's why Stacks couldn't let Ashley go just yet? Regardless, he was certain that he was hard to deal with at times, too.

He supposed he was too ambitious, always put stacking his cash above everything else. If he was earning money and performing his duties as a Warlord, then he couldn't be with a woman all damn day. Sacrifices had to be made. It was at times difficult to balance that with his voracious sexual appetite, but his self-discipline allowed him to accomplish the feat nevertheless. Women were like art to him, but sometimes, they were far too worrisome to deal with. Better left hanging on a wall and admired from afar.

The sound of the dripping faucet on the unwashed dishes, playing an out-of-tune song, interrupted his thoughts. He turned the cold water handle, putting a stop to it, then returned to his thoughts. Sometimes, he couldn't keep women off his mind despite his best efforts. *I don't need the aggravation right now... I really don't.* And though he was able to handle staying away from relationships, he found himself changing. He used to be indifferent. Now, he wanted companionship, but his life was complicated. Even dating one of his own didn't seem to scratch the itch.

If he dated a Latin Queen, they usually understood his circumstances, his frequent absences, but then there'd be inner-circle fights, jealousy, rumors in order to cause a rift. If he dated just a girl from around town, one who was not gang affiliated as they'd say, it was rare that it ended well. Sometimes he surmised these women were only with him for the thrill of it. Some chicks just dug gangbangers. He was a fetish in some circles, and he knew it. These type of women liked to fuck them, flaunt them, use them as threats – a flesh weapon walking on two legs with a big dick to drill their mouths and pussies behind closed doors. He got tired of that shit, too. It wasn't as fun and exciting as it used to be. Now that he'd was in his thirties, he wasn't in the mood for any more bullshit.

"Viper… Yo, Viper!"

He quickly turned and found himself looking into Jose's pink, hooded eyes. The man was high as the moon and stars.

"I've been calling you for like ten seconds. You all right?"

"Yeah… yeah." He wiped his hands on the dish towel and faced his friend. "What's up?"

"Wanna play dominoes? We're starting a game."

"Yeah, I'll be in."

Jose nodded and left. When he resumed looking out the kitchen window, the truck was taking off from the house across the street. The lights remained on, and out of a front window, the blinds moved. The same little boy that had been running around appeared at the window. Seconds later, a taller shadow stood behind him, ushering the child away. This was followed by the blinds being completely closed, one window after another. He pulled out a kitchen drawer, reached for a fresh cigar, lit it, and made his way into the living room. It was time to win a game of dominoes, and take all of these bastards' money…

CHAPTER TWO

Music to my Ears

"WHAT IS ALL of that thumpin'?" Destiny asked her through the speaker phone.

"The motherfuckers across the street. They play that shit all night. It's usually reggaetón, rap, or some Latin music. Between that and the dogs barking sometimes, it's crazy... Damn! Where did I put that box of Troy's socks?" Majesty tossed her phone onto the new couch still covered in shipping plastic, hunkered down onto the white tile floor of the new house she'd moved into, and tore away at yet another box, hopeful her nine-year-old son's socks were inside.

"Just my costume jewelry. Shit. This isn't it, either." She pushed the box against the couch, her frustration reaching a higher level than she imagined possible. *This is what I get for not labeling everything.* The last few days had been hectic, and she was running on fumes. She'd enrolled

Troy in school, which took hours. She still needed to get his room set up, too. There was simply too much on her agenda. Work, school online at night, and then unpack and try to turn that house into a home. But she'd gotten them out of Allapattah, and that was all that mattered.

"Majesty, the music is so loud I can recognize the song!"

"You can? What are they playing?" she asked absently, not really caring about the answer as she pulled open another box.

"It's 'Mentirosa' by Mellow Man Ace. It's old. They must be some older Latinos or somethin'. How can you stand it?"

"I *can't* stand it, but every time I make plans to go over there and pay whoever lives there a visit and ask them to turn it down, I get sidetracked. There's just too much to do… I'll take care of it. Eventually." She'd taken a half day off at work just to get caught up on getting her house in order.

"This weekend me and Trisha can come by to help you. Just like we said. It doesn't all have to be done at once," her friend urged, no doubt picking up on her anxiety.

"You know I can't let this house stay like this, Destiny. It'll drive me crazy… boxes up to the rafters."

"Why doesn't Anthony's lazy ass come by and help?" Majesty sucked her teeth and got to her feet. That box was yet another dead end, full of magazines and old books from her youth. She dusted off her knees, removing bits of grime and debris that clung to her jeggings.

"Anthony is not tryna fool with me. Since I told him I don't want to be with him like that, he pretty much has left me alone. I was lucky he and his brothers helped me move, considering he was pissed off about it." She marched into the kitchen, grabbed a freshly unboxed and washed glass from the dishrack, and filled it to the rim. She took long, deep gulps, needing to cure her thirst in the worst way.

"You still never told me why you don't want him?"

"Didn't you just call him lazy? That's why!" Destiny burst out laughing. "Besides, Anthony isn't really my type, like I told you. He's cool and all, but he doesn't have a lot of ambition. He acts like life just happens. Plus, he was cool with Kevin, and that makes me uncomfortable." Her friend was quiet on the phone for a bit. Kevin was Troy's father. Before the woman delved deeper into a conversation she didn't wish to have, she broke the silence, exit strategy style. "Destiny, let me call you back. I have to pick up Troy from school in a little bit, but before I go, I wanted to make sure at least the rest of his underwear and pajamas are in his drawers for tonight."

"Okay, call me back tonight, okay? I still need to tell you what happened to my other cellphone."

"All right. I will." She disconnected the call and shook her head. Destiny was notorious for losing her phones, or having them stolen. She stood at the sink and finished the glass of water, then made her way back into the living room, her feet in only socks patting against the floor. She crossed her arms, feeling the vibration of the music from across the way. *How can someone have their music that loud? I mean, shit, I like loud music, too, but that has to be painful! I wonder why no one has called the police on these people?! I thought I had gotten Troy and me away from this kind of shit.* It was one of the few houses that had a lot of land around it on the street – a corner lot. She'd often see nice big trucks in the driveway, shiny black and gold motorcycles, and Hispanic men and women coming and going like a damn parade. She could see dogs at times, too, beyond a white fence. Whatever family lived there played music from the afternoon onward like they were getting paid for it. They were loud and obnoxious with it. She approached her front window and looked out. A Cuban flag waved in the slight breeze above the back patio, as well as another one that was yellow and black.

Running her fingers against the clear teardrop-shaped pendant of her necklace, she sighed and took a deep breath, then continued to sort out more of the boxes piled in the living room. She screamed when a sudden boom rent the air. This was followed by 'Oye Mi Canto,' by N.O.R.E. Ft. Daddy Yankee, Nina Sky, Gemstar, and Big Mato.

"Oh my God! It's so loud it's rattling my house now!" Having had enough, she marched to her front door, slid on her white and silver Nike sneakers by the entrance, and made a mad dash down her front walkway, her big hoop earrings slapping her cheeks as she practically flew like a bird towards the street. She looked both ways, then raced across the road until she was finally at the nice house surrounded by palm trees, the place responsible for making her ears practically bleed. She stood at the entrance; certain the people inside wouldn't be able to hear her as she pounded on the door. Then, she noticed a camera with a red light flashing. It moved, as if someone had used it to zoom in on her. Suddenly, the music stopped, and she heard heavy footsteps approaching. The door swung open, and it felt like the air was sucked out of her lungs, her surroundings, the street, and the entire city.

Standing in the doorway was a tall, broad-shouldered man with piercing light hazel eyes, and tattoos on practically every inch of his neck, chest and arms, including a crucifix in the middle of his forehead. He glared at her, and she instantly filled with trepidation and concern, but fought the urge to flee. He stood barefoot, clad in only a pair of baggy white shorts, his dick print more than apparent, despite the loose fit of the apparel around his hips. Long, muscular legs, covered in black hair and more tattoos, caught her eye, and on his chest was something she'd seen a time or two: symbols for the notorious street gang, the Latin Kings.

There was no way you could be born and raised in Miami and not recognize them. Black, menacing ink of snarling kings, vicious lions, attacking snakes, screaming skulls, and jeweled crowns covered his brawny frame. *Shit… This motherfucker is a gang banger. What in the hell is he doing livin' here?!* She fought to find the right words, a way to approach such a bastard without something bad popping off, but then loud barking broke her out of her trance.

"Sarge! NO. Quiet." The man kept his eye on her, but turned his head ever so slightly in the direction of the dog.

The barking stopped immediately. His deep, booming voice made the music that had been playing sound like a whisper.

"Hello." She worked up her nerve, holding her head high in spite of a racing pulse. "I live across the street." She pointed to her house. He casually glanced over, then brought his gaze back to her. "My name is Majesty. I just moved in." The big man said nothing. As she stood there, she expected people to be roaming about inside his home. After all, it sounded like he had daily parties—but there was no one there. At least, not in the visible part of the living area. As if sensing her trying to get a better look, he crossed his ankles, then his arms, and leaned against the frame of the door, blocking her view. "I wanted to—"

"...talk to me about the music."

"Yeah. It's too loud. I work... school. I have a kid. I moved out here for some peace. I like music, too, but—"

"I'll turn it down." He moved back from the door, then slammed it in her face. Within seconds, DMX's, 'We Right Here' was blaring. Same volume. Same thumping. A swell of anger erupted inside her like a volcano that had been trying to explode for decades. She knocked on the door, so fast and hard, her knuckles stung. The door swung back open and music poured out of the house like an invisible avalanche, while a haze of smoke drifted behind him. She smelled cherry incense and saw a dog run past in the background.

"It's still loud!" She shouted over the music. Sure, even if he didn't hear her, the motherfucker could read lips. He rubbed his hands together, bit into his lower lip

and grinned. Just then, about six motorcycles pulled up—
a bunch of motherfuckers dripping in gold chains and
black and yellow attire, with women sitting on the back.
The bunch of tatted-up misfits started to snap their
fingers, dancing, cackling and cursing as they held what
looked like bags chock full of wine and beer bottles. As
they approached the door, they acted as if they didn't see
her. In fact, one of the big guys, bald with a big gut,
slightly bumped into her as he made his way inside the
house, pushing the screen door into her shoulder.

"Hey. You hit her…" The monster who answered the
door whispered so low, she almost missed it. He took a
hold of the big guy's arm and pulled him back. The man
paused, staring at the both of them. She'd never seen such
a thing. With a few words, this big man showed reverence.
The respect, tinged with apprehension, was palpable.

"Oh, I'm sorry, baby." The fat man chuckled. "I ain't
even notice you, mami. You Dominican? You look like
you might be Dominican."

"No. I'm Black, as if that matters, and the music is too
fuckin' loud!" Both guys burst out laughing while the rest
of the gang marched inside, business as usual.

"Dominicans can be Black." The big guy shrugged.
"You look it is all I'm sayin'."

"Well, I'm not Dominican. I didn't come over here for
an Ancestry.com discussion."

The angrier she became, the more they cackled. The
big guy walked off, leaving the Monster at the door with
her. He shook his head, as if there were some inside joke
she wasn't aware of. Just then, 50 Cent's 'I Get Money'

began to play. She loved that song, down to her damn bones, but refused to acknowledge it.

"Look, I'm sure you're used to people bein' afraid of you, sir, and you know that I know your affiliations. It's all over your body, and I can read just fine. But you can't move into a place like this and expect to be a thug. My son has homework, and so do I, and some of us got to get up in the morning. We have jobs. Turn it down!" She turned and walked off, her heart pounding so hard in her chest, it hurt. Suddenly, as she was heading back onto the sidewalk to cross the street, the music stopped.

"Hey, hold up! Majesty, the Black Queen of England and music volume police!" he hooted.

She huffed and spun back to face him.

"What?"

"Welcome to the neighborhood. You're sexy as hell, you know that? And brave, too." He winked at her, and her blood ran cold.

"I don't give a damn what you think of me. I couldn't care less if you think I'm titillating and courageous. You have *no* respect. You are the last person on this street, in this city, in the country, and on this entire damn planet who I would take any stock in wantin' to impress."

"Ewwwww! So mean, *Mami Chula*!" He burst out laughing, showing all his glistening, white teeth, then reached low and rubbed the top of his dog's head. It was then that she realized it was a blue Pit Bull. Gorgeous dog. It was also then that she saw the butt of the gun jammed into the back of his shorts. Perspiration broke out on her face. *Oh shit... see... my mouth always gets me in trouble...*

"My name is Viper," he stated calmly, smiling even. "Look, Majesty, nice name by the way… I've got a party goin' on tonight, so the music will be loud, and there isn't shit you can do about it." He shrugged. "But, sometimes, if I'm in the mood, I can be a nice guy, so I'll make you a deal. The ordinance out here says loud music has to be turned down at ten. I will turn it off at eleven. Sweet dreams."

And then, he slammed the door once again…

CHAPTER THREE

Snitchin' and Lyftin'

"**T**HEY'RE DEFINITELY SNITCHIN'." Pedro sighed as he slumped back in a black plastic chair in his new one-bedroom apartment in Little Havana. The bastard had returned to his roots, but the controversy and trouble soon followed. Many of the kings were gathered inside, drinking beer, smoking cigarettes and weed blazing, and the sounds of the big screen television mounted on the wall played in the background. Viper stood and pulled out his keys from his jeans pocket.

"Nothing we discussed today leaves this apartment. I'll find out what's going on. I told y'all last week that someone is talking to the police," he stated angrily. "I told all of you to lay low! Play it cool. You were being watched. We're not out here in the streets drawing attention to ourselves! We learned from the past. I had already heard from the inside that that is what was happening. Someone wants to take over that territory. We were warned. You got caught slippin'. I told y'all to be cool, chill, not drawing attention to ourselves, and now with the heat on, some of you decided to get flashy. No one listened. I'm not even supposed to be over here right now, but I had to come to this motherfucker and find out what the fuck happened because Showtime is dead, and Wild is looking at least at twenty to thirty, no questions asked. Someone fucked up. Big time."

Everyone drew quiet as he raged, pissed about it all. What was the point of being in charge when people sometimes did whatever the hell they wanted to do? But as soon as shit hit the fan, he was expected to come out and fix all the chaos and confusion.

"You wanna make me step out of character, huh? You want to undermine me?! YOU MOTHERFUCKERS SHOWIN' OFF FOR WOMEN AND CLOUT CHAS-IN'! Honking your horns, flashin' your money, bringing haters to the block! Then you at first only tell me half the story of what went down last night, afraid I'd shoot one of you, that I'd teach everyone a lesson. I am going to teach a lesson all right, but I first need all the facts. I will find out. Your lies don't work on me. Do you take me for a fool?!"

"No, Viper," several of them said.

"I told you, if you're fair with me, I'll be fair with you. Stacks," he pointed angrily at Pedro, "I told you to not get back in the game. You were just at Wild's crib, and had you not left thirty minutes earlier, you'd be back in the joint for life!" Pedro hung his head. "You've been busted for drugs, narcotics distribution, too many times to count in the past, and your luck is runnin' out. You have to be smarter, Pedro. What the fuck is wrong with y'all?!" Viper kicked a chair over, feeling like he was talking to mere children. "*¡Voy a matarte!* That's it. We're in deep shit. If Wild gets a long sentence, you know what's going to happen: you're all going down. The Council will demand answers. *¡Te has equivocado!* The police don't give a shit about him, you, or me. They want the big kahuna."

"Wild got picked up. We know someone dropped a dime. We'll find out who did it, Viper," King EC, for East Coast, spoke up. "I know you're angry, man. Your orders were disregarded by some of us, but not all of us. You sent direct orders, and now things aren't right, but we'll *make* this right. I promise you and Jaguar."

Jaguar was second in command. What he said went, and if anyone stepped out of line, there were always consequences.

"It doesn't matter. Damage has been done. If anyone, and I mean anyone, in this room is responsible, I will be given orders… and I think you all know what those orders will be." If they were lucky, it would be a beatdown of epic proportions. The other scenario involved a headstone and a prayer.

King Wild was a good buddy of his, true blue, but even the bravest of the brave, and the most loyal, could snitch if the pressure was just right. Wild was different though. He was one of the few kings Viper knew who was built to last and wouldn't fold at the drop of a dime. Wild had been dealing dope out of his apartment; the police pulled up the evening prior and nabbed him. Wild hadn't been slangin' on the street in years, but always kept that window of his open, doing business. Watching everyone, too. The man had been there in that apartment for so long he was like a fixture, and the local beat cops were well paid, but someone wasn't on the payroll. Someone was talking.

Wild was important, a lookout. That was his post while business was being taken care of. He could be trusted; he knew what to peep out, and how to warn the crew. Now, he was gone. That entire street was Latin King territory and ever since the new police chief came into office, things had changed. Their enemies had just been looking for a weak spot, and found it. Between the cops and the Haitian gangs trying to get a foothold, things were a tangled mess. Wild could be replaced, that was no issue, but the fact that he was now facing time in prison due to the cops finding almost a kilo of cocaine in his spot meant he would be serving some serious time. That also meant some people would become paranoid, think he might become desperate and rat them out to lessen his sentence – anything to be set free from the cage of lifetime incarceration.

"I need to head back. Everyone, be cool. I'll be in touch. In the meantime, handle all of your deals on burner phones exclusively. No new customers. No one is to be out on the street, either. Stay away from Wild's apartment and that entire block for drop-offs. I've already got several lookouts there, trying to piece together what went down and what's going on now. We can't let anyone think the street is unprotected. Don't keep product on you, either.

You could get pulled over or detained at any time. Put it elsewhere, some place no one will look at, and tell no one where it is. I know I've been out of this game for a long time. I don't slang, never did; the drug game is not my thing because we all have our talents – and you all know what mine is. But even though that wasn't my assignment, I know what to do to keep you protected. I know what I'm talking about. Just ask any of the old heads. I know what the cops look for, all right? If anyone disobeys me again, your life is over. I will not hesitate. You will bring down others with you because of carelessness, and I can't have that. Be on top of your shit, twenty-four-seven!" They all nodded in agreement as he headed towards the front door. "Pedro, I meant what the fuck I said to you."

"I know..."

"I don't think you're taking this seriously, Stacks." He glared at him. "If I find out you're involved in selling any of this shit, in any fucking shape, form or capacity, be that online, in person at some club, on the street, through the pussy of a bitch holdin' bags for you, I'm going to break your fuckin' neck. I'd rather kill you than have you disgrace the Nation, or your mother have to deal with you being locked up for life. To some, that's worse than death." Snatching the door open, he slammed it behind him.

He headed to his black Bugatti with gold chrome and custom paint job, and got inside. He kept the beauty in his garage, protected under lock and key, and only took her out for special occasions. Today, he had business to attend to, but had also visited some of his family in Little Havana earlier in the day. He wanted to assure everyone that he was doing fine, that everything was under control. The best way to do such a thing was to look one's best, and he did that so well. He stared at himself in the car mirror for a spell, then turned on some music. 'Mas Maiz' by N.O.R.E blasted through the speakers, and the white Pit Bull air freshener swayed back and forth as he zigzagged out of the parking space and merged into traffic.

He cracked his window and the scent of grilled meat and marijuana from outside filled his vehicle. He noticed all of the beautiful women standing around checking him out in his ride, some calling out to him… more than likely creaming in their lacy panties, wishing to be near him. Be seen beside him. Fuck him. They knew him by name.

"Viper! King Viper!"

"Dominic!!! Hey! Wait up!"

He smiled, offered a wave, and kept rolling until about an hour later, he was back in Boca Raton. He turned off the music as he pulled into his driveway and pressed the garage opener, beckoning for the door to rise while listening to 'I Love My Life,' by Norega. He enjoyed the earlier rap hits more than recent music as of late. His father called him a knucklehead with an old soul.

Out of the corner of his eye, he noticed the Black queen known as Majesty across the street as he pulled in. He'd not spoken to her since the day she'd come to his home, demanding things, her hand on her hip and a sneer on her face. Her car hood was up, and from what he could make out, she looked downright frustrated. Moments later, he was out of his car and inside his home.

After taking a swig of cold coffee, he headed out the front door to see what was going on. As casually as he pleased, he crossed the street and headed in her direction.

"Of course I can't." She had her back to him as she gripped her phone to her ear. "But I can't miss work today, Porsha. That's the whole point. I already had to take a few days off for this move… No… by the time you come get me, I'll be extremely late. Besides, I don't want to take you away from your job right now… I know… It keeps making this knocking noise, too. I have to drop off Troy at the babysitter. Now, I'm runnin' late… I know, but it's not working out! I don't have time for this… Who? I told you that Mitch didn't fix it right. I just spent five hundred dollars on this piece of shit and here it is, doin' the same thing again. Some mechanic he is! I swear that—" She spun around, stumbled back, and her eyes widened when she saw him. "…I swear that he is trying to rob me… Let me call you back, girl."

She disconnected the call. He looked her up and down, taking note of her button-down pink blouse that hugged her tits just right, and her tight black pants and low heels. Her long black hair was pulled back in a ponytail, and her sweet, sexy perfume filled the air, mixing in with the smell of oil and grease. A black smudge stained her cheek, and her right hand was covered in soot. Stepping in front of the car, he looked down at the engine and began to tinker around.

"What are you doin'?"

He picked up a nearby wrench and got to work.

"What's this? A 2018 or '19 Dodge Charger?" he asked

after a few moments.

"…'18. Do you even know what to look for? How do I know you're not making it worse?" He ignored her and kept at it. After a few minutes of messing around, his fingers now black and slick with oil, he figured it out.

"These are the wrong transmission rods. They don't fit right." He pointed downwards. "It was an accident from the manufacturer. The car is stalling, right?" She nodded. "That's because of the voltage regulator. Your mechanic fixed the wrong thing. You gotta take this to the dealer. They'll fix the rods free of charge. It was a recall from years ago."

"You're a mechanic?"

"No. My stepfather is, my biological father is, too. So are two uncles, and a few cousins. I grew up around it." He closed the hood. "I like cars too, so I stay on top of things like this." He rubbed his hands on a paper towel he found lying nearby. "You've got some other car complications too, like this filter here, but they're easy fixes. Get your purse and your child. I'll drop your son off and drive you to work."

"No," she barked defiantly, then cleared her throat. He could see in her eyes she was afraid, but trying to stand her ground. He was used to people being afraid of him. It came with the territory. "I appreciate you comin' over here, Viper, but I'll take care of it. Thank you." She made her way to her front door, her heels clicking against the concrete. He stood there for a spell, holding that wrinkled paper towel, staring at the closed front door. Then, he slowly walked up her driveway, towards her porch. And waited. He could hear her on the phone; she sounded frantic. Desperate. It wasn't long before he heard a child in the background, and her asking the boy to quiet down.

He slid his phone out of his pocket, and made a call. Then, he knocked on the door. Everything inside became quiet.

"Majesty, it's me. I know you know that I'm out here. Now you know that I never left. Look, I'm going to leave and go home."

"Please do. I don't mean to be rude, and I appreciate you coming by, I do, but you're a... you're not—"

"I don't need you to tell me what you think I am, or how much you appreciate me, and all of that other shit. You don't owe me any explanations, and neither do I. You don't know me, and I don't know you. I offered you a ride; you said no. Cool." He threw up his hands. "I can't make you come with me, but uh, I arranged a Lyft for you. It'll be here in ten minutes. The ride is arranged from my gift account, so you can drop off your son on the way, too. No charge to you."

"I didn't need you to do that," she said after a moment of hesitation.

"I didn't *need* to do it, either. But I did anyway."

Having heard enough, he headed back home. It got to him – the hopelessness in her voice, how she could lose her job, how she didn't have the money to call a cab or anything like that. She'd sunk all of her expendable income into that house she was renting to own, from what he could make out. Something about the way she'd looked him in the eye, shoved her fear aside when they'd first seen one another, resonated with him. She'd practically started shaking, but she'd stated her case about his music, and she'd meant what she said. She wasn't the first one to complain – but she was the first one with balls big enough to confront him face to face versus taking the cowardly way out and calling the police anonymously. Perhaps she hadn't known who he was before she'd come trouncing across the street, but once she *did* realize, the woman hadn't backed down. He'd caught her eyes fixated on one of his 'Latin King' tattoos, a serpent wrapped around the letters.

She'd pushed her fear aside and done what she'd needed to do. Because of that, he had in fact turned the music down at eleven that evening, right on the dot. He'd kept his word.

It didn't hurt that she was beautiful – her face and body were incredible. Something truly lovely to adore. It didn't hurt that she smelled like soft music, reggae, and ocean waves. It didn't hurt that she seemed to be fiercely independent, but possessed a soft, sweet femininity that called to him, deep within his soul. It was obvious she was a single mother. No real man would let their woman struggle with their car that way, at least not one worth his salt.

As he re-entered his home, he was playfully jumped on by his dogs as if they'd not seen him for weeks. While he freshened up their food bowls, he looked out the kitchen window and saw a black Toyota RAV4 pull up. Moments later, Majesty stepped out of her home, her son in tow, and got into the car. He smirked as he poured himself a drink, and watched them drive away…

CHAPTER FOUR

'Tow' the Line and Ain't that Peachy?

"**M**Y WIFE USED to do it." The tall, thin Black man with tight, white kinky curls, and a prominent bald spot on his head, stood on Majesty's porch holding a peach pie. The smell wafted in the air like invisible flags waving in the wind. He had a kind smile, his dark skin was aged from the sun and time, and he smelled of tobacco and earth. The whites of his heavily hooded eyes were a bit yellow, and straight black and gray hairs peeked out from his wide nostrils. He held the tin pan containing a dessert as though it were a delicate child. "She died seven months ago. She used to welcome new people to the neighborhood with a homemade dessert. I've picked up the torch since she passed."

Majesty stepped outside her door.

"That's nice of you. Thank you." She took the pie from him. It was still warm, and although she hated peach pie, the fact that it was just out of the oven filled her with comfort. It was truly the thought that counted. "Do you make it from scratch, too?"

Just then, she spotted Viper pulling out of his garage in his black Bugatti with gold trim. The loud Latin music pouring from the car made the entire street vibrate, and it seemed as though the bastard was inside of a giant dildo. *He is a bit of a dick.* She smirked at the thought. The show-off revved his engine before speeding down the block. Meanwhile, the old neighbor from two doors down kept talking about not using too much butter in the crust. As if noticing her distraction, he craned his neck and watched the black and gold expensive car disappear down the road.

"That's Dominic," he offered.

"Dominic? That must be his government name. He told me it was Viper. Of course, no one would name their son after a snake." She chuckled. "Uh, I'm sorry, sir, speaking of names, I didn't catch yours."

"Earl. Earl Dickens. Some call me, Mr. Earl."

"Mr. Earl, would you like to step inside?" She realized she'd forgotten her manners. She'd been so frazzled with unpacking, working overtime the last couple of days, helping Troy with his homework, making sure he got his hair cut at the barber, and trying to get her car fixed, that it seemed her basic home training in hospitality had gone out the window.

"Okay, thank ya. Thank ya."

The old man timidly followed her inside. She kept the front door open, then closed the screen behind him.

"Let me put this pie in the kitchen and get you something to drink. I'll be right back. Please have a seat."

"I'm okay right here. Need to stretch my legs anyway."

Mr. Earl crossed his slight arms and hands, and waited like a statue in his army green button-down shirt, slouchy brown pants, and worn shoes. She placed the pie on the counter, then pulled out a pitcher of a concoction she often made for Troy from the refrigerator. His favorite drink: a mixture of pink lemonade, Sprite, fruit punch, pineapple juice, strawberry flavoring and a little blackberry puree. After pouring a glass, she marched back into her living room, then to the foyer area where Mr. Earl remained.

"You've got a real nice home. I like seein' younger people movin' here."

"Thank you." She handed him the glass and he graciously took a sip. "I didn't ask if you were thirsty. Just assumed you were since it's such a hot day."

"This is good. Real good." He smacked his lips. "Woulda been better with some Vodka though." They both burst out laughing.

"I agree." She shrugged. "But I make it for my son, too."

"Oh, yes. I saw your boy runnin' 'round the other day. How old is he?"

"He's eight, about to turn nine soon. In the fourth grade."

The old man smiled big and wide.

"Children are a blessing." She nodded in agreement. "I've got seventeen grandchildren!" he stated proudly.

"Oh, wow! That's a lot of children to keep track of."

"It is, but I manage. Check it out…" He then started to rattle off every grandchild's name. "Me and Arnette had six children. Five of 'em still alive. I had a son prior to meeting her, my first marriage, so that's seven children for me. He's Earl Jr." Majesty mustered a smile. Truth be told, she was bone tired, but refused to rush the fellow home. He was a widower and had come out of his way to welcome her to the neighborhood, bringing her a fresh pie. "Well, I won't tarry too long. I'll get goin'. It was nice meeting you, Ms. Majesty Wilson."

"It was nice meeting you, too." She opened the door for him, and as he made way to the steps, she called out to him. "Uh, Mr. Dickens, I mean, Mr. Earl, do you mind if I ask you a question?"

"You can." He turned back towards her. "Don't mean I'll know the answer, but I'll try."

"Dominic… Do you know him well?" She pointed to the big pretty house across the street where the asshole lived.

The old man tapped his finger against his chin, then smiled, as if remembering something near and dear to his heart.

"Well, let me start from the beginning." *Oh no…* "I moved ova here with my retirement money when Arnette got sick 'bout five years ago. Wanted to give her her dream house. These houses are expensive. Nice part of town. Golf courses. Beaches. Once she got diagnosed with stage 4 breast cancer, I knew I had to make sure she had everything she wanted, 'cause wasn't no way I was going to have her last days be anythin' short of glorious.

She didn't act like she was sick, though; she looked beautiful up until her dyin' day." Majesty reached for the fabric of her shirt and twisted it when the melancholy struck.

"My wife was as sweet as that pie." He shook his head, donning a sad smile. "Went to church every Sunday. Sometimes, I went with her. Cooked big dinners for the whole family. Volunteered at the homeless shelters. Played her card games and loved to babysit the grandbabies. Oh, but uh, let me get back to your question… Dominic… We saw Dominic movin' in one day while we were sittin' on the porch together. A bunch of biker type guys was wit' him. Big ol' mean lookin' dudes!" The man's face became animated as he spoke. "We knew these white folks was gonna lose their shit once they caught sight of that big ass Latino man wit' all them tattoos walkin' around, lookin' like a coloring book! Oh, 'scuse me, didn't mean to cuss in front of no woman. My wife used to get on me about that! I used to be in the navy. Once a sailor, always a sailor… this mouth still a sailor, too." His complexion deepened right before her eyes.

Majesty burst out laughing. "It's fine. I've been known to say my share of colorful words. I know you're right, too, about what the neighbors would think."

He grinned. "They didn't pay me and Arnette any mind, guess 'cause we're old, but they kinda stuck up out here. Stick to themselves. So, Arnette said to me, 'Well, better go bake a pie for the new family.' She yawned, got up off the swing, went on in the house, and set out all these ingredients to make an apple cobbler. *Oh, so Viper's ass gets a delicious apple cobbler but I get the stinky peach one? Why didn't you make me an apple cobbler, Mr. Earl? I sure would've enjoyed that!* Majesty kept her wayward, silly thoughts about the pie to herself. "I sat out there and watched him and his friends load stuff in, and then, to my surprise, they all left… 'cept for him. We was expecting him to have a wife 'nd kids. He has a bunch uh dogs, though. I noticed him putting in lights and cameras over the following days, and putting a fence up. Then he—"

"What happened when your wife took him the pie? How'd he respond?" she cut in, then regretted it, feeling rude. *It takes him so long to get to the point.* "I'm sorry for interrupting you."

"Naw, naw." He waved to her. "That's all right. If I recollect right, she said he said, 'thank you,' but not much else. Not really a talker. Gave her one word answers, but seemed nice enough."

"Oh. I see."

"I started noticing he was trainin' them dogs." He shook his finger in the direction of Viper's house. "See, I take two walks a day. One in the mornin', after breakfast, and one right before dinner. That man would be out there with some clicker gadget doohickey in his hand, sometimes suited up in those protective body suits so when the dog bite, it don't get cha too bad. The boy bad! I'm tellin' you, it was like watching a movie." The man grinned from ear to ear. "I ain't nevah seen a man make Pit Bulls, Bull Dogs, big ol' German Shepherds, Rottweilers and Great Danes bow down with the snap of a finger! I'm tellin' you, dem dogs bowed and prayed to him when he got through wit' 'em. Treated him like God. I don't know much about him personally though, Ms. Wilson, so maybe I didn't tell you what you were lookin' for. That's all I know."

"Please just call me Majesty, and you've been a great help. I was just curious is all."

He nodded. "I know he likes loud music, like me. But mine is loud 'cause I can't hear shit." They both burst out laughing again. Mr. Earl was funny, and boy did she need the laugh. "Are you uh… are you takin' an interest in him? A suitor? You thinking of courting Dominic?" Mischief shined in his timeworn eyes.

Her heart thumped, and her throat constricted like she'd swallowed food wrong.

"Uh…no. Not really." Running her hand along her collarbone, she shook her head, a bit taken aback by the question.

"Hope I'm not imposing. Didn't mean to make you uncomfortable or anything like that."

"No… no, you're fine," she lied.

"It's just that you're a real nice-lookin' woman, and if you live here, must mean you doin' all right. He's doin' all right apparently, too. I bet you two are around the same age, too."

So now Mr. Earl is a matchmaker. She suppressed a laugh.

"I'm not interested in Viper, Dominic, whatever name he goes by. See, I was just curious about him because we had a… situation, I guess you could say."

"A situation?" His brow rose.

"Yes. I had to ask him to turn his music down. I work and have classes at night, so having a concert right across the street is not exactly ideal."

"Oh, I see. Where do you work if ya don't mind me asking?"

"I work full time as a customer service rep for a retail company, and I work part time as a Human Resources assistant. I also have an online service where I help kids who've had some trouble getting into college or trade school. On top of that I am in school getting my Master's degree in Human Resources. Almost finished, too… just a bit more time to go."

"Whoa! I like that!"

Her face felt hotter as she flushed.

"Yeah… I keep busy. Just trying to make a good life for me and Troy."

"Ambition! You're pretty *and* smart! What a jackpot. I love to hear about us bein' busy, and doing great things." She nodded in agreement. "Me and my wife made sure our children went to college if they wanted to. We made a way. Put three of 'em through school, and our eldest daughter, Linda, is a doctor now." He beamed with pride.

"That's wonderful. She is blessed to have you."

"Your parents live around here?"

She briefly glanced at her watch. "No."

It took a moment for him to get the hint she wasn't saying any more. The last thing she wished to discuss was her some-timey mother. Nor did she wish to discuss her father, whom she didn't have any desire to speak with.

"All right." He offered a smile, his eyes narrowed. No doubt he'd figured out that was a sore spot to be avoided and left alone. "Now, 'bout the music situation you said you had wit' Dominic. Usually, these White folks just call the cops on him, but that never goes anywhere." He shrugged. "They stopped callin' about his music after a while. I would see the police pull up, talk to him, then off they'd go. Five minutes later, it would be turned up even louder." He chuckled and shook his head. Mr. Earl didn't seem terribly concerned about Viper. In fact, it was as if he found him to be a source of entertainment. He started to walk down the steps.

"Okay, well, thank you for talking to me, and for the wonderful pie! I am sure my son will enjoy a slice tonight with some vanilla ice-cream."

"You're more than welcome. If you need anything, you let me know."

"Thank you so much for that offer."

"Ain't too many of us over here. They think we don't belong here, Majesty, but we do. We do..."

Mr. Earl made his way back to his driveway. Back in the house washing dishes, she reflected on her conversation with the old man who was full of personality, good conversation, and truth. *Mr. Earl reminds me a little of my grandfather. Not in how he looks, but the way he moves and acts. Grandaddy has been gone for fifteen years, but I will never forget him. He used to give me oranges from his tree and tell me I was his favorite granddaughter, but not to tell anyone.* She smiled at the memory. Then, she heard a car pulling up in her driveway.

"That must be Troy. He's a little early today."

Majesty had made a quick association with one of the moms at the fancy school Troy was now attending. The woman didn't live too far away, and Troy and her son were in the same class. The deal was that Troy could ride home with them if Majesty would join the PTA. As she dried her hands off, she heard a beeping sound.

What in the world is that? She made her way to her front door.

"Hey!" she hollered out as a tow truck backed up, ready to haul her car away. "I paid this month's bill!" An Asian guy wearing a dark green beanie hat got out of the truck and began to hook her car to the pulleys. "Get those off my car!"

"Relax, lady," he said with a smile. She wanted to smack it clean off his face.

"What are you doing? I said I paid the damn bill. I am not delinquent."

"This is not a repo." He smiled wider now, a toothpick dangling from the corner of his mouth. "It's boss' orders. Your car isn't being towed. Well…" He smirked. "Technically, it is, but it's being taken in for repairs. No big deal."

"But I never called anyone to come get my car. I made some calls to get estimates, and I called the dealership and tried to explain to them about a recall, but they said they couldn't get me in until next week, so I tried to—"

"This is already paid for in advance. Get your stuff out of the car if you have anything in there."

"You can't take my car until I get some answers on what is going on. You could be any ol' body."

"Don't give me a hard time. I'm not giving you a song and dance, just doing my job."

"You're about to be doing that Tik Tok, 'I'm a Savage'

mothafuckin' dance as you tryna get my foot out of yo' ass, if you don't tell me why in the hell you're trying to tow my car away!" *He has made me go complete Loud Ass Black woman on him! I have tried, Lord knows I did, to stay cool and keep my composure! Mothafuckas be trying it!*

He huffed, then nonchalantly reached for a clipboard, and flipped through the paperwork. "You're getting some scheduled repairs at Martinez Pérez Auto shop in Little Havana on West Flagler Street. Says here they'll have your car back to you in forty-eight hours, and everything is squared away."

"Little Havana? That's a whole hour away. I never scheduled this." She stood there dumbfounded. Then, it hit her... *Wait a minute... Didn't Viper say his uncle and father have a shop in Little Havana? HE DID!* Her body heated with an emotion she wasn't quite sure how to identify, let alone speak of.

"You said your boss told you to do this. Who is your boss?"

The driver chuckled.

"You *know* who he is..." And then the man got right back to work.

I can't get my car into the dealership, and there are other repairs that need to be made which I can't afford right now. I need this taken care of. I am damn sure not taking it back to my other mechanic; he messed up. Viper did know what he was talking about. I looked it up online and he was right. There was in fact a recall of those parts. How he knew that off the top of his head is crazy to me... I don't have a lot of expendable money right now. I spent almost every dime tryna get myself and Troy away from that neighborhood and him into a good school system. If I let Viper do this, he'll want something in return though. I know his type. I've been around street dudes, thugs, drug dealers and the like my whole damn life. They try to butter you up, then bam! The bullshit starts. This motherfucker thinks he's slick. First it was the Lyft service, now this…

Shit, I need my car fixed, though! I can't keep paying for driving services like I have been, or having my friends pick up Troy in the mornings, then take him to the babysitter when I have to work late. Okay, I'm going to allow this, but this is the last favor I'm going to let him do for me. Men always want something in return, and it usually involves our bodies. That man is a whole motherfucking Latin King – that's nothin' to play with. I ain't fuckin', suckin', or trickin' for nobody.

I know what I'll do… I'll pay him back the money when I can. That'll be in a few weeks, easy. Yeah. This is the last favor. THE LAST!

She ran through all of her thoughts, trying to figure out how the hell to proceed. But truly, there was only one thing left to do.

She quickly grabbed two tote bags she typically used for groceries out of the back of the trunk and began to fill them with a few of her items and Troy's toys that were lying about.

Just then, a white Toyota Camry pulled up and out popped Troy, sporting his fresh fade haircut and crisp white shirt and jeans. He waved to his little blond-haired friend, Anderson, as he slung his backpack over his shoulder. "Thank you, Katie, for dropping him off today. I appreciate it." She offered a wave and a forced smile as the tow truck driver continued making a racket in the background.

"No problem, Majesty! See ya tomorrow." The woman threw a quizzical look at the tow truck, judging her, thinking her car was being towed for non-payment no doubt. As Katie drove off, Majesty couldn't help but notice one of her neighbors' curtains moving. A wave of embarrassment washed over her. Several years ago, while living in downtown Miami, she'd been evicted from her apartment. To add insult to injury, as she'd been moving out with her then toddler son, a tow truck had pulled up to take her parked Mazda. She'd watched helplessly as her vehicle had been towed away, and her home gone. Though that exact scenario wasn't happening again, and she'd come a long way, her body and heart didn't seem to know that. It was almost as if it were happening all over again. The memories swelled within her, forcing her to relive the trauma.

"Mama... don't you hear me?" Troy grabbed her wrist and shook it. "I said I gotta B on my math homework today."

"A B? Oh... Well, that's still good, honey."

"Ms. Pritchel said you was wrong on two of the answers, but right on the others. I expected better from you, Mama. You let me down."

"Huh? Boy, hush!" She didn't miss the silly smirk on his face. "I told you to stop telling your teacher that I'm helping you with your homework like that! You were supposed to let her know I *helped*, not do it for you!"

"But I didn't want her to think I got the problems

wrong, Mama. I wanted her to know it was *you* that got 'em wrong."

"You didn't get any of them wrong, and you didn't get any right, because you didn't understand any of it. That's why I did what I did. I probably was rushing, trying to get it finished after I realized you weren't understanding how I was trying to explain it to you. We'll work on it some more tonight after my class. This time, we'll do it together, and I won't rush."

"I don't think I can trust you, Mama, because you got two of the answers wrong. Maybe you need help with the homework, too."

"Thanks, Troy." The boy giggled, knowing darn well what he'd done. "So you're just gonna throw your mother under the bus like that?" She laughed and playfully swatted at him. "Come on, baby. Get in here and wash your hands. Dinner will be made in a little bit. You can eat a few apple slices until then. We need to go over those math timetables again since you seem to be struggling with them." She turned to walk back inside, then paused. "Forty-eight hours it'll be ready, right?"

"Yes, and they'll drop it back off here, too. No need to make arrangements to come pick it up." The man then dug in his pocket and pulled out a piece of paper. "Here's the number of the place. The owner's name is Esteban Martinez." The guy got in the truck, then drove off.

"Mama, will you pack my lunch for tomorrow? The food at school is nasty. 'Cept for Fridays. Fridays are Pizza Day."

"Yes, baby… I'll make you a peanut butter and jam sandwich, and toss in some chips and a Capri Sun. Come on, we have limited time and a lot to do…"

CHAPTER FIVE

It's Raining Trained Cats and Dogs

I REMEMBER *STANDING out in the rain when I was five.*

I can think about it now, with an adult mind, but my vision on that day was a child's. That made everything ten times harder, rougher.

My hair felt heavy, like a helmet against my head, my bones clung to an ungodly coolness, and my clothing glued itself to my skin like a second layer of flesh. I stood out in the rain with my big brother, Diego. We were safer out there, chancing catching pneumonia rather than being within those cursed walls. Inside my childhood home, the tiny house with the sloped roof rang sharp screams and the shattering of goblets and dishes that poured from the closed windows, beating on the glass panes and breaking free to reach our ears. Our belongings were being destroyed. We didn't have much to begin with. Despite the queasiness and my body shivering, knees buckling, I remained standing. Twisted curse words and wishes of death drifted from the house. I could not turn up the music this time to block them out. I loved my music loud enough to drown out the demons. The music became my guardian angel, but she was nowhere to be found.

No song could kill the wicked witch of wretchedness. She refused to go under. I yearned for it to stop. To go away. Our parents were gasoline and fire. Their love was air, fanning the flames. Toxic kisses and codependency, fucking all morning, fighting, and screaming all night. We heard orgasms and calls to the police all in the same day. Freezing temperatures and rain. Their pain climbed the mountains of sound and stood on top of that peak, drenched in the blood of despair. At last, the screaming stopped. But only for a minute.

My father walked past one of the windows, his back hunched. He looked like a monster, only I knew him well, and he was not hiding in my closet or under my bed. His towering frame was like a looming dark shadow against the broken light. He was walking away now. Far away. He'd been walking away for years, only his feet hadn't been moving. My mother, with her fragmented mind and festering dejection, pulled him back to her, blocking his way, grabbing him by his shirt. She sank her teeth into his arm, then slapped him with the strength of giants and drained his last bit of hope like a vampire.

He grabbed her, and I screamed out. Diego pulled me to him and placed his hand over my mouth. Silencing me. Made me hiss like a snake, for no words came out as he held my lips tight with his palm. My father dragged her through the house, out of view. Screaming. Laughing. Crying.

We stood out in the rain, our lives falling apart and disappearing into the blades of half dead grass. My mind drifted away, as it did when I watched a movie. I'd never seen my father do such a thing. Mi padre *fought her. He beat her. We could not see, but we could feel and hear it as Mamá laughed and cursed him. Each blow to her tore at my heart. It felt like a ruptured rumble, a trickle of our souls melting away. Life in slow motion.*

No one came to help us. No one interfered. In that moment, the house looked as if it were covered in a million spiky thorns, with wilted red roses that stunk of decay. I imagined it being crushed by the foliage, and the walls were folding in, smooshed down into the ground with the two of them inside of it. The thought gave me a sense of peace. Things got quiet, but I didn't budge. I didn't want to go in the house just yet. For some reason, I hesitated...

Diego and I seemed to have the same reservations, for he didn't move a muscle, either. I was shivering and cold. Hungry, too. I hadn't eaten in days. My stomach growled as though a bear cub lived inside of me, desperate to claw his way out. It hurt so badly that soon, I felt nothing at all. Just a dull ache. After a while, I didn't feel that either. I just stood in the rain. Hungry for love but refusing to ever love again. How could that be? I was so young, and already, I hated it so much. If love made people act this way, I didn't want it...

Dad came out the house, bursting from the front door with a black bag in his hand and a look of complete defeat and shame on his face. Yes, even at that age, I knew what shame looked like. The same face as when my cousin had been arrested by the police for murdering his wife's son in a jealous rage.

Tears fell from his eyes. The scars on his face were blurred with moisture, softening his appearance. I had only seen Dad cry at his father's funeral. Su padre fue el pilar de la familia. *Dad bent down and kissed me on the cheek, Diego on the forehead. He told us that he loved us. He then said he had to go before he killed her. We knew he meant it. I don't remember what he said after that, but I* watched him get in his car with that one bag and drive away. He drove off, abandoning us, and then, Diego and I looked at each other. Diego's black hair was practically covering his eyes, and raindrops dangled from his earlobes and dripped from his nose. He couldn't see me crying; it was raining. Or at least I thought he couldn't.

Our parents never lived together again after that day.

Diego drew closer to the door, holding my hand tight, pulling me along. We hesitated in front of the same exit Dad had walked out of. He looked down at me and shook his head, almost in disgust. 'I told you to stop that! No more! Wipe your face, Dominic. Never cry. Crying is a weakness. It's for pussies. We have to be strong for Mamá.' I wiped my face and the snot from my nose with the back of my wet hand, and he helped me get rid of the tears, too. When he was satisfied that I looked the part, we walked back into the house. He looked down at the floor, then picked me up in his arms; I had on no shoes. There was broken glass all over our small living room. Mamá was sobbing in her bed, a little ways down the hall.

We could hear her, make out her form. I know she had to have heard the crunching glass under Diego's sandals. I know she heard us coming. She didn't look at us for a long time. We stood quiet at her door, and then, she finally looked up from her bed. Her face had been shoved in the pillow as if she'd wanted to suffocate herself. Her eyes were flushed, her skin splotchy pale pink and yellow. Her black wavy hair was all over the place, her blue butterfly ankle tattoo vibrant against her flesh. Her red nightgown drooped down her shoulders, exposing her breast. She pointed to me and smiled. It was not a typical smile. Not joyous, or a happy-to-see-me smile. It was a gesture filled with oscuridad- darkness.

"I need you to go away." Her smile faded away like an ink drop

in a bucket of black dye, and more tears fell from her mahogany eyes.
"I can't look at you right now. Especially you, Dominic." Her dark
eyes tapered into slits. Te pareces a él." She pointed at me.
"Just look at you. I hate your father. Go away!"

I backed up, then fled into the room Diego and I shared. And I
cried in silence. I sat in a corner; my eyes fixed on my reflection in a
mirror above the dresser. A rosary hung from it. The beads were
gleaming in colors of bright gold and blood red. It started to swing. I
covered my mouth with my hands. My sight was blurred with hot
tears of disbelief and fright. The rosary swung back and forth like a
pendulum. How? Why? Who was moving it? I ignored the insects
crawling around me, and the scurrying of mice. I ignored the odor of
mildew and mold. I ignored the booming lightning, and the way my
skin itched from the wet clothes. The rosary chain suddenly stopped
moving, and then, I heard a broom slowly swaying from left to right,
right to left. It was Diego, cleaning up our parents' mess.

Diego always cleaned up the mess. Maybe that was why he
eventually left me, as well? Or maybe he thought he was a mess that
needed to be cleaned up, too…

Viper gasped as he suddenly awoke and sat up straight.
He blinked, opened his eyes, and focused. *Am I awake? I*
am. His muscles ached; an odd stiff pain radiated throughout his sweat-drenched body.

It was raining outside. *I must've heard it in my dreams.* He
hated that nightmare. Only, it wasn't a nightmare. It was
true, one of many pages of his book of life. He closed his
eyes and touched the gold chain around his neck, the
cross pendant with Jesus nailed against it, his head
wrapped in gold thorns. His heart pounded painfully in his
chest. He took a couple deep breaths, then reached for a

bottle of water on his black marble nightstand and gulped it straight down.

He cleared his throat and grabbed his cellphone, taking note of several missed calls and voicemails. He was shocked to see how late in the day it was. 3:14 P.M. He yawned, stretched, then got out of bed. As soon as he opened his bedroom door, the dogs came for him.

"Yo, hey!" He grinned as he dropped to his knees and loved on them. "I slept late, huh? You had food and water. You were okay." He rubbed them and scratched behind their ears. "You've got automatic feeders. Toys, too." But he knew in his heart they wanted more. They wanted *him*.

After taking a quick shower, he got dressed in a pair of oversized overalls and his Nikes. He put his Los Angeles Dodgers snapback on his head then headed to the kitchen, only to be surrounded by his furry friends once again. *"Mis perros están enamorados de mí!"* He made himself a cup of coffee, leaned against the counter, and peered out his window. The rain had finally stopped, and the sun was coming out. He always likened the sun as being a woman. She, too, had awakened late. Shoving a handful of dog treats in his pocket, he retrieved their three leashes from the foyer area. They pranced about, excited as ever.

"No accidents today. Good." He'd trained them to go out of a special dog door that led into the backyard. It was rather small, so they had to move their bodies just so – to exit and enter, and it had a special lock. He'd also installed an electric fence, as well as a dog hut for shelter in case of a sudden downpour. He set the alarm and opened the front door. The air was scented with the promise of another bout of rain. He inhaled, exhaled, then started walking. It was strangely quiet outside, so different from Little Havana and the various places he'd visited throughout his lifetime.

His phone buzzed in his pocket as Sarge paused to sniff a tree trunk. The other two joined in. A piss sniff fest.

"Hola, Marie." He yanked the leash, forcing Sarge to come closer. *"¿Cómo estás?"*

"No lo estoy haciendo bien, Viper."

He paused.

"What's wrong? Are you okay physically?"

"Physically, yes." She took a labored breath, as if she could barely breathe.

"Is it Stacks? It's Stacks, isn't it? Is he in trouble?"

"No, Viper. Stacks is fine. I was told you came by and had a talk with him and some of the others. From what I understand and see, they're following your orders. I'm calling because Javier got into a fight with Dice."

Javier and King Dice had never liked one another. Ego. Pride. Competition. It had begun due to a woman many years ago, but the animosity never ended, even after she'd left. When it came to internal Nation fighting, they were at the top of the tier, always at each other's throats. Javier was immature, but very good at tattooing and getting fast money.

"I thought Dice had moved to California to be with his wife's family? I haven't seen him in months."

"He came back last week. I meant to tell you. It wasn't

planned. He had a falling out with his wife's father. Everything was fine for a couple of days, then they went out drinking."

He rolled his eyes, then began walking the dogs again.

"Javier can't control his alcohol. *Su lengua se afloja.* Belleza!" he hollered, then whistled. She'd snarled at a cat on someone's porch then tried to make a mad dash towards it. "Belleza. Sit." The dog immediately stopped pulling the leash and sat down, still as a soldier. "So, I take it, this time, things went too far, and Javier is in trouble?"

"*Sí,* but he did not strike first."

"Does Jaguar know?"

"*Sí. La policía disolvió la pelea.* Dice was arrested."

"Shit." He took a deep breath, tossed on a smile, and waved when one of his neighbors drove down the street—a little Jewish woman originally from New York who never smiled or waved back. Now there were two Kings in jail within a matter of days, and the police wanted information. Things were being made too easy for them. Perhaps they'd pit Wild and Dice against one another, make it seem as if each was dropping dimes. Viper knew the game and how it was played. He'd been around too long to not catch on. "Marie, find out how much his bond is. Wild isn't getting out anytime soon, they made sure of that, but Dice's bond should be cheap unless they've tossed other trumped-up charges at him. We have to get him out of there."

"Okay. I will call you back when I find out."

"*Gracias.* I'll handle it."

"I know you will. You always do."

He disconnected the call, then turned around at the corner. Absently aware of his Glock-19 against his hip as he walked back to his house, he sent several text messages to fellow Kings, asking what they knew about the situation, as well as trying to get an update on Wild. It was challenging to keep his thumb on his brothers when not right amongst them, but after he paid the pop-up visit, he had a better hold of the situation. It reminded them who was in charge, and any fuck-up would result in a severe punishment. Then, he saw a text from Jaguar. The inevitable had come home to roost.

Vibora, tenemos un problema.

Yeah, we have a problem all right…

He approached a few tall trees and allowed Chance, Sarge, and Belleza to roam a bit less close to him while he dialed Jaguar. This warranted a verbal conversation.

"*Hola*, Jaguar. What's up?"

"I understand Wild got into some trouble."

"*Si.* I'm handling it."

"He is weak under pressure. He will run his mouth. Are you bailing him out?"

"The judge made the bail too high, but I got him a good attorney."

"When the opportunity presents itself, take him out." With that, he ended the call.

Viper slipped the phone back into his pocket, then called to his dogs, and ordered them to keep walking. His legs felt heavy, and the scent of rain in the air made his mind flood with visions of being soaked in the torrent, beside Diego. He kept moving ahead, his thoughts swinging like that rosary on the dresser mirror. This was his concern: that Jaguar would fear that Wild would talk, and his entire operation would sink down to the ground. Everyone had been so careful for so long. Wild knew everyone's moves; he had the inside information. It was his job. He was a lookout, after all. The perfect target. Viper wished he could've been surprised by Jaguar's call, but he wasn't.

King Jaguar was in prison, serving a ten-year sentence for assault and weapons charges, with three years served. He still ran his local operation with an iron fist, behind those bars. He always had access to cell phones, the internet, whatever he needed. He'd had several members killed for what he deemed was disrespect, bucking his authority. Jaguar was the epitome of no fucks given. He had an estranged wife and two ex-girlfriends, his baby mamas, several children with each, and made sure all of them were living well. He had drugs coming and going so fast, the money was almost *too* easy to make. With all of that power, all of that dope, and all of that command, problems were imminent. Jaguar wasn't the quiet child he recalled so many years ago.

When they were kids, they were close, like brothers, though Jaguar was a few years his senior, the same age as his big brother. It came as no surprise that he and Diego had joined the Latin Kings on the exact same day, both of them jumped on and beaten within an inch of their lives. Viper was soon to follow. Less than a year later, he was brought into the fold. At the time, at the mere age of fourteen, he was certain that this was the life he wanted.

Protection in an uncertain world. A family at last. Shelter from the rain.

He'd worked hard to prove himself, to show he had what it took, to try and be even better than his brother. Stronger. Smarter. After a while, the beatings and murders got easier to handle, until he felt nothing at all. Numb. Everyone had to earn their stripes and their keep, to bring in dough, and maintain honor. Rather than be involved in robberies or dealing drugs like many of his Nation brothers, he got into acquiring weapons and soon garnered a reputation for his vicious assaults in retaliation for the slightest infractions. He stayed in the gym, kept his weight up, and never let his guard down. Some people didn't know how to take him; he wasn't a braggart, he didn't kiss ass, and he didn't kiss and tell. He kept his business to himself, his friends close, enemies closer— some of those enemies being fellow Latin Kings—but family, including his Latin King brothers, was crucial to him.

When Marie called him and requested a coming home bash for Stacks, he didn't shillyshally, but something about looking into her eyes as she prepared food, sang in his kitchen and laughed broke his heart. He'd been away from Little Havana, and in that time, it seemed his mind had begun to play tricks on him. His desires were changing, his thirst for being in the thick of it all waning. Marie was getting up in age; the life she'd lived shone on her beautiful, mature face. She looked far older than she was and had buried most of her children. How was this nirvana? He saw himself in her, but imagined he'd be in a box six feet under with a gunshot to his head by the time he reached her age. Execution style. The same had happened to her eldest son.

She was in the life, had slowed down but was still quite active. She was still trying to protect and serve, calling and warning him and other officers in the Nation of things she'd seen and heard. His last stint in prison had made him weary, so he'd stepped back from the weapons commerce and focused on what he'd done since he was a boy: train dogs. If he got serious about this business, it would be lucrative, and perhaps, subconsciously, he knew it would also be like insurance. A way out.

He was a natural at it. He loved animals, especially dogs. It had begun by accident. He'd found a stray dog and brought it home to his mother. She hadn't wanted it, but he'd begged her to keep it. She'd said, *Dominic, I don't want that filthy animal in our home, but you've been begging me for days, and you keep sneaking him back in here. I will make you a deal. If you can make it not shit or piss in my house, and do tricks and obey, you can keep it. If you can't, and he acts up, he's gone.'* Mamá had been certain the dog would be out the door soon. There was no way he, at the age of 11, could have trained a wild, stray street dog to do any of those things.

But he'd taken her challenge and taught the mutt multiple tricks, potty trained it, and even trained it to fetch her slippers and the remote control. She'd been sold.

He soon reached the bottom of his driveway. His thoughts scattered like jumbled puzzle pieces. Then, a noise sounded in the distance. He turned and stared at the house with the slightly sloped lawn where the pretty

Majesty dwelled.

Her car was back in her driveway, fixed. Viper had paid for everything, without a second thought. She'd shown no interest in him whatsoever, yet he'd insisted on helping her.

Or maybe it was the challenge of it. Fact was, he was thinking about her far too much, and he was beginning to get on his own nerves. Instead of a thank you, she'd left a curt handwritten note in his mailbox letting him know she'd found out the total for the repairs, she would appreciate it if he would not interfere again, and she'd be paying him back in full. The script was in dark purple ink, flowy and elegant. Pretty. As he looked at the note, smelling it, the sweetness of the paper perhaps inadvertently soaked with a drop of her perfume, he wondered why she didn't have a man.

Could she be crazy? A lesbian? *Well, she had to have liked dick at least one time, because she's got a son… Maybe she'd just gotten out of something?* He had questions, and he wanted them answered. His singlehood was by choice. Was she the same? Inside the house, he turned off the alarm and the dogs dashed straightaway to their individual water dispensers and food bowls. He took his time hanging up the leashes, then made his way up the steps to his weight room.

He turned on the music system in his home gym, and "Tres Deliquentes" by Delinquent Habits blasted through the speakers. Taking off his shirt, he started with the weight bench, grunting with each push of the two-hundred-pound weights. After a short while, he increased the weight, then some more, bursting into a drenched sweat and growing angrier and angrier.

I'm tired! I'm sick of this shit! Jaguar has no clue what he's doing. He's taking out too many people, way too fast. That's going to draw more attention from the wrong people. We'll look unorganized. Fractured. I understand his concerns, but killing Wild is a bad idea. It's not the answer unless we have concrete proof he snitched. Yet I know he won't listen to me. He thinks he knows better than everyone else. King Million should've never crowned him in this position. Jaguar wasn't ready. It doesn't even matter now… I've been fed up for a while. I can't leave my brothers, though. The Nation is losing soldiers. If I leave now, more lives will be lost. These guys can't make it on their own. They need me, King Beast, Juan, and the rest of us, especially the enforcers. I help these young guys get on the right path. Try to show 'em other things they can do instead of hanging in the street. They've got to be cleverer. Work smarter.

The streets are different now. People walk around strapped, but not everyone knows how to shoot. The police are crawling everywhere. They want to drive the poor out by arresting and targeting them, so the buildings can be bought up and gentrification can commence. Why can't these idiots see that has been the plan all along? They're pussies! They don't think! It's just a bunch of noise. No strategic planning. They just rush in and fuck everything up. I don't need teardrop tattoos. I know the bodies I've got, and so does everyone else. I've been wettin' motherfuckers up since I was fourteen! Nobody knows how to fight anymore! Nobody knows how to shut their fuckin' mouths, either… These idiots are smoking their own product. Lame. People who aren't from where we're from don't understand our thinking…

He gritted his teeth as he kept pumping, his arm muscles and biceps burning along the way.

They say, if you gangbang, you'll be dead before you know it. But little do they know, many of us would've been dead if it weren't for the Nation… for bangin'. Our lives are short, but longer with a tribe. People judge! But they don't get it. I get it… They don't know my story; no one but Diego and I know the truth. And now, I want to do something else with the time I have here on this planet. I don't know if I'm goin' to heaven or hell, but I know I want a piece of paradise right now, and this ain't it. I am so fucking tired… I know there's more out here for me. The world is so fucked up. And I'm fucked up, too…

I don't want to take out any more of my brothers for petty shit, or shit that wasn't their fault. Yeah, they need their ass kicked, but to wet them up for being ten minutes late to the meeting? It happens… I'm sick of that, too. Some of this no longer makes sense. I can't keep doing shit that doesn't make sense to me anymore, just for the sake of tradition. Life within itself isn't precious to me, but a chance to believe in its worth is gold. I wonder what that feels like? To care? I don't remember. I'd like to remember, though. Maybe I'm getting too fucking soft in my old age? Nah, I just want somethin' else. Ya gotta grow, right? I feel stagnated. Stuck. Mamá said I'm like my father. She's told me that my entire life. Said she loves me, but she could never control me. She blamed Diego when she found out I had joined the Latin Kings, but it wasn't Diego's fault. She had two sons lost to the streets, and she cried about it. She knows that deep down, Diego wasn't to blame. I needed something she couldn't give me. A sense of belonging. Shelter out of the rain. I needed no shattered glass, no black duffle bags, and no windows blocked by demons, dancing on the backs of angels born of the light.

I can't just walk away… Well, I could, but then of course…

there's THAT. I'm on a mission... I have to do it. It's mine. I must finish the cycle... FUCK EVERYONE.

He pushed the weight up for the last time, placed the barbell back, and sat up, his entire body drenched in sweat. After stewing in his own thoughts for what felt like an eternity, he got to his feet and jumped in the shower of his master suite bedroom. Cypress Hill's, 'Insane In the Membrane' played as he rinsed off and stepped onto the plush black rug to dry off. He proceeded to check his schedule on his computer. Two new dogs would be coming over soon for an initial consultation for training, but he had about an hour to kill beforehand. *I'll eat a little something.* He tossed on a black V-neck T-shirt and black cargo shorts, then a pair of no-show white socks under his red and black GOAT Jordans.

Moments later, he was riding down the street on his BMW F 900 XR motorcycle, making his way to the Taco Inn Food Truck, located next to the local brewery. The spot had strange business hours, but he was in luck. They were open. The delectable scent of fresh salsa, grilled pork, beef, and chicken wafted in the air, making his stomach growl in anticipation. This was one of the few spots where he could find authentic Mexican cuisine. He ordered some Birria tacos, one of his favorites, and headed back home, checking the time every so often. As he approached his house, he noticed Majesty's son playing with a couple of other little boys in the front yard.

He slowed down, noting that one of the kids was White, and the other Asian. They were tossing a ball between them, laughing and carrying on. He smiled at the sight, then slowed when the ball rolled down the driveway, into the street...

CHAPTER SIX

A King's Ransom

ONE OF THE boys screamed, and they all stopped and stared in horror, expecting he'd run over the ball and smash it to a pulp. Viper pulled over and parked his bike along the sidewalk, grabbed the ball, and tucked it under his arm. Brandishing a smile, he walked up the driveway towards the youthful trio.

"A, don't worry. That's my mama's friend," the handsome little Black boy said, as if he were responsible for putting everyone at ease. "His name is Diaper." The other two boys burst out laughing, beating on their knees as their faces turned red.

"Diaper!" one of them kept repeating, barely able to get the word out before falling to the ground, totally taken asunder by the giggles.

"Viper," he corrected, swallowing a chuckle of his own. "Vi-per." He tossed the ball to Majesty's son. "What are you playing?"

"Just toss. Bored. Mama is supposed to take us to the park, but she said she might not have time, so Sirus and Lou came to play with me. They wanna go, too." He looked as if his feelings were genuinely hurt.

"I'm sure she'll let you go another day."

The boy nodded half-heartedly, then tossed him back the ball, engaging him in a bit of play. He caught it, then tossed it to the Asian kid, who passed it on to the dark-haired White boy. He recognized the children from the neighborhood and wondered if perhaps they were all the same age. They appeared to be.

"Tell your mother hello for me." He smirked as he tossed the ball one last time to the kid. He caught it, and a mischievous gleam crossed the boy's face.

"Maaaama! Viper said hello! He out here playin' with us!" he screamed at the top of his lungs. Suddenly, the front door swung open, and there stood Majesty in a light gray crop top, long-sleeved cotton hoodie, and baggy gray jogging pants, pierced navel exposed. Her hair was parted on the side, flowing down past her shoulders and breasts.

"Mama, tell him I'm not lying. Didn't you say his name was Diaper? You were on the phone and said that the big Cuban man across the street was named Diaper."

Viper stared at the woman who looked completely mortified. He crossed his arms and sucked his teeth, pretending to be pissed, when all he really wanted to do was burst out laughing. *She's been talking shit about me to other people. That's good, actually. Means I'm on her mind, too. Looks like she might like me after all…*

"I never said his name was no damn Diaper, Troy. Now what sense does that make?!" Her face turned to a deeper hue along the cheeks.

"Yes, you did. You said, he ain't S-H-I-T, and then you said that his name fits, 'cause it's Diaper." The two boys burst out laughing again. Boy did Majesty look angry.

"I'm a diaper, huh? Viper and Diaper. That rhymes. I get it. Good joke." He flashed his teeth at her. "What brand am I? Huggies or Pampers? I hope I come with wipes, too." This really got the boys giggling.

"Troy, I've got something special for you." She pointed at her son, her threat loud and clear. She looked around, as if suddenly remembering she had company. "I'll take you and your friends to the park in five minutes." All three boys began to jump up and down, cheering, soon forgetting about the running joke. "Viper, what are you doing here?"

"Your son, I just realized his name was Troy since you've just now said it, lost his ball in the street. I was bringing some food home, stopped, and picked it up to give back to him." She nodded in understanding. The boys began to laugh and chase each other around the yard. Holding herself as though she felt chilly, she inched closer across the porch, then looked both ways as though a train was coming before making her way down the steps. She now stood close enough for him to view all her beautiful imperfections. A smattering of beauty marks. A small scar on her chin. Her eyebrows were pitch black, natural, and arched to perfection. Her lips were full and succulent, and her neck was long and lovely.

And boy did she smell amazing.

"Damn, you look good."

"What?" She rolled her eyes. "Look, Viper, I just wanted to tell you, thank you for what you did for my car, but you overstepped your bounds. I don't need anyone bailing me out. Regardless, I know your heart was in the right place. I thanked your father, too, when I called over there. If you wait right here, I can give you a hundred dollars towards the bill."

"I don't need it." Ignoring him, she walked in her house, the screen door slamming behind her. He watched the boys playing as he waited. They reminded him of him and his brother with their next-door neighbor. Those had been innocent times. Good times. Times long gone.

"Can I have some shoes like yours?" the White boy asked, bits of grass sticking to his sweaty face. Lust for the sneakers shone in his bright blue eyes.

"You like these, huh? These cost a lot. Maybe if you go to college and get a good job, you can have some." *That's the politically right thing to tell kids, right? Maybe? Hell, who knows. I've never been politically correct. How would I know?*

"He'll be old by then, man, and they'll be outta style, too!" Troy protested.

"Well, you have a point there. So, why don't you ask for a pair for your birthday, or Christmas?"

"I did. My mother said they were too expensive for just a pair of sneakers. What I don't get is she spends way more than that to make me take piano lessons! I hate playing the piano!" The little kid turned away, disgruntled.

Majesty came back out, money in hand. Taking his

hand, she spread out his fingers and placed two fifty-dollar bills in his palm. When she touched him, electricity flashed through him. He slipped the cash into his pocket.

"This wasn't necessary, but if it makes you feel better, that's fine."

"It does. I know that barely scratches the surface, but I'll have the rest to you in the next couple of weeks. No such thing as a free lunch out here." Silence stretched for a while. She looked awkward, as if not certain where to rest her eyes. Her stomach grumbled. Her cheeks turned deep red once again, and she burst out laughing. He followed suit.

"You're hungry."

"I have food in the house."

"That's not what I said. Check this out." He grabbed his bag of grub from his motorcycle and approached her. "Look what I've got?" Grinning, he reached into the bag as if it were full of candies from Halloween and un-wrapped one of the tacos from its greasy parchment paper wrapping. He knew the aroma alone would seduce her. "Best damn tacos in town. Taste this." He brought it closer to her face.

"No, that's all right. Thank you though." She took a step back.

He stepped closer and her eyes widened.

"Open your mouth…" *I want to put something tasty, warm, and heavy in there…*

Her smile faded, but then, she parted her lips and bit into the taco. Her lips curved in a smile. He caught a bit of lettuce she was having trouble getting into her mouth with his finger, and let it fall to the ground.

"It's good, isn't it?"

"I'd be lying if I said it wasn't. What is that? Some kind of steak?"

"They're called Birria tacos… Mexican recipe. It's stewed beef with many different seasonings. Cooked real slow until it's falling off the bone. Every now and again, you might go to a place that makes 'em out of goat meat, but these are the best."

"It's peppery, but sweet and flavorful all at the same time." She patted the side of her mouth with the back of her hand. "Delicious."

"Here… take another bite. Better yet, take it all."

"No, no, I'm okay. I can't eat your dinner, Viper."

"I insist. Come on. I have three more of these. I'm *really* greedy, so I always buy plenty."

"Thank you." She took the taco and dug in.

"If you think this is good, you should try Cuban food. Ever been to Little Havana?"

"Driven through many times, but never stayed for any length of time. You told me you grew up there. What part did you live in?" She took another bite, then wrapped the remainder up.

"East Havana. The place everyone talks badly about."

She offered a crooked smile. He could see in her eyes she'd heard the stories about East Havana, too. How dangerous it was with all the high crime, murders, rapes, and thefts.

"What about you? Where'd you grow up?"

"Allapattah."

"What?!" He burst out laughing.

"What is so funny?" She looked somewhat confused.

"My boy asked if you were Dominican, Majesty. You said no, and that's fine, he was just curious, but you grew up in a Dominicano and Nicaragüense hood! You better check your DNA. Oh my God! How dare you be offended. What the fuck?" He cackled.

She rolled her eyes, smirked, then giggled.

"It's a coincidence, and there are *far* more Blacks and Cubans there than Dominicans. I have quite a few Dominican friends though, but I'm not one. You'd think I'd know Spanish due to having so many friends that speak it, but I don't. Well, I know a little."

"*Un pequeño?*" He brought his index finger and thumb close, indicating a small amount.

"Yes! *Pequeño.*" Her smile lit up the atmosphere.

"So, why'd you move away?"

"I moved downtown for a few years after I had Troy, tried to get a fresh start, but then went back to save some money."

"I take it you didn't like it where you grew up?"

"No, I didn't. It's unsafe, especially for me and trying to raise my son. Some parts are safer than others, but you know what I mean. I was afraid something bad would happen." She hesitated, as if she wanted to say more, but stopped herself. She snuck a brief glance at her kid, playing with his friends. "So, speaking of neighborhoods, I also had wanted to tell you that I love your house, Viper. It's one of the prettiest in the area. How do you pay the bills to keep it?"

"Damn, you're nosey. You just come on out and say it, huh?"

"I am. Are you gonna answer or what? I might need another part time job, as long as it's not something illegal," she teased.

"Nah, I make my money above the table. I train dogs. The kind no one else can. Many of them are in danger of being put down without an intervention. I have rich people coming to me due to little FiFi tearing up their shoes, all the way to your average guy who can't control his dog and if he doesn't get help, his pet will be taken away by the city. I train them here at my home, and I also teach a class out in Wellington every now and again, at one of the training centers. I want to eventually own my own instruction facility, and have staff, then have it be a franchise all over south Florida."

"That is a big goal, but I bet you'll pull it off. You seem passionate about it."

"I'm passionate about a lot of things. If you only knew…" Silence lingered in the air as she scratched her neck, then cleared her throat.

"I, uh, saw one of your blue Pit Bulls the other day. Gorgeous animal."

"Yeah, I have three of them, actually. So… while we're on the topic, how did you come about renting this house?"

"How'd you know I rent?" She grimaced, as if she'd somehow been violated.

"There was a 'For Rent' sign in the yard before you moved in, Majesty," he stated dryly, mirroring her expression.

"Oh… that's right." She laughed. "Um, well, it's a long story."

"I've got time," he lied. In fact, if he didn't get home soon, he'd be late for his appointments, but this was the chance of a lifetime. That ball rolling into the street changed his fortune. Majesty had come out to play.

"Well, my mother knows the guy who owns it. I had been wanting to move. I had saved up a lot of money, but I wanted to move into a house. No more apartments. I wanted Troy to have a yard, and a good school district." He nodded in understanding. "So, on my behalf, my mother asked if I could rent it, since the guy was having trouble keeping good tenants in it. They always stopped paying rent or left it in shambles. The owner lives in Texas now. He just wanted it occupied, and well taken care of."

"Yeah, I'd heard he moved to Texas."

"He and I spoke, worked out an agreement, now, here we are." She shrugged. "I work, take good care of my child and go to school. I budget. I work hard, and I will work even harder to make sure we're good. Better than good."

"The night you came by complaining about my music, you said you were in school. What's your major?" He knew he was pushing his luck by asking her personal questions, but he had to try. He wanted to know every damn thing about her.

"I'm going into Human Resources and I'll be finished soon."

The more she spoke, the more turned on he was. Her

determination, love for her son, goals and fiery personality hit all of his buttons. She set him ablaze with desire and hatched sinful fantasies of him doing all sorts of sordid things to her. He loved her get-up-and-go attitude, and how she refused to fail. She was like him, resilient, and he'd hardly ever met anyone that could match his ambition.

"I *did* say your name was Diaper to my friend."

"I know you did." He laughed lightly. "Your son couldn't have thought of that on his own. He's too young to have reached that level of smart-ass just yet. That was a grown woman move."

She pretended to swipe dust off her shoulder then grinned proudly.

"I meant what I said earlier. You look so damn good. Definitely my type."

"You need to stop." She shook her head and sighed.

"I can't stop. You're sexy to me. Now that we've spoken for longer than one minute, I see you've got a good head on your shoulders, too. That's good. I like that. Motivation and determination are a big turn on to me."

"Well then, let me drop out of school right now, stop payin' rent, neglect my child and play video games all day," she teased, making him laugh.

"Stop playing hard to get and let me take you out. Can you dance? We can go dancing, get a bite to eat."

"You're probably married with fifteen children, Viper."

"Fourteen. Only fourteen kids, and three wives. Looking for a fourth. If you're lucky, that's you."

She twisted her lips and put her hand on her hip. But soon, they succumbed to mirth all over again.

"Nah, not married… never been married." He scratched his elbow and glanced at the children for a moment. "I don't have any fruit of my loins, so to speak, either. If I did, I definitely would claim them."

"Really? No children, huh? How old are you?" She looked unconvinced.

"I'm thirty-one. You?"

"Just turned thirty."

"Well then, happy belated birthday. So… you gonna let me take you out or what? No Netflix and chill. A *real* date."

She took a deep breath, looked away at a passing car, then eyed him again.

"You know that's not going to happen. I know what you do, how you operate, and the circles you hang in. I can't have that sort of thing around my son, Viper."

"Mmm, I see." He licked his lower lip and absently cracked his knuckles. "You think a guy like me makes it to age thirty-one by bein' stupid?" He narrowed his gaze. "I've had plenty of women, baby. You can ask anybody about me, and they'll tell you I'm not the one to try shit with. None of the women I've dated or been in a relationship with have gotten into any shit on account of me, or the company I keep."

"You can't guarantee that. There's no way to guarantee that."

"You really have no idea who you're talking to right now. I don't have to tell you anything, explain anything.

Just ask around. My reputation precedes me. I'm well known. Not here, but in the dark corners of Miami. Ask people who my brother was. My family. I'm not what you think I am. Not by a long shot."

"But see, I bet none of the women you were with had—"

"Some of 'em had children. I knew what you were about to say. I've dated women with children before. I'm funny about family, Majesty. I'm protective of children. I keep my lifestyle away from them, and when dating a woman who isn't a Latin Queen, I keep it away from her, too. It's really not that difficult."

She regarded him long and hard.

"Are you active? Because let me tell you, Mr. King Viper, I don't want that shit around *me* either." Her smile was soon replaced by darkness... Hurt swelled to the surface, as if she'd stood by a motherfucker like him before, only it was a different face, different race, and different place.

"Do you know why they call me Viper?"

"No, but I bet you're about to tell me."

"They call me Viper because I lie low. I plot. I plan. I stand on my own two feet. Ten toes down in my *own* honor. Years can pass, and the prey can think it's gotten away. But then, I strike. I'm slow. Then fast. Methodical, until it's time to attack. I'm never in a rush. I take my time, then build up... keep it steady..." He scanned her sensual form from the top of her head to her feet, real slow, then looked back up until he met her eyes once again. "I speed up, bit by bit, moving around and around in that garden until I'm fully engulfed in the brush, deep in the jungle... *deep* in that bush... A snake, dipping in and out... in... then out... over and over, never getting enough. The earth around me grows warm and wet with rain as I move with precision within it. I go faster... and faster... and faster... until the whole damn world around me explodes. Pulsing. Nothin' but stars. The earth vibrates, as a grand finale, and then, I make my way out, leaving nothing but satisfaction." He winked at her as he waved his hands about in the air.

She sucked her teeth and her face twitched.

"And last but not least, Majesty, I rest there. Held close by Mother Nature. My cold, reptilian heart beats slower as I curl against the wet warmth of the oasis. I lie there and reminisce, still tasting my prey on my forked tongue... Because you see, before the chase, and all of that moving around in that sweet rainforest, I ate what was in my way. It was a tiny, succulent pink flower, a beautiful bud, sitting in a little sailboat all by its lonesome. Gulp!" He burst out laughing as she turned a million colors.

"Uhhh..." She sighed, her face beet red now. *Black girls definitely blush...* And he loved it. "You're nasty." She waved her finger at him and laughed.

"Nah." He threw up his hands. "I'm just talkin' about being a Viper is all."

"Satan was a snake in the garden of Eden," she chided. "Just like you."

"And Eve just couldn't resist temptation. Just like you..."

"Mama!" Troy called out from across the yard, the ball now cradled under his arm. "Can we go to the park now? Dang. We been waitin'."

"Okay. Yeah, let's go. We'll walk over. Well, it was nice talking to you, Viper. Thanks for the taco." She waved the food in the air and turned to hurriedly walk away. Reaching out, he gently grabbed her wrist, stopping her. Her eyes fixed on his fingers wrapped around her arm.

"Talk is cheap. I want to spend some time with you. Call me."

"As charming, resourceful and, dare I admit, sexy as you are, Viper, you know I'm not calling you."

"My number is, 305-555-0100. Remember that, and keep in mind what I said. Family preservation is crucial. I would *never* allow anything or anyone to mess up my plans, hurt something, or in this case, someone that I want." He glanced at Troy who was sitting on the porch, retying his shoelaces.

"Like I told you, there's no guarantee, even with the best of intentions."

"That goes for everything and everyone, Majesty. You think you'd be safer dating an accountant? He could get robbed, and you could be killed in the process. I'm not dealing drugs, I'm not dealing weapons anymore, either. I protect my brothers. Period."

"Everyone thinks they're different until it's proven they're not." He stood close to her, so their bodies almost touched. As he drowned in her beautiful dark brown eyes, the lashes lush and thick, he could see the worry, pain, trauma and hurt in her face. She had no idea it was tattooed on her, but he could smell and feel it, too. Practically taste it.

"I'm not like the rest, baby, but I am the fucking best. Give me a chance. Don't stereotype me. Not all Kings play chess the same way. Some are newbies, then there are professionals. Like me. I know how to work the board, and your jungle. Latin Kings do it better…"

And then, he turned, got on his bike and rode the rest of the way home…

CHAPTER SEVEN

Get Along Like Oil and Water

"**I**T'S FINE, ACTUALLY. I haven't had any problems. I'm going to eventually replace the refrigerator that's here though. It's a little older, and the ice maker isn't really the best." She'd picked up a few hours to work weekly, from home, as a customer service rep for a bank. The extra cash would give her a nice buffer and allow her to rebuild her nest egg. It was an easy gig that permitted her to even do chores around the house while she worked, such as dusting and folding laundry. Lounging on the living room couch, Majesty flipped a page of her Women's Health magazine, her feet curled up and the glow of the television filling the room. She'd been debating getting a gym membership but knew she wouldn't have time to work out. A few stubborn pounds refused to get off her, and the tightness in her jeans proved that, but she wasn't quite ready to give up her Häagen-Dazs ice-cream.

"Can you afford a refrigerator right now? Seems to me that would be the least of your concerns, Majesty."

Majesty turned the magazine page and swallowed the reply she *wanted* to say.

"If I couldn't, I would not be considering it. I think you know I can be frugal. I budget. When I say I'm broke, it's not most people's kind of broke. Broke to me is having less than ten thousand in the bank, so yes, I'm not where I was before I moved into this house, but I can afford a decent, new refrigerator."

"Yes, well, if you don't need one right now, that is a waste of money. You know, Majesty, I think you need to start dating again. A man could help you with some of these expenses. Then again, you usually choose men who are bad for you, so maybe you should scratch that."

"Mama, first, thank you always for your vote of confidence. Luckily, I don't require anyone to co-sign on my self-esteem. Secondly, I have my finances under control. Don't make me regret answering the phone, please. I have no idea why when you get insomnia, you always call me. I doubt you call and wake up Michael. Allison avoids this, too. I'm probably the only one who answers your calls. All we do is argue."

"I prefer to call them spirited conversations." Mama laughed, as if their chronic dysfunction was funny.

She rolled her eyes at the snooty way her mother enunciated her words, as if she'd never spent one day in the hood. Now that Mama had married some rich man twenty years her senior, no one could tell her anything. She had always been rather snobbish, sticking her nose up at others as if she were not riding along in the same boat, on the same ocean, and feeling the same waves, but things had gotten dramatically worse since she and Mr. Gerald tied the knot in Jamaica. She was certain the man didn't know the *true* Josephine. Mama had a way of being a chameleon when it suited her.

"Oh, and thank you again, Majesty, for the peach pie."

"I figured since you asked for some, you did me a favor. Troy didn't eat much of it, but he liked it. You know I'm not a peach pie person, but Mr. Earl is so nice. It looked good when he brought it over. I just can't get past the smell of cooked peaches." She wrinkled her nose. "Makes me nauseous. Did it taste good to you at least?"

"Oh, heavens no, honey. The pie wasn't for *me*! You know I don't eat just anyone's cooking. I wanted Beijing to have a nice snack! She loves pie, and since it was her birthday, I thought I could treat her a little."

"Beijing? You gave that man's homemade pie to that nasty, old ass dog, Mama?" She gritted her teeth and tossed the magazine on the coffee table.

"How rude! She is not nasty, Majesty! She has a sinus condition that causes her to have an overproduction of mucus, and I've had her for almost seventeen years now. She's practically a fourth child to me."

"I wouldn't care if you had her for four score and seven years, she'd be pushin' up daisies if it was up to me. It's selfish to keep that dog alive, Mama. The vet said she needs to be put down."

"Do we put down our elderly when they're sick? Place them in a field to die? I don't give a shit what Dr. Arnold says. Beijing will be with me until she draws her last breath."

"She's got tumors and can barely walk, Mama, and now you done gave that mangy, stinkin', matted poop brown toupee of a creature Mr. Earl's pie!"

"You said you hate peach pie, so what does it matter?! And I repeat, she's not going anywhere. Yes! She ate your neighbor's pie. What is so wrong with treating her to a bit of dessert? You would've tossed it in the trash soon enough anyhow."

"You made it seem like you wanted it for yourself. I would've just kept it here, let Troy and his friends eat the rest of it had I known your true intentions." She sucked her teeth. "Forget the pie, Mama. It doesn't even matter at this point and I really have some nerve being surprised. This is typical of you. I wanted to tell you about the—"

"Typical of me? You don't get to rush me along like that! You know what, Majesty? Seems you've gotten too damn big for your britches." *I have. This damn ice-cream and I have been the best of friends, but if I say that, she'll accuse me of getting smart...* "You think you'd show a little gratitude. I am the one who got you that house! I am the one who had the—"

"No. You spoke to your friend, Mr. Carmichael, the owner of the house, and vouched for me. I got this house with *my* money. Yes, you helped, but I'm the one who saved the money and worked the deal with him. Don't try to twist the narrative. I even thanked you a million times for your assistance and gave you two of my designer purses, which I could have just put on Poshmark instead. You had been wanting that Kate Spade and Michael Kors purse for quite some time now and because you couldn't find them to purchase your own, them being limited editions, that was my thank you for your contribution. You didn't offer one dime, and you made literally a five-minute call on my behalf, knowing he was havin' trouble keeping decent tenants. I did not ask for your money, I didn't want your money, and I proved I was grateful."

"Without me, Paul would have never let you rent that house, Majesty, and you know it. That is my point. I can't believe this argument all started because of some damn peach pie! Geesh! You're really defensive lately, you know that? I'm still your mother and I demand a level of respect from you, regardless of how old and grown you think you are. I have always been there for you, and yes, I want to be acknowledged. You had a child at a young age. I was too young to be a grandmother. You tried to move out on your own and take care of Troy, then had to move back home. You failed like I said you would, and who rescued you? Opened their home to you? Me. It was *I* who helped. Again. Your father sure didn't offer. I have been helping you, as a mother should, but I told you that I would no longer serve as your training wheels. You have to roll out on your own."

"Like you? Are you rollin' out on your own? When was the last time you worked a nine to five, Mama? It must've been when 'I Want it That Way,' from the Backstreet Boys, had come out! You went to beauty school, never did anything with the certification and training, and that was it! You used what you had to get what you wanted. Daddy had money at the time, you went after him, and the rest was history."

"Girl, you can imply that I was a gold digger all you want, but I sure as hell never wanted for nothin'. You, on the other hand, had a car that wasn't running just two weeks ago, sitting up in yo' driveway, leaking oil like it had a Jheri curl. And you had to take planes, trains, and automobiles just to get Troy to school and the babysitter, and you off to work!"

"And I took those planes and trains and automobiles gladly, Mama. I'm not ashamed. You were the girl all the men wanted back in the day, and it helped you in life. I'm not judging you, but that's just not me. That's not how I want to live my life."

"Majesty, you've learned nothing from all of the pain you've experienced, some of it self-inflicted. Absolutely nothing." She glanced at the television where a soup commercial was airing. It was strange to see so late at night. A silver spoon dipped into the broth, swirling slowly round and round. She felt a little like that spoon, in hot water, only she wanted to drag the person dipping her into the deep end of the bowl, right along with her.

"Mama, you must get strength, points, cash prizes, a trip to Maui or superpowers from arguing with me. You twist things around to fit your perspective, things that aren't even true, and you have always thrown me having Troy up in my face. That's what this is about. It all bounces right back to that."

"I'm just telling you that I didn't want you to back-track, Majesty! You are my oldest child. My *first* daughter. I needed you to help set an example for Michael and Allison. At the end of the day, Troy is my grandson, and

I've always wanted what was best for both of you, but you moved out far too fast, got evicted, and then your credit was destroyed. All to prove me wrong, and it backfired."

"You didn't want me to move out because you wanted full control over me and to always feel needed. You always have to feel in control, and when someone, especially one of your children, tells you they don't want you to have dominion over them, you freak out."

"Oh, bullcrap, Majesty!"

"It's true. I didn't need you anymore. I *wanted* you around, but I didn't need you, Mama, and you could not stand it. And don't act like you don't remember the details of what happened. It wasn't because I was irresponsible or anything like that. I got evicted because Troy's father died so I wasn't getting anymore child support. Kevin would help take him while I studied and went to my second job, so him being gone changed everything, as if his death in itself wasn't bad enough. I was already workin' two jobs at the time while being in college, but instead of telling me you were proud of me, despite all the mountains I had to climb, you kept talkin' about how I couldn't even keep that apartment, and now I was back home."

"I had warned you, Majesty. I told you that boy wasn't going to help support you and Troy forever. He was a criminal! He sold drugs and lived a fast life! I begged you to stay home, not to control you, but because believe it or not, sometimes I know best for my children. Sometimes, surprise, surprise," she laughed sarcastically, "I actually know what I'm talking about!"

"All I know is that you made things worse. It's been

long overdue, this conversation, because I've been sitting on this powder keg of rage about how this all transpired and went down with you for years. I was grieving, strugglin', trying to get back on my feet, and you rubbed it in my face. Just because Kevin and I had broken up before he was killed didn't mean I didn't love him anymore, and it didn't mean that he was unlovable either, just because he was doin' the things he was doing. I never approved, but I knew he had a desire to get himself together, although he never had the chance. We were young! Didn't you ever make a mistake? I know you hated him, but he was my best friend. Yes, he was out in the street, Mama. That's all he knew was the streets. He didn't have a place to stay growing up like I did, a mother and father, so he had to teach himself how to be a man. Still, he loved his son and was a good father and you know it! You know what happened about that situation... You know how that messed me up so bad."

Her heart pounded, an ache spreading in her chest as her distress climbed high and squeezed her skull, demanding to initiate a headache.

"Everything about it was surreal," Majesty continued. "I wasn't okay after that. I'm still not okay after that... after all of these years. You know how badly Kevin's death affected me, and now you're using it against me because I told you the truth, and you didn't like what I said. How could you?!"

"I'm sorry you're upset, Majesty, but I am telling you the truth, too. Sometimes, the truth hurts. Fine, let's drop all of that, okay? Let's focus on the real issue. You are always talking about college and these low paying jobs you get, and where has it gotten you, honey? College is great, don't get me wrong, but you lack clear direction. Human Resource jobs are oversaturated. You're finishing a Masters in a field that isn't in high demand, which will cause you to do what you do best. Struggle. You're going to be back at square one, and it seems like since you got pregnant all those years ago, that's when your progress stopped… like arrested development."

"I thought you said you were done talking about the father of my child?" She fisted and unfisted her left hand, while her rage festered. Violence was on her mind.

"I am. I'm speaking about him indirectly now." Majesty rolled her eyes and slumped on the couch. "Just listen. It's like you got trapped in time. I sure as hell didn't get trapped in time. I left your father as soon as I was able and continued with my life, instead of wasting valuable years with a fool, and I damn sure wasn't silly enough to have another child by him. Thank goodness you didn't get pregnant again! We have to learn from our mistakes, honey. That's all I'm saying."

"What was my mistake, Mama? Was I a mistake of yours? Was havin' my baby a mistake too?" The woman grew silent on the other end. "You know darn well I was not a little kid when I had my child. Yes, I was young, and I shouldn't have been havin' kids because I didn't have enough money to support a child, but I don't regret him. He's my whole world! I was legally grown, mature for my age, and had graduated high school with honors. But instead of bein' happy about my grades and how I stepped up to the plate as a new mother, and encouraging me, you kept pointing out all of my flaws. Just like you're doing now. I am so sick and tired of—"

"I've told you for years how pretty you are, Majesty." She couldn't believe her ears… "I've given you compliments since the day you were born. Everyone remarked about how you should've been a Gerber baby. That's the only thing your father gave me that was worth having. He had good genes, a great smile, lovely eyes and a nice head of hair, and he gave all of that to you, so don't act like I never praised you. Don't put that guilt trip on me."

"Pretty looks. That's a dime a dozen. I walk past pretty girls every day, Mama. We're in Miami! Nowadays, a pretty face isn't enough. These girls are getting their boobs and booties done, their waists snatched, and their wigs and weaves cost a thousand dollars, easy. Pretty faces and nice bodies aren't enough to make it, to sustain me or any man I may be interested in. A pretty face attracts… but what about after that, Mama? I'm talking about you lovin' on me for my educational pursuits, and just because I'm your daughter, and I'm a good person. I'm not sayin' I'm an easy person all the time, I know I can be hardheaded and stubborn, but I was a good child, Mama!" Her voice cracked with anger, more so than sorrow. "You could've praised me for the type of woman I was tryna grow up to be. For walkin' in your footsteps, wanting to be classy, just like you. I wanted to wear those nice white and black suits with the beautiful jewelry and matching hats, but in an office, runnin' the show. You are the one who inspired me, and you don't even know it! Not once did you tell me you were proud of my report cards. I was always tryna impress you. Not once did you encourage me seeking out my education.

"Instead, you wanted to enter me and Allison in pageants, silly mess like that... oh, and before I forget, let me jump on a point you made earlier before it slips away. I need to set something straight, so you know you didn't get over on me. Michael and Allison's fathers weren't any better than Dad. In fact, both of them were worse, so let's not act like you left my father and went on to greener pastures. Talkin' about you learned from your mistakes like you've always progressed and never took two steps back, saying I had arrested development, well what was that? Obstructed improvement in warp speed!"

"Jake and Don weren't shit, either, but the point is, Majesty, that I never gave up on bettering myself and others! Those pageants may have been silly to you, but it was a way to help you build self-worth, and self-esteem. I never wanted you to have to break your back to make it in this world, and after all I did, the dance classes, encouraging you to be in theater, the whole nine, you still ended up with the likes of Kevin's ass. That broke my heart that my daughter was runnin' around town with a known drug dealer, and until your child goes out into the world, and you see them making life-altering mistakes repeatedly, don't lecture me about what you think was going on in my head, and my motives."

Majesty took a deep breath and closed her eyes. Her heart was beating entirely too fast...

"Look, I've made blunders, Mama. What human being

hasn't? But you make it seem like I was wild and out of control. I wasn't out here sleepin' with all of South Florida, and I wasn't on drugs or drinkin', either. I wasn't perfect, but you never had to come to a jail to get me or call the police on me. I haven't asked you for money in years, and you volunteered to help me get a house. I never came to you and asked for *any*thing. The one thing you keep holding over my head is Kevin and that I was too young to have a baby in your opinion. You also didn't want to be a grandmother, felt like it would make you look older in the dating arena. You were disappointed that I got pregnant, but I dated Troy's father for two years before I had gotten pregnant, and even though it was not something we'd planned, and I was upset about it initially, it happened. And I busted my ass to make sure I could take care of my son. He didn't ask to be here."

"I know that, and you know I love my grandson to death, but like I said, until you're in my shoes and feeling how I felt about you and how your life spiraled out of control after Kevin came into your world, then you can't judge me."

"I don't know everything you had to endure as a parent, that's true. I know you had dreams for me, even if they weren't *my* dreams. But I also know I needed more from you, Mama, than what you were willing to give, yet you rarely listened."

"I *did* listen to you."

"No, you didn't. You're not even listening right now. I never want Troy to feel like he can't come to me and talk to me and be honest about it whatever it is on his mind, no matter how bad it is. Sometimes, the mother is right. Sometimes, she is wrong, and that's okay." She sighed. "I don't like arguing with you like this. It happens too often, it's exhausting, and I'm constantly biting my tongue. Only for you do I watch my mouth, but Mama, you know how to push my buttons. I think I'm a good mother, but I know I'm not perfect, and I won't be able to do everything right all the time. It just would be nice to hear you acknowledge that sometimes."

"What for, Majesty? Is that going to erase the past ten years? I'll admit wrongdoing when *you* admit you made bad choices and instead of trying to be a martyr or victim of my alleged bad parenting, perhaps you can take accountability? Isn't that what you want me to do? You could always lead by example." Mama snorted.

Majesty's head was about to explode. Someone had doused her with cold gasoline and lit a match.

"It's late. I finished two exams tonight that took me several days to study for, so I'm already behind on my sleep. I'm tired. I am not about to argue with you right now. I'm gettin' off this phone before I say something I regret."

"Oh… you don't regret what you've said already? Let me do you the honors." The call suddenly ended.

She tossed the phone on the couch and turned off the television, then got to her feet and stretched. She glanced at the clock on the wall: 1:21 in the morning. Yawning, she grabbed the phone again and trekked down the hall, as she did every evening. She paused in the darkness of her beautiful home, wrapping her satin aqua blue robe tighter around her waist as she caught a chill. She stood there for a moment, feeling fury, bitterness, while simultaneously fighting a need to simply fall asleep and forget it all for a few hours. Wrapping her hand around the knob of her son's room, she gave it a slow turn, careful to not wake him as she entered.

On either side of his room were two Spiderman night-lights. She crept in, her bare feet on the soft, plush navy-blue rug. As she stood before his sleeping body, she couldn't help but smile. Troy was lying in the fetal position, his knees drawn up and his little head pressed firmly against his large Spiderman pillow. Blue and red sheets were flung everywhere. He was such a wild sleeper. She bent down and slowly caressed his cheek, then kissed his forehead before tiptoeing back out of his room and closing the door softly. As she made her way to her room, she heard the faint strands of music. She couldn't quite make out where it was coming from.

She went to the large bedroom window facing the street and pushed the blinds apart to peer out into the street, the sole light coming from a lamppost. Across the way, most of the houses were shrouded in darkness. A porch bulb or garage lantern shined here and there. She drew quiet, even monitoring the sound of her breathing. She could not recognize the tune but the sound was undeniable, like an angel's whisper. She pushed on the latches and raised the window, opening it. She inhaled the sweet summer air and heard the frogs and crickets. Now, the music was much clearer, too. It was coming from Viper's home. Her lips curled and then she quietly laughed. *Shame on me for not guessing that sooner. I'm tired or I would've known.* It wasn't his rap music, nor the Reggaeton he seemed to relish so much. It sounded old, yet new. An earthy sound, smooth with hard guitar riffs blending perfectly into a jazz like tune. She rested her arms on the windowsill, bobbing her head to the beat. She then held up her phone and recorded for a minute or two, trying to capture the sounds…

Placing her phone down, she kept listening, enjoying the melody. After a while, she locked her window, removed her robe, allowing it to flow to the ground, and crawled into bed. The cool sheets felt so good against her skin. She yawned again as she reached for her iPad.

"Siri… what is this song?" She played the recording from her phone and had her tablet listen. 'Santana, Tales of Kilimanjaro,' came the automated female voice. She placed her electronics down on her nightstand, and with a smile on her face drifted off to sleep, the song repeating in her head…

CHAPTER EIGHT

A Bill of Goods

You've got that good shit… that real shit… that dope shit.
You've got that razzle dazzle and gunmetal sunshine
With brilliant diamonds flowing out of your mind.

Your tongue is made of gold and your lips have secrets to hold.
You crawl in my brain, like a memory-to-be told,
But I hope when I'm gone, you still remember me as
Iced out and cold…

"**A**GAIN!" VIPER STOOD in the stiff, padded bite suit as the crazed Boxer raced towards him, snarling, growling, and in need of blood. The dog jumped on him, just as he had before, and had it not been for his attire, he'd be missing a chunk of flesh. "Again!" he yelled at the dog after the bastard sprinted off, anger and fury in each step. Victor was a four-year-old Boxer who was on the chopping block. He'd been badly abused by his owners and used in illegal dog fighting. A rescue agency retrieved him, but due to his extreme aggression and PTSD, he was believed to be unredeemable. He'd killed two other dogs, not in self-defense or provocation, and had badly injured someone who'd fostered him for a week. Allegedly, that owner was playing too roughly with the dog and waving a wooden spoon in his face, a trigger for the canine.

Dominic knew how that felt. To be antagonized, tested. It was like state prison, the DOC. He'd gotten into trouble for protecting himself and shooting someone in self-defense. He'd ended up serving time, angry about it, and then when someone dropped a kite on him, he wet their asses up as soon as he was released. The killing and flipping never stopped. If he wasn't shooting or stabbing someone, he was beating the fuck out of them. Then there were the illegal weapon sales and distribution. It was a revolving door…

The PTSD was real. The rage was real.

I can't be thirty-one doin' the same shit I did when I was four-teen and fifteen. That's crazy. Guys in the streets are not growing. They're stuck. Stagnated. *I want to keep moving. A viper always keeps moving forward. I need to live up to my name, my nature. I got this name for a reason. No one knows my next move. It's too late when I get to them—they never see me coming—and I have the patience of an angel. I can wait to exact my revenge for a damn decade if I have to. I don't give a fuck. When I say I'm going to get you, I'm going to get you. And that's on my dead brother…* Descansa en paz, Diego.

He'd always be street in his heart, but the streets were tearing him apart…

He focused back on Victor and felt a kinship as soon as he looked into the dog's crazed eyes. Someone had contacted him anonymously, pleading for him to have a go at the canine before it was too late.

"Again!"

The dog raced towards him once more, his eyes gleaming and his mouth wide open, exposing glistening teeth. With one hand in mid-air, he caught the dog by the throat and glared at him.

"Victor. No! Victor, no attack!" He dropped the dog, and the beast whimpered at his feet. Viper didn't follow typical dog training protocol. What was the point? That didn't work on dogs like Victor. The animals that came to him were often mentally ill. He couldn't understand why some people didn't comprehend that animals, especially canines, could have the same responses to life as humans: jealousy, rage, relief, elation, sadness... He raised his arm as high as he could and made a fetching motion. The dog raced away, searching. Once the poor guy realized he'd been fooled, he returned to Viper and stood at his feet.

"Do you see what happened? You've been tricked. Not everyone is trying to trick and hurt you, Victor. That's disappointment you feel. I did not give you the command. Now listen this time." He tossed a treat far in the air, and it landed approximately fifteen feet away. Victor made a motion to run, but then paused to look back at him. Viper smiled. "Fetch!"

As soon as the word left his mouth, Victor took off like a lightning bolt and found the chewy bone-shaped treat and began munching away at it. Viper laughed when he spotted Chance, Sarge, and Belleza with their snouts practically smashed into the patio door glass, observing the session. He had to keep them inside when he had dogs like Victor around. It was far too dangerous. As he continued to work with his four-legged client, he would gradually integrate him into the population with fellow dogs, and then humans; but he had to be patient with Victor, something no one had done previously.

He issued more commands, and time marched on. Slipping out of the suit, sweaty and hot, to his T-shirt and shorts, he raised his arm in the air as Victor made another mad dash towards him, then snapped his tongue and the animal clicker, and the beast sat at his feet, obedient. No attacks. No teeth. No barking. He patted his head, then chained him in the back, giving him fresh water and food. As he entered the house, he noted his phone flashing on the kitchen counter. After washing his face and hands, he checked his messages. Several were from women who wanted a bit of his time, a hello from an old probation officer checking in to see how he was doing, one from his mother asking if he would consider going on a family trip with them to Chicago in a couple of months, another from Jaguar seeing if things had calmed down… and then… one more.

His lips curled in sweet satisfaction.

Majesty… She memorized my number after all.

He hadn't heard or seen her in days. He hadn't even seen Troy playing outside. He hated to admit it, but he missed that. He liked looking out of his window every so often and seeing the kid happy, enjoying himself. Perhaps he was busy or spending time with family for the weekend. He wondered where Troy's father was, too. He hadn't seen any guys coming over to visit her, except for an elderly Black man named Earl who lived on their street, and whose wife he believed had passed away some time ago. Earl tended to take morning and early evening walks and would slow down to a crawl and watch him if he was out with his dogs from time to time. *Is she seeing someone?* If she was, he wasn't sure how he'd feel about that. Perhaps jealous. He read the text message from the woman and smirked. She asked if she could stop over and give him two hundred dollars when she got off work at six.

She's serious about paying this money back. Damn. She wants to make sure I don't ask her for anything, like expecting she should give it up because I did her a favor. He burst out laughing.

Leaning against his kitchen island, he replied to the message:

I'll be here. Stop through.

He grabbed a beer from his refrigerator, gulped it down, and turned on some music. While Kid Frost rapped the old classic, 'La Raza,' he stepped back outside to find Victor relaxing under a shady tree. It was then that he heard more music, a vibrating, booming sound coming from up the street. He wondered if someone was having a party, but it was a bit early in the day for that. Nevertheless, he soon made out the song: 'Atomic Dog,' by George Clinton. He wondered who could be playing that song? Most of his neighbors didn't seem to be the type to enjoy such a tune. He liked the beat as it blended in with his own. He also appreciated what his life was bringing. He was breaking through with a dog everyone else had given up on. The lady across the street that he'd been feeling was stopping over, and he had plans for her, knowing he would no longer take 'no' for an answer. His mother was doing well, his father was still alive, his stepbrothers were still breathing, too, and he hadn't had to take anyone out to pasture in months.

Today is a good day...

MAJESTY STARED AT the house for a second, then turned off the car radio. One of her favorite recording artists, Doja Cat's, 'Juicy' had been playing but she'd zoned out long ago. She took a deep breath, knowing the house cameras were on her. They flickered in the distance. She sat a little longer in her car in that big driveway, then grabbed her purse off the passenger's seat and exited, making her way to the large red front door. The cameras began to glow bright and rotate, and the motion detector came on. As usual, she could hear music coming from Viper's home, only this time, it wasn't nearly as loud. After waiting for what felt like an infinity, he opened the door. Shirtless, except for a gold chain around his heavily tattooed neck and chest. His muscles glistened, as if he'd just taken a shower, and his long legs were encased in a pair of dark loose-fitting jeans. Farther down, white socks covered his feet. He opened the door wider and stepped to the side.

"Come in," he offered.

She mustered a smile, stepped over the threshold, and heard the music a bit clearer now: 'Exchange,' by Bryson Tiller. The smell of incense hung in the air, mingling with the distinct odor of food that had been cooked perhaps earlier in the day, and what smelled like cleaning products. She waited as he disappeared into a back room, leaving her there without an explanation. She could hear the scampering of dogs, barking, and doors closing. From her vantage point, she had a view of the marble and granite kitchen and living room. The man's home was absolutely gorgeous. He seemed to avoid clutter. Not quite minimalistic; he had his fair share of paintings, furniture, and mirrors, but all the pieces made sense. They fit well. She could see her reflection in his floors.

He has all these damn dogs but I can't smell them really, and his house is so clean...

She hadn't expected this, not from him, considering his occupation. She enjoyed dogs, too, but knew they had a distinct scent, one many deemed unpleasant. And then, she got a whiff of a delectably sexy musk cologne. She sniffed the air, cleared her throat, and straightened up as he approached, hearing his heavy gait first. He held a long silver chain in his hands, possibly a dog leash. Stopping about six feet away from her, he waited for her to say something.

"Were you busy?" She crossed her arms.

"I'm always busy, but willing to make time for important things." He mirrored her stance, and the chain rattled in his grip. Silence stretched between them while she studied his face. The way his light hazel eyes, with hints of green, amber, and gray glowed when the kitchen lights hit them. They were narrow, slightly slanted, and piercing, like hell bound bullets headed straight for one's soul. Slightly unruly black eyebrows dipped naturally, making him look as if he were always concentrating on something important. Concerned about an outcome. His high cheekbones gave him an almost regal appearance. The bridge of his nose was long with a slight bump in the middle, as if perhaps at one point it had been broken and healed. It gave him more character.

His succulent pink lips were framed by a black mustache and nicely trimmed, short beard. He was a beautiful man, from his crucifix-marked forehead, down to his toes. She swallowed, then stuck her hand into her purse, pulling out an envelope.

"Here. That's two hundred twenty. Now, that's three-twenty paid back thus far, if you include the hundred I already gave you. I still owe four hundred twenty and will have that repaid in the next few weeks."

The man cocked his head to the side, put the chain down on the counter, then took the envelope from her hand. He opened it but kept his eyes on her. She noticed that whenever they were in each other's company, he would look at her hands first, then go up to her eyes. He'd done the same thing when he'd answered the door, and then, again, just at that moment. She wasn't certain what that was about, not even sure she should ask. Maybe it was all in her mind. He briefly glanced down into the envelope and counted the money, or at least appeared to be doing such, then slapped it onto the counter beside him.

"How can we speed up the inevitable?" he finally said as he leisurely adjusted his watch. The damn thing was loaded with big diamonds and gold.

"Speed up the inevitable? What are you talking about?"

"You're going to be mine."

"Oh, really?" she quipped.

"This can happen now or later. Though I'm laid back, I don't like wastin' time, so let's just stop the bullshit and get on with it."

She chuckled at his words and shook her head.

"You *really* don't give up. I came over here to give you your money and—"

"You could've CashApp'ed me, or sent via Apple Pay, online bank transfer, money order, PayPal, shit, gone old school and wrote a check and tossed it in my mailbox. Instead, you asked me if you could come by. You wanted to see me. Up close and personal."

"Don't get it twisted, Viper. That's because I want a receipt." They glared at one another, and she hated the way his lips curled in a smirk.

"That may be true, but it doesn't explain why you sat in your car for so long, fixing your hair, takin' deep breaths, playing with the collar of your shirt to make sure it wasn't too low, or too high… but just right. Just enough to let me see a bit of a show, but not too much to make me think you're a ho." He sneered. She felt warm all over. "Yeah… you didn't think I could see all of that, did you?

Or maybe," he tapped on his lower lip, "just maybe, you were aware that the cameras were on you, and you put on a little show anyway… Yeah, that's probably more like it. You're too smart and perceptive for it to be anything else."

"Can I get a receipt please? I'm sure even *you* have some professional receipt stationery because you run your own business." She refused to elevate her voice, to let the man see her struggle, buckle, or react. That's what he wanted after all. At that moment, it felt like it was the last thing she controlled that he could not have…

She cleared her throat once again as he turned away, then disappeared again. She assumed he was honoring her request and getting receipt slips. That gave her time to look around some more. She noticed a picture stuck to the stainless-steel refrigerator with a margarita glass magnet. It was an older Polaroid of two boys with wild black hair, hanging onto one another, smiling. One boy looked much like him. She drew closer and looked harder, then smiled. It was definitely Viper. He looked to be about thirteen or so, was thin, his limbs long and lanky, sporting a promi-nent cleft chin, and grinning from ear to ear. Soon, the man returned. Pulling out a drawer, he picked up a pen and began to scribble down some words onto a receipt pad. He ripped it out and handed it to her. Everything appeared in order; he'd even included her earlier payment without her asking, and put the date, too.

"Thank you." She folded it, then slipped it into her purse. "One time I accepted money from a friend. That friend turned around and said I owed them money, when

I'd never asked for a loan, but they volunteered to help me because I'd fallen on hard times. When this friend of mine decided she needed some money, she asked for it back. I reminded her that it hadn't been a loan. She said it was. After all of that and a few other issues I've faced, I promised myself I'd never accept money without documentation again. I don't ask for loans, and I don't take so-called monetary gifts anymore, either. I do thank you for your generosity though. It bought me some time while allowing me to get my car back sooner rather than later."

Viper stared at her, his expression hard to read. He didn't look angry. He didn't look happy. He looked perhaps somewhere in the middle. She turned to walk away.

"It's me and my brother." She stopped and turned towards him again. He tapped the counter a few times, then pointed to the picture on the refrigerator. "My big brother and I... Diego."

"How'd you know I was looking at it? Were you spying on me? Camera or something?"

"I could hear you. I have very good hearing. I heard you walking, and this area of the kitchen sounds different from over there." He gestured to the table in the nook by a bay window. "The floor is different in the kitchen versus the eating area. You can hear it and see it. It's subtle, but there's a difference." She looked down. He was right. "You stopped in front of the refrigerator. I know the sound because it dips slightly right here. There's a small hollow to help collect water if the freezer leaks." Sure enough, there was a slight dip in the floor right in front of the refrigerator. "I don't have anything else interesting over here, so I safely assumed you were lookin' at the picture."

"I find that you knew all of that from just listening impressive and at the same time, disturbing." She smiled at him and he smiled back, then shrugged.

"When you're like me, paying attention is really important."

"Like you? What are you like, Viper?" She bit her lower lip and crossed her arms, feeling flirty and not liking that at all.

"You'd have to go out with me to find out. I'm not an open book. What do I look like telling you anything about me when you've given me nothing in return?" She shook her head and averted her gaze. "And I'm not talking about pussy."

"Sure you are."

"No, I'm not. If sex is my main motivation, regardless of who the woman is, then I make that clear."

"Do you want sex?"

"That's not the point. I told you it's not my main motivation. You can't handle sex with me right now anyway. It would be too intense for you. We need to talk for a bit, so you can be more comfortable. That requires spending some quality time together." At this, she burst out laughing. When she stopped, she realized he was serious. "I'm for real. You're not ready for that. This dick and tongue of mine will ruin your fucking life."

"Boy, your ego is hilarious! I give you credit for confidence though. You're a different breed, huh?"

"I am. I don't need to tell you that though. My actions and how I carry myself should speak for themselves."

He had a point there. The man owned his own house. She'd already looked it up online. He wasn't renting. From what she could tell, he had a lot of friends, and of course dogs came and went, but she never saw any signs that he was dealing drugs out of his house. She'd recognize the tell-tale signs and knew she couldn't go down that road again. She flat out refused. Yet, she was interested in the man. The problem was, she had a history of being attracted to treacherous males. Was history repeating itself?

"You've been to prison, right?"

He looked at her for a moment, then nodded. "Yeah."

"I told myself I would never go out with another man who'd been to prison. You guys are stuck in a damaging mentality, and it causes you to go right back there sooner or later."

"I'm not like your exes, other men you've dated, screwed, whatever. It's none of my business what you told yourself you wouldn't do. I don't care. I only care about what you *will* do, with *me*. You know I'm interested in you. I've put it out there multiple times. I tried to be nice to you by turnin' my music down that first time you came over, respecting you, trying to help you with your car, being nice to you, trying to be... what's the word... chivalrous... all to prove to you that you can trust me enough to go out with me, but you want more and more. I can't give you more information, my time or my energy unless you give me something, too."

See? All of these mothafuckas are the same.

"What?"

"Time."

That's not what she expected to hear at all. He was standing firm on that, and something about the way he spoke and looked at her made it sound truthful.

"I have things to do and I'm not going to keep standing here repeating myself. You gave me the money you wanted to give me, I told you what I want, so now it's time for you to go." *This rude ass son of a bitch.* "Think it over if you want, but I'm not going to beg you, especially when I know you want to spend some time with me, too. This is becoming pointless. I don't play silly games." Her eyes grew wide when he suddenly took her by the wrist and started to lead her back to the front door. He opened it. "Adios, Majesty." His deep voice made her insides vibrate.

There was a chill in the air, and the sounds of a song she'd recognized: Rusherking's, 'Ademas De Mi.'

"Viper, why do I feel like I need to go on a date with you to quell my own curiosity, if nothing else?" she blurted.

He leaned against the door frame and crossed his legs, shrugging. He looked slightly irritated. She found his expression, the scent of his cologne, and his attitude sexy. "You're like candy, Viper. I know you are nothin' but sugar. You're going to rot my teeth out. Give me diabetes. Make me hyper so I'll crash. But your flavor... your freshness... the promise of sampling you make me want to do it anyway." She winked.

"I'm not sweet, but whatever. I get the point you're tryna make just the same. What time am I picking you up this upcoming Saturday night?" The man was no-frills. For some reason, that gave her some comfort. As if he wasn't in the mood to bullshit or pour it on thick just in case she changed her mind.

"I work Saturday."

"I can't do any other day, so what time do you get off?"

It depends on what you do to get me off... I can't believe I just said that in my head.

"Seven."

"The place I want to take you is open late. Get a babysitter. I'll be coming over at nine, and I'll be on time."

And then, he closed the door...

CHAPTER NINE

Good Fences Make Good neighbors

Her mind has been played with; her body used as a toy.
Her arms reached for heaven; God gave her a little boy.
Her daddy left her home, her mother sought comfort in men,
She was told she was pretty, and that would be her greatest
sin...

MAJESTY ADJUSTED HER purse along her shoulder as she pushed her grocery store cart, otherwise known as a buggy, down the aisle, humming to the sounds of 'Love is Blue,' by Johnny Gibbs drifting from the speakers. A strange White woman with honey blond hair curled tight at the ends glared at her from behind black and pink rimmed cat-eyeglasses, filling her with anxiety. This went on while Majesty studied the oatmeal brands selection. She hadn't had oatmeal since high school but felt like trying something different. She picked up the Quaker Oats, peaches and cream flavor, and read the nutritional information on the back of the box. The woman in the glasses was now shamelessly gawking.

"What do you want?" Majesty barked before tossing the box and Troy's favorite cereal, Fruit Loops, into her cart. The woman's pale pink lips twitched. The sparkle in her light blue eyes dulled and she lifted her pointy chin, sporting an unnerving grin.

"I'm so sorry for staring. You just look familiar is all. Do you live over on 10th Street?"

Majesty looked deep into the woman's eyes. She had a dead face, the kind that knew nothing of love and life, desire, passion, blessings, and gratitude. They were about ten feet apart from one another, but the space felt small, the world shrinking around them, the air stifling. Her throat developed a sudden tickle, as if she were about to come down with a cold.

"Who are you?" Majesty crossed her arms, cocked her head, and waited.

"I live not too far from you… I think. You have a little boy, right?"

"Your name? Again, who are you?" *Why is this weird ass woman all in my business? She's ducking my questions like this is a game of dodgeball. I don't know her. She seems to know a lot about me, though.*

"If you don't mind me asking, how can you afford to live there? In that house?" The woman's smile morphed into a pretentious smirk. "I know it's one of the more moderately appraised ones on the street, but it's still pricey. You're a single mother, right? Where do you work?"

Majesty's body flushed with heat. One thing about her,

contrary to her mother's concerns regarding discernment, she could feel people's bad energy a mile away. She knew when someone was a devil in the flesh, or an angel in disguise. This intuition had gotten her far in life, and this bitch right here was Lilith. Lucifer's wife had come to pay her a visit… in the cereal aisle of all places. The woman tilted her head to the side. Majesty envisioned it rolling about on a silver platter. She noted the lady's attire, putting her in mind of a 1950s housewife in her mid-30s, give or take a year or two.

"Did you hear me? Where do you work, sweetheart?"

"Where do I work?" The woman nodded. "Oh, I work down yonder on that there plantation that your ugly White daddy run, pickin' cotton all day for you and yo' family, ma'am." Majesty stated in a phony Black Southern drawl as she pointed ahead at nothing in particular. "And I like to be out in that heat from sunup to sundown, singin' songs 'bout Dixie, all day long!" The woman bristled, her expression twisting as she muttered something unintelligible under her breath. But the look of mortification on her face was satisfying enough. "I don't even know you, and don't *wanna* know you. You have the damn nerve to stand there and question me, riddle off a survey, like you're entitled to an answer about me and mine, my personal life. Who the hell do you think you are?"

"There's no reason to become belligerent and angry. I'm just trying to be neighborly."

"No, you're trying to be nosey and disguise your racism as concern. If you don't get yo' dumb, racist, Stepford wife lookin' ass the hell outta my face, you won't be worried about how I make my money anymore because you'll be too busy paying your emergency room bill with your *own* coins after I'm finished with you!"

People around them paused to observe the scene. Majesty stood taller, her blood boiling to the point she was certainly about to detonate. She'd had it up to here with her snooty neighbors, the moms on the PTA and their snide, judgmental remarks, the White people at her job asking if her hair was real and then trying to touch and play in it. Everything had come to a head. BOOM! Explosion now in session...

The woman looked suddenly flustered and afraid. Her cheeks turned beet red as she undoubtedly slipped into victim mode. Clutching her necklace, she pushed her cart quickly a great distance away, as if she needed to get to safety, her white heels clicking. She looked like some terrified little white rat in a swing skirt. The woman glanced back a time or two before she turned the corner, as if afraid Majesty would jump on her back like some enraged, sharp-toothed animal and bite her clutched-pearl neck.

Her heart thumped and danced as though in the middle of a performance for a sold-out arena. Heat consumed her. Racism came in all shades of ignorance, such as those who did not understand how a Black person could live in such a neighborhood without tearing up their credit or doing something illegal. If it wasn't one thing, it was another. Like some police officers who abused their power by stashing drugs and weapons on an unsuspecting someone they'd pulled over and profiled, framing them in an elaborate setup and trumped-up scheme. This had happened to her own cousin, Xavier. The man was serving a twenty-year sentence for something he hadn't done.

Gathering her composure, she finished her shopping.

During the drive home, her mind was on a million and one things, not the road. Troy was with his paternal grandmother. It was in actuality Kevin's foster parent, Ms. Deidra, who'd been a great mother to him when he was growing up. She'd also run a successful daycare center many years ago, and had always been there for her and Troy, regularly checking in to see how she and her child were doing. Mrs. Deidra hadn't been able to save Kevin from his demons, but she'd tried. The older woman considered Troy her grandson and was one of the sweetest ladies to walk the planet. In fact, one of the few people that Majesty felt safe leaving her kid with. He'd be with her for a couple of days while she caught up on some work and went out on her date with Viper.

A date… A damn date with that man.

She'd been second guessing her decision the entire week. She'd usually see him coming and going every now and again. He'd take off on his motorcycle, or in his truck, or that incredible car of his. She despised how she felt when one day she saw an incredibly beautiful woman with long black hair all the way to her ass standing in front of his house, talking to him. Flirting with him.

At last, she made it home. She started to put the groceries away quickly, wanting to get on with things so she could get cleaned up and dressed after a long day at work.

As soon as she got into a groove, her phone rang. She no longer fooled with separate ringers for different people who called. Either she answered, or she didn't. Stretching to loosen up her tired limbs, she looked down at the phone lying on the island and smiled.

"Hey, Destiny." She put her friend on speakerphone.

"Hey, girl! It's been a minute. I'm used to talking to you practically every day."

"I know. It's been crazy. I barely have time to sleep some days it seems. It'll calm down. I'm almost finished with school. That'll make a big difference."

"I suppose I'm spoiled. Used to having you close." She chuckled, though she knew her friend didn't find her absence funny. It was hard on them both, honestly. "You didn't call me back last week, girl. I should put you in time out."

"I know, I am so sorry, Destiny. It's been so hectic, like I said. I have a plan, and then I'll have more wiggle room and we can get back to the way things were. Actually better. Thanks for coming down last month and helping me with the house. You have no idea how much I cherished that."

"Would you stop thanking me? That's what friends are for! Hey, it's too quiet over there. Where's my husband?" she joked, referring to Troy.

"With his grandma." Majesty smiled as she washed down a Vitamin D capsule with some room-temperature water.

"Your mother is watching him? I thought she was too cute for that? Still tellin' people she's forty-five."

Majesty shook her head and snorted. "She *is* too cute for it. Nothin' has changed. You know my mama is a trip. She gives Troy presents, calls him and talks to him, and she came for a visit, too, but she is not tryna do that whole grandma thing like baking cookies, reading stories, and all of that stuff. Not even with Michael's daughter. No, I'm talking about Kevin's foster mother, though. You remember Ms. Deidra?"

"Oh, yes! I remember her. So he's spendin' the weekend with her then?"

"Yes. I dropped him off this morning before work." She opened one of the cabinet doors and placed a couple cans of boiled peanuts inside. Her guilty pleasure.

"So, when are we going out? Your friends miss you. I just think you're aiight." They both burst out laughing. "Seriously, real talk. You've got the weekend to yourself, and I can get a babysitter for Kia – my sister will watch her. Let's go! Time for you to get back to Miami, baby, and live it up! It's all lame, sterile, boring, and White where you're at. Did I mention White?" Destiny chuckled.

A flicker of the incident at the grocery store flashed inside her mind. Majesty quickly shook it away.

"Yeah, well, you and Joy act like I moved a hundred miles away. It takes me less than forty-five minutes to get to y'all. Forty if I'm speeding."

"I know, I know… but it's not the same without you here all the time, Majesty." She could hear the sadness in her best friend's voice.

"I miss you too, Destiny. I miss all of y'all. I had to do what was best for Troy though. Plus, change is good. I have to be honest; I really like it here."

"You do?"

"Stop sounding all surprised! Yes, I do." She placed the new box of oatmeal in a different cupboard.

"Well, if you're happy, I can't ask for much else. I'm proud of you; I think you need to know that. I don't want to seem selfish or anything, and I know you're less than an hour away. Girl, I just want to grow up and be like you."

Majesty retrieved a carton of brown eggs from a bag and placed them inside of the refrigerator. After a bit more small talk, Destiny brought up turning the weekend into a getaway once more. The topic that refused to die.

"So, you comin' down? Yay or nay?"

Majesty placed some dishes in the dishwasher after taking note of the time from her watch.

"I can't."

"Working again? School? Well, you're always working, but I mean... damn. Come on out tonight, Maj! I'll have you back by Sunday morning. Well, late mornin'."

"I can't go because I have a date." She sank her teeth into her lower lip and squelched a chuckle.

"A date? With *who*? 'Ms. Cicely Celibate' going out with someone belonging to the male species? Say it ain't so! You belong to the streets now, huh?"

"Girl, stop!"

"You told me when I was there at your house to stop trying to hook you up and stop asking when you were going to settle down again. You told me you weren't interested in that sort of thing. I believed you. The big question is, do you even know what a man looks like anymore?"

"Well, damn. You don't have to make it sound like I'm some recluse! I never said I didn't want a guy ever again. I just didn't want ninety-nine-point-nine percent of them." They both burst out laughing.

"All I know is that I've tried to get you out to meet men and you always snubbed them, got your drink from them and dashed off, or went out with them like twice, then stopped returning their calls. You're the queen of ghosting these negroes."

"Now that's not true. I dated Pierre for like… a month. And remember Jason? They just weren't a good fit for me." She shrugged. "If I don't feel the vibe, I just don't feel it, Destiny. I'm not forcing anything. Not my size nine foot in a seven shoe, and not a relationship just for the sake of having one." She slipped out of her sneakers, then stuffed her socks in them.

"Oh, girl, let me tell you. Joy's sister, Hope, you know, the one we don't like…" Majesty rolled her eyes, knowing Destiny was about to tell her some shit she didn't want to hear. Hope was the biggest hater, always bitching about people she couldn't hold a candle to. "She said you only want to date ballers, but you're broke. Girl! Joy shouldn't've told me that, 'cause sister or no damn sister, I called Hope's ass on her phone and set her straight!"

Majesty rocked her hips to some music playing from across the street as she arranged a few lemons and limes in a bowl just so. She was certain it was Viper being the neighborhood DJ, once again. He was probably getting ready for their night out, too, or maybe he'd wait until the last second to do so, like most men. "What'd you say back to her?"

"Back to Hope's humpback whale, SpongeBob Square Pants built ass? I said that you ain't broke, number one. You just moved to Boca Raton, in a good ass neighborhood, and secondly, I told her there was nothin' wrong with wanting a baller, a shot caller, even if you were. Why is it that can't nobody want anything better than their own circumstances? I mean, damn! Do we all have to be destitute and miserable? I hate heffas like her."

"Me too." She sucked her teeth and studied her cuticles. "She knew not to say that shit to my face. She would've been looking for her own after it came out of her mouth. How gutless do you have to be to talk big and bad about someone when they've moved away."

"Joy can't even stand her, Majesty, and that's her own sister. I'm not fucking with that envy energy. It's toxic. I've been reading about vibes, and gratitude." Majesty recalled the recent conversation she and Destiny had had about such things. It had got her thinking about it, too. "Any woman who shows me that she can't abide another woman gettin' ahead, I cut 'em off. No explanation. That's some devious shit."

"It is. I can't stand it one bit, and I've cut people off for far less. I don't have the patience for that kind of stupidity. I'm just trying to get my life in order and give my son happy memories, keep him safe, love him, and fill his head with education. This is one thing my mother taught me that I can totally vouch for. She said women will be your sisters and your worst enemy, Destiny, all at the same time. They'll do you dirty, worse than a lyin', cheating ass man. If we ain't got nothing, we never want the one next to us to have anything, either. Always being negative, putting each other down, being happy when someone's dreams get crushed. And we love to see people acting nasty to one another. We wanna join in on the action and get our laugh on." Her stomach knotted with thoughts of her own past when far too often she'd ended up being the butt of hateful jokes. "I'm too grown for that now." She turned on the faucet and ran some water in the sink to wash a few glasses. "If I don't like you, I don't like you, but it sure as hell won't be due to me wanting something you got."

"Girl, sometimes it's not even that they want what you have. They just don't want *yo'* ass to have it!"

"Preach!"

"Women puttin' other women down is gross. Pure stank coochie energy. Ewww, bitch! Uplift or set adrift. No one wants you here! You and your jealousy are dismissed!" Majesty burst out laughing. When annoyed, Destiny certainly had a way with words. And she loved her best friend something fierce. "So, anyway, since you're blowing your girls off for a dick, tell me about this man, chile!"

Majesty dried her hands off, poured herself a glass of wine and settled down at her kitchen nook. She took a sip and looked off into the distance.

"Girl, he is fine as fuck. I mean… stop-dead-in-your-tracks gorgeous. He's rough though. Not just around the edges, but everywhere. He's not a pretty boy at all. But he's… striking all the same, if that makes sense? Looks like he'll walk on broken glass barefoot and not even blink."

"What he look like?!" Destiny didn't even try to hide her eagerness to get the details. It tickled Majesty so.

"Well, he's Cuban, and—"

"Black Cuban or White Cuban?"

Majesty chuckled. She knew what Destiny meant. There were definitely two different kinds.

"White Cuban."

"Hmm, again, what he look like?"

"I was tryna tell you! You keep interjecting." She laughed. "So, he's about six-three or six-four, and he—"

"Ohhhh! He's tall! Yaaasssss, baby!"

"Would you stop interrupting me?!" They were both cracking up now.

"All right, shit! You ain't gotta get huffy," her friend teased. "Finish."

"So, yeah, he's tall and he has tattoos all over his damn body, girl. Very sexy. He has black hair and a short beard. Muscular… whew!"

"Like a bodybuilder?"

"He ain't swole up like Mike O'Hearn, if that's what you mean, but you can tell he works out. He's a big guy. Okay, so that's the physical. Here's the nitty gritty. Destiny, I'm not really certain what's going on, I need to get more information about the depth of his involvement, but… he's a L.K."

"An L.K.? What's… Oh, shit! A Latin King? Bitch! Is you crazy?!" Destiny burst out laughing before Majesty joined in.

"I must be." Majesty wouldn't stop struggling with her own emotions over the situation. "He's thirty-one, so I don't think he's in real deep like that anymore, but he still keeps tabs, and he's still friends with his brothers I guess they call them, the other gang members. I doubt he's involved in anything illegal. He told me he wasn't. Not that that means anything, men are always lying, but trust me, I was checking, and I know what to look out for. No signs of any shady shit whatsoever. What really makes me think that though is that he lives out here, literally right across the street from me, and the police don't bother him."

"Is he on probation or something?"

"Nope. He grew up in Little Havana, moved out here almost a year ago. He told me he needed to lie low, get a fresh start. He didn't want to be around the stuff he was around before twenty-four-seven."

Destiny drew quiet. That hamster wheel brain of hers was working overtime.

"Does he have kids?"

"No, he doesn't have any. What's interesting is that he seems to get along well with children. Troy had a few of his friends over here some time ago and he was playing with them, and they were talking to him like it was nothing. You know how mistrustful Troy is. I didn't say anything, but that kind of blew me away."

"Yeah, Troy is real funny about strangers. That's good actually."

"It is. Troy also told me later that night that he thinks

Viper likes me. Of course, I played it off like I didn't know what he was talking about." She smiled before taking another sip of her wine. "You know I don't let random men around my son."

"True. True."

"Now, check this out. The kicker was that Troy's old ball they'd been playing with was a little deflated. The next morning, a new ball just like it appeared on our front porch. He ain't leave no note, no nothing, but I knew it was him that left it."

"Hmmm, that was nice. Girl, look, you know you can look these guys up now. Since he's an LK, we already know he has a record, but you can just—"

"I actually called Erica and she gave me the 411." Erica was a friend they'd all went to high school with who was now a police officer. The only one she trusted. She and Majesty had always been cool. Every now and again, from time to time, Majesty would let her know about things she'd heard in their old neighborhood, on the down low, to possibly assist in solving crimes, and Erica would give her information about guys she might be interested in. Erica was also the one who'd helped solve Kevin's murder. A chill ran down Majesty's spine when she thought about the night she'd found out someone had shot and killed her first love.

"So… uh, yeah. He's got a rap sheet. A bad one, I'm not going to lie to you, but most of it is old, like four or five years ago was the last thing I saw. And there's nothing involving rape, beating women up, messin' with kids, or anything like that."

"Well, that's good. Girl, living out here, we'd be hell pressed to find someone without a record. Plus, the cops ride Black and Brown people so hard."

"Tell me about it." She finished off her wine, rinsed the glass out, and set it in the sink. "Well, sis, I gotta get dressed to go out with him. I'll find out more tonight, and if I even see a piece of a red flag, I'm out."

"Hold up, you never told me his name and I need information in case your ass ends up in a ditch. You know we don't play that!" Destiny was right. Whenever they met a new man and either of them went out with him, they'd give each other all the information about the guy. It had been so long since she'd been on a date, she'd nearly forgotten.

"His name is Dominic Martinez. He goes by the nickname, 'King Viper.'" She proceeded to run off his address, his occupation, his number, and a few other details.

"All right, got it. I'm going to check him out online, too. Is he on social media?"

"Yeah, but his pages are private and he isn't on there much, at least that was what he said when I asked to add him onto mine. I did find a couple of photos of him on there though. I'll send one to you. For research purposes, of course." She chuckled.

CHAPTER TEN

A Snake in One's Bosom

MAJESTY AND DESTINY continued to talk for a couple of minutes, when she promised to text her friend at the start and end of the date. She then switched on her music and listened to Stwo's, 'Neither Do I', featuring Jeremih as she showered in the large ivory and silver bathroom, one of her favorite rooms in her entire home. She had it lit with candles, and a beautiful silver and ivory pineapple shaped diffuser that perfumed the air with lavender and peppermint essential oils. This was her tiny retreat, her sanctuary.

She stood under the hot stream of water, washing away the stress of the day. Her body shivered as she set aside the pain and frustrations of life, thoughts of which kept coming to the forefront of her mind, trying to take over.

The strawberry scented lather from her Victoria's Secret bath gel, another gift from her mother, helped to soothe her. When she was finished, she stepped out of the shower enclosure, dried off with a soft, baby pink towel, leaving a little moisture along her legs and arms to mix in with her scented almond body oil and gardenia lotion.

She sat at the bedroom vanity in her robe and fingered through her tresses, twisting the strands and pinning them up with an Oriental style black and red clip. Then, she proceeded to moisturize her face and apply a makeup primer. She'd wear basic makeup for work, but for dates, she spent a bit more time on her desired look, lashes and all. It had been quite some time since she'd been out with a man. She had her share of male friends and associates and would sometimes meet them for lunch on her breaks or for drinks when the time allowed, but this was an entirely different ball game. She searched inside her drawer for the eyeshadow palette she wanted, and though a bit rusty at applying a full glam look, it was like riding a bike – it all came tumbling back.

Twenty or so minutes later, she was done, and applied a finishing spray to set in her makeup. She looked at herself in the mirror, turning her head slowly from left to right. The highlight of her cheeks, the rich plum of her blush against her brown skin seemed perfect, and the matte wine-colored lipstick she'd opted for, versus her go-to clear or pale pink glosses, pulled off the look she wished to achieve. She took a deep breath and managed a smile, almost not recognizing herself like this. Giving herself a wink, she rose to her feet, put on her underwear, and slipped on the black off shoulder jumpsuit she'd purchased two years prior from TJ Maxx but had never worn. Next came the faux gold necklace, small gold hoops, and the release of her hair from the clip. She sat back down at her vanity, sprayed a conditioner and water mixture to make her natural curls and waves pop, then scrunched it with hair mousse before tussling it over one shoulder. For a final touch, she reached for the perfume her mother had bought her for her birthday three years prior and which she used for special occasions: *Lancôme la nuit trésor à la folie.* After spritzing it behind her ears, along her wrists, neck, clothing and hair, she set the elegant burgundy glass bottle down, and checked her image a final time.

Her stomach flipped, feeling like it teemed with butterflies high on sugar cookies sprinkled with cocaine. She tried to drum up some shame for being attracted to yet another 'wrong' man, and yet, she felt none. Such an emotion didn't resonate with her soul at the moment.

She rose and slid on a pair of elegant heels. *Anklet... I should put on a gold anklet, too.* She opened drawer after drawer of a tall black dresser full of scattered accessories — knock-off fake designer sunglasses, amazing costume jewelry rings, beautifully printed scarves, bracelets, and the like, desperately trying to find her gold and diamond anklet that she hadn't worn in years.

DING DONG! DING... DONG...

The sound of the doorbell startled her, and in a panic, she looked at the clock.

"Oh shit, it's nine. Like he said, he's here right on time."

She grabbed her purse and made a mad dash out of her bedroom, then down the hall, until she forced herself to slow the hell down. *Why am I running? Make that mothafucka wait. Act casual, like you almost forgot he was coming…* She took slow, steady steps to the front door. As she glimpsed through the peephole, those damn butterflies rose high to the tallest ceilings now, doing somersaults and snorting cocaine and crushed sugar dust like pros. On the other side of the door stood a gorgeous man dressed in a button-down black shirt and matching pants. She got a peek of his black chest hair above the collar, where a subtle gold chain hung around his neck. His jet-black hair was combed away from his face, allowing her to see the full gorgeousness of his bone structure. His fingers sparkled with gold and diamonds. She opened the door and her lungs filled with the intoxicating scent of his cologne. They smiled at each other.

"I told you I'd be on time."

"I had no idea how to dress, so I tried to not go overboard, while dressing up a little." She stepped out of her home onto the porch and locked the door.

"You're dressed perfectly. You look beautiful, too."

She shot him a glance before slipping her keys into her purse, then tugging onto the front door handle for good measure. The lock tended to stick.

"Well, thank you. You look nice, too." Her cheeks flushed with heat. "Where are we going? I want to know before I get into your car and you drive me off to Lord knows where."

He raised a brow.

"I wanted to surprise you, but since you want to know, I'm takin' you to dinner, then dancing."

Pulling out her cellphone, she sent Destiny a text with that information, and also to let her know she was leaving her home. Once she sat in his Bugatti and practically OD'd on the scent of leather, she snuck a quick glance at him out the corner of her eye as he put the key into the ignition, which looked more like a USB stick. A bunch of lights lit up in shades of electric light blue as he pulled out of her driveway and worked the shift. *I ain't never been in no car like this! It's like some spaceship! Damn, this car is bad! I wish Destiny and Joy could see this.*

"How many cylinders are in this car?" she asked as she put on her seatbelt.

"Sweet sixteen."

"Sixteen cylinders? Wow!"

Viper had on a serious expression as he drove, but in truth he always looked that way. The ride was so smooth, it felt like they were damn near floating. He turned on the radio and Mokenstef's, 'He's Mine' began to play on the R&B oldies station.

"You listen to R&B?"

He nodded, then tossed her a look as if to say, *'Of course. What a silly question.'*

"You don't look like the R&B type." She started to snap her fingers to the tune that had hit the airwaves when she was a young girl. She'd had the nerve to sing the lyrics back then, too, as if she knew anything about the perils of toxic love and the tortured minds of men.

"What? You thought I'd be playing 'La Bamba' or some shit like that?" He grinned. Meanwhile, they approached the expressway.

"I don't know about all that. It just surprises me is all." They enjoyed the ride in silence then, and she was feeling the music and the vibe. Viper was silent, ignoring all the people checking out his car as he drove past. Maybe he was used to it. *Broke people don't have cars like this... houses like his... the clothing he's wearing and the jewelry he flashes.* She wasn't her mother, always focusing on her looks in her relentless chase after a man's dollar, but curiosity ate at her. He didn't appear short on *any*thing.

Money or not, there would be no second date unless he passed her battery of tests and answered her questions to her satisfaction. She damn sure wasn't fucking him tonight, risking giving herself and developing feelings for a guy who only wished to toy with her emotions and sell her a bunch of rainbow-colored dreams to hide the actual nightmares covered in shit.

"So, training dogs brings in good money?" she asked flat out.

"Ask me what you *really* wanna ask me..." he said, tapping his fingers against the steering wheel. 'Anniversary,' by Tony Toni Tone was playing.

"What do you think I really want to ask you?" She was too entertained for her own good.

"You want to know if I'm doing something crazy to afford my shit." He stroked his beard as he kept his eye on the road.

"I do. I was in your house. Great furniture and set up,

and I only saw a small portion of it. I know you may think I'm overstepping, but to me, in this day and age, to not ask the important questions from the jump would be stupid… and stupid I am *not*. Your house obviously is really nice, and I can't see how dog training can support that." Flashes of the bitch in the grocery store flooded her mind. Was she doing the same thing to Viper? *I sure as hell am. That heffa isn't dating me. This mothafucka wants to fuck me. Little does he know, I've been in such a drought that his damn voice alone makes me sprinkle my panties and if I were to give in to temptation, a piece of overcooked chicken and a dried-up string bean was all that would be needed to part these damn thighs like the Red Sea. Thankfully, I have self-discipline. But still, I deserve to know.*

"Do you even know what dog training entails and how much potential money can be made, Majesty?"

She swallowed. She hadn't even thought that far. It didn't matter. It just didn't seem realistic. *Who the hell gets rich training a mutt to fetch a newspaper?!*

"Well, you're right. Most dog trainers don't make a lot of money."

She inwardly sighed with relief, yet also bristled with concern.

"I'm not most dog trainers though, number one, so those numbers don't apply to me, and yeah, I made a lot of money when I was in the life, too." He hooked his fingers in the universal gesture for quotes.

"Now that you're not in the life, as you call it, what made you decide to change it up, money-wise?"

"When I was in prison this last stint, I got myself a financial advisor, and my money grew. I've always been industrious about finding new ways to bring in cash. Also, I wanted to make sure that in case anything happened to me, I was leaving something behind for my family. My father has his own shop, as you know, but he works hard, and his earnings aren't as high as they should be. My mother is okay, but she could use more. Soon after I got out, I wanted a house, a new car, and I wanted to start my own business with the dogs. It was time to do something different. Be resourceful. Use my talents. I had seed money to do that, though. Seed money I earned."

"Earned how?"

He smirked. "Don't play with me, Majesty."

"I'm not!" She feigned ignorance, irritated that he didn't fall for her trick to make him disclose his dirty dealings.

"I got the money in ways I'm not going to talk about. But I don't do those things anymore, and that's the only part you need to know."

"You expect me to believe that, Viper? Seems the money was *real* good to you, and that can be addictive."

"Since you want to count my money, want me to expose my pockets, let's see how the—"

"Okay, hold up. I never said—"

"You mean *gold* up?" He sneered, his implication clear.

"I'm not a gold digger."

"Why? What's wrong with being a gold digger?" He tossed her a glance, his eyes dark and foreboding.

"I'm just not like that. I don't go for men because of what they drive, or where they live, or their job."

"You should. Your standards are too low, then."

"So you're tellin' me men want a gold digger?"

He shrugged. "You tell *me*. Kanye West made a whole fuckin' song dissin' them, then married one." She laughed at that, but he was right. "Nothing wrong with a woman wanting a man with money. You honestly think most men would approach you if they found you unattractive? That's the male version of gold digging. Men find women who make us look good. Make us feel good. Women we think other men want."

"Isn't that a bit shallow?"

"Nah, it's Mother Nature. It's deeper than you think. Most men want a woman who we feel is going to bring us the best babies. So, that means she needs to look a certain way. What each of us finds attractive is different, but that's one of the reasons men want what we consider the prettiest chick in the bunch. Even if we're not feelin' a certain look of a lady, we pretty much know when she is aesthetically pleasing, I guess you could say. We want someone our brothers would want to fuck. Someone we'll fuck them up over if they try to touch her though. Once all that newness wears off, and we stop salivating over her, *only* then will we dig deeper. It's at that point that we want to find out if she's nurturing, smart, resourceful, supportive, all the things that make a good wife, mother, and homemaker."

"Uh, Dominic Viper, this isn't 1956, sweetheart!" She guffawed. "I know what you mean though."

"I know you do. It doesn't have to be 1956 when this shit is hard programmed into us. Doesn't matter what year it is. We have the same basic desires. Basic human cravings don't know what day, month, year or century we're in." He switched lanes in the fast-moving traffic with the greatest of ease. "You do realize that most men get nice cars, clothes, all that shit not just for other men to envy, or for ourselves. We do it to attract a woman. It's like a mating call."

She burst out laughing. "Viper, you need to stop."

He laughed right back. "Nah, I'm serious, Beautiful." Her cheeks flushed from his compliment. "See, we don't think of this shit consciously. It's not like we're out here actively looking for women with childbearing hips. This is old shit, from our ancestors. It doesn't care about our race, either. It's in our DNA. Being human is all that is required."

"So, what happens after *that?*"

"After *what?*"

"After you get the girl with the childbearing hips and nurturing personality straight out of 'Father Knows Best,' only she is wearing a bodycon dress with a frilly apron at the dinner parties, a plain Jane business suit in the light of day with her hair in a librarian bun, and nothin' but a G-string at night before you ravish her and she's your personal fun-time freak?"

"Then, a real man continues to do all the same shit he did to attract that woman. He has to keep her panties wet, her eyes dry, and her heart in love." Her stomach clenched at his words. "We don't want to invest all of that time, money, and attention into someone we don't plan to keep."

"Oh, bullshit, Viper." She sucked her teeth. "Do you

know how many men with fancy cars have tried to talk to me and my friends, all with *no* intentions but to hit it and quit it?"

"We have practice years, but eventually, we start getting serious. Playtime is over."

"You mean ho holidays and gigolo durations. Practice years my ass." She rolled her eyes and chuckled. Who did he think he was trying to fool? "You ain't a damn doctor... This ain't your practice, and it's always playtime for a player. Y'all out here trollin' for pussy and forget our name after you cum."

"Are you bitter?"

"Never. Just better."

"I had no idea you were sick," he jabbed.

"Sick of the bullshit. I took a prescription for it. It said, Call Viper out on his crap twice a day after every meal and spiel, then see a *real* doctor, not the doctor of deception, in the gotdamn morning."

He burst out laughing. Gorgeous. His teeth were so white and pretty, and when he laughed, his eyes narrowed to slits.

"You're funny. Hilarious, even."

"I know." She quipped as she crossed her legs and readjusted her position in her seat. "I'm glad you know how to hold a conversation. I'm also glad you have a sense of humor, too."

Reaching toward his back seat while keeping his other hand steady on the steering wheel, he grabbed a bouquet of pink roses and handed them to her. She felt warm all over as she brought them close, then took a hearty sniff.

"These are so pretty. Thank you, Viper."

"*De nada, querida.*"

What does, 'querida,' mean? I know 'de nada,' means you're welcome. Never mind… I'll just assume it was a compliment.

"I love pink. I don't wear it often though, I don't think it looks good on me, but I'm really drawn to this color, and these roses are my favorite shade of it." He nodded in understanding, almost as though somewhere inside of him, he'd *known* this would be her preference. Moments later, they arrived at a restaurant, Abe and Louie's on Glade's Road.

She'd never been there before and wasted no time in alerting her friend, sending a text to let her know the location. Viper turned down valet parking, definitely not liking the idea of some random guy—who was ogling the car—getting his paws on his ride, so he found his own parking space. He helped her out of the car, gently taking the roses from her hand and placing them back on the back seat. Then, he took her hand.

Her insides churned like butter at the touch. Strong. Demanding. Protective. When they entered the establishment, awe struck her and her heart beat a wild melody. The place was gorgeous – fine dining, bright lights, and elegantly dressed men and women. Feeling a little under-dressed, she hugged herself.

"Relax. It's a steakhouse, not the Ritz. You look beautiful," he whispered as they were led to their reserved table.

The waiter pulled out her chair and she took her seat, then they listened to him rattling the specials of the day, including a vast selection of wines.

I haven't been out like this in so long. I need this, too. I really need just a bit of time to remember who I am, what I enjoy, let off some steam. And it doesn't hurt that it's with Viper. I barely know the man, but he's proven to be able to hold his own so far. Gotta give credit where credit is due.

"…That sounds good. I'd like the shrimp and scallop cavatappi," she said. The waiter asked what she wished to have on her salad and promised to bring out a basket of hot, fresh bread.

"I want the bone-in New York strip."

"Twenty-ounce, sir?"

"Yeah… and for the sides, let me get…" his eyes narrowed on the menu as he stroked his chin with those long, thick, tattooed fingers of his, "lobster mac and cheese. What do you want, Majesty? What side?" He waved his finger in her direction.

"Oh, that's fine. Whatever you want."

"No, baby." He smirked. "We get to choose two. They're big. We share 'em."

"Oh, uh, didn't they have asparagus? I'll get that." She felt a wave of embarrassment come over her for she felt clueless about how this shit exactly worked. She'd never been to a place like this, and though at various times in her life she could've probably splurged and done so without dire financial consequence, it just never really crossed her mind.

"Great choices." The waiter promised to return with their wine and refresh their waters momentarily.

Viper sat back in his chair, stroking his glass of water… a lascivious, sexy look on his face.

"What?" She clasped her hands, then leaned forward.

"What I like about you is how down to earth you are."

"How do you know I'm down to earth?" She took a sip of water. "I could be petty, fake, and materialistic. People play roles all the time to get what they want. Just ask my mother." She immediately regretted the words as soon as they left her damn mouth. Something about the man made her feel extremely comfortable. Too comfortable. Much to her surprise, and relief, he didn't press her about it.

"I know when people want to just use me, versus when they have a genuine interest in me as a man. I wouldn't be alive right now if I didn't."

She nodded. How could she disagree?

A glass of white wine was set before her, and a red glass for him. They engaged in a bit of playful flirting and small talk, during which she realized how much she liked… no *loved*, the way Viper's body moved. Each movement of his limbs was slick, seamless, his entire vibe oiled down to perfection. It wasn't forced, but simply the way he was. Despite all his tattoos and intimidating physical presence, he was able to set her and their wait staff at ease. The man could blend in with the best of them. He spoke to the waiter with respect, even joked with the guy, relaxing him. She hadn't missed how the man had kept glaring at Viper's crucifix tattoo on his forehead when they'd first walked in, but then Viper broke the ice so perfectly, pouring cold water on those concerns.

"Earlier, you mentioned when you were 'in the life.' Do you consider yourself no longer a Latin King?"

Viper pushed his salad around with his fork, then ate a mouthful.

"Once a Latin King, always a Latin King."

She took a taste of her wine. It was so damn good.

"Arc you concerned about being back under the influence, I guess you could say?"

He seemed thoughtful, as if trying to find the best way to answer her query.

"I'm not easily influenced. I do the influencing."

She wasn't certain if he was being cocky or he believed his words. She imagined it was a combination of the two.

"My ex wasn't in a gang, but a lot of his friends were. He sold drugs." She kept her voice low. The bite of salad she just had was difficult going down. Perhaps she'd bitten off more than she could chew. Viper kept his face planted in his food. Then, he sat back in his seat, sighed, and rested his fork on the napkin. He stared at her.

"That's Troy's father, I assume. He's dead, right?"

A chill came over her. *How the hell does he know that? Am I wearing a sign?!*

"Yes. Kevin." She quickly looked away, poking at her salad. This was not the light-hearted dinner conversation she'd hoped for. "Why did you assume he was dead?"

"I can tell you're concerned about certain people and influences around your child. Nothing I said convinced you at first to spend some time with me. You made it clear as to why. I figured somethin' fucked up had to have happened to you in the past... a guy like me that you cared about, or at least one you *think* is like me, and it didn't end well. Bigger than a breakup. Something there was no coming back from. Death is the only thing we can't come back from." He shrugged, and casually began to eat his salad once again. Soon, their entrees emerged, and the smell and look of the food made her practically drool.

The mood lightened after that. She lit up like a Macy's parade Christmas tree from the funny tales he shared involving him and some of his friends. The stories were ordinary ones, with kids having fun and causing mischief. She wasn't fooled though. The man hung with murderers, thieves, and con artists. He called them his brothers. *Mis hermanos.* Did birds of a feather flock together? Those motherfuckers flapped their tattered wings until they were bloody…

"What made you join the Latin Kings?" She reached for a roll and bit into it.

"For many of the same reasons you've probably heard… and I wanted a family."

"But you had one. Not the best, from the little you've told me, but it seems like you know your mother loves you, and your parents tried to take care of you and your brother even though they were poor."

"When you think of a great family member, like, the best you can imagine ever having in your entire life, what do you think of?" he asked as he reached for his glass of wine.

"What do you mean?"

"What attributes would they have?"

"They'd be trustworthy. Loyal. A good listener. Fun. They'd have my back, give good advice and care about me... love me unconditionally."

"Well, I had the love, but nothing else."

She drank some more wine, her throat feeling a bit dry.

"You can have parents who love you, Majesty, but don't know how to show it." Boy did she understand *that*. "I couldn't talk to my parents about much. Discussing things that bothered us really wasn't acceptable."

"You said you were close with Diego, your brother. Didn't he pick up some of the slack of what you were missing?"

Did he follow in his brother's footsteps?

"Some. Not all. What could he do? He was a child, too. I looked up to my big brother and wanted to be like him, but I believe I would've become King Viper anyway." Once again, he seemed to know the true intention of her questions. "I wanted exactly what you said you would want from a family. Loyalty. A good listener. Trustworthiness. I wanted someone to have my back, not just pay the bills to the best of their ability and put food on the table. I love my mother, my father, and my stepfather, but sometimes, that love isn't enough. I was living around a lot of violence and chaos, inside the house *and* out. I was looking for a constant. Something that didn't change."

"You were looking for stability. That's something all children need." *...or they feel lost. And then, the wrong things or people can find them...*

"Yeah. I couldn't articulate it the way I can now, but we don't need words all the time to say how we feel. The way we live our lives shows it."

She jabbed her fork into a shrimp, brought it to her mouth, and about fell in love when the buttery, succulent food hit her palate. As she chewed on her food, she also chewed on his words. It all tasted familiar.

"When you look back on your life as a gang member, do you regret it?" she cocked her head to the side, genuinely interested.

He smiled. "I regret nothing."

They studied each other for a long ass time after those words left his mouth. After they finished their dinner, he asked her if she wanted dessert.

"I better not!" She giggled, waving her hand. "I had to practically slather myself with Crisco to get into this jumpsuit. I'm surprised the chef didn't come out and ask if he could dab his spatula on my leg to fry up some grub." Viper burst out laughing, and it was contagious. "Hell, it's true. I've been stress eatin' lately. Just keeping it 100. I'm ashamed, but it's the truth." She was pretty shocked at her own frankness.

"You're beautiful… Crisco and all. All right, let me pay the check, then we can be on our way to the Funky Biscuit."

"The Funky Biscuit?" She chuckled. "What a silly name."

"Yeah, it's a club not too far from here. Great drinks and music."

"All right. I'm down. Thank you for dinner. It was so

nice. The food was good, but the company was even better."

"That's what I like to hear." He winked at her, put his card in the bill envelope, then excused himself to go to the men's room. Once she was certain the coast was clear, she dug in her purse as if she were searching for a bomb to turn off before it exploded, grabbed her phone, and sent Destiny a text:

Dinner went well. Too well. Determined to poke holes in his story, but he only equipped me with a spoon to do so. LOL. We're about to go dancing. Some place called the Stinky Biscuit, I mean, Funky Biscuit. I'll update you later.

She slipped her phone back in her purse.

Viper, please make me hate you... Better yet, don't. I'm not vulnerable, but I have my guard up for good reason. Too bad I'm peeking over the fence I built to keep you out. And too bad I really like what I see on the other side...

CHAPTER ELEVEN

Ballooned Out of Control

MAJESTY LOOKED LIKE heaven, and she made him crave her like hell. She made him wrestle with both demented demons and altruistic angels. Viper's desire for something more substantial than just a fuck buddy forced him to review and study women in ways he'd never cared to do. He'd always had great control over his sexual proclivities, refusing to return women's phone calls even during a self-imposed carnal drought. Though rather promiscuous by normal standards, he considered himself picky on who he served cock to. Not everyone was up to par, and as several of his ex-girlfriends had said, he possessed a *pene del diablo*, a 'devil dick,' and he knew how to use it. As they lounged about at the bar in the Funky Biscuit, enjoying drinks and a fun conversation, he found himself staring at her through a cloud of Cuban cigar smoke from a patron standing nearby. Somehow that hazy halo fit her perfectly; maybe tonight, she was his temptation and his salvation, all wrapped in one woman.

"So, they have live performers like this every night?" She sipped from her glass of wine.

He swiveled in his chair, now facing the patrons and the glowing stage. The main performance hadn't yet begun. People were milling about, talking in loud voices, drinking their hearts out. Majesty stood for a bit, as if she needed to stretch. *I can stretch you out all right...* He smiled at the thought, which ebbed as the smoke from Cigar Guy, who was now walking away.

When she sat back down, she seemed to feel his gaze on her. She smiled, her eyes gleaming as if she were coming to, from a long dream.

"Why are you looking at me like that?"

"Because I want to." She grimaced in an exaggerated sort of way, making him laugh. "So, at dinner tonight, you tossed questions at me like I was on a witness stand, and that's cool." He threw up his hands, while she folded her arms and pursed her lips. "But now, it's my turn."

"Okay. What is it you wanna know?" She took another taste of her drink.

"You told me you work in customer service for a couple different companies, and you teach some online classes, but what do you really enjoy?"

"Like hobbies?"

"Kinda. Our dream job should feel like a hobby, too. So, if you had your dream job, what would it be?"

"I want to be the Human Resources Director for a major company. I want to help ensure that employees get quality healthcare, and that the company I work for has integrity. I want to deal with all of the legal issues as far as first point of reference for the company and the employees, and I want to help create employee guidelines and—"

"Okay. Stop." He waved his hand. "I know what an H.R. director does. This isn't an interview."

"You can't ask me a question and tell me how to answer it."

"I want you to tell me why you're passionate about that though. What drives that desire of yours to fulfill that role for all those people?"

She dropped the attitude, and her shoulders slumped as she mulled his question.

"That's a good question."

"I know it is. Do you have an answer?"

"I sure as hell do." She sat straighter, seriousness in her eyes. "I want to be what I wish I had, at so many different jobs. Like I told you tonight, I hate my job. What makes it bearable are some of my co-workers, but I don't like much of the management. They don't know how to treat people and in fact treat me like some token Black since I am one of the few in there. I was passed over for customer service manager twice, by two White women who were far less qualified." He could see the hurt and anger in her eyes. "I needed that promotion. But see, I let that anger drive me to continue getting my education. It motivated me so that one day, I'll be able to tell all of them to kiss my ass. I want to be one of the good guys when I climb up this corporate ladder.

"I want to be the person employees can turn to, that they can trust. I want to be the person they know has their best interest in mind, not just the company's. It's hard to do both, but not impossible. The reason why I'm also passionate about this, as you say, is because I honestly enjoy that type of work, Viper. I was an assistant H.R. manager at one job, a long time ago, and I loved it." Her eyes lit up. "That company closed down, but it was the best two vocational years of my life. It didn't pay enough, but it showed me exactly what I wanted to do."

"I can respect that."

"Well, that's good, 'cause Lord knows if you didn't respect it, Viper, I wouldn't know what to do with myself!" She rolled her eyes, then burst out laughing. He shook his finger at her, amused.

"Looks like they're setting up." He gestured to the stage.

"Oh, good!" A few seconds later, she glanced at her watch. "Let me call Troy real quick. He might be already asleep, but I want to make sure he's doing okay." He nodded in understanding as she went somewhere quieter, cell phone in hand.

As he sat there for a bit, he pondered his work schedule, then decided to check his own phone. He'd turned it off while on this date, something he never did. Tonight, he didn't want any disturbances. A waitress came by. He looked at his empty beer bottle, his usual draft, and decided to try something else. *Sometimes this place has authentic Cuban beers.*

"Do you have Bucanero Fuerte? It's a native Cuban beer."

"Yes, we do."

"Bring me that, please."

"Sure." The waitress nodded and sauntered off.

He looked down at his phone and noted several missed calls and text messages, mostly to do with dog training and a party he and his King brothers had been invited to in Orlando. Then, a message caught his eye.

King Brick (Jose): *King Golden Boy got flipped and shanked at chow-hall.*

He wrote back.

Viper: *Is he dead?*

King Brick: *No, but he's fucked up. Bad.*

Viper: *Who did it?*

King Brick: *Jaguar got King Cadillac to do it, and a couple of his boys who are in the same prison.*

Viper: *Why?*

King Brick: *Said he was talking shit about Jaguar. Said Gold had said Jag was setting people up he didn't like. He accused Gold of working with the Feds. Ahora es un hombre marcado.*

He slipped his phone back in his pocket, a million thoughts swirling through his head. The waitress returned with his beer, and he asked that she refresh Majesty's wine.

Viper crossed his arms and watched the band set up, while the people got riled with excitement. He liked this place quite a bit, but nothing beat the clubs back in Little Havana. His brain searched, swam, and dipped in the deep end of his consciousness. Memories and emotions were often covered in heavy cloaks of voluntary forgetfulness.

His heart was ice, his feelings elusive, skipping into the depths of weary shadows and swallowed whole by gold and black holes – deficits in his own cosmos.

I am so fuckin' sick of this shit. I can't even take a honey out, have us enjoy ourselves without someone getting flipped or merked due to Jag. He's supposed to contact me first. He went over my head. He knows he doesn't have to answer to me; he's Second Crown of our Miami, Florida division, our VP, but I'm right under him. I'm Warlord, the Third Crown, and some in the nation consider us practically equal. We're both high-ranking, and the pride of men will destroy.

He wasn't man enough to be Warlord. He can't handle the blood but likes to cause it and then look away. He wants the glory without the guts. His cousin got him on board. Without that family tie, without King Snoopy, may he rest in peace, he would've been nothin'. I'm smarter than him, that's for damn sure, because he lets his emotions dictate his next move. That's weak-minded. Some pussy shit. Jag is charismatic though, and he knows how to make large sums of money fast, but so do I, if I must.

Still, he doesn't know how to handle business beyond that. He just pretends that he does. I'm always makin' him look good, as I always do. I'm the muscle. No one is supposed to get cut, beat up, worked over, punished, or taken out without my approval, and if it is real serious, we have to go through King Blood. Jaguar knew I'd tell him this was a fucked-up thing to do, so he didn't bother to call me this time around. It's all about his ego.

Even if he goes over my head, we had an unspoken rule that he's supposed to fucking tell me first! Now I'm getting text messages that he got work done on Golden Boy. Golden Boy always says what he feels, so no surprise his mouth got him in trouble, but this is ridiculous. It's juvenile. We're supposed to have evolved beyond this. Golden Boy and Jag never liked each other anyway. Jag is still runnin' shit for our division, prison bars be damned, but he's out of control. Golden Boy is in his way. I know he wants him gone. Golden has high favor with several high-ranking Kings in Florida and Georgia. Golden is up for promotion. Jag got called on the carpet about that botched sting operation two years ago. That's the REAL motivation right there.

I wonder if King Blood knows that Jag is trippin'? I could call a meeting, but then that would bring light to the fact that I've got beef with Jag. Jag knows I'm pissed. I told him about this shit before, that it wasn't right. Regardless, I need to keep these communication lines open with this fool, even if he does pick and choose what to tell me. Some information is better than none. Marie and the brothers will fill in the rest. If he realizes I see him cracking, he'll either avoid me or try to start some shit to have me targeted. I can't let that happen right now. I need him to believe that I think he has everything under control. Gotta play this cool...

Just then, Majesty returned, looking out of sorts.

"¿Hay algo mal?"

"Huh? What did you say?" She frowned at him, scowling.

He laughed.

"I said, is something wrong?"

Blue, purple, and pink lights spun all around and the lead singer of the band began to test the microphone.

"Troy has been acting up."

"Acting up? He got into a fight with one of the other kids the babysitter has tonight or something?" She shook her head. "Well, what is it? You had mentioned she had some other children over there that he plays with and—"

"No… well, yes, there are other kids, no fighting… kinda fighting… but not like that."

"Now it's my turn to say, 'huh?'" He chuckled.

She swallowed and looked away, her complexion deepening. "I found out they had a birthday party for one of the kids there tonight. Troy was helping to blow up the balloons, and… and uh…"

"And what?"

"Nelson, another kid there at the party, caught Troy in a spare bedroom, bent over, his pants down and a balloon up to his damn ass." Viper sucked his teeth to keep from changing his facial expression, and God forbid, laughing. "Right before that, he was slipping out of the kitchen where they were blowing up the balloons, going into that bedroom, and privately farting in them. Then he was returning to the kitchen, where everyone was, and releasing them into the air. He kept doing it, and no one knew where the smell was coming from until Nelson caught him in the act."

Viper held out as long as he could, but then he erupted in laughter so hard, it made his stomach clench like never before. He was practically sliding out of his chair, melting right in his skin. His muscles gave out on him as his body lulled about in the chair, and he couldn't catch his breath! His eyes watered until moisture was soon cascading down his cheeks, and he'd come undone. He could hear Majesty faintly going off in the background, something about, '…*It's not funny, Viper!* By the time he had gotten himself together, she was sitting in her chair, rapidly rocking her leg back and forth and staring at the stage, doused in anger like gasoline – and he was the fiery match.

"Majesty…" he said with a snort as he tried to stop from laughing again. It was a tall order. "Majesty…" She kept looking straight ahead. "What's wrong? Do you think I have a strange scent of humor?" And once more, he surrendered to the laughter, his gut hurting, his face hot, and his body trembling. She seemed unimpressed. "Baby… baby… Hey, how do you know when a clown farts?" She kept ignoring him. "…It smells funny. Hey… how does NASA pass gas, baby? They do it using ass-teroids! One more… one more…What do I have if I fart in my wallet? Gas money!"

This time, her mouth twitched as she tried to keep from giving in. The music began to play, drowning him out. She seemed satisfied with this, until he whipped out his cell phone and texted her:

Majesty, if a ho farts, is she called a prostiTOOT?

She clutched the phone and looked at the screen, the light bathing her face. And then he witnessed the angry mother-of-one's eyes light up and narrow as she laughed her head off.

They went on to enjoy the music when the first song played, a Caribbean style fast jazz tune. People meandered to the dance floor. The pretty lady beside him jumped to her feet and grabbed his arm, a big smile on her face.

"Come on! Let's dance!"

"Nah, you go ahead."

"What?!" she yelled over the music and commotion.

"You told me you were takin' me out dancing. We're here now, come on." She pulled harder at him, but he wouldn't budge. He curled his finger, motioning her to bring her ear close to his mouth. She hesitated for a moment, then did so.

"...I wanted to take *you* out dancing, so you could hear some good ass music. Live. I don't dance, baby. I wanted *you* to blow off some steam. Now go on... dance. Have fun."

He leaned back and waved her off before taking another swig from his bottle of beer. She waltzed off and at some point, she became engulfed in the crowd, but he could still feel her... knowing she was twirling and moving about, dancing to her heart's content. She came back into view. The curls in her hair had fallen over her face, a sheen of sweat covered her skin, and she looked so sexy. Beautiful. Strong. Soft. Incredible.

She danced as if she'd been holding inside the weight of the world, and gave birth right there, to her own freedom. Something about moving and swaying to the beat of a good song would make everything all right. Music soothed the savage beasts. Music was a universal language; everyone had the urge to tap their feet every now and again. Music made angry men pause, made vipers tango and salsa. Another song came on, and she was still at it.

A man approached her to dance. Viper slowly sat up, watching.

He clasped his hands, trying to ignore the fact that he felt froggy and hot all over. He observed as she smiled and talked with the stranger… far too long for his liking, but then, she pointed at him, and the man turned toward him. Viper smirked, raised his arm, and waved at the fucker. The man walked off, leaving her alone. *Yeah, that's right. Keep it movin'…*

A few hours later the good times at the Funky Biscuit came to an end. They left, laughing and talking, the cool air feeling good as they made their way to his parked car. He ignored the drunk guys trying to engage him in car chat—wanting to know where he'd gotten it, and if they could take it for a spin. He helped her into the car, got in, and drove off back towards their homes. When he turned on the radio, Queen Naija, featuring Ari Lennox, was crooning 'Set Him Up.'

"Oh, this is my shit! Turn it up, Viper!" She was loose now. Between the dancing, conversation, laughter and the wine, the woman was in her zone. He leisurely leaned forward and turned it up while she rocked those sexy hips to the beat. When he pulled into her driveway, his heart was beating a mile a minute. It was three in the damn morning, but it felt like they'd only been out for a couple of hours.

This was one of the best dates I've ever had. I like how she looks… how she smells… how she talks. I love her humor, her modesty, and her confidence. I'm going to do this right. She's definitely a candidate. Makes a motherfucker seriously consider turning over a new leaf. Well, I already was, but she could make it all the easier…

He cut off the car, hopped out, and opened her door. As he helped her to her feet, the fresh air caught the scent of her perfume and natural aroma, and it sent him into a lust-filled, hedonistic place. His dick hardened and throbbed, overdosing on all that was she.

Taking her hand, he walked her up to her front door, she holding the flowers, and him pretending to be the perfect gentleman.

"I had such a fun time tonight, Viper. Even if you're lame and can't dance." She placed the bouquet of roses on a nearby windowsill.

"I didn't say I couldn't dance. I said I *don't* dance. In actuality, I do dance sometimes, but I wanted tonight to be about you." She gave him a curious look, as if trying to pick his mind. Perhaps she believed she had some super-power to do that. After a few seconds of silence, she pulled out her keys from her purse.

"You should've danced with me like I asked you to. I would've had more fun. Men kept hitting on me, thinking I was alone. Or was that a test? Did you want to see how I'd handle that?" She opened her front door but didn't enter yet.

"Nah, no testing. It just seems to me that you're so busy all the time, you never get time to yourself. You needed to unwind, but the main reason I did that is because dancing, even fast dancing, can be sensual. I'd be too much for you."

"Oh, here you go!" She laughed.

"You were so concerned with thinking all I wanted to do was fuck you, I didn't want you to feel as if I was up to something." She crossed her arms, clearly not believing him. "I'm serious."

"Sensual? It was a bunch of fast songs, Viper. Who bumps and grinds to Caribbean jazz tunes and 'Beautiful Life,' by Ace of Base? That was the last song they played tonight."

"Close your door."

"What?"

"Close the damn door," he repeated. "Wait right here on the porch." Making a mad dash to his car, he turned it on and selected a song from his collection: 'Please Me,' by Cardi B and Bruno Mars. He rocked his body back and forth, moving to the beat as he approached her, arms in the air, a grin on his face, then lifted his shirt, exposing his eight-pack, making his abs roll.

"You ain't shit!" She burst out laughing. "All right. Fine. You can dance, but this ain't no fast song! This is a 'do-it' song. A 'come out them draws' song!" When he finally stood before her again, they were both cheesing at one another, building on a growing connection. They stood there, dancing together, their eyes on one another. He grabbed her around the waist, bringing her close so he could feel her heart beating a mile a minute now, too. He looked down at her, and their lips parted at the exact same time.

And then, he was swallowing her cries as he bent down to claim her lips, tasting the wine she'd been drinking. He ran his hand along her back, his other hand still at her waist, then cradled the back of her head, bringing her impossibly closer. He moaned before pulling away. She smiled up at him.

"You're a good kisser." She touched her mouth with

two fingers, pressing into the soft flesh. "Thanks again for tonight." Leaning to him, she gave him a peck, then opened her front door wider.

"It's a long ride back to my place. Aren't you going to invite me in?" he joked, making her cheeks plump.

"You are a trip, man. Call me tomorrow, okay?" She grabbed the flowers and stepped inside… but slowly.

"I'll do that. Sleep tight. Don't let the Viper bite…"

She giggled and closed the door. He heard it lock, then jogged down her steps, a bit of pep in his step. He was thankful that his back was towards her, so she couldn't see the big ass, corny smile on his face. It practically split him in two…

CHAPTER TWELVE

He Watches Over You

V IPER COULD FEEL his eyes twitching, but he was caught in the dream. No matter which way he attempted to turn in that big, empty bed to wake himself, it didn't work. He remained trapped in his own mind. He kept hearing his own voice, saying the words aloud. Who was he talking to? All he needed to do was ride it out... Perhaps his own subconscious was trying to tell him something?

There is such a thing as sacred ground...

There were places you didn't go and stir the pot. Things you didn't say, and things you didn't do. Sometimes, it's a mix of these, such as things you didn't do or say if you happened to be in that place considered sacrosanct. Where you were born was your womb. Home was blessed, no matter how bad of a place it may have been. You don't shit where you eat. We'd all agreed when we were much younger, my King brothers and I, that some things could never occur on Little Havana soil. Sin odio entre cubanos.

The prayers of our dead ancestors from Cuba are written above our heads in the clouds. They'd prayed to be here, to get freedom from Castro, while others revered him and would split someone open if they spoke ill of him. Some of our ancestors were forced to come to America against their will. Others willingly made a life here, starting all over from nothing. Marielitos. Their sacrifices were the blood, their work, the sweat, and their ambition, and faith, the tears shed to get to this place whole, in one piece. Regardless of their reasons for leaving their native home, they made a life in this new country, creating new spaces for themselves. One of those spaces was Little Havana.

Over time, fractures surfaced in the tight knit community. Poverty reared its ugly head and gave birth to the twin bastards: desperation and greed. Families fell apart, crime skyrocketed. Groups, organizations, and factions were needed. A call to order. A sense of belonging, of normalcy in an upside-down place. These groups developed further, some of them morphing into gangs. My uncles didn't call themselves a gang until much later. That terminology was adopted from other places. They were just a social club. Once more of the Puerto Ricans, Dominicans, Venezuelans, Mexicans, Nicaraguans, Salvadorians, more Cubans, Ecuadorians, Hondurans, Peruvians, Colombians, and Panamanians came to Florida, there was influence in how these factions ran. Some of that guidance was good, some not so much, but one thing was certain: it fostered much needed organization and created sensibility out of chaos. At least, according to my mother's brother, mi tío Oscar.

He told us the gangs that were already well established in the United States back in the 1970s and 1980s flooded into the South from Chicago, Newark, Los Angeles, and New York City. All states surrounded by water were prime pickings, for obvious reasons. Dope floats. Ya need a boat. The power spread, and one of the most dominant organizations to land in South Florida was the Latin Kings. The Latin Kings have been coined one of the most, if not the most, violent gang in the United States, with a considerable and growing membership. For every three you see, there'll be three more that didn't make it. For every one of us killed, there is a new gang member taking their place, and twenty more being born who will be full blown LKs by the time they reach the age of sixteen. For every individual behind bars, there are two or three being released back into civilization. The power behind the LKs is woven tight. That's for good reason. We are very serious about our brotherhood, and our business.

We're particularly well-structured. We follow protocol and protect one another, and if anyone gets out of line, internally or externally, they are dealt with. That notwithstanding, one thing I learned early on was this: Your best friend will be a Latin King. So will your worst enemy. We hold close to many traditional values, despite the bad rap we've received. One of those values is treating fellow Latina women with respect, as well as any woman of any race we're involved with romantically. What one may see as respectful, another may not, so I suppose the area is kind of gray there—but a Latin King beating up a Latin Queen or orchestrating violence against her is strictly prohibited. Doesn't mean this doesn't happen, it does, but it's frowned upon. We're also taught to show respect to our elders.

I must be honest though...

The new generation is not following procedure. They are doing things that require disciplinary actions. In some cases, death. Some of these teenagers coming into the game now are reckless. They're feral. Selfish. Ignorant. Stupid. Egotistical. They only think of themselves, not the collective. We survived by thinking of our brothers. We'll die *by hoarding and giving in to our aspirations. They have no self-control and don't think things through, but it wasn't always that way. We used to move with purpose. Many of us still do, but there are concerns from the OGs that are still drawing breath. Marie has told me many times that she fears for our future. Florida is home. It's where we lay our heads. It's where we make our money. It's where we raise our families. If that is disrupted, a war will ignite. This wouldn't be the first time money caused the fall of our personal Rome.*

I went to community college for less than one year. I took a class in philosophy—my favorite. One lesson was about how outside influences change our minds, forever. At first, the gang was formed due to discrimination, the desire to create a haven for all Latinos, but somewhere along the way, things changed. Here in Little Havana, we still had many of the older guys influencing us, and we respected them. We made a promise to them because of that respect. We made a pact, and it went down as law. Anyone breaking that law would be punished. Sometimes, depending on the severity of the disobedience, it also meant death.

The ways of the old will always be instilled in the snake. The snake will always protect the oath. The Viper is not the enemy; he is the protector. Misunderstood. Feared. The snake slithered through Little Havana, and he did the same in the Garden of Eden. He brought with him death, where God had created promise, light, and life. The Viper waited in the tree, the moonlight streaming across his black and green shimmery scales, and when the beautiful naked dark woman approached with a head of wool, he asked her to step aside...

Viper swallowed hard, trying desperately to wake up once again as his dream took a strange and sharp turn out of the blue. He was suddenly in a black, silver, and purple lush garden with high trees, red skies, and jade birds with black and coral beaks flying high. He could smell wildlife, rotting fruit, and femininity… Trapped in this world, he was unable to wake up. He relaxed once again, giving in, far too tired to keep struggling…

The snake hissed and said, 'It's not you I wish to give the golden apple to, my Love… It's the one from which you protect. He will lie in the stories of your Lord, and say it was you who fell into temptation. You will be to blame for every woe, and he will be praised for every gain. He will deem you overly emotional, weak, silly, responsible for the downfall of man, and say that your monthly blood is a curse for all that you have done, and your pain while bringing his seed into the world is your punishment for listening to a cast out, fallen angel like me. I say mostly lies, 'tis true, but this, my Love, is my one truth…"

"I was taught to never trust you, snake. I will not listen to anything you say." The dark woman, with smooth skin the color of plums and teeth white like the insides of bitten apples, stood before him while he stayed coiled in his tree. She showed no fear.

"There will be a story written about you, Eve. The first book of a long series of distortions, the truth shall be buried deep within it, the important bits ripped out and scattered in the desert, never to be seen again. They can't control you if you know the truth. So, you must believe the lie. This, my Love, is what they fear. Hear me, and never forget the true tale of the Viper.

The dark woman with the wooly hair, her breasts soon to be swollen with milk—though she had no idea she was with child— looked at him in disbelief.

"You are to never be trusted. My mate would never betray me."

'He will, and worst of all, you will not remember this warning once you and he are cast aside. He is the one who wishes to be like God and take his place. Right now, you can save yourself if you walk away, and let me have him.'

In the distance stood a tall, fit, dark man made of clay and Earth. The man was afraid of him, a coward waiting in the wings.

"He is trying to sacrifice you, right now. He can hear your thoughts because you allowed him to crawl into your heart. It is not YOU who disobeyed God's word first. It was listening to the advice of your mate, who told you to do it, after he took the first taste of death by tricking you to stand before me. You will think you are dreaming, but seven days from now, everything I am telling you will come to fruition. Adam is weaker than you in all ways, except for his brawn. He will fool you time and time again because of your guilt over the lies he has fed you."

"He showed me proof that you are evil, and that the fruit is good, and that is why you don't want us to have it!"

"His proof was written by him. How can you trust someone to tell you the truth when this would cause their own demise? Would you trust a storm to promise to pass you by? How can you trust someone who enslaves you? That is his plan. To own you."

"Lies!"

"You will have to fight for everything you get in seven days! Your paradise will be destroyed. You will be beaten! Blamed! Shunned! Lied on from now until the end of time. Centuries later, your body will be sold against your will. Your spirit broken. He will steal from you and kill your sisters, mothers, and daughters. You will support and help him, and he will still blame you for his struggles and downfalls. You will pick him up from the ground, and once you do, he will knock you down. He will point out all your flaws and claim *none of his own. He will start war after war, spill blood from the moment he awakens to the second he falls asleep.*

"He will destroy your planet; the air will be polluted from these odd machines he builds, the oceans and rivers will be poisoned, important resources will be pumped dry, the animals will be sick and die off, the soil will be barren and produce no fruit or grains. And he will still not learn, and he will want more, and more, and more, and worst of all, he will teach you to do the same. He will make deals with me so that he may be legendary in the eyes of men. He will be greedy and vile. He will lie on God and call himself a shepherd. God needs no marshals. He is Alpha and Omega. That male wasn't even here first… YOU WERE. If you fail this test, Eve, there is no turning back."

"Give me the apple. I trust my mate. He asked that I retrieve it from this twisted tree you sleep in and look over the entire garden from the highest branch."

"This fruit is not for you. Now step aside! Do not listen to him!"

"You are evil! You are Lucifer! You are a viper… Eres una víbora!"

"I am all of those things, but it is HIM that I want. It is him I will have… Step aside. For the final time—I am the Viper he rightfully fears, but your mate's desire for power will force him to sacrifice anyone and anything to get it. Including YOU being forced to walk ahead of him and ask for the apple! It's the only time he will ever put you in the front— and that is to ransom yourself! Otherwise, you, your sisters, your mothers, and your daughters will walk two steps behind. He will take all the praise and none of the condemnation. Why are you here alone? Or are you? He lurks in the darkness, like a deserter, sending in his mate to do his dirty work. I

can smell him. I want revenge, for he betrayed me, too." The large snake's forked tongue whipped out and tasted the air. Vengeance was so close...

"Betrayed you? How did he betray you?"

"He befriended me, then told me to ask God if I could work beside him. He told me I deserved it, and that God was simply waiting for me to show the initiative and ask for what was rightfully mine. I did as he encouraged me to do and was cast out of Heaven, and he became God's favorite. Adam is devious, my Love. He skulks like a cat. He laughed when we were cast out, me and the dark angels, who'd been created in the sun but are now damned to the darkness of Hell."

"I will not be fooled by you."

"My dear, you've already been fooled, but not by me. The diabolical deception will cost you your sanity, your womb, and all of civilization. Did you ever consider that you've been tricked so well, you cannot decipher reality? Did you stop and think that perhaps it is Adam who is the biggest devil of all? It is my time, my Love. This is my day to taste the blood poured from your mate, and end my sorrow, as well as your future pain that he'd inflict, for centuries to come. I can save the whole world, if you simply step aside. My golden apple is delicious. It is poisonous, just like my kiss. Just like my bite, and my might... For I am Genesis, and Adam is the Revelations. Eve, you are the removed words from the text... pages ripped, burned, while others were spread out, carried away by the winds of the desert. You've brought shame to yourself now, not because you've sinned, but because you fell in love..."

Viper slowly awoke, in a daze. He rubbed his sweaty face, then stared at the clock on his nightstand. It was 4:44 A.M., on the dot. Since he was a child, he'd often have vivid dreams and awaken at 3:33 A.M., or 4:44 A.M. This one had a sense of familiarity. Perhaps he'd dreamt it before? *No… I would've remembered that.* He plopped back down on the pillow, desperate to go back to sleep, but it would be damn near impossible. There were things to take care of, work to be done. Calls to be made. After that, he needed to drive to Little Havana. He had stuff to take care of there, too.

MR. EARL DICKENS was mowing his lawn. Majesty noticed the daunting rain clouds gathering as if they were about to have a good cry and soak everything that dared to stand below. The buzz of the old lawnmower was now interrupted by the occasional burst of lightning, but the old man seemed determined to finish his front yard. Clutching her purse and wrinkled lunch bag from work, she hurried into the house, Troy right on her heels. She washed her hands, then got out the fixings to make spaghetti and garlic bread for dinner while Troy played on his iPad and ate an after-school snack at the kitchen island.

After a short while, she stepped onto the porch to see if the old man was still out there. Sure enough, Mr. Earl was still tempting precipitation fate. *It's going to be raining soon. He is too old to be mowing that big lot all by himself, and it is too hot, too.*

She went back into the house and marched into the kitchen.

"Troy, I need to be able to trust you."

"I didn't do it, Mama!"

She sucked her teeth and rolled her eyes.

"Boy, I ain't even accuse you of nothing, and you're screaming at me about how you didn't do it. Makes me think you *did* do something I just haven't found out about yet. Now listen, I want you to get washed up." He nodded in understanding. "Wash your hands real good, too, and do your homework."

"I already washed my hands, Mama."

"That five seconds of you flicking water around in the bathroom sink doesn't count. Now, after you're done with that, you come right back in here and sit right in this kitchen, with your milk, crackers, and pineapple. I'm going to get changed, go to Mr. Earl's for a bit, and I expect you to be right where I told you to be when I get back." She wagged her finger at him.

The boy's face split in a grin, no doubt thrilled he would have the run of the house. He was always excited when she stepped out for a minute or two, doing a bit of gardening. Made him feel like a big boy.

"Don't get any ideas. I'm going over to Mr. Earl's, just like I said. The man lives two houses down."

"The old man who gave us the peach pie. I know where his house is."

"Good. You'll be able to look right out this here window and see his backyard, but you'll have to come out on the porch to see the front, which is where I'll be. I'll be back in about ten minutes tops. I should be able to trust you for ten minutes. Right, Troy?"

"Of course, Mama. I'm a man now. I'm just short is all." She grimaced and crossed her arms. "I'm for real! And why don't you let me stay in here for longer than just a couple minutes? Wesley gets to stay at home alone for two hours now!"

"That's Wesley, and you're *you*."

"Mama, if you think about it, kids should be runnin' things, anyway. Grownups don't know what y'all are doing. You don't see kids fightin' about presidents and votin', laws, and racist stuff. Y'all the ones who shouldn't be left in the house alone. You just can't be trusted."

"Troy, if you weren't my own flesh and blood, as God is my witness, I'd... God give me strength!" She shook her fist at the ceiling. "You're too young, and I've told you a hundred times that I will not have you here in this house by yourself. Now, you're lucky you get these ten minutes. Instead of thinking you can take this time to help build my trust, you start getting grand ideas about world domination. Keep on, and you won't be here alone until you're seventeen!"

"But Mama—"

"But Mama, nothing. I bet Wesley wasn't fartin' in balloons at a birthday party and gassin' everyone out. I bet Wesley wasn't eating all the pepperonis off the school pizza back in the kitchen when he was supposed to be helping to serve, and then everyone had to have 'cheese pizza,' and my ass was called up to the school due to the new change of menu, thanks to Chef Boy-I-Know-You-Lyin'! Talkin' to me about some damn Wesley! I bet his parents didn't have to take him to the E.R., like I had to take you, for supergluing your damn underarm closed!"

Troy's rich complexion deepened.

"It was a dare!"

"And you was foolish enough to fall in line. You was walkin' around like a toy soldier. I turned you around to see how to wind you up! You're lucky you didn't lose any skin, boy, but I am certain you'll never grow hair in that spot once puberty gets a hold of you. It'll be smooth as a baby's behind for the rest of your days!" Oddly enough, he remained quiet as she lit into him. "Boy, that bill 'bout took me to Jesus when I saw it! All because you want to be a little, pint-sized Steve Harvey and make everyone laugh! You ain't a king of comedy, and you ain't got Steve Harvey's money to pay that hospital bill, either. Hell, you can't pay a telephone bill, a water bill, or a duck's bill! Nothin'! Tellin' me adults need to stay home!" she mumbled as she snatched open a drawer looking for her wine corkscrew opener to set out for as soon as her child's head hit the pillow.

His eyes widened, and the utter look of defeat and disappointment took over.

"Now you sit here and be quiet, Troy. Understood?"

"All right, Mama."

Minutes later, she was heading over to Mr. Earl's house. It was now sprinkling. As she approached, he turned the loud machine off.

"Hi there, Ms. Majesty! Nice of ya to stop by!"

"Mr. Earl. I'd like to help. You shouldn't be out here, and it's started to rain."

"Oh, I'll be all right! Go on back home." He shooed

her away and got ready to start the mower up again.

"Let me finish it for you."

"You? No, no. I can do it, Majesty. Besides, look. I'm almost finished."

She looked around, and he had about three more rows to do.

"What if I told you that I love to mow the lawn? I know you see me out there sometimes. When it's not too hot, I really enjoy it. Please let me. It would be a real shame if you caught pneumonia. Besides, it's my way of thanking you for the pie."

He looked at her thoughtfully, wiped his forehead with the back of his hand, and peered at his porch.

"All right, but only because I'm almost finished."

The poor man was breathing hard, and his shirt was soaked through. Gripping the lawnmower handle, she pushed it over the lawn, her thoughts swarming and her mood lifted. She loved the smell of freshly cut grass. It reminded her of so many beautiful childhood memories, the times before reality set in. The rain began to fall harder, and by the time she was done, taking pride in her perfectly straight rows compared to Mr. Earl's nice but wobbly ones, she was soaked. She found the man sitting on his porch with a big glass of ice water. She pushed the lawnmower towards him, suddenly realizing the rain had gone away, although probably not for long. It would come back with a vengeance.

"Where should I take it to? Your garage?"

"Just leave it right there, honey." She nodded. "You know what? Ain't nobody ever offered to help me mow this here lawn. You surprised me. I still feel mighty bad about letting you do it. And look at you, you're drenched."

"I'm just fine, Mr. Earl." She smiled. "Besides, I like cold showers." They both had a good laugh at that. "All right, I'll head on back home. Thanks again for the pie and try to get some rest."

"Hold up now. I poured this water for you."

"Oh…" She thanked him and drank, the cold beverage tasting like the best damn water she'd ever had.

"Young lady, your parents should be mighty proud of you." She smiled weakly—couldn't muster more—and kept on drinking. "I don't get to see my children as much as I'd like. It gets a little lonely sometimes."

She handed him the empty glass, then crossed her arms.

"Well, you must've not seen it in the paper I suppose, but I happen to be up for adoption."

The man burst out laughing. "Your parents… hmmm… difficult relationship?"

"Sometimes things are fine. Sometimes they're not so fine."

He nodded in understanding.

"Mr. Earl, I'd be more than happy to check in on you and spend time with you, just like I do with my own family."

"Well, aren't you the sweetest! If I adopted you, you'd be my youngest one, almost my eldest grandson's age. I wouldn't mind a smart daughter like you!" He smiled so big, it made her heart melt. "All jokes aside, thank you for your help. I do appreciate it, though I hate that you took the trouble." She walked up his steps, gave him a kiss on the cheek, then turned to leave.

"Uh, Majesty, do you mind some fake, pretend fatherly advice?"

"You being my father is fake, or the advice?" she teased, making him chuckle. "I suppose not. Go ahead."

"All right." He wiped his forehead once again. "I ain't got shit to do but look around and see what everybody else is doing 'round here. It's like a free TV show, without havin' HBO or one of those damn streaming services people on the computer are always tryna sell me. All I gotta do is look out this here window and see pay per view!"

She burst out laughing. "I can only imagine what goes on around here when I'm at work." It was starting to sprinkle again, so she stepped onto his porch, seeking protection from the awning.

"I think Viper is sweet on you."

She ran her hand along her arm, not certain she really wanted to get into all of that right then and there.

"You ain't gotta say anything, Majesty. I just wanted you to know. He is out there trainin' them dogs early in the morning sometimes, and I see him walking them, and he'll fetch your newspaper outta your yard, put it on your porch. Sometimes, this lazy ass mailman doesn't close the mail hatches; he'll just rush around putting the wrong stuff in people's boxes and such, letting everyone driving around see if we've got something interesting in there to steal by leavin' the flap open. I've seen Viper walk over and close your mailbox for you a time or two. I've also seen him pick weeds outta your yard after that notice came around about folks not tending to their lawns, and he put numbers on your mailbox, too."

She'd wondered who'd done that! Some busybody from the HOA had emailed her talking about she needed the numbers on the mailbox, but she hadn't gotten around to it. She figured the woman had just come over and done it herself.

"I asked you before if you knew him, Mr. Earl. You said you didn't... not well, anyway."

The man stood and stretched.

"I don't. He keeps to himself. I just know he reminds me a bit of a friend of mine I knew a long time ago, before I had gotten right with the Lord and settled down." She wasn't fooled the man was speaking about himself. "I know he works hard with those dogs and he's good at what he does. He keeps a low profile, despite all of that loud music. He was playin' Parliament the other day. Now that's some shit I can boogie to. I play it sometimes, too. Got all the records! Flash. Light! Reeeed Light! Neon light! Stop. LIGHT!"

"Shinin' on the funk!"

"Oh my God! Whatcha know about that, girl?! You and Viper too young to know about that good music! Must've been in ya mama's albums!"

They both burst out laughing again. Her stomach was hurting from the silliness of it all.

"But anyway, yeah, as I was saying. I also know when a man is sweet on someone, really into her, but doesn't always know how to show it."

"Oh, he's made it clear." Her cheeks warmed as she let the cat out of the bag.

Mr. Earl giggled.

"Honey, I don't mean with words. He could be the smoothest talker in the South, the most honest man to walk the streets of Boca Raton. I'm talkin' about men like him probably find it hard to trust folks is all. To open up. They don't do nice things to gain points with you, per se. They do it, so they can prove to *themselves* they can walk the walk, not just talk the talk. He's going through changes."

"And you can tell all of that just from him picking up my newspaper and putting numbers on my mailbox?"

"Naw. I can tell because he sits in his backyard, late at night sometimes, drinking a beer, listening to music, those big ass dogs around him, and he'll be in that lawn chair or that hammock, lookin' right over at your house. When your lights go out, he goes in. He watches over you like some protector. That's a man who's fallin' fast. And definitely fallin' hard…"

CHAPTER THIRTEEN

Bless the Child that's Got His Own

VIPER SAT NEXT to his mother in her small home that smelled of rich coffee and strong cigarette smoke. His thoughts drifted to the previous day when he and Majesty met for lunch. The evening before that, they'd started a long text message conversation after Troy had gone to bed, which had led to an even longer phone call, and then to them sitting on her porch, talking face to face as the stars sparkled in the sky. And kissing. Plenty of kissing.

He craved her so badly. *Oh, the wonderful things I could do to that pussy if given the chance. I'll get it. Soon...* He could still practically taste her strawberry lip-gloss and smell her perfume. Things were progressing well, though he kept their connection a secret, as with all things that mattered to him. He didn't want it jinxed, or put it out into the world, making it everyone's business. Each day, he looked forward to her 'good morning' texts, often accompanied by a meme or some inspirational quote of the day. He was enjoying himself with Majesty, and though things were moving a bit slower with her than he'd like, he was happy with the time they shared, the conversations they had, and her warmth and humor.

A Hispanic soap opera played out on the TV, and the sounds of children playing outside was at times louder than even the buzz of hair clippers coming from the back bedroom, where his stepfather, Ricky, was cutting one of his cousins' hair.

"*¿Dónde has estado?*"

"I've been where I told you I've been." He tapped his knee and bent forward, looking down at the ash covered magazine on the table. *Vanidades.*

"*Tu padre me debe dinero.*"

"Why are you telling me that papá owes you money?" He shrugged before flopping back on the couch, his chain belt rattling as he moved. "Go take that up with him."

"*No le hablo.*"

"Well, if you don't call him or talk to him, then how is he supposed to know you're hard pressed to get it?" She rolled her eyes at him as she lit a cigarette. Her hair was down to her waist now, the jet-black color streaked with silver. She seemed to have lost weight; maybe she was trying a new diet as usual, even though she'd always been petite. He'd been in the house for a little over thirty minutes, during which time all she'd done was nag and complain.

First, he was told how he doesn't answer his phone, or

how he should train her friends' dogs for free. Then she went into a spiel about how her car needs to be fixed, and she wished for him to buy her a new one, even though he'd just bought her the one she currently had, a blue Lexus, two years prior. She then tried to lay a guilt trip on him about Grandma's death, when all else failed to get the reaction she so desired, harping about how he'd missed the funeral because of him being in prison. But he refused to play her games. He just sat there and yawned as she ranted. He'd hoped she'd be in better spirits, considering she was going on one of her many trips soon, but he'd been wrong.

"When are you giving me a grandchild?" She plopped on the chair across from him. It was beige with a palm tree print, and a stain on the arm from spilled coffee. "Something wrong with you or something?" She waved her cigarette, gesturing towards his pants. "You're thirty-one."

"Mamá, this is my first time in I don't know how long being out of jail for more than four years in a row. Would you *please* stop naggin' me, and just let me live my life in peace?" He took a sip of his coffee. On the screen was a ghostly pale Hispanic woman with bleach blond hair and blue contact lenses, crying and yelling in Spanish about how her husband had run off with her twin sister.

"I have no more sons! No daughter, Dominic!" Her voice quaked as her eyes sheened over. "I only had you and Diego! Your father has many stepchildren and grandchildren, while I have nothing. I know you're not gay, so what is going on? Are you still punishing me?"

Many years ago, he told his mother during one of their notorious arguments that he wasn't having children. All his friends, LK brothers his age and a bit younger, had kids. It was like a rite of passage, so he was almost like some mystical unicorn amongst his peers. Mamá had burst in tears, but he'd been adamant that though he didn't blame her for all that had happened in his childhood, the last thing he wanted was to bring an innocent person in the world and watch them struggle and be subjected to possibly he and the child's mother fighting day in, day out. Mamá had expressed how crushed she'd been by his words, for being a grandmother was one of her greatest aspirations.

"Dominic, I'm speaking to you. Do you still not want children?"

"I want them. I *always* wanted them. I just said I wasn't going to have any, regardless of that."

"That's ridiculous. It doesn't make any sense!" She flailed her arms about.

"Wanting something doesn't mean it's meant to be. People want things they shouldn't have all the time."

She took a drag of her cigarette then smashed it out in a gray ashtray.

"I got to get ready to go."

They both stood. She seemed so frail, like a tiny flower with wilted petals, but determined to hang on. He walked around the coffee table and wrapped his arms around her. She struggled a bit, being stubborn and angry, but then she laughed and hugged him back. They kissed on the cheek.

"Say goodbye to Ricky, Carlos and Daniel for me." He heard the buzzing still going from down the hall.

She nodded. "Move back here… to Havana," she said as she followed him to the front door.

"I told you I needed some time away so I wouldn't get into any more shit, Mamá. I don't want to go back to prison. If I'm here, I know I'll go back. It's best I just come to take care of business and visit. One day I may return, but it won't be anytime soon. Things are the way they should be for now. Besides, I'm still close."

"There's a girl I want you to meet. Very pretty. She works at a coffee shop," She pointed ahead, as if that narrowed down the location of the place. "Her name is Camila. She's tall, like you. Nice smile. Shapely. She's twenty-one."

"Too young." He chuckled and grabbed the doorknob to exit.

"No. It's perfect. She's your type!"

"Mamá, what do you think my type is?"

"Big boobs and booty!"

He burst out laughing, his eyes filled with moisture. Mamá was crazy.

"I'm serious!" She slapped his arm playfully, grinning from ear to ear. "I know what my son likes. And she's nice."

"I didn't hear anything about smart…" He toyed with her, thoroughly entertained even though he had no desire to see whoever this woman was that his mother undoubtedly believed would be her daughter-in-law.

"Oh, but she is! I told her next time you come visit, I

will have you two meet. She knows who you are." Mamá crossed her arms, looked him up and down, and sucked her teeth.

"Then you told her my name was Viper, instead of Dominic." His brow raised, he waited for her to reply.

"What can I say?" She shrugged. "Everyone knows you by that horrible name. So, will you go and meet her?"

"Nah. I'm seeing someone, Mamá." He opened the door all the way, and the burst of hot sun felt so good against his face.

"Oh, well, whoever she is, she better know how to make a good cup of coffee, and how to cook for my son!" She spoke with such venom, as if blood would be shed if Majesty didn't do such things. All he could do was laugh. He leaned in and gave her another kiss, then walked to his vehicle. "You brought out your big truck today? *¡Me encanta!* Will you buy me a new car, Dominic? Come on, I brought you into the world! Do it for your mother. I deserve a new car!" She hollered out, sporting a toothy grin that made her dimples stand out even more.

"We'll see, Mamá. We'll see." He got into his car, turned on the stereo, and started the engine to go pick up a dog, a Rottweiler named Ruby, that had destroyed most of the doors in her owner's house. Maluma's '11 PM' began to play through his truck speakers. Feeling the rhythm, he slapped the steering wheel as he drove down the street. When he got to a red light, he picked up his cell phone and made a call.

"You have reached Majesty. I can't answer my phone right now, but please leave a brief message and I'll get back to you. If you're an ex, a bill collector, or trying to sell me something, no, I don't want you back, the check is in the mail, and I don't want your cleaning supplies, vacuum, quick cash loan, or whatever the hell it is you're being paid to peddle. Toodles!"

He smiled and shook his head, then spoke at the tone.

"Hey, it's me. I wanted to know if you wanted to go to the movies tonight. I know this is kinda last minute, so, if you need to bring Troy, that's cool. We'll just go see a kid-friendly movie. Oh, and as a side note, one of the ladies up the street runs a twenty-four-hour daycare. 4.8 stars on Angie's List, so ya know, I thought that may be an option for you sometimes since she's so close and all. I know about it because I trained two of her dogs. Hope your day has been good. I'll catch you later." He disconnected the call, turned the music back up, and drove on...

CHAPTER FOURTEEN
Eve in the Garden of Eden

MAJESTY PLACED THE chicken legs in the air fryer, then set a lavender candle in the living room. Clapping her hands to PJ Morton's 'Say So,' featuring JoJo, she proceeded to turn on the television, shut the blinds, and pull the sheer curtains closed. She smiled when she heard the faint sound of the hall toilet flushing, followed by the water running in the sink. *Here he comes.*

"You're frying chicken?" Viper's deep voice rumbled as he toyed with his zipper. Her breath hitched when she spun around and caught a brief glimpse of his dark gray boxer briefs and the huge bulge inside it, making her think of a snake wrapped around itself three times.

What the hell. Is that shit real?! I've seen some big dicks in my life, but damn. Is he even hard? Lord have mercy.

"Uh, yeah. When we were leaving the movie theater and I invited you over to hang out for a little bit, you said you were hungry." She scurried to the kitchen, averting eye contact as her cheeks warmed.

"I like your set-up in here." She looked over into the living room as she poured them each a glass of wine. "It's classy. Nice." He sat on the couch, directly in the center of it. Viper places his arms on the back of the sofa, hands almost reaching the ends. His legs wide apart, he looked around.

"Thank you. It's not as nice as yours, but once I'm ballin', it will be." She laughed. "When I save up a bit more money, I can use some of the extra to get the rug I want, things like that. It's coming along." She placed his wine glass before him on the glass coffee table, then sat beside him. He wrapped his arm around her and squeezed, making her feel so safe. *I didn't think I was in harm's way... but why do I feel like this? Like he could protect me from anything and everything?* His muscular arm felt like a fortress.

She took a sip of her wine, placed the glass down, then handed him the remote control, which he put back on the coffee table. Before she could say a word, he was pulling her in an embrace and kissing her passionately. A moan escaped him, and she melted and just like that. She realized all her mental pre-planning was going to waste. She'd told herself she'd be good if she invited him in, that she would fight temptation, but she was losing. In fact, she'd been losing all damn night. Once her sister had agreed to watch Troy, all bets were off. Inside the movie theater, when the lights had dimmed, they were kissing and all over each other. *If my life depended on tellin' someone what that movie was about, I'd be dead…*

And now, this. The final nail in the coffin. She stiffened when his large hand made its way inside her blouse, but she didn't dare stop him. Soon, he was cupping her breasts, giving the left one a gentle squeeze over her black satin bra. He circled her nipple with his thumb and it hardened at his touch.

A slow drag of soft flesh against her ear, then the warmth of parted lips…

"You're my walking, talking fantasy." Her pussy throbbed at his words. "*Vamos a joder hoy por la noche…*"

"I don't know what you just said, but I know we shouldn't do this." Yet despite her words, she reached for the top button of her blouse, and then the next. "Talk me out of it."

She was met with nothing but a deep, throaty laugh.

"Now you know I can't do that, baby…" He sat up on one knee and tore his shirt off, discarding it on the floor. Then, he proceeded to remove his shoes and socks, flexing his arm muscles as he moved.

"Let's go to the back." She got on her feet, chugged her wine in one big gulp, then drank his, too, before going to turn off the air fryer in the kitchen. Her heart was beating damn near out of her chest as she practically ran to her bedroom, Viper on her heels.

They removed their clothing so fast, she was certain she looked like a damn worm being electrocuted, while he somehow managed to still look suave and cool. When she stood in nothing but her panties, reality settled in. *I haven't had sex in a long while. Am I ready for this?* She ran her hand along the back of her neck, curing a nervous itch as Viper placed his watch on her clear nightstand. *It's not the length of time that concerns me. It's like riding a bike… It's just that I know how much I like him, how much I am enjoying him, and if for some reason he's managed to fool me, this'll really hurt.* She turned on her iPad, which lay next to her laptop on a small table and plugged in an external speaker she kept nearby. Then, she selected one of her favorite playlists. Dvsn's, 'Between Us,' featuring Snoh Aalegra, was the first song to play. She was about to turn around when a heavy, intense, sexy presence loomed from behind. He massaged her breasts, her shoulder, and snaked an arm around her waist, pulling her to him.

His big, hard dick pressed demandingly against her lower back, then he slipped his hand from her shoulder, down to her core, his forearm resting against her stomach. With no warning, he picked her up, using one arm to support her like the seat of a chair, while with his free hand, he strapped her in for the ride. Her legs dangled as he walked in reverse, kissing the side of her neck, ushering her towards the bed. He hadn't even gotten to the next base, and she was already falling apart.

"How long do we have before Troy's home?" he asked in between kisses along her neck as he sat on the bed, bringing her with him. She leaned back into his touch, sitting on his lap, her ass against his crotch.

"Breakfast. She's dropping him back off before I have to leave for work tomorrow."

Sliding both of his arms around her waist, he grinded against her, slow and nasty. She sighed as he pressed that dick into her flesh, over, and over, as if he were fucking her from behind. She trembled at the touch of his hand, slipping away from her hips and reaching in front of her, pushing her thighs apart with a deft hand. His chin rested against her shoulder, he layered the side of her neck with delicious kisses, pushed her panties aside, then worked his digits in the slick creases of her wet pussy. She bucked to his touch, getting off on his breathing, his scent, and the way he moved.

"Ahhh…" she cried out when he slipped his finger inside her, opening her love. He glided another finger in her, and she watched the digits going in and out, slick with her juices.

"Your papaya… ohhh, baby… so tight, juicy and wet for me, Mami… *Tremenda manguita.*" His voice rasped while the words rolled off his tongue, and though she didn't understand what he'd said exactly, somehow, she got the gist of it. He had to get a kick out of being able to say whatever he wished, with her being none the wiser. He finger-fucked her nice and slow, rotating his hips from left to right beneath her until she could barely take it anymore. She gasped for air when he slowly slid his fingers out of her pussy, then kissed her neck.

"Stand up."

She got up from his lap, and he tugged at the front of her panties, then slid them down her legs, his gaze on hers. When he was done, he wrapped his hand roughly around her neck and pulled her in for a kiss.

Their tongues danced and played, and her breaths rang in her ears. She couldn't fight it anymore; she wanted

Viper in the worst way. He laid her down on the bed, and she was now able to see his dick, without barriers. The guesswork was gone. She salivated and bit into her lower lip as her pussy ached and screamed his name. It was huge. A gorgeous monstrosity. The perfect pairing with his unbelievably taut abs. Bending slightly to the right, it bobbed every time he moved, the veins thick and prominent, the head wide and a bit lighter than the shaft. He stroked it as he looked down at her, then retrieved a couple golden wrapped condoms out of his phone case with pockets, slapping them on the nightstand.

Viper got into the bed and moved one of the throw pillows that was propped against the headboard down towards the bottom of the bed, then yanked her to the middle of the mattress by the hips. Nestling between her thighs, he kissed on them, on the front... the sides... then along her stomach and navel.

I should've shaved! Shit!

A wave of heat coursed through her entire body at the realization she had more than just a bit of peach fuzz. He didn't seem concerned as he kept showering her with affection, his need and desire for her evident, making her lust for him soar to impossibly higher heights. A chopped and screwed DJ remix of 'Don't You Know That' by Luther Vandross, was playing, setting the mood.

Pressing his hands into her ass cheeks, he lifted her off the bed, and slipped a pillow beneath her butt. He placed a tattooed hand on her stomach, two fingers adorned with rings, and used the other to open her petals. His sexy hazel eyes turned to inky slits as he wiggled his tongue back and forth all over her pussy, then laved her with slow, intense strokes. Up… down… up… down…

"Shit!" She snatched a fistful of his hair with one hand and the sheets with her other hand, holding on for dear life.

"I've been waiting too long to eat this pussy, baby. I train dogs, but I was born to make your cat purr and cum when I call."

She shivered at his words.

He wrapped his lips around her clit and sucked. She released her hold on him, arched her back, and her thighs began to shake as she came. The liquid explosion between her thighs began as a mere tickle, then a flood leaked from between her legs. Nonstop eating her pussy, not even coming up for air, he shook his head vigorously back and forth before, during, and after her mind and body-bending orgasm. Aftershocks rushed through her, and her skin broke into sweat all over. At last, she let go and lay there listlessly, her eyes fluttering. Kwaye's, 'Runaway' now played through her speakers.

Long legs wrapped around her own, strong arms grabbed her tight, and an urgent kiss on her cheek brought her back to the present. Using all the strength she had, she rose onto her hands, cradled his jaw, and brought him in for a kiss as they rolled onto their sides. He gently caressed her ass, the enchantment between them spreading like a beautiful illness that neither seemed to wish to get well from.

He gently pushed her hair out of her face and looked into her eyes, smiling.

"You good?"

She nodded.

"All right." He grinned wider, kissed the tip of her nose, and fell onto his back. KAMAUU, featuring Adeline & Masego sang 'Mango,' in the background. She laughed as he began to bob his head to the music, then sing the lyrics.

"You know this song?"

He smirked and rolled his eyes.

"Majesty, why do you keep asking me silly shit like that? You keep being surprised that I know about good music."

"Like I said, you just don't look the type." She chuckled and crawled on top of him, resting her chin on his chest.

"And you don't look the type to fry chicken in an air fryer."

She swallowed the urge to laugh and curse his ass out. She wouldn't give him the satisfaction. Instead, she started to kiss up and down his chest. The hair... the art... the beauty of him. She kept going, meandering lower and lower, pausing at his silky black pubic hair, then studying his gorgeous cock once again. Inhale... exhale...

He smelled like love.

He smelled like bad decisions.

He smelled like fresh fruit, rain, and new chances...

He groaned when she lifted his heavy shaft and ran her tongue up and down his sensitive flesh. She reached up with her free hand and intertwined their fingers. His eyes hooded, he pumped his hips to the rhythm she set.

Soon, she needed both hands to wrap around his wide nature as she engulfed the head, going down as far as she could, over and over while rubbing his balls. She sucked hard, then light, varying her pressure on the shaft, careful with the head, loving that she was giving this man maximum pleasure and putting her all into it.

"Majesty... my Majesty... fuck..." His head slammed into the pillow and all she could see was his extended neck, the veins bulging, and his chin. His arms stretched out on either side of him.

"I love the taste of your big dick, baby." She moaned to him as she kept sucking and sucking, promising to be his undoing. The one to ruin him. The one to suck his soul and swallow it whole. Now, he was even harder.

"*Me vas a hacer cum,*" he slurred.

"Cum?"

"*Sí!* You're gonna make me cum!" He fisted the sheet. She kept on sucking and licking and watched as his balls drew tighter. She delighted in the way she had him in a weakened state, something she was certain rarely happened in his life.

"Stop. I don't want to cum right now... I want to fuck you first."

She yelled when he sat up and dragged her off him onto her back, then mounted her and began to bump and thrust against her pussy. He shoved his tongue in her mouth, grabbed a fistful of her hair, and roughly banged his pelvis against hers, simulating a brutal fucking that made her orgasm from the fierce impact alone.

"Shit! SHIT!" she hollered as he reached between their

grinding bodies and slipped his fingers along her clit, torturing her. He drew her nipple into his mouth, the flesh tender and ready for the pleasure he gave. Kissing and massaging them, he kept dry humping her like a pro. It was unnerving. Disturbing. The final straw.

"Motherfucker! Viper, stop playin'. You know I want it!"

Grabbing one of the condom packets off the nightstand, he tore it open and quickly sheathed himself.

"You think you're ready, huh?" He smirked. "I told you before, it's going to ruin you. You'll never want to be fucked by anyone else after *I* fuck you."

"Yeah, yeah." She rolled her eyes. "Enough with the foreplay and bragging. "Come on. Teasin' ass... You're probably full of shit."

"We'll see about that." He gripped his cock, aiming it right at her pussy as he rose slightly on one arm. She braced herself, suddenly realizing this may be a rodeo with the wrong damn bull. Looking into her eyes, he rested his weight on top of her and bumped the head against her pussy lips, over and over, as if knocking to come in.

"Ahhh! ...Uh! ... No! I mean, yes! ... Oh God! Shit!"

He pushed the broad head in. Her pussy felt so full, and the mixture of pleasure and discomfort merged, thankful that he'd gotten her juices flowing before attempting to do such a thing. *I underestimated this! Shit! Viper's dick isn't anything to play with! Every woman wants a man with a big dick, till they get a big dick up in them! Damn! Okay... I can do this. We just gotta go slow...* He kept moving, in and out, just the head, pacing himself. He watched her, and though he didn't say a word, he looked so caring as he controlled his pace and speed. He took her lower lip into his mouth and sucked, then kissed all along her jaw.

"Shit! Viper! Shit!"

He pushed more of himself inside of her, then cradled the top of her head with one arm as they kissed.

"You feel fucking incredible, baby…" he whispered in her ear, his thrusts a little faster now. He reached for her hand, paused his movements, and placed it on his shaft. "Touch me. You feel that? I'm not even halfway inside you yet, baby, and you're already acting like you can't take anymore. You want me to stop right here?"

She moaned once again, determined to get the upper hand. Refusing to be shown up as he showed out.

"Viper, I've had a damn baby! Pussies stretch! Your dick is nothin' compared to that nine-pound child I gave birth to."

"Pussies *do* stretch for babies, but they have time to do that in preparation, because of the hormones your body releases while you're pregnant. You're just getting *screwed* by a guy with a big dick, and I know how to fuck you good, okay? So, you're going to feel it. All of it. Every bit of me. The right way." He said 'fucked' with such emphasis, it jarred her, but what disturbed her the most was that he called her bluff, and this smart-mouthed motherfucker knew what he was talking about. Most men didn't seem to know that… How dare he!

"Uh uh…" She panted and shook her head, sweaty and nervous and horny as she was! "Whatever. Just don't stop. I want the whole thing. I want what I paid for."

"Paid for? Someone put me on Craig's List?" He chortled.

"They don't sell cock on Craig's List anymore. That got shut down. I found you on Only Fans, in the 'Annoying Neighbors' section. Barkin' dogs, Cuban cigars, and loud Latin music sold separately.'"

He burst out laughing. "You're a liar, baby. A beautiful liar, but a liar all the same."

She smiled up at him, then he kissed her once again.

Wrapping her legs around his waist, she held on tight to him as he drove himself slowly in and out of her, then deeper... and deeper. Her eyes rolled and her muscles clenched, body shuddering as a more intense wave of pain and pleasure merged, making her fall apart. She took a couple deep breaths while her pussy stretched and pulsed, then silently prayed, too!

"You okay, baby?" he asked, placing a tender kiss on her lips.

"Yeah. Just need a minute. I'll be fine."

He nodded and began to kiss and suck her neck, and everywhere he touched, stroked, and nibbled felt so good. She rocked her hips, meeting his short thrusts, inviting him for more as she sighed with relief, finally over that initial intrusion. He'd taken his time, doing it right.

She could see in his eyes he was following her lead. Such a damn good lover he was. Stroking his hair, she demanded another kiss. She loved the feel of his warm lips against hers. He moved faster and deeper now, groaning as his hips worked hard for each skillful thrust. He slipped his arms beneath her thighs and brought her impossibly closer, now moving inside of her at a sharp angle.

"Mmmmm." He emitted an earthy, deep, rumbling groan…

She cried out as he slammed into her, cupping her ass and forcing her to take the nasty blows. Harder and harder he went, the loving too damn good. Her pussy had died from his killer cock, and now it was in heaven with his sweet, sinful loving. He stirred his hips from left to right, then in circles, brushing upward against her clit with each steady, hard stroke.

"Oh shit, yes! Fuck me, baby," she cooed as she exploded, her climax leaving her feeling dizzy. He'd been right; she hadn't been ready. This shit was addictive. *He* was addictive. He paused, kissed her breasts, then up and down her neck and shoulders. The tenderness, mixed with the unforgiving fucking, made her weak with desire.

"The Viper and his Majesty…" Damn, the words sounded so good… "That's what we are."

"That has a nice ring to it." She smiled up at him, looping her arms around his neck.

"You know, baby, I wanted you since the first time I saw you. I wanted your body, to fuck you, I'm not going to lie to you, but I also wanted to get to know you." She sighed with contentment. "You intrigued me. You're not a fling to me. I care about you." He began to pump his hips again, making love to her just how she needed it.

"I care about you, too." There was no way he could know how much she needed to hear what he was saying. How her heart craved those words. "Sometimes, when we talk, or we're alone just chillin' together, I feel like it's just us in our own little world. Feels like we've got our own garden of Eden... Maybe I could be your Eve?"

He suddenly jerked, his eyes growing larger for a split second, then closed. A wave of warmth flooded her gate when he emptied his seed into the condom. Laying against her, his heart beating, he gave her lazy kisses. They looked at one another, playing with each other's hair.

"Such a pretty smile," he complimented, then kissed her and got out of the bed. "This is probably the bathroom over here, right?"

"Yes, that's it."

He grabbed his dick and removed the condom as he walked to the restroom and closed the door behind him.

He'd left her there with his inebriating scent lingering in the air, and her pussy suddenly empty, missing him already. She slowly got up from the bed, her body sore and feeling good all at once. She made her way over to the music and turned the volume up as Nasty C and Ari Lennox's, 'Black and White' started to play. Snapping her fingers to the music, she made her way back to the bed and sat down. Slowly. Thinking.

I don't know if I did the right thing or not, but I'm not going to overthink this. I like him... A lot. I did what felt right. End of story.

She ran her hands up and down her arms and fell into a daydream as the music played. Viper emerged from the bathroom and the first thing she noticed when he approached the bed was a new erection. She burst out laughing when he grabbed another condom, tore it open, and quickly slid it down his dick.

"I thought we were going to take a minute?"

"We did. It's been at least ten minutes. Get on your hands and knees on the bed. I want to fuck you from behind and watch that ass jiggle."

They were both laughing now as she complied. Standing behind her, he gripped her waist and kissed up and down her spine. Her pussy began to weep in anticipation.

"I want you inside me." She urged him on as he stroked her, then pushed his dick within her. She screamed and writhed about, flattening her breasts on the bed in the process. Massaging her shoulder, he kept pumping his hips. Doggy style with him was even more intense. He made love to her slowly, then ruthlessly, speeding up and cursing over her screams, delivering deep blows until she was shaking and quaking.

His dick was pure fucking magic. And he knew how to use it. She couldn't recall the last time she'd orgasmed so much. In fact, this was probably the first time she'd had so many, in such a short span of time. He came once again, groaning and trembling. It wasn't long before they were cuddled in the bed, fast asleep. Several hours later, she awoke to see that Viper was gone from the bed. She found him standing by her window, looking out. She could only make out the outline of his body for it was dark now in the room, except for the illumination of her blue nightlight that reflected on his skin. She imagined the sun would be rising soon, but right then, *he* was the sun. He'd turned her inside out, and she knew it would be hard to let him go now, just as she'd both hoped and feared.

He turned away from the window, and without saying a word, slipped back under the sheets with her. Wrapping his arms around her, he kissed and held her, then rolled her on her side, facing him. They looked at one another in the darkness, breathing slow and easy. Reaching for her breasts, he gently caressed them, then placed his hand against her pussy, lightly stroking her folds, kneading her clit. He increased the pressure, rubbing and massaging her pussy until she burst, releasing an orgasm that caught her off guard. With a gentle hand, he coaxed her trembling body flat on her back, then disappeared between her legs…

His tongue taut, he weaponized it against her in the most beautiful of ways until she came again… and again… and again…

CHAPTER FIFTEEN

Blood and Onions

THERE WAS BLOOD everywhere…

A deep, red, angry scattering of terminated life and fresh death sprayed like paint upon the walls. Furniture and lamps were turned over. Bloody handprints stained the linoleum floors. Three dead bodies, one of whom he didn't recognize but was informed had been a Latin King, occupied the room. One was face down, lying in a pool of blood. Another was slumped on the black couch with two bullet holes in his head, his fingers still loosely holding onto an unlit joint, eyes wide open. The last lay dead in front of the television, the video game he'd been watching still on pause. Viper was being told for the second time how several members of the Crips had broken in, looking for a stash of cocaine that wasn't even there. There had been no lookout replacement since Wild had been apprehended and incarcerated, only guys doing half-assed shifts, and everything was going to hell.

"They thought it was Blood territory," King Joker announced, his face splotchy and voice cracking. One of the deceased was his second cousin. "They thought Day's friend was here, too." Day was a drug runner who was cool with several of the Bloods that came in the area to purchase weed, grub, or fuck some Cuban women. "This is fucked up, man. Real fucked up."

"It will be taken care of." Viper sighed. "In fact, it's being addressed as we speak. I've sent out someone to bring me back some names." Hands on hips, he once again surveyed the scene.

"Kill them and their fuckin' mothers. Kill them all!" Joker yelled as he knelt over his cousin and gently brushed his eyes closed.

Grief was a strange thing, but in the end, it didn't matter. The souls of the damned were doing what they did best. Destroy. It was a dog-eat-dog world, and Viper trained the leaders of the pack. *This wasn't our fight.* Bloods and Latin Kings got along; they weren't enemies, and it wasn't unheard of for them to help one another in various situations, especially behind bars. King felt somewhat distant, devoid of emotional triggers. The sight of these bodies didn't make him flinch or recoil in disgust. The smell of death no longer resonated with him. He'd been to too many funerals, seen too many dead fuckers in the streets and alleys, and at his very own feet, to give a damn.

This sense of detachment, the lack of feeling or concern for the horrors facing him, was something he'd been experiencing for quite some time. He'd become immune to it long before this moment, but this gave him food for thought. *Nothing shocks me anymore. If I saw a priest getting a blow job from a nun in broad daylight, and then she shoots him in the face with heroin while singing a Frank Sinatra song in French, I wouldn't even slow my stride as I walked on by.*

Nothing could make him scream, jump, or lose his cool. He'd taken out so many people over the years, he'd lost count. *Many times, you don't wait around and watch. You spray and go.* He was a Warlord. It was his job to keep order, punish and give the go ahead for disposals, and he did the shit well – was one of the reasons why he'd climbed the food chain so quickly. He'd choked, stabbed, tortured, beaten to a pulp so many men during his lifetime, if he tried to write their names in a ledger, his hand would grow tired.

That's just what this life was about: Kill or be killed. He didn't relish this, but it was part of survival. No one grew up in the life he lived, the one he inherited, without ever having to waste someone. Most people had no inkling what was really going on in the streets. Once the sun set, under the cover of night, an entirely different world would emerge. The police had an idea, but even they only saw the aftermath, rarely the acts that led up to such behavior. Poverty. Strife. Depression. Need. Greed. Lust. All doorways to what he'd been born into. He understood that in some factions of society, he was perceived as a savage, but savages were created by the same society who judged them. *People didn't care when I was a child in need. They don't need to care about what the fuck I do now. It's just that simple.*

He was the same little boy who'd witnessed his father shoot a man in the gut for stealing from him, the same kid who had cuts in his arms and hands from shattering glass during a botched robbery in a small family restaurant that resulted in four people being shot to death. He'd grown up around gangs, violence, drug usage, physical abuse, and more. As a child, he'd witnessed atrocious crimes he'd tried to scrub from his mind over the years… crimes passed off as everyday life.

The last straw, he believed, was when he was forced to witness his own mother being assaulted by an intruder while he and his brother were held at gunpoint. Their father had left months prior, and someone took advantage of the situation. A woman living alone with two boys. She'd never disclosed what happened to her during those twenty-four minutes when their tiny home was ransacked by a couple drug addicts, and she was behind closed doors with some man who was making her scream, beg, and cry. *'I'll do what you want! Just don't hurt my children…'* He and his brother were never without weapons again after that night, which was still etched in his mind. How else would anyone expect him to turn out? He was born from blood and death. He'd lived in blood and death. He'd die in blood and death.

Viper knew one of the dead men, but they weren't friends. It was another Latin King, a brother not by blood, but by Reye. Protect the crown, protect the nation. He bowed his head and whispered in prayer, "*Amor de Rey.*"

"There's no forced entry." He casually pointed to the front door. *They knew these guys.*

"You sound like a cop," King Vodka joked, but no one laughed. "Uh…" He cleared his throat, taking the matter a bit more seriously. "Yeah… but Day's sister said they broke in."

"She was here when it happened?"

"Yeah, but she climbed out the back window."

Viper slipped on some gloves and did a search, looking for any other clues. Moments later, about thirteen Latin Kings and Queens arrived with bottles of detergent, buckets, garbage bags, coverlets, rags, mops, towels, and various other cleaning agents.

"Did you all leave your phones at home and on like I asked?" They all nodded in the affirmative.

"Where do you want us to start, Viper?" King Red asked as he removed his dark sunglasses from his eyes and placed them atop his short, buzzed cut head. A teardrop tattoo, prison blue, sat below his right eye.

"Right here in the living room." They instantly began to prepare. "Use the sheets and blankets you brought to wrap the guys up in, just like the times before. Then…" he glanced at his watch, "at two o'clock, take the first person out to Franco's truck. Put him in the bed, be respectful. No bruises or bumps. Wait ten minutes between each body. Break out into groups. I need all this shit cleaned up within two hours. Clean the entire apartment." He waved his finger around. "Even in the bedroom and bathroom, just in case one of the fuckers who did this tracked blood everywhere they went. If they couldn't get the cocaine, trust, they weren't leaving empty-handed. They got a hold of something other than money.

All their pockets are empty, too, including their cell-phones, but they took anything small and fast no doubt, like jewelry, weed, shit like that. Take the UV light and go over this room especially good to make sure you didn't miss one square inch. Take the rugs off the floor, throw 'em away. Get into the creases of the linoleum. The corners of the baseboards. Use the OxiClean, dish detergent, and the peroxide. No bleach. Then, when you're finished, call me."

It was a common misconception that bleach got rid of all traces of blood. In fact, it was often a red flag to police homicide teams confirming that something amiss had in fact taken place. Gone were the days of South Florida Latin Kings leaving shocking massacres for the authorities to walk in on. Headline news. They'd adapted. No crime scene. No problem.

"Yes, Viper." The team worked fast.

"Contact their families once you've spoken to me. Tell them we'll take care of the funerals." He grabbed his keys, ready to head out.

"Viper, let me kill the motherfuckers responsible. Fuckin' crabs."

King Coin, who Viper had known for about five years, had come to help make all this shit disappear. Young guy with lots of heart, in Viper's eyes a Warlord in the making. He was a natural, which was a shame, a blessing, and a curse.

"Coin, I don't want any fuck ups, so we have to go easy on this. Space things out. Keep 'em guessing. If they know we figured out who it was, they'll run off." Coin nodded in understanding. "If someone does what happened a year ago, it's a fuckin' wrap!" They all knew exactly what he was talking about. Someone from Naranja had shot a seven-year-old girl. No one seemed to know which amongst them had done it. It was all hush hush. Then, people started disappearing – other Kings. "They were trying to get at Snaps, and I very well may be looking that motherfucker in the eye right now who covered for the coward." Everyone drew quiet. "Then I heard that one of you motherfuckers said that it was a Black kid, the little girl who lost her life, as though that made it okay. Did you fuckin' forget who we are?!"

A rage that had been burning inside of him swelled up, bursting free. "We're all linked!" He locked his fingers together, which symbolized the chain of people. Comrades. "These are our people! I know most of you don't think that way, but enough of you do to put a smear on our name, on the nation. No one disrespects the crown! If I ever hear anyone say some shit like that, that so and so doesn't count because they're Black, or because it's a chick, it's off with your fuckin' head!" He made a cutting motion with his finger, as if decapitation was imminent. "We've been down with the Bloods since the 1960's. Since before any of us were born. You don't shit on what our King forefathers put together. It took a lot of time and investment to form those pacts. You *need* allies, or you're fucked. And y'all are fucking it up. Some of you knew who did it, and you tried to hide the one responsible. Protect him from me and the other warlords. You know the magnitude of that."

"Do you want us to take care of that too, Viper?" King Torch offered. Torch was cool; he got shit done. He respected the old ways, but Viper suspected he could fold under pressure.

"Take care of it?" Viper repeated. He sucked his teeth, then smirked. "No. I've got it under control." In fact, it was already done, only most of the Nation was unaware of that. Once word had spread that he was in over his head, the guy's family had shipped the motherfucker off to Texas, but Viper had gone right after him. He could have assigned this task to somebody else, but this had been personal. In the end, he'd made sure the girl's father knew he'd had to ice his own king brother to keep the peace.

He'd also made a public statement at their annual ALKQN meeting in Miami, that that sort of thing would not be tolerated. If you fuck up and miss your target, hitting an ally's child instead, death was coming for you, from your brethren. It had to be so for them to keep peace. Unlike some of his brethren, he didn't need to brag about his exploits or report how he ran business, he just produced results. Period. If he hadn't done what he had, there would have been blood in the streets, and the damage and thirst for revenge could have potentially lasted for decades. Regardless, one always needed to move in silence. *That's their fucking problem. They talked too damn much.*

"King Loco was upset about that, too," Joker added as he began to pick up debris and toss it in a bag. Loco was now dead but the man had made it known that whoever in their family had been responsible for that little girl's death would pay the ultimate price.

"As he should've been. The Bloods are part of the People Nation, just like us." King Hell added. "Those are our brothers and sisters."

Many nodded in agreement.

"Vice Lord Nation, and the Black P-Stone Nation. We respect one another. That kid, her name was Kerisha… beautiful little girl. She was the daughter of a P-Stone, man. His name is Jacob, but he goes by Wizard," King Hell went on to explain as he slumped down in a chair, clutching a bottle of cleaner.

"Whoever did that to her fucked up big time. It almost started a feud. You want this to turn into a Black and Latino thing? Like the shit they try and pull in prison? Like how some of the Mexicans and Blacks go after each other in the penn? Those White guards eat that shit up! It's entertainment for them. Black and brown men fighting each other to the death over bullshit! Wake up! We're not them! Is that what you want?" Viper yelled at everyone in that room. "Us pitted against each other?" Several of them shook their heads. "Let Combat 18 and American Front do all that dumb shit! We all bleed red." His voice echoed throughout the room. "We don't die, we multiply, and we *need* the numbers. I don't like what's going on. I'm seein' an uptick in bullshit. You've even got other Latino gangs fuckin' with the Black gangs, and vice versa, out in Chicago and L.A. That's what some of the police and government want. It keeps them in a job. Divide and conquer. So they can look like the good guys, and we look like scrubs. Let's just look us for a minute.

Do you know how powerful we'd be if each and every Latino and Hispanic gang united? We'd be unstoppable, but we're even split amongst each other. You fuckers only call me when the shit hits the fan. Next time, call me before you take a dump and turn that motherfucker on full blast."

He stormed out of there, furious as ever.

"GO ON, I'M serious," Viper said as he poured himself a glass of ice water from the pitcher on Majesty's kitchen counter. The woman kept giving him an uncertain look.

"Mama, go 'head!" Troy said, rolling his eyes in an exasperated fashion. "Viper can stay with me. Us men don't need you here all the time."

Majesty sucked her teeth and grimaced at her son. Viper placed his hand over his mouth to keep from laughing, then pulled out one of the breakfast bar stools and sat down, getting comfortable. Majesty put her hand on her hip and twisted her lips.

"Okay, Majesty. Fine." Viper threw up his hands. "Just let me do it. I can go. I'll buy a pre-made crust. Let me get my keys." Viper started to head to the grocery store.

"No, no. I'll go. It's not far." She waved her arm, then grabbed her purse from the kitchen island. "I can't believe I forgot the flour to make the crust." She glanced at her watch. "Yeah, it's getting late, so I guess I will just pick up one of the pre-made ones at this point." She was making a homemade pizza and didn't realize her mistake until it was too late. "I won't be gone long. Troy, behave. Don't you talk this man's ear off or try to do anything slick," the woman warned, wagging her finger at him. Majesty was very protective of her child, with whom she shared a beautiful bond. He respected that. Viper stood up, wrapped his arm around her waist, and drew her in for a kiss. He could feel Troy's eyes on them, but the kid remained quiet. It wasn't long before they heard the sound of the front door closing behind her.

"Well, it's just you and me now, Troy."

"Yeah, finally! Mama treats me like a baby, Viper, but she don't even know I got a hair growin' on my left leg now." Yet, he pointed to the right one. "For you know it, I'm going to have a beard and mustache and uh bunch of muscles just like you. Probably in a week or two." He spoke with such seriousness.

Once again, Viper fought the urge to laugh.

"Help me cut up these green peppers for your mother's pizza. Let's save her a little time."

"Okay!"

Troy seemed eager to help, donning a big smile as he rounded the kitchen table. He watched as the dark-chocolate-skinned boy turned on the faucet, then washed his hands. *Damn. She's got him coached well.* Viper chuckled inwardly. Troy had big dimples that reminded him of his own mother. His thick, jet black hair was like Majesty's, only his was faded on the sides and in the back, and he had eyes that appeared naturally sad, but a smile that was something magical, balanced things out.

"All right, first, are you allowed to use a knife?"

"Hell, yeah! I'm a G! A ninja, too."

Viper realized that not laughing at Troy's antics would prove more difficult than he'd initially hoped.

"Cool. This cutting board here is ready." He reached for one of her boards sitting off to the side, then grabbed a couple of knives, one that was rather dull for Troy's safety. "Now, when you cut these peppers, you want to make them thin, and you do that by—"

"Are you bangin' my mama, man?"

Viper turned the pepper lengthwise and cut off the stem. Then split it open to remove the seeds.

"Am I bangin' your mother... Hmm..." He cut the pepper in two, then shoved half of it towards the kid, handing him one of the knives. "No, that's too thick. Cut like this. Nice 'nd easy..."

Troy began to watch how he was doing it, then followed suit.

"Perfect. You'll be a chef before you know it." Troy smiled, his dimples super deep. "So, what you *really* want to know is if your mother and I are serious, right?"

Troy nodded and kept on cutting.

"Yeah. We are. We're in a relationship, and I really like her."

"That's good. She likes you, too. Mama doesn't like a lot of people. She says most people are assholes. Don't tell her I cussed. I'm just repeatin' what she said is all."

"I won't. She told you that?" He tossed some of the chopped peppers on a plate, then continued to slice the rest.

"She ain't say that to me, but I hear her all the time on

the phone with her friends. Mama hates people, but that's okay. She loves me, and that's all that matters."

He laughed.

"I don't think your mother hates people, I just think she's frustrated sometimes with how some of them act and so she stands up for herself. I think she likes people a lot, actually. Isn't she nice to your friends and their parents?"

Troy shrugged. "Yeah. She's nice to a lot of people, but that don't mean she likes 'em. She had a boyfriend before you."

"Yeah? Was he cool?"

"Nope. I ain't like him. I don't like a lot of guys Mama has went out wit'. The one I hated the most was this guy named Ashton. She was with him for a little while. I was young, but I remember him." He noted how Troy's voice trailed. Sadness tinged his words. "He ain't treat my mama right."

"Let's cut these mushrooms, too."

"I don't like mushrooms on my pizza."

"Well, we don't have to put them on the entire pizza. Let me wash them here in this bowl. Mushrooms are dirty." Viper made haste, washing the vegetables in a colander. He then dried them off and divided them up between the two of them, to cut into pieces.

"Somebody popped my daddy and killed him."

Viper kept chopping. Troy said the words out of the blue... but perhaps, it wasn't out of the blue at all.

"How old were you when your father passed away?"

"Um, I forget. I was young though. I don't remember

him. I've seen pictures of him. Mama gave me his wallet, his jewelry, stuff like that. I still got a teddy bear Mama said he bought for me when I was born. My grandmama said he wasn't a good man. She said he was a no good nigga. Mama said he *was* a good man; he had just made some bad choices. She said he loved me, too. Loved me a lot. Said she didn't want me to grow up and do the same things my daddy did, so she moved us out here."

They kept cutting, and Viper let the boy talk. He wanted to hear what he said, as well as all the things he wasn't saying. He had a feeling the boy didn't get to talk freely like this much. Besides, there was so much one could learn from speaking to children.

"You got a lot of tattoos, like my daddy had. Why have you got so many tattoos?"

"It helps remind me where I've been. Where I am. And where I want to go. I like them."

"Don't they hurt to get 'em?"

"Eh, it's different for everyone. I guess I have a high pain tolerance, so for me, not really. Tickles a little. I like the way the art looks."

"That was kinda confusing, you know, what you said about them helping to remind you where you wanna go. But I think I understand. Like, they tell a story?"

"Exactly."

"I wanna get a tattoo, too."

"Do you? Of what?"

"It'll be my mama's name, and my daddy's, too."

"That sounds like a good first tattoo, little man. I've got my mother's name, too."

"Do you? Wow. Where?" Troy stopped slicing, his eyes lighting up.

"You can't see it right now, but it's on my chest surrounded by roses."

"That means you must really love your mama."

"Yeah, I do. We only get one mother. Majesty really loves you, Troy. She talks about you all the time to me."

Troy smiled, showing all his teeth. Viper imagined the boy felt like now, they had something in common.

"I like you, Viper. You seem cool. I bet you act like my daddy did. I heard he was big time. People were scared of him, too. That's what my auntie said."

Viper swallowed... but kept working on the mushrooms.

"You're doing a great job, Troy. We'll leave the onion for your mother."

"Good. Onions stink. I hate onions."

Viper grinned at him, then they both went to the kitchen sink to wash their hands once again.

"Viper. Can I have one of yo' dogs? Mama likes dogs, too, and if you give me one, I bet she'll let me keep it!"

"Come on, we can talk in the living room. Let's go watch cartoons together."

"You like cartoons?! This night is just getting better and better!"

Viper cracked up at this.

When they settled on the couch, he handed the boy the remote and the kid chose to watch Teen Titans Go.

"So, can I have one of your dogs?"

"A pet is a big responsibility, Troy. You'd have to talk

to your mother about that first, and—"

"Awww, come on, man! I've got experience. My grandmama got this ugly dog, Beijing, that she makes wear little sweaters, and it's always throwin' up. It must take this little doggy pill every day, and that thing look like one of my grandmama's wigs. Grandmama said she don't wear wigs, but I saw one sittin' on her dresser one night. At first, I thought it was the dog, but it didn't have no tail or ears. She was in the bed asleep, and her head looked like a big brown Q-tip with a little gray fuzz on it. Like when a lollipop falls on the carpet and you pick it up, but you can't lick it, 'cause see, it has dirt and lint on it. She was lyin'. That thang I thought was her dog is her hair."

Viper burst out laughing, but quickly put on a straight face. Troy sported a serious look as if for the life of him, he didn't see what was so funny.

"Were you nice to the dog, even though it looked funny?"

"I was really nice to it, Viper, and I like to play with it when I go over there, but I want a big dog! Not one that could be mistaken for a wig. I want a dog like you got! You got Pit Bulls, I've seen 'em, and Mama said you train dogs."

"I do."

"That's cool!"

They sat in silence for a while. His gaze rested on a framed picture of Majesty and who he knew now was her mother. He appreciated the times they shared here after that first night. Majesty would arrange it for them to spend some private time together, though with her finishing school and work, and his schedule, too, some-times it was difficult to make plans. Still, they managed to go out on dates and make love as often as possible, one time on her lunch break, a quickie in his truck in a deserted parking lot. But, he yearned for more.

"Viper?"

"Yeah?"

"Did you want to be a dog trainer when you were a kid? Like, did you always know that's what you wanted to do?"

"I did, actually. I just didn't know what it was called."

"I don't know what I want to be yet. Maybe a doctor. But I like music, too, so maybe a producer."

"That's normal. You're young. You might change your mind many times. I wanted to work with dogs, but sometimes I wasn't sure where I'd end up. I'm glad it all worked out."

"'Cause you could be dead like my father?"

He stared at Troy for a spell, then nodded.

"Yes. I believe I could've been."

"I think sometimes, people make bad choices, like Mama said about my daddy, not because they want to, but like, they feel that they have to or somethin' worse will happen."

"I think you're probably right." Viper sat back and crossed his arms.

Sometimes, people are like onions. We must look beyond that first layer of skin to see what's really going on.

"Viper, I wish people would stop lookin' at others and thinkin' stuff that isn't true. Like… judgin' 'em, I guess."

The boy shrugged.

"What do you mean?"

"Like, my grandmama judges my mama all the time. Mama don't tell me anythin' but she always looks sad and mad after she get off the phone with Grandmama."

"You seem to overhear a lot of conversations." Viper playfully pushed the boy into a side pillow, making the kid laugh.

"Mama tells me a child should stay in a child's place. But I learned a lot about her from hearing her on the phone. I learn how she *really* feels."

This kid is smart. Real smart. Look at the words he uses and how he talks. How he pieces things together. Troy is a bright child, and I know that is due in part to Majesty. He'd seen the boy's room. She had an entire bookshelf in there, full of books about space, great Black inventors, math workbooks, and Biblical tales. His room was decorated nicely, with a big world globe on the desk, as well as framed art on the walls with inspirational sayings. Viper's love for Majesty grew in part due to her love for her son. He found it sexy. Admirable.

Just then, he heard the front door unlocking, and they both turned to see Majesty walking through it.

"It was crowded in the store tonight. I decided to get a couple liters of pop, and some chips and ice-cream, too... Thank you," she said when Viper got to his feet and took the bag from her grasp.

"Troy, did you give Viper any problems?"

"No, Mama." Troy then burst out laughing as he pointed to the television.

"He was great, Majesty. He even helped me cut up some of the toppings for the pizza."

He kissed her on the cheek, then headed to the kitchen with the bag. As he removed the items and set them on the counter for her, he heard Troy say, "Mama, guess what? Viper said I could have a dog if you say I can! He also said you'll probably say no, 'cause you're real mean."

"Boy, I know you lyin'! He ain't say that about me!"

Viper shook his head and chuckled, his heart light and content...

CHAPTER SIXTEEN

On the Eve of Awakening

S OUTH INLET PARK on Ocean Blvd, in Boca Raton, was a scenic, secluded beach off the beaten path that many didn't seem to know about unless the secret was given away by a generous local. Majesty's feet sank in the soft sand as she observed her man putting in work on her behalf. She couldn't wipe the big smile on her face, even if she wanted to.

Viper placed a large white wicker picnic basket inside the bulky tent, then disappeared for a spell inside of it. Free National's 'Beauty & Essex,' featuring Daniel Caesar & Unknown Mortal Orchestra, played from his phone. She moved her body to the music, swaying back and forth, left to right. It was a definite bop. He re-emerged, focused as ever. She'd offered to help twice, but each time he refused her assistance. As she watched him, bare-footed, his well-built torso bare above loose white cargo shorts, she felt her pussy clench at the mere sight of his muscles flexing as he maneuvered about. His amazing physique was the result of a habit stemming from routine prison workouts, and somehow it didn't bother her one bit.

She turned away, her hair blowing in the wind and her new Target bathing suit still wet from their romp in the ocean. He'd thought it silly that she didn't want to get her hair wet and had made it his mission to terrorize her by threatening to dunk her under. So, they'd spent most of the time chasing one another back and forth and splashing water like children. The crazy man had even brought a water gun and blasted her with no warning. Although she'd cussed his ass out, she'd secretly loved it.

It's been so long since I've been to the beach. This is nice.

It would be getting dark soon, and she loved this time of day when the air was sweeter, and the sky stretched in enchanting pastel hues.

"Come here," he beckoned. "Lie down with me."

Wrapping her thin white coverall around her shoulders, she crawled inside the tent.

"Oh, my goodness," she gasped, placing her hands over her mouth. "This is so pretty!"

He'd lit two small tin can candles, and the basket was open, revealing two champagne glasses, a bottle of bubbly, chocolate covered strawberries, a veggie tray, cold cuts, and slices of rye bread. Viper popped the cork and poured them both a glass. He raised his glass in the air, a sexy smile on his face, and she followed suit.

"To many more days like this." He gave her a peck on the lips, then they clinked their glasses together.

"Cheers!" The bubbly made her throat burn oh so good. Rich, a bit sweet, and of good quality. She lounged on her side, feeling comfortable.

"Romantic… That's another way to describe you," she said flirtatiously, then took another taste. *Mmmm.*

"Don't tell anyone that. Might lose my street cred." He winked, teasing her.

She sat up to kiss him and in that moment, she felt herself falling harder for the man. *If I go any deeper, I'll be in the land down under.*

Neither of them had uttered the 'love' word. Yet, she recognized the signs. She hadn't felt this type of connection with someone in a long time. She'd liked several men after the death of Troy's father, even had strong feelings for a couple of them, but never as strong as what she was experiencing now. Viper slipped his tongue inside of her mouth, jarring her from her pondering, working it in and out, making her hot and bothered all over. She exhaled when he wrapped his arms around her waist and squeezed her to him with strength and possession. In a flash, she drained her glass and set it aside. He got on top of her, grinding between her legs in slow, hard gyrations, and kissing all over her neck. Their moans overlapped as they held one another, rubbing all over each other, and she craved his touch, his kiss, and that thick, long, big snake that was tucked away in his shorts, pressing against her.

Then… he stopped.

"What's wrong?" Her heart was beating like a clock as she looked up into his gleaming eyes. She grabbed tight onto his wrists, not wanting him to move until he answered her. Her chest flooded with warmth, making her restless, and every damn inch of her craved him. She'd do anything to get him to keep going.

"Nothing is wrong." He scooched away from her, then began to plate up food. She stared at him, confused.

"What's going on, Viper? Why did you stop all of a sudden?"

"I just remembered that I don't have any protection with me. I was just planning to bring you out here and have a nice time. Eat. Talk. Shit like that. Then I saw you in your bathing suit…" He grinned and shook his head. "Anyway, you want a lotta strawberries, baby, or just a few?"

"…Just a few."

She bit her lower lip and smiled. Something about the way he spoke and looked while explaining himself made her feel special. It was in moments like these that she was gently reminded he wasn't going to fit into her little box of expectations and disappointments. More than once they'd fallen asleep together on her couch, and he hadn't tried to have sex with her. In fact, just the week prior, she'd woken up in her bed, with the sheets wrapped around her, and realized he'd actually carried her in and laid her down. When she got up and moving, she noticed a note on her dresser that read:

I've gone home. You were tired from all that studying for your exam and I didn't want to wake you. I'll call you later.'

He'd been truthful when he'd said sex wasn't the only thing on his mind, and now, he had enough control to power through, regardless of how hot and bothered they were. She didn't tolerate most birth control pills well, so couldn't get on that. She was exploring other options. In the meantime, there was nothing to do about it.

The music kept playing, and the sounds of seagulls blended in with the ocean waves. There was plenty to appreciate.

He handed her a plate, then fixed himself one, and they sat practically on top of one another, talking, laughing, and eating.

"I love olives. The green ones." She ate a couple.

"I like the black and the green ones. I used to hate 'em as a kid." He handed her a bottle of water from the basket. "I hated most vegetables as a kid, though. I only willingly ate meat, cheese, potatoes, and rice for the longest time. I wasn't really into candy, either. Not a big sweets eater. Now that I think about it, I was kind of a strange kid." He chuckled. "My mother would have to hide vegetables in other food."

"Troy is the same way! I have to sneak them in his food."

"Yeah, I've kinda figured that out with the whole pizza party thing the other day. Speaking of parties, one day soon, I'm going to have some friends over and they're going to cook. I want you to taste some good Cuban food. I've got a friend, she's like the matriarch of our group, and she can cook her ass off, Majesty." He sucked his fingers, then popped a slice of pineapple in his mouth. "I'm talkin', the shit that my abuela used to make, like tostones, arroz con pollo, picadillo, masitas, ropa vieja! Mmmm! I'm gettin' hungry just thinkin' about it." He chuckled then looked at her out of the corner of his eye. "Why are you lookin' at me like that?"

"I love how you speak, especially when you're happy or passionate about something. I want to... I want to meet your friends."

"Oh, *really*?!" He laughed. She playfully swatted his shoulder.

"I know, I know. I gave you grief about it, but you seem really close to these people. I've seen them from time to time, and I hardly know them. You said they're like your family, so I'd like to try and get to know them." She snuggled up to him and rubbed his arm. "If that's all right with you?"

"Yeah. It's cool with me." He grinned at her, looking mischievous as ever with a twinkle in his gorgeous eyes. "Come 'ere..." He put his plate down and coaxed her down onto the blanket.

"What are you doing? I thought you said you didn't have protection?"

Viper ignored her, and she soon found herself clutching the blanket beneath her as he pushed the crotch part of her swimming suit to the side and proceeded to flick his tongue against her pussy. Warm breaths tickled her sensitive skin, and her body bowed and waved, flowing like the tide.

"Shit..."

The sounds of his hungry lapping seemed to echo all around her, and he devoured her as though she was all the delicious foods he'd told her about earlier, and more.

"Stop running." He grabbed her hips and yanked her back to his mouth. His muffled moans turned her on as he feasted upon her like a ravenous monster.

"Dominic... Dominic, I'm about to... I'm about TO...! Ugh!" He kept on sucking and licking with vigor as she exploded, her body falling apart like broken streamers. Her pussy pulsated and poured, her heart pounded, and her legs quaked. He held her calf in the air, keeping it steady as he wagged the tip of his tongue slower, then slower.

Pause.

She released her grip on the blanket while he slid up her body, stealing her breath away. She shuddered as he kissed all over her shoulders, then pulled the top of her swimming suit down, exposing her breasts. Wet heat surrounded her nipples as he took his time with her, making her yearn for him in ways that words could never describe.

"Are you sure you didn't bring any condoms? Saran wrap? Tissues? Seaweed?" she teased and was met with rumbling laughter. Dropping a kiss on her breasts, he rolled off her and began to quickly throw things in the picnic basket.

"Come on, let's go back to my place, baby, and we can finish what we started. You said Troy doesn't come home for a few hours, so if we hurry, we should have enough time."

She fixed her swimsuit, got to her feet, and dusted off her knees.

"Wait a minute." She re-wound his words in her mind. "Go back to your place, Viper? Oh, I don't think so! Hell, naw!"

"Why not?"

"You've got that werewolf in there now, that's why! And he's not Derek Hale from Teen Wolf, either. He's not from the television or the movies. He's a full-grown menace, and I'm not tryna be in his rolling credits. The Black person always gets killed first."

He burst out laughing. "Stop being silly and exaggerating. He's just an American German Shepherd."

"Viper, I don't give a good damn if it was a fuckin' French poodle, *oui, oui*! With the way it was actin', its breed doesn't matter to me, only it's bite, and last I checked, teeth are universal. He could be Scottish, British, West African, or a pigmy, I don't give a shit. I'm not about to have that damn dog draggin' me across the floor as his next Scooby snack!"

This made the man laugh all the harder.

"Majesty, stop."

"I'm serious. Now, the last time I was in your house, he was growling and snappin' at me. You expect me to be okay with that?"

"That's because he'd never seen you before. I had it all under control." He waved her off. "His bark is just loud, so it scared you." He slipped his white wife-beater over his head.

"You know I like dogs, but I don't care what you say. I

don't want to be around him. You take in the worst of the worst. When will you be finished with him so he can go back to his owner?" She gave him a disgusted look. She wanted that damn dog to vanish.

"Soon. And all the stuff you described is why I have him. He's getting better."

"Better ain't good enough. I need him to be well or get gone."

"Sometimes creatures can't get better without a little help, Majesty. I'm not just going to give up on him. He's already had enough of that."

"But if you can't fix him, then he'll be a danger to society. Some dogs are a threat, and there isn't anything that can be done about it. They just need to be put down."

"I see it like this. If you break a dog's spirit, then send them out into the world after that abuse, or whatever is making them act like that, and it's never addressed, then we set them up for failure. They get blamed for what someone else did to them. How is that right?" He shrugged. "It's kind of like breaking someone's leg then being angry at them because they're in pain and can't walk. I give the dog a mental cast and emotional crutches, then show them how to walk again. On their own."

She looked at the back of him as he kept cleaning up and working. *I bet he's talkin' about himself. We're no longer talking about that dog. Viper sees himself as that terrible German Shepherd. Maybe even as all the dogs he's had under his care at one time or other. My God...*

"Are you sure I can't help you clean up?" she offered after an awkward silence.

"No, baby, I've got it. Don't worry about the dog. I'll put him outside while you're over, okay?"

"All right."

"Go back out the tent. I have to take these poles down."

She made her way out the tent and waited as he disassembled it, the sounds of his toiling reminding her of windchimes. The whoosh of the wind and waves made her keenly aware of her surroundings and of how amazing and beautiful life and nature were. She looked over her shoulder at Viper who was now folding up the blanket, seemingly oblivious to her gaze. The sun had begun to set, and there was hardly anyone around. He looked so majestic at that moment. Strong. Giving. He was doing things that, in her mind, didn't match his appearance. Saying things that she didn't think she'd hear from a man like him. And the way he treated her and her son at times made her speechless. When she was too busy to get together, he was understanding. When Troy interrupted their alone time together, he welcomed her child with open arms, even inviting him to sit between them.

Every now and again, he'd open up to her… like when she'd asked about his childhood, and he'd answered. A part of her wished she'd hadn't even gone there after he'd described some painfully sad situations that had happened. The pride in his heritage and culture was obvious, the love for his brothers and sisters in the Nation, yet he'd also expressed his struggles with the way things had been changing in his world. He no longer felt like he quite belonged, although he still felt protective of his LK family.

She never expected him to denounce his allegiance, but it was crucial to her that he keep a safe distance and protect himself at all costs. Obviously, he felt the same, or the man wouldn't have moved away from Little Havana in the first place. But then again, Viper was reserved, and she always felt like he fed her in small increments, mere bite-sized pieces of who he really was, deep within his soul, and how he truly felt. He didn't discuss emotions. He spoke about facts and events. He never looked sad when discussing horrific things, and he wasn't faking or pretending to be strong. He *was* strong, hard on the outside and inside. And guarded. A tough man to figure out.

Yet, when they were together in the quiet of the night, just the two of them, sipping wine, their fingers inter-twined, and nice music playing, he'd look at her and share a secret or two. He'd say atrocious things, vague confessions of sorts, as if he were speaking of regular days in his life. In truth, the more time passed, the more he trusted her. So in those moments, he'd spill his guts. That was a big deal. It was more than evident that Viper was a private person by nature. She respected that. In fact, she respected so much about him. More than he could ever know.

I'm falling in love with you, Viper, and I'm scared. I don't want you to go back to the way you were, a way that I never saw, but I see the aftermath of it in your eyes. You've stepped away from that, but it's left holes in your spirit. Yeah… love. I love this man.

She turned back towards the ocean and hugged herself.

She thought the words but couldn't yet say them. The

241

'L' word was so hard to utter, for when she declared her feelings, there would be no way to take it all back. To renege.

About ten minutes later, they were in his car, heading home. She leaned back in the passenger's seat and closed her eyes to the sounds of Lucky Daye's, 'Access Denied.' Viper was chewing on a piece of spearmint gum, his long limbs stretched out and his head cocked to the side. He smelled like decadent cologne, the beach, and mint. *I love how this motherfucker smells. Damn!* A black Yankees cap and a pair of gold and black sunglasses made him even sexier as he thoughtfully stroked his beard with one hand and held the steering wheel with the other.

"If you keep lookin' at me like that, Majesty, like you want something from over this way, I'm going to beat that pussy up when we get in here."

"Oh, really?" She smirked. "Well, you aren't threatenin' me, mothafucka. Come on and bring it."

"Bet."

When he said the word, he pulled into his driveway. Before she knew it, he'd put the dogs away and was leading her inside, picking her up in his arms, and kissing her hard and slow as he carried her up the steps to his bedroom…

Q'S, 'GARAGE ROOFTOP' played in high volume, making the walls practically vibrate with life and lust. Majesty sat naked on the edge of his bed that was dressed in gold and black sheets. His clothes also discarded, he drew the curtains shut, shrouding the room in almost complete darkness, then turned on a corner lamp on the lowest light setting. A stream of light crept through, enough to hug the curves of her soul, taste her energy, and touch her vibration. On the nightstand sat a handful of Magnum condoms and a bottle of lube.

She got under the sheets, covered to her waist. He salivated at the sight of her big, soft breasts, the dark nipples erect and begging to be sucked.

"You in love with me?" He picked up his gold lighter and lit a small amber and musk candle by his bed. The light flickered and danced before settling. Sliding into bed with her, he snuggled close, wrapping his arms around her waist and drawing her near. She seemed guarded, stiff, scared, maybe of something beyond her control. "I asked you a question." He went for one of his favorite spots on her body: that lovely, sweet smelling neck. As he kissed her, she shuddered and held him tight.

"What made you ask me that?" Her airy voice, tinged with an ever-so-slight Southern dialect that he loved, broke the barrier of her silence.

"Because you look like you're in love with a mother-fucker." He sucked and licked along her collar bone, then went right back to her neck. Sneaking his hand between her hot thighs, he cradled her moist pussy. Her whimpers and coos sounded so sexy, they made his dick throb and lengthen with need. "And you *feel* like you're in love with me."

He kissed her then. Her body trembled as he kept

stroking her pussy, faster and faster, working her clit into a frenzy. "Cum tell me the truth…"

"Ahhh!" She twisted in his arms, squirming as her pussy dripped juice on his feverishly fast digits. "Fuck!"

Her head fell back and her body shook hard. She seemed to have lost complete control of herself. He kept on pleasuring her until she quieted. A live recording of Jhené Aiko's 'Chilombo Medley' serenaded them as he looked into her eyes and stroked her arms, then placed a gentle kiss against her succulent lips. He closed his eyes and felt her soft hands wrapping around his neck. Then, her warm breath caressed his ear.

"Yes…"

It was all she needed to say. All he needed to hear. Gently, he drew her down towards the end of the bed.

"Stand up and turn your back towards me."

She did as he asked. After bringing the lube bottle on the bed, he slid the condom on his hard cock and bent her over, keeping his touch like a hundred rain drops against a leaf, making her bend. He melted into her, relishing the feel of her while caressing her back, her neck, and layering her soft, brown, beautiful skin with kisses. Intoxicated by every drop of woman that she was, he cupped her ass and gave it a little squeeze, then opened the bottle of lube and slathered his dick until it was practically dripping wet.

"Tonight, I'm going in deep, baby…"

"Ahhhh…" She jerked and shuddered when he entered her tight, juicy slit. Slow. Deep. So damn deep. He held onto her waist, moving in tune with the music. Taking his time.

"Damn, Majesty..." Her warm pussy felt like wet velvet gloves wrapped around his dick. Squeezing and loving it. "You've got some good pussy, baby... Shit."

He reached around her with her one hand, cupped her pussy, and stroked her clit. Easy like.

"*No importa, estoy aquí y no me voy a ir a ninguna parte, Majesty.*"

He knew that she may not understand everything he said, but she'd feel his sentiment. The language needed no translation for his feelings for her poured out with each thrust. The shit he couldn't say, he could show her in other ways for the rest of her days. He groaned and grunted as he went balls deep. Faster. Harder. Up until this point, he'd always used restraint. Tonight, she was going to feel *all* of him. Her screams of anguished ecstasy and aching delight shattered the space around them. Their moans intersected like crucifixes... like fingers intertwined... like twin flames... like double souls...

He sped the pace even more, sweat pouring down his body like a waterfall. There were no gaps, no space, no room for even a butterfly's whisper to slip between their bodies. They were one. Skin on skin. Light tan and dark cinnamon combined. Connected. Linked like Eve to the serpent... Perhaps Viper had been her one true love. Perhaps she'd been designed for him, but because of his disobedience to the Creator, he was punished, cast out of Heaven, and had to watch her go away with Adam as the final stake in his black, now reptilian heart. A fallen, exiled angel.

She was his heaven. She was where he'd been but was

never welcomed again. She was his—

"God!"

She cried out, her fists grabbing the sheets. Shaking, she started to fall but he caught her in time. Her thighs trickled with nectar. The golden apple had burst...

There it was, the liquor of the Immortals living between her thighs.

He stood her on her feet and caressed her stomach from behind as she turned her head to look up in his eyes. As he kissed her, he kept pumping within her, diving as deep as he could in harsh, fast jabs until her eyes sheened over. She pleaded for him to stop, begged him to keep on going, to love her hard, love her soft. To never let her beautiful ass go. Rearing back, he left only the tip of his hungry dick within her, throbbing with lust inside her addictive garden. And then he slammed into her over and over, making her scream. Loud clapping echoed throughout the bedroom, until he exploded within her.

Her fingers dug into his arm, nails dragging against his skin as she held on while he emptied himself into the condom. They remained connected. Still kissing. Still cumming.

Still telling her to step aside in their Garden of Eden... and yet, out of his same mouth, with that same forked tongue, he begged her to stay, to let him have her, what was always rightfully his, once and for all...

CHAPTER SEVENTEEN
PREYing for a Change

VIPER SWIPED A cloth across the top of his prized
possession, his black Bugatti, then headed inside The
Shops at Midtown Miami. He snuck a glance at his car,
parked sideways, way in the back of the parking lot to
keep other vehicles away from it. It was a lovely day. His
diamond bracelets, watch, and rings sparkled in the
sunlight.

King Sting, his cousin on his father's side and three
years his junior, with whom he was on the phone, was
running off at the mouth and he was only half listening.
Catching his reflection in one of the storefront windows,
he also noticed several women laughing and staring at
him, pointing and blowing kisses.

He was dressed in Psycho Bunny white jeans and a

black and white checkered tank top, adorned with two gold and diamond Cuban link chains around his neck and diamond studs in his ears. He rarely wore his earrings anymore but had felt in the mood to be completely blinged out when he'd jumped out the shower that morning. After sprinkling on some Versace cologne, one of Majesty's favorites, he slid on his black and white Jordans and headed to the barber, then to Miami to take care of a few errands.

"*No voy contigo.*"

"What do you mean you're not coming, Viper? You have to."

"I don't have to do a damn thing." He paused briefly to adjust one of his bracelets.

"But it's already planned out." King Sting sounded desperate. "They're doin' the hit next week. There's three kilos of coke, and they need—"

"I told you when I got out of prison the last time that I would no longer be involved in any of that."

"But we're not asking you to go in, or even to deal. Everyone knows you don't deal! You're too busy, and—"

"I'm not coming out there to be your muscle if something jumps off, either."

"Awww, man! Viper, you're losin' it! This is big. *No puedes abandonarnos. Nosotros hemos estado allí para ti.*"

"Bullshit! I never abandoned y'all, and I've always been there for all of you, so much so I did time for it, and I never fuckin' snitched. I've done cases for my own shit and for someone else's, but not once did I try to save my own ass, even if a motherfucker deserved it. I was even in jail for three months once because Jugo snitched on me. After everything I had done for that bitch. No fuckin' loyalty!"

"Viper I'm not talking about all of that though. You have a chance to make some serious money! I know those dogs ain't bringing in six figures a year. All you gotta do is—"

"But dogs are loyal, and there's no amount of money that can compare. My freedom also has no price." *I don't want to be another statistic. Another brown man in prison with a life sentence...*

"But Viper, we're depending on you."

"I never decided to do anything. In fact, I said the exact opposite. Depending on me..." He rolled his eyes and sucked his teeth as he made his way past a Coach purse and luggage store. "And that used to be my fucking problem. I couldn't depend on anyone but myself. When I needed some of you the most, you weren't there. I was always loyal to my Reyes, but some of y'all wouldn't give me the time of day if my life depended on it, and I'm done with that shit, Sting."

"Let me come through and talk to you in person about this. We gotta—"

"Coming and talking to me in person won't change a fucking thing, man. You've known me your whole life. I don't care if someone is across the world talkin' to me on the phone with a gun to their head, or right in my fucking face, pleading and crying. The same answers apply. I swear you guys keep trying me, and you're not going to like how things turn out. There's bad blood being shed, and I'll be damned if I let another motherfucker wearing a got damn crown, Amor de Rey, spill mine!" He paused, noticing he was attracting some attention as he went off. He turned away.

"Viper, I never really hear you talking like this, so obviously you've got some shit on your chest. But that doesn't mean you turn your back on all of us. I had nothing to do with that shit they did to you back then. I'm asking you to do this. Just me, Sting. Forget about everyone else. This is a chance for me to bring in a big bank roll, and besides, Jaguar said it was fine. He gave his blessing."

Fuck Jaguar. He doesn't give a shit if any of them live or die. He just wants his piece of the pie. His cut.

"You are my past and present disappointment, man, and truly, it's hard to disappoint me because I don't trust anyone as it is."

"Your disappointment? Man, Viper, I've always been down!"

"You didn't do what you were supposed to do, either. Only my mother, father and stepfather on occasion, Marie of course, and some of the bitches who wanted to be with me when I got out came to see me when I was locked up all of those years. I never got any calls, letters, or emails from your ass. Nothing. The people I named were the only ones who checked on me and made sure I was straight, and behind those bars, I was still putting in work! I'm incarcerated working like a slave, while all of you were enjoying yourselves on the street. I had to keep the correctional officers quiet, the snitches in check, the brothers at peace, and our enemies flipped or dead, without leaving a trace. I know you heard about why I went to the hole."

Sting got quiet. His silence said it all.

"I know you know what happened. Everyone does. I killed that motherfucker. He was a fucking Chomo, and this wasn't rumor or speculation. I saw the proof. The details of his case. He was fucking disgusting, and I took him out because I was told to by higher ups in the ranks, and to help keep myself established in there. You know our adversaries love trying Warlords! And I'm a two-for-one, because in our chapter, I'm also the Cacique. Anyone can get status if they take me out. It's like a game of chess. King Viper is a top prize. So, that move helped. It reminded people what I was capable of. It took planning and perfect execution. That's how I got my name. Viper. I'm patient as a motherfucker, and I lay low, blending in with the brush, then go for the jugular. I strike when everyone else has forgotten, underestimated me, moved on, or gone to sleep."

"I heard about it. I look up to you, Viper."

"You're missing the point. I'm not saying it to you to brag or to get your admiration. It's a cautionary tale. If one thing had gone wrong, that would've been it for me. I refuse to return to that hell. It was risky because he was protected. He had money. Elite. Thankfully, they couldn't prove that I was the one responsible, so that was that, but no one else had the balls to do it because it was like a guaranteed death sentence, and maybe, in some way, that was the smarter choice, you know? I didn't have shit to prove, but I was prideful and wanted my respect at all costs.

"I'm no longer willing to risk it all. You guys are planning something that if one of you does anything wrong, you're blown. If anything happens that is not accounted for, you're blown. For all you know, they may be onto you. Don't underestimate people, *primo*. You'll be in prison for possibly the rest of your life, Sting. I was built for that, you're not."

"Viper, that's bullshit, nigga! I got balls! Fuck you, man!"

Viper stopped walking and gripped the phone harder.

"What the fuck did you just say to me?"

"I'm sorry. I just, uh, I felt offended by what you said."

"I don't give a shit about how you're feeling, what premenstrual emotions you may be going through! I'm giving you some knowledge, telling you my story, some shit very few people know the details of, and you turn this around and want your ego sucked. I'm not suckin' or soothing shit. I *eat* pussy, but I'm not one. Watch who the fuck you're talking to. I'll flip my own cousin, beat your ass one step away from 'Peace,' in R.I.P. I'll beat you like I don't even know your fucking name. Don't get it twisted. Cousin or not, don't you ever say 'fuck you' to me again. Do you fuckin' understand me?"

"Yeah. I apologize."

Viper started to walk again, his temper cooling down just as quickly as it had flared up. Sting was family, but that was a huge pet peeve of his. Someone saying 'fuck you' to him. Everyone knew not to say it, except Majesty. With her, he let it slide. Plus, he knew she never meant it maliciously, and it would escape her mouth most often when he was making her cum. *That*, he could forgive.

But not the rest. He may have been triggered by it because that was the last thing he'd heard at the age of sixteen, right before someone blew his friend's brains out right in front of him one day while they'd been sitting in the park. To this day, he still recalled the smell of the gun smoke and the feel of brain matter, bits of shattered skull, and blood all over his arms and chest.

"Wake the fuck up, Sting. You've got a two-year-old daughter and your girl is pregnant with your son, man. Think twice."

"Viper, you know this is how we make our money. No one is going to hire us to make the kind of cash we could robbing these guys. Besides, they deserve this shit! They invaded our territory. We're taking all their stash, and we're going to sell it and triple the profit. Who in the fuck is going to pay any of us that kind of dinero, huh? It would take a lifetime to achieve that, to make what we can make in one hour of work in the streets." Sting had a point, but it still didn't matter.

"Sting, there's always a loophole, a way out. I've done my own thing to get my money, and it was no better than what you're trying to do. In fact, in some ways, I'd say it was worse, but it's up to us to find the best way."

"I'm not like you though, Viper. I'm just not. I guess you found God… You're judging me, man."

"It's not about judgment or morals, and I can't find

God if I never lost Him. It's not even about right or wrong, motherfucker. You think I give a shit about those guys getting jacked? They're scum. I don't give a fuck about them, but I do give a fuck about you, so this is about keeping your ass alive and out of prison. Oh, and another thing. I'm not saying you don't have any juice. You're a tough motherfucker, okay? You are. If you were a pussy, I'd say so, but long prison terms will change you, man. They make what's hard harder. The crazy gets crazier. I was still on the Nation's clock. Body drop. Twenty-four-seven." He opened a restaurant door for a woman struggling to get out with a large carry-out bag and purse in her arms, along with shopping bags.

"Thank you so much," the older, attractive White woman said with a smile. "That was nice of you."

"*Está bien.*"

He continued on, checking out the various displays in the stores he passed. Fat Larry's Band's, 'Act Like You Know' played out of some old Black man's car as he sailed by in a long, gold Cadillac. Something about the guy reminded him of his father. He raised two fingers at the old player, and the man waved back.

"How'd you get to do what you did?" his cousin asked after a long silence.

"How'd I get to do what?"

"Start over."

"Before I got out of prison, I knew I needed to figure out some things. I was looking back on my life, and I was torn. With all the time I had, I'd just sit and think. I don't believe in regrets, but change needed to happen. So, I started writing down what I wanted in a notebook, my goals and plans, shit like that, and I wasn't going to let anyone stop me. No excuses. I knew, like you said, the chances of me landing a good job with the criminal record I have were slim to none, so that made me even more determined to start my own business. I wanted property, too, my own place. I wanted to help support my family, and to eventually get married as well. At the time this wasn't at the top of my priorities, but I'm a long-term planner.

"So, the idea of getting married meant I'd need to be able to support myself and my wife. Regardless of whether I married a Latin Queen, which wasn't out of the question but not guaranteed, my future wife would need protection. She'd need me by her side for mental, financial, emotional, sexual, spiritual and physical support, and if I'm incarcerated, I can't be there for her to the same extent as if I were free, now can I?"

"Yeah, yeah, I hear you."

He could tell his cousin was truly paying attention. Soaking it all in.

"So, those were my driving forces, the framework to push me forward. Money and business. Family. Future wifey. As soon as I got out the joint, Sting, and got my money right, I invested whatever I'd saved before I got locked up, see? And then I was able to buy a home, pay off my mother's house and get her a new car, pay off some of my father's debts for his car repair business, and start my own business that I had been writing down the plan for in prison. Once I was able to put work on it, I realized just how big of an undertaking it was, but it was worth it, and no one helped me. I did it on my own. I'm self-made."

"But see, that's just it, Viper. You had money already to help you. I don't have anything."

"You don't have to steal and sell dope though, man, to make it. You're an amazing rapper, and you can play the guitar. I want you to record your songs and put them on iTunes and Spotify, man. I want you to do gigs in the city for free to get your name around, then start charging. Start a podcast to discuss music and things you know about. I want you to start teaching guitar lessons. You can advertise online for free on social media. It doesn't matter how you start, just start! There're so many ways to make money now, Sting. With the way technology is now, you can make money in your sleep. Get you some. Stack your currency."

"You really think people would buy my music?"

"Like I told you, you're so fucking talented, you can do this. I know you can. You just gotta be patient, and you've got to be resourceful. Go get a trade if you want while you do it at the same time, so you can get a house for Gloria and your babies, man. Sting, I've been where you're at. My brother…" Viper felt a migraine hit him as soon as his dead brother entered his thoughts. "My brother was where you are, too… and now, he's not here anymore."

"I hear you, Viper. I'm kinda surprised that you feel like this. You're so high up, you know? I mean, you're a Warlord, man."

"I've got more to me than just being Warlord. You think anyone gives a shit about me being a Warlord outside the Nation, law enforcement, and gang affiliation, huh?" He was met with silence. "If anything, they'd use it against me. Say that I was beyond rehabilitation or see it as a reason to try me, to get points."

"People look up to you though. Everybody knows who King Viper is, man. That's power."

"And I like the power. I'm hungry for it, I'd be lying if I said otherwise. I wanna be paid. I like nice shit. Expensive shit. I like nice looking women, high-powered cars, and I enjoy knowing that people want what I have. But I'll tell you something. I will never be broke again, Sting, and by broke, I mean my mind and my spirit." He tapped his temple. "I'm done with the crazy shit. I would rather be chillin' with my dogs in my backyard, partying hard in Miami or L.A., in some amazing five-star hotel eating steaks as big as my face, or screwing the shit out of my beautiful girlfriend all morning and night long, than trade in my freedom just to prove what a badass I am again. Real talk.

" I'm sick of all of these simps, pretending to be pimps. All of these actors pretending to be real McCoys, all these betas pretending to be alphas, and all of these disasters pretending to be someone's blessing. I have nothing to prove to anyone, but to myself. Same for you. That's right… it's about me now. People want to act funny when I try to focus on myself for a change, improve things for *mi familia*. Funny how when that shit jumped off in the Union Correctional Institution, everyone wanted me to fucking fight and kill with them. No problem. But when I needed help, they stayed behind me and let me get stabbed."

He'd had a faint stab wound scar on his shoulder for years to prove this, now covered and blended in by a crown tattoo. "Wasn't the first time, but it definitely was the last time. My allegiance to the Nation is stellar! Don't you *ever* put that shit on me. Now that I'm getting older though, I want to distance myself from some of these… activities," he looked around, making sure nobody was listening, "but not my brothers. If someone doesn't like it, that's not my problem."

I paved the way. I walked the mile on broken glass, so mother-fuckers like Sting could crawl a mere yard on sand. Intact. Three of our boys are still in the pen for that fuck shit from six years ago. Gio has a life sentence. Javier is a fucking vegetable. Monopoly will never walk again. That could've been Sting. That could've been me.

"I get what you're saying, I do, and I mean no disrespect, Viper. I know you give me more of a pass because we're cousins, and I can talk to you differently. I didn't expect to have this heart to heart with you. This is the most you've spoken to me ever. Probably to anyone. You're the quietest, and yet most treacherous mother-fucker I know. That's called sneaky."

They both laughed at that. It was true. For some reason, Viper felt like expressing himself right then; perhaps in an effort to spare Sting some of the pain he'd endured in his lifetime. He wasn't convinced the young man would listen, but at least he tried, and that gave him peace.

Three fucking prison stints, countless jail stints, sending money to the families of our dead brothers and sisters, sometimes when I didn't even have it to spare. Attending each and every meeting. Squashing internal beefs, righting wrongs, trying to bring peace when one of my Reyes got into it with one of our allies. It was I who was called on, I who was trusted. This shit just last month, when they had to clean up the apartment? I got that shit squared away. And then, I was the one who found out exactly who was involved and made sure they were wiped off the map. People like to jump in after I've done all the heavy lifting, all the dirty work, then put their name on it like it's theirs. I say nothing. I'm sick of this shit… I've paid my dues. I want a life that doesn't always include having to merk, rob, stab, beat, flip, or hide a fuckin' body. Let me fuckin' live…

"We'll never let you go," his cousin said.

Viper looked into the window of a store selling classy men's apparel.

"I have no intentions of leaving you or the Nation. I just move differently now. I'm always going to be Viper. I'm too far entrenched in this to ever be anyone but *me*. I'm always a Latin King. Amor de Rey."

"Amor de Rey. You're damn straight, and I don't want you to forget that."

"I'd never. I love you all. For real." He pumped his fist against his heart. "But I'm done sacrificing myself for things that no longer fit in with what I'm trying to do, and where I'm trying to go, and if you know like I know, little cousin, you'll do the same. I don't want you going to prison again. I don't want you dead." Sting was breathing heavily on the other end, as if he was breaking. A lot of pressure was on his shoulders. "You're in deep, but this doesn't mean you can never swim away and get back up to the surface. You'll be tired and wet. No one enters this life without some battle scars along the way, but at least, you'll be alive." Viper disconnected the call and entered the Footlocker.

An employee greeted him and told him to let him know if he needed help. As he checked out the inventory, he thought about his baby. *I just want her heaven, her peace, to kill my hell and murder my anguish. I need my baby's warm thighs wrapped around me as I drill her so deep, she knows my language — not of my tongue, but of my heart. May it be that our souls blend and combine, so that even God can't tell us apart…*

He pulled out his phone and sent Majesty a text.

Viper: Hey baby, I know you're at work, but answer me if you can. What size shoe did you say Troy wears?

He waited a few minutes, and then his phone buzzed.

Majesty: 5 or 6 depending on how it's made. Why? What are you up to?

Viper: His birthday is in three days. I'm taking care of something.

Majesty: You're so sweet.

Viper: No, I'm not.

Majesty: LMAO 😂 You hate when I call you sweet! It's funny. OK. TY anyway. That's nice. You spoil him. I'll see you tonight.

Viper: Ok. Te quiero mucho, Mami.

He slid his phone in his pocket and approached the sales guy, a slender, short light-complexioned Black guy with a low Caesar haircut.

"Hey, what's up?" They slapped hands. "My girl-friend's son's birthday is coming up, and I want to get him those new Jordan Retros. He wants a pair like mine. I don't have them on right now, but you know the ones, right?"

"For sure. Bet. What color? White, Carolina, or Black?"

"White. Size six."

He followed the man to the display area.

"The display model is gone. I think I have one pair left in that size in the back, though. They've been selling out fast. I'll be right back."

"All right."

Viper rubbed his hands together as he waited. D'Angelo's, 'Spanish Joint' drifted from the speakers, a tune he liked. Meanwhile, he picked up a snapback for the kid, and a T-Shirt, too.

"Last pair, man!" The employee emerged from the stock room door, a big smile on his face. "You're lucky 'cause we're not getting any more for a while."

"Cool. I know my little guy will love them." Viper whipped out his wallet and paid for all the items in cash. After he walked out the store, he strolled around a bit to blow off some steam before his three o'clock appointment with a new canine client, a Labrador puppy prone to accidents in the house.

It felt good to be back in one of his favorite Miami shopping areas, even if only for a few hours. He slowed down by a bridal shop, a store he didn't recall seeing there before. Perhaps it was new. He looked at the shiny-faced, featureless mannequins in the window display, all donning different wedding dresses, veils, and their stiff hands holding fake bouquets of flowers. He stood there for a minute, and his lips curled in a smile.

One day, ya know? My lady could be coming to a place like this, to meet me down the aisle. I think I found the one though. I really do. Majesty is exactly what I want in a woman. Beautiful. Smart. Funny. Sexy. Nurturing. Truthful. Strong. She fits me well. We get along amazingly. Chemistry off the chain. Majesty makes me feel different from anyone else I've ever dated. I'm in love with her. Yeah. I'm definitely in love with that woman.

As he thought about picking up a bite to eat before heading back to Boca Raton, his phone buzzed. It was his cousin again.

"Yeah?"

"Hey, Viper, I had to call you back, man!"

"*¿Oye que bola?*"

"Did you hear the good news?"

"What?"

"Jagger's getting out early."

"Oh, is he now?" He opened the door to Crab De Jour, figuring he'd get one to go and smash it once he got home. It had been a long time since he'd enjoyed some crab legs.

"Yeah, man! Worked out a deal. He'll be home in a few months!" His cousin was clearly on cloud nine. Like so many others, Sting saw Jaguar as some superstar, but honestly, it was more out of a notion of an expected way to behave, versus authentic emotions and love for a person. Jaguar caused fear in most around him. He had influence and clout that men dreamed of, and with a snap of his fingers he could make someone disappear, if he so chose. One of the many perks of being high ranking. Viper wasn't afraid of him in the least. But of course, Jaguar knew that all too well. His cousin rattled out the details, play by play, of how their homeboy, their brother from another mother, was escaping the iron whore, better known as that funky ass jail cell, and rejoining society.

"That's great news, Sting. Glad to hear it. Keep me updated."

"Bet."

Viper disconnected the call and slipped the phone back into his pocket.

"May I take your order?" a Black woman with a short afro asked.

"Yeah, I want a to-go order. Let me get two lobster tails, shrimp with the head off, a pound of your King crab legs, and half a pound of scallops. I want the original Cajun sauce, hot, along with boiled eggs, potatoes, sausage, and corn on the cob."

"Would you like anything else with that?"

"No. That's it."

"Okay. It'll be ready in fifteen minutes. You're more than welcome to wait at the bar."

He was sitting at the bar, waiting for his carryout order, when he saw another Latin King enter the restaurant. It was clearly a Reye based on the guy's tattoos. They immediately zoned in on one another and brandished their gang signs discreetly.

"Sir, would you like to order a drink?"

"Yeah. Let me get coffee please. Black. Don't give it to me until my order arrives, though. I'm going to take it with me on the drive home." The bartender nodded and walked away.

When he was alone again, his mind went wild. Thinking… thinking… thinking…

I used to keep that old journal in prison. Just like I told Sting, I'd write down all my dreams, my ambitions, and how I was going to get it all. Everything I've been wanting, I'm getting. Everything that is happening, good or bad, is coming to pass for a reason. It's like the tortoise and the hare. I don't question timing as it doesn't matter. The result of your efforts matters. That's why I'm such a good Warlord and businessman. I focus on results, and if I say so myself, I'm good with Majesty, too. The result is, she's now with me… I said she was going to be mine, and now, she is. Not because she's easy, but because I know how to get what I want. How to move effectively, if not necessarily fast. She's been through a lot of shit. So have I. We don't make things harder for one another; we make things better. That takes patience. Everyone is in such a rush now, but I'm fine with biding my time. Waiting. My father, uncles, and brother taught me well, by their mistakes, more than anything else. I saw an opportunity so long ago, and I seized it. It's a thing of ugly beauty.

Funny how no one seems to see what's coming until it's too late. Maybe because they're sitting too high up and can only see the crown. I'm situated down low in the grass, slithering about, and I can see everything from the east to the west, the north and south. I see all the flaws of the land and the sky, things that others miss. No one notices the viper until it's too late. I'm camouflaged in the colors of the grass and earth. I'm lethal, never having to rush to get my point across.

Once I see an opportunity to strike, then and only then do I move with haste, injecting venom from my long fangs. Mothafuckas never know what hit 'em…

Soon, it will be time to feast.

"Here's your order, sir. Enjoy!"

"Oh, trust me, I most certainly will…"

CHAPTER EIGHTEEN

The LIFE of the party

"STOP IT, DOMINIC! Oh my God! See? You play too much!" Majesty giggled and swatted at the crazy man. Viper reached for her arm to yank her back to him in his backyard, but she evaded him and went to claim a lawn chair, a beer in hand and her belly full and hurting from laughter. Viper had moments of silliness, which were amplified when he was in his element, around friends and family. She took a swig of her beer and looked around. She rarely drank beer but had grabbed the first cold thing she'd seen to quench her thirst. Viper's friends were making a ruckus inside and outside the house with their partying and drinking.

The space was filled with an abundance of guns on hips, yellow, gold, and black bandanas, bold black eyeliner on many of the women's faces, and tapestries of tattoos on most of them, telling stories she was certain she'd never fully understand.

"Majesty! Did Viper tell you the time he got locked in a closet with the Bogeyman?" one of Viper's drunk friends, King Javier, slurred.

"Shut up, Javier." Viper chortled from across the lawn and tried to shoo the guy away with a wave of his fingers. "Don't tell her about that shit!"

Majesty shook her head. "No, tell me!"

"All right. Check it. The Bogeyman was this old guy from our neighborhood who was always high. Loaded. Viper was about, I dunno, seventeen or so, and I was probably around thirteen. So, there was a party goin' on, and the Bogeyman coasts through. He asked to speak to Viper alone, so they went into this big ass closet, right? Like a pantry. He told Viper to get him some weed 'cause his dealer wouldn't give him anymore for some reason I don't remember. So…" Javier came to stand right before her, a cigar in one hand and beer in the other. His light brown eyes lit up and he was animated, getting into the story. "They were in the closet of this house, right?"

"Yeah… yeah," she said, anxiously waiting for the punchline as more people gathered around Javier.

"We'd go to this abandoned house for meetings and shit. Nothing strange with us all being there; we partied there all the time. The music was loud. We had a boom box." He took a toke of his cigar and continued, "So, he gave Viper the money to get the weed, right, and of course extra to take care of it. But when Viper went to open the closet door after their little talk, the door was locked. Viper starts bangin' on the door for help, but none of us can hear him. He's in there goin' crazy! See, he's a little claustrophobic and doesn't like being in tight spaces." *Hmmm… I didn't know that.* "So, he starts panicking 'cause he's also in there with Bogeyman, of all people. The old guy was talking shit, going crazy, screaming about they needed to get the fuck out of there. At one point, Viper got tired of Bogeyman's mouth, so he picked this fucker up, turned the guy sideways, and used the dude's entire fuckin' body like a police battering ram, the kind they use to fuckin' kick doors in. He broke through the damn door using Bogeyman's head!"

Everyone in the backyard erupted in laughter, including Majesty and Viper.

"Bogeyman had to get a few stitches, but he was okay. The fucked-up part is that he still wanted Viper to get him the weed, bloody head and all, and we all partied afterwards like didn't shit happen. Even Bogeyman."

Viper stuck out his tongue, showed him both middle fingers, then continued to talk to another guy standing beside him. Majesty was taking it all in. She'd never seen a party like this in her life.

Even though most of Viper's LK brothers and sisters were speaking Spanish during the party, and she could only understand a little here and there, the women were friendly and welcoming, and spoke in English when addressing her. She did notice that when some of the men said something to her, they seemed a bit flirtatious, yet remained respectful. Majesty figured some of this may have been cultural. She'd never dated a Hispanic man before Viper, but she'd been around enough of them to know that many came across that way, even if they were only being friendly and meant nothing by it. Nevertheless, she more than once would catch Viper glaring if one of the Kings kept a conversation going with her that lasted more than a minute or two. It was always innocent banter, but his potential for jealousy was stark clear.

He never told her to keep away or chastised his Reyes for engaging in sociable conversation, but she couldn't deny he was a control freak. One wrong look from Viper, and those guys wrapped that conversation up fast. She smiled inwardly at the notion. *No one is to flirt with his girl...*

It was getting late, but she had to admit, she'd been having a fun time with the boisterous crowd. Marie was the only one in attendance who seemed quieter and wasn't partying quite as hard, but most notably, damn could that woman cook. Viper had been right. Majesty was a bit embarrassed at how much food she'd wolfed down, many dishes she couldn't even pronounce the name of, but she just couldn't help being such a glutton. It was too delicious to let it go to waste.

"...I know, right?!" One of Viper's friends, King OP spoke in a booming voice, drawing attention. "Motherfucker was in there for being caught with a biscuit while he was on parole. His White ass got locked up with us, called Deuces a jalapeño. They were battlin' it out. So that night, Deuces got him some shit from the Juice Man as a peace offering, pretending he didn't want no beef, but the shit was spiked. White boy got fucked up! Officers saw him the next morning talking about he was Spiderman, drooling, and tryna climb up the walls and spin a web from his wrists! They took his ass out of there and he said, 'Let go of me, villains. Do you know who I am, mother-fucker?! I'm Spiderman! Don't make me call Batman and the Hulk in here, too! We'll take you all down!" These words were followed by an outburst of laughter from the crowd. The man had been entertaining the masses most of the day.

Jalapeño? Juiceman? Biscuit? What are they talking about?

She shrugged her shoulders and took another sip of her beer.

"Gotcha!"

She screamed when Viper snuck up from behind and put her in a bear squeeze, then kissed her cheek and lips. She longed for him. Every fiber of her being desired his touch. As if picking up on her excitement, he kissed her again, then whispered in her ear. "As soon as they leave, I'm going to fuck you… tear your beautiful ass to pieces…"

"Make sure that you do." She winked at him and he winked back. "You know, your friend, King OP, seems to be quite the comedian. I wish I could understand what he was talking about though." She'd noticed that every time the stocky Cuban LK told a story, the entire place would laugh their heads off.

"He's hilarious. A clown. But don't get it twisted. He's sharp. Smart as hell." Viper knelt beside her. "I don't really think about it, you know, the words he uses. We just understand it. It's prison slang." She nodded in under-standing. "Like, that last story was about a White guy who was in prison with us for drug possession and gun charges. He got in there tryna act big and bad, ya know, called our boy Deuces a racial slur when they'd gotten into it. A jalapeño is what the guy called him, so Deuces went and got some prison wine with drugs mixed in, gave it to the White boy, and the guy was hallucinating 'nd shit all night and morning long."

"Ohhh! So, a biscuit is a gun? The Juice Man is the guy who makes the illegal wine in jail, I mean, prison?"

"Yeah, now you've got it. Should I make you like a little prison pamphlet or something so you can understand the lingo and follow along?" he teased. She rolled her eyes at the man. "I mean, I can. You've never been inside a prison, but a little bit of prison, via me, has been inside of *you*."

She swatted at him and the fucker backed up just in time, laughing. Getting to his feet, he kissed the top of her head then disappeared inside the house.

The music blared all night long, song after song and she was certain she had a second-hand high from occasional whiffs of marijuana smoke. Troy was with his friends for a playdate, which also included him spending the night at his friend's house. She glanced at her watch. He'd be at a restaurant at that moment, then head to a ball game. She had the entire day and night to herself.

"Majesty, do you want something else to drink, *cariña?*" one of the Latin Queens offered.

"No, I've got a beer, Tia. Thank you though."

She was impressed by how nice everyone was to her. Every time she tried to go and do something herself, like serving her own plate, someone would jump in and help.

The hospitality was over the top, but she wasn't a fool. Viper had it like that. People would be damned if they'd pissed him off, and as one King stated, any friend of Viper's was a friend of theirs, too. When Viper approached, people would move out of the way. They offered him things, wanted his opinions, and showed the utmost respect to him, all while having a good time. It was evident who was running shit and in charge.

A new song thumped from the speakers. Another Latin rap tune with a catchy beat and ample curse words in Spanish. The sliding patio door opened once more, and out came Viper's three Pit Bulls. The three furry amigos. They raced right toward her, practically tackling her in excitement.

"Hey! No! Leave Majesty alone," Viper yelled, then whistled, following the dogs into the backyard.

"They're okay, Viper!" She smiled at them as they tried to lick her face. Placing her beer under the seat of the lawn chair, she began to shower them with affection. She loved them all, each one with its unique, special personality. Especially Sarge who was a big, overgrown baby and demanded nonstop belly and head rubs. Viper and three other men now stood close to the grill, some holding cigars or cigarettes while they all spoke in Spanish, sometimes in hushed tones. Suddenly, the vibe seemed to change. She could tell from Viper's facial expression; he wasn't happy with whatever was going down. Moments later, the small crowd dispersed, and Viper came on the hammock close to her. As he typed texts on his phone, his brows furrowed, and he looked mad as hell.

"Is everything okay?" she asked after a while.

"Wild is dead."

Then just like that, he got off the hammock and stormed into the house, slamming the patio door behind him.

Majesty took a deep breath, rubbed Sarge's head one last time, and went inside the packed house with a forced smile stamped on her face. She searched for Viper, but he was nowhere to be found.

Upstairs. I bet that's where he went.

She made her way up the steps, then knocked on his bedroom door.

"Who is it?" Viper barked.

"Me."

After a few seconds of silence, the door swung open. She walked in, and he locked it behind her. The man was pacing back and forth, looking down at his phone every now and again. Preoccupied. Angry. Hurt.

"If I remember this correctly, Wild was your friend, right? He'd gotten locked up recently. You told me he'd been a lookout, but the police had set him up. Same guy, right?"

"Yeah."

"I'm sorry for your loss, Viper." She approached him and wrapped her arms around him. He was so stiff. Icy. Distant.

He avoided eye contact.

"Do you know how it happened?"

"It was planned. Our own killed our own. You can't have a better friend than a Latin King. You can't have a worse enemy than a Latin King… I asked Jag not to do this. I told him not to do this shit!'" He closed his eyes, shook his head, and then, as if a light switch had been flicked, he opened his eyes, and all she saw was death in his face. Emotionlessness. Aloofness. "I don't want to talk about it." Shaking loose from her grip, he hurried into the bathroom, leaving her standing there, alone. Majesty fought the urge to bang on the bathroom door and make the man talk.

He just needs some time…

She got ready to leave the bedroom and head back downstairs, then paused. Something stopped her from walking away. Walking to the bathroom door, she placed her hand against it. She stood silent for a spell, then cleared her throat.

"Viper… you don't need to respond. Just listen. I know how you feel. I've lost so many people I've cared about over the years, and it never gets easier. Some people, I haven't lost physically, but emotionally. For example, my father. He's here, but I don't fuck with him like that. Back to the point, though. I know it hurts. Losing a friend… Honestly, that's another reason why I moved away. I just didn't tell anyone that. Too many bad memories." She paused, taking a deep breath. "I know you don't want to be upset in front of me, or anyone for that matter. It's just not your style. But it's okay to be sad about it, to even feel a sense of responsibility. You told me that you can't leave your brothers. You told me, once a Latin King, always a Latin King, but you've grown over the years, and there are some things that just don't entice or excite you anymore. Nevertheless, your heart is with them, and that's all right. Viper, you can't save everyone, but I applaud you for trying."

The door slowly opened, and he stood there, staring down at her. He crossed his arms, pissed off at the world. She reached up and stroked the man's cheek, feeling the rough stubble. His hazel eyes were hooded, as if he were fighting something. Trying to shut her out from seeing just how dark he could go. Something so disconcerting, he wouldn't even show it to himself.

He sucked his teeth, then lowered his gaze to the floor.

"Baby, talk to me. It's just me and you here, Dominic." She tugged at his elbow, making one of his arms drop, then took his big hand into hers.

"Something else went down."

"What?"

"Something happened. Something unrelated to Wild. There was a plan to get some money. Now, I'm waiting to see if my cousin, King Sting, is dead."

Two horrible announcements all within one day. God, Viper...

"Oh shit. I'm sorry... Hopefully you'll hear something soon. This is a lot to deal with."

He shrugged. "I'm a gangbanger, baby. Doesn't matter if I'm on active duty or not. This is our life. It's what happens."

"Why do you think your cousin might be dead, Viper? Maybe he just—"

"I found out that a plan they had backfired big time. They got ambushed. That's all I can say. I don't want you to know more about this than you already do. Come on. Let's go back to the party."

He maneuvered around her, then made his way out. They went down the steps together.

Viper put on an award-winning smile and began to chop it up with his friends. It was all a show, or perhaps it wasn't. Maybe he was able to morph like that, shed the skin of pain and appear brand new because he'd had a lifetime of practice. Luis Fonsi's, 'Despacito,' featuring Daddy Yankee, was playing as they both re-entered the living room, which was alive with dancing and chatter, the place now even more crowded than before. She spent the rest of the evening dancing her head off with Viper's female friends. One of them, Aymee, had been especially nice to her, but authentically so.

Aymee had straight, shoulder length, dark brown hair, slanted green eyes with thick lashes, and skin the color of vanilla wafers. She was short, no more than five-one, sassy, and just as pretty as she wanted to be. Aymee's nickname was Queen Tarot, and she had a tattoo of a spiderweb on the side of her face.

"Now you've got it, Majesty! Come on, girl! Work those hips!" she encouraged, showing her how to dance the Rumba.

The women in the room were beautiful, even with their overdone black eyeliner. They were all different heights, weight, and shapes. Full of life, feisty, and their stunning smiles lit up the room. One wouldn't even guess by a mere glance that they were gang affiliated if it weren't for their tattoos. This was one of those times when

Majesty had to go inward and reevaluate her own stereotypes about people. It was hard not to. She used to even be annoyed, when she was younger, at illegals supposedly taking jobs from Americans, and didn't understand until she got older that many Americans she knew didn't want those damn jobs anyway. It was hard labor and didn't pay enough, but to someone coming over to the country trying to escape true atrocities, those jobs were nothing short of a blessing.

But gangbanging was different. She was fully aware of what these people did behind closed doors when others were not looking. They did unspeakable things to make money, honor their LK colors, and take care of their families. Regardless, not every book matched its cover, and not everyone could be put in a box. Not agreeing with someone's choices didn't mean that they were a bad person, or predictable. In fact, some of these women were married or gainfully employed.

Some had attended college, and some had graduated. Some of them just focused on their families, or enjoyed their singlehood, but one thing was certain: they were still a tough bunch of ladies who didn't give two shits about who didn't approve of them. They were strapped just like the Kings, and she'd overheard enough conversations throughout the evening to prove they'd curse someone out just as badly as their male counterpart, too. Majesty didn't feel in danger, threatened, or alienated, regardless. There was no racial tension, and in fact, they kept drawing her in, asking if she needed anything or if she wanted to play dominoes. A couple of the ladies even asked for her number so they could all go out together sometime. Despite being aware they were trying to walk the straight and narrow for Viper, she could sense that if they weren't digging her, none of that would've happened. They'd be cordial, but not go out of their way to be so friendly.

She made her way into the kitchen where Marie was sitting at the island, checking her social media. A few Kings and Queens were in there, too, talking and enjoying themselves.

"Hello, Majesty. Are you hungry?" The woman greeted her with a big, beautiful smile. Her Latin dialect wrapped around the syllables like a shawl.

"Marie, if I eat one more thing from you, my stomach is going to explode. You know you are wrong for cookin' all of this tasty food." The woman's face turned red, but she was undeniably pleased with the compliment. "I won't be able to fit into my clothes after tonight and I have the nerve to contemplate packing up a to-go plate. Well, there's no contemplating it: I am. Viper needs to ask you to move in so you can do this all the time."

The woman burst out laughing and slapped the table.

"You liked it, huh? Good! I'm so glad I got a chance to finally meet you. Viper has told me so much about you." Their eyes locked. Then, silence. "Sit down, sit down!" The older woman pointed at a chair across from her. Majesty grabbed a bottle of iced water and sat down. "You're so pretty! *Qué mujer tan bonita*."

"Thank you. So are you."

Marie stroked her own arm, her dark eyes full of life, love, and pain.

"You've got a great man, Majesty."

"I think so, too."

"I'm serious." The woman's expression turned grave. "He's rare. Hard worker. So, so smart. I knew when he told me he had a new *novia*, that he was in love. Viper isn't exactly the type to talk about his love life."

A new novia. *I know that word. It means 'girlfriend'...*

The woman clasped her hands and offered a careful smile. "He brought it up to me... discussed you with me." The woman seemed to look through her, as if dissecting her. It was a bit unnerving, but there was something so motherly about Marie that it didn't ruffle Majesty too badly.

"So, what was said exactly in these discussions?"

"Oh, the usual... What you looked like, how you two met. What you do for a living. That you had a son." Majesty nodded in understanding. "Viper likes children. He said your son is bright."

"He is very smart. And a smart ass, too!"

They both burst out laughing, then Marie drew serious again.

"Majesty, Viper loves you. Do you know that? He loves you very much."

"Yeah, I know. I love him, too."

"We're protective of him. We're family and he's like another son to me. He's been good to me. Generous. Helpful. He scares people, not always intentionally, but inside, he's loving. He has a big heart. Only the people he trusts get to see that, though."

"I agree with you completely." Majesty broke the seal

of her water and took a big gulp.

"*¿Puedo ofrecerte un consejo?*"

"I'm sorry, my Spanish is limited, Marie."

"Oh, okay. I said, I'd like to give you some advice, if that's okay?"

"Of course."

"Accept him for who he is." The woman's eyes grew darker. "He's a King. He will *always* be a King. It's not a word or title; it's what is in his heart. He was born this way. If you don't accept him for the man that he is, you will hurt him deeply. When men like Viper get hurt in love, they move on as if nothing has happened, but inside, they are never the same. He trusts you. That's a big deal. He trusts very few…" The woman's gaze bore into her. "If you take my advice, you two will be just fine. He will give you the world on a platter. He's come a long way. Now, he's ready." The woman sighed, stood and walked around the island to her. After patting Majesty's hand, she walked out of the kitchen.

Majesty sat there for a while, mulling Marie's words.

Later in the evening, the house began to clear out. People said their goodbyes, kissing and hugging, some holding to-go plates of delicious Cuban food. The Queens kissed and hugged her on the way out, and the Kings were ever so cordial. *Polite gangsters… Wow.* She chuckled on the inside.

Majesty, Viper, and a few others cleaned up the house, and then, at last, it was just the two of them.

Viper turned off the music, poured himself some tequila, then plopped down on the big living room couch.

Turning on his remote-controlled fireplace, he rested his head on the sofa, looking every bit exhausted. Majesty sat beside him.

"I hate to tell you this, but we haven't cleaned up the backyard yet."

"Awww, fuck!"

She burst out laughing, then got back up and left out the patio door. It was so quiet and particularly light that evening with the moon and stars shining bright. She began to clear some of the backyard tables of empty cups, used napkins, and so forth. She wasn't out there for more than a couple of minutes before Viper joined her, a trash bag in hand. They steadily got the job done, working as a team.

"Thank you for helping with this. You were my guest, though, like I told you. Go back inside and relax," he said.

"No, I've been relaxing all night already. Your friends were waiting on me hand and foot." She chuckled, then looked at her watch. It was three in the morning.

After a few more minutes, they had everything put away.

"All right. We did it!" she squealed. "Since I'm spending the night, I figure we can go inside and—"

"You ever fucked on a hammock?" He didn't wait for an answer. Viper was suddenly undressing, tossing his clothing down on the grass.

"You bet not get naked out here! What if someone sees you?!"

He laughed lazily, then crawled onto the hammock, clutching his shirt. Draping it over his big, erect dick, he waved her over.

"Come here, sexy."

She went over and tugged at his arm.

"Come on, get your ass off there. You must be drunk."

"I'm not drunk." He reached for her and caressed her face. "Ride me, baby. I want some of that good cha-cha."

She abhorred how her pussy palpitated at his words.

"I'm not fucking you outside, Dominic."

"Get on this dick and ride it." He yanked her to him, making her scream so loud, he quickly covered her mouth to muffle the sound. The hammock swung wildly back and forth as he pulled her up, then steadied her against his chest. She kept squealing.

"I'm going to move my hand. If you scream again, someone might hear you and the police will be over here. If that's not what you want, don't do it." They glared at one another. "Nod if you understand me."

She nodded, then he slowly moved his big palm away from her face.

"You asshole."

"Fine. I'm an asshole. Now, suck and fuck your man," he said with mock-sternness.

He discarded the shirt and she gingerly scooted down his body, afraid she'd fall as the hammock rocked to and fro.

"Keep going… I've got you."

She moved past his waist and came face to face with his big, juicy dick. Her heart pounded and her pussy swelled with excitement, nipples growing taut. The starlit sky twinkled above them, as if giving them its approval.

He groaned when she enveloped his cock in her mouth. Sucking it with fervor, going as deep as she could go, she closed her eyes, loving the way the smooth, velvety skin felt against her tongue. Up and down she went, trying to take more and more of him in, but she went too far and ended up gagging, forced to pull back.

"Easy now... You can do it. Try again."

Her eyes watering, she then returned to the task grabbing the base with both hands and massaging him as she delivered bottomless sucks with gusto.

"Shit, baby... Feels so fucking good. Damn, Majesty... Keep suckin' it just like that!" He groaned.

Working her head up and down, the slurping noises from her mouth seemed to emit in stereo, along with her heartbeats. The risk of being seen or caught, as well as the way she risked falling off the hammock and the pleasure he expressed, excited her in ways she hadn't imagined. Soon, her thighs grew sticky with moisture. He ran his fingers through her hair as he rocked his hips up and down, delivering more of himself inside her mouth.

"Mmmm! Baby... Come on!" He grabbed the base of his dick and pulled her off him. "Get on my dick."

She removed her capris and panties, grabbed his dick, then slowly... gradually... carefully inched down. The girth spread her pussy open, and she took her time guiding herself down the monster cock. They moaned in unison when she took him all in, then started to move, her palms pressed against his chest. He wrapped his shirt around her ass and hips to shield her body from prying eyes, giving her a sense of protection, and held onto her waist as she jostled up and down his shaft. His lips parted and a look of longing danced in his eyes that took her breath away.

When he started to move with her, it was pure magic. Her clit swelled with exhilaration; an orgasm imminent as he bumped his pelvis against her clit.

"Shit, Dominic! You feel so good inside me!"

He rocked back and forth, his teeth sinking into his lower lip as he took full control. She suppressed a scream when he pushed himself upward in rapid speed, the slapping noise of his balls beating against her sensitive flesh driving her crazy. The hammock rocked wildly, but somehow, he managed to keep them on it. It was like fucking on a rollercoaster, a precarious seesaw, and the dull pain and pleasure that radiated between her legs from the pounding of his dick was too much to take. She came hard and he quickly pulled her flat against him, squelching her euphoric screams when her mouth collided with his hard chest. He kept fucking her, never stopping, long after her orgasm had come and gone.

"Get up, get up, get up. I'm about to nut."

She quickly lifted her body and he snatched himself out of her. White streams of cum shot from his dick, and she could see he struggled to not let go with his usual loud moans of pleasure. He threw his head back, his eyes rolling, neck veins popping, Adam's apple bobbing, and his complexion darkening. Harsh breaths exited his mouth, and he looked positively drained. He slowly sat up, kissed her lips, then cleaned the cum from her stomach with his shirt. Helping her off the hammock, she quickly redressed. He picked up his clothing from the grass and they walked back inside, hand in hand, with the bright moonlight and stars guiding the way.

They took a shower together in calm silence, the warm water streaming down their bodies so soothing. After they rinsed the soap away, he embraced her, holding her tight and resting his chin on the top of her head. They stayed that way for a long while.

Once they'd dried off and changed into comfortable clothing, they crawled into the huge bed together. She fell almost instantly asleep against his chest.

When she came to, she felt his weight on top of her. She groggily held on, wrapping her thighs around his waist as he entered her in shallow thrusts. He made love to her slow and easy, then she felt the locking of his muscles followed by a slight tremble, and the warmth of his cum flooding the condom. After a quick clean-up in the bathroom, he fell back to sleep on her breasts. She ran her fingers through his hair, stroking him until she heard him lightly snoring.

After a while, his cellphone began to glow and vibrate. He remained asleep, but she glanced over and saw a message:

Sting: *Hey, Cousin. It's me. I had to lie low today. The block is hot. Obviously, you see I'm alive if you're reading this. I didn't go. I backed out at the last minute because I thought about what you'd said to me. They went without me. Now all of them are dead, Viper. I'm fucked up about this. You saved my life.*

MR. EARL ANGRILY tossed his binoculars on the porch floor.

I can't see a damn thang!

He often had insomnia and would be up early in the wee hours of the morning. This time, at a little after 3:00 A.M., he heard the faint sound of moaning drifting from across the street. Some sounded deep and masculine, others feminine and high pitched. That's when he realized someone was fuckin', and it was coming from that big Cuban man's house – Dominic.

The night before, he'd seen Majesty hightailing it over there wearing tight pink capris that hugged that nice ass of hers, along with a white tank top and sparkly sandals. He hadn't seen her leave Dominic's house though, and it had gotten to be past midnight. All the cars on the street had vanished, so unless those dogs of his were getting it on, and he highly doubted they'd sound that way, that only left two suspects…

Retrieving his binoculars once more, he tried spying again, but the damn things wouldn't focus, and he couldn't see over the fence no how. He'd have to walk up to the man's home to get a full view, and he refused to do such a thing though for a split second, he found the idea tempting. After a few minutes more fumbling with the binoculars that did nothing but cause a blur, he gave up on the notion of catching a sneak peak of the action.

Still, he cracked a smile anyway.

NOW HOLD ON JUST A DAMN MINUTE! I *know you sittin' over there reading this, judging me, thinking I'm some dirty old man. AND YOU KNOW WHAT?*

I AM! SO WHAT?!

I ain't got no wife no more, no girlfriend either, and even if I did, I doubt my thang is working the way it used to. I can't remember the last time I was hard. Probably when Reagan was in office… I'm just kidding. It wasn't that long ago, but I haven't used it in years, since right after my wife got sick, and I never cheated on that woman a day in my life. Just 'cause I'm old and the pecker don't salute no more don't mean that I don't get titillated and excited every now and again. Mmm mmm mmm! The two of them are an item, that's for sure, and I'd like to think I had something to do with it. They courtin'. Back there on that there swing, or whatever the hell those tree nets are called, boilin' each other's cabbage.

He burst out laughing, tickled so.

Ain't love beautiful?

And then he clasped his hands together, completely satisfied with himself…

CHAPTER NINETEEN

'Cause this Kind of Shit Happens Every Day...

"DAMN. I FORGOT my phone charger, Viper."

Keeping his eyes on the road, Viper reached over Majesty's lap and grabbed a portable charger he kept in his glove compartment. Troy lounged on the backseat, his headphones on, playing a game on his iPad.

"See? You need to relax. It's cool. I've got you covered." He winked at her and blew her a kiss as she took it from his hands and slid it inside her purse.

"Thank you. I've been so forgetful today." She sighed. "I think I'm excited for Troy. He's never been before, and this is like a dream come true for him." She smiled with her eyes, as well as her mouth. They'd just finished eating breakfast at IHOP, bellies full of pancakes, bacon, and eggs, and now back on the road to Disney World. Viper had been when he was younger, just for the hell of it. Once Majesty had told him in casual conversation that

Troy had never been, he knew he had to change that right away, so after she took her final exam for school, they planned this weekend trip.

Comfortable in his new tricked out silver Ford Explorer, which he'd bought to transport multiple dogs with ease, they listened to radio tunes and chatted. 'My Ex's Best Friend' by Machine Gun Kelly featuring blackbear was the current selection.

Business was booming, probably due to the social media group he'd started, and the fact that a celebrity rapper had recently utilized his services and bragged about him on Instagram.

"*Tengo hambre. Quiero jama*," he mumbled.

"How can you be hungry again after we just ate, Viper? You're like a human vacuum!"

Viper laughed. "Ahhh, you understood me!" She looked quite proud of herself. "Your Spanish is getting better I see. That's great." He switched lanes on the highway.

"You're like a goat. Constantly munching."

"I know… I could go for something though. I'll wait until we get closer, then pull over and make a pitstop."

They kept going and Troy eventually removed his headphones, fell asleep for a spell, then awoke revived and full of silliness and energy.

"Mama, didn't Donte say he just got a dog? I wanna dog, too. Viper can get us a dog. Come on, let's make this happen." Viper smiled at Troy's use of words. He was a natural born salesman.

"Troy, I already told you we're not getting a pet right

now. I'm too busy with work, and you're not responsible. I can't even trust you to take a bath properly."

"Awww, Mama! Stop saying stuff like that in front of Viper!"

"Oh, now you want to act embarrassed. Don't be ashamed. You weren't ashamed when I saw how black the collar of your shirt was the other day. You gonna have those teachers thinking I bathe you in mud!"

"Viper, don't believe Mama. I know how to take a bath. You turn on the water, put in the bubbles and get in."

"You missed the most important part: Washin' your behind! You act like you're allergic to soap half the time, Troy."

"And you act like you're allergic to bein' nice to your only son."

"Troy… Keep on, hear? You're on thin ice."

"And didn't you say that you were allergic to dogs one time? You not allergic to dogs, Mama! You made that up."

"Boy, I don't have to lie to you! I'm the parent here. Not *you*." Majesty craned her head around so fast to look at her son sitting there in the backseat, it was a miracle she hadn't given herself whiplash. "I *didn't* make it up, and I'm not allergic to the point that I can't be around them. I've been around dogs my whole life, but they make me sneeze a little is all." He knew Majesty was telling the truth. Her allergies did seem to flare up a bit when she was at his house, but it didn't prevent her from playing with the dogs.

"So, I can't have a dog 'cause you allergic?"

"No, you can't have a dog right now, but that's not the reason. I already said why, Troy."

"…Oh yeah… you did. I forgot. I was gonna say, though, Mama, like, 'cause if it was because you was allergic, then you could sleep outside on the porch or somethin', and me and the dog could be inside. Until it was time for you to come in and cook dinner for us though, or to use the bathroom. We'd let you in for stuff like that."

Viper burst out laughing, unable to take it anymore. He could feel Majesty's heated glare upon him, but it did no good. He couldn't stop.

"Troy, I swear fo'e God!"

"What, Mama?"

"Keep tryna show off in front of Viper by cracking disrespectful jokes, and I'll have him turn this here car around on account of you being suddenly allergic to Disney World! How'd ya like that?! We'll see who's laughing then! It ain't too late, Troy." The boy drew suddenly quiet and recoiled in the corner of the seat. "You can just relish the *thought* of Mickey, little boy, 'cause you sure won't see him in person!"

"But Mickey isn't a person, Mama. He's a mouse…"

"That's not what that means, and you know it! Viper, turn this shit around!" She was losing it. Viper reached for her arm and then looked back at Troy, giving him the universal expression for, *'Be quiet before it's too late!'*

"Calm down, Majesty. He's just—"

"No, I won't calm down, Dominic. He thinks this is cute. All this money being spent to take him here." She glared back at Troy. "We're takin' your smart-mouthed tail home."

"No, Mama! I'm sorry!"

"Once we get to the house, you can think about what you've done, all while sittin' on the same porch you wanted *me* banished to!"

Viper was now shaking with mirth. It didn't help that neither seemed to understand how very silly it all sounded.

"All right, come on now," He patted her thigh, but she gave him a look of death, then began to stare out the window. "Let's just try to have a good time." Troy was at the age where he was starting to push boundaries. The precarious in-between stage of not being a baby anymore, but nowhere near a teenager.

Every time Majesty and the boy went at each other like this, he'd fall apart with laughter, sometimes even having to excuse himself. Both quick witted and naturally hilarious, he loved how they connected with one another, despite these occasional trivial flare ups. Majesty didn't want to hear it, but he'd told her more than once that Troy was just like her and that was why they bumped heads. Same personality, different face.

Soon, things settled down, and the smiles and laughter returned.

"Look at that, we're only about forty minutes away now," Viper announced, pointing to the GPS. Troy began to bounce up and down excitedly. "Now, the lines are long to pay and park sometimes, so let's take a quick pit stop to use the restroom. I'm going to get some chips or something, too."

He turned on his signal to change lanes and get off on the next exit. There was a bit of construction on the highway, slowing things down, but he managed. Suddenly, a police siren came on.

"Shit," Majesty said under her breath as Viper pulled over to the curb.

"It's all right. I wasn't speeding or anything. My license is fine, too." He glanced back at Troy through the mirror, and for some reason, the boy looked deeply concerned. After a few moments, the officer got out of his car and approached his window.

"Good morning," Viper said, throwing on the charm. "Is there a problem?"

The cop, a middle-aged White man with a thick salt and pepper mustache, glared at him.

"Yeah. You didn't use a turn signal. Let me see your license and registration."

"But he *did* turn his turn signal on. I heard it," Troy uttered, his voice a bit shaky.

Majesty's shoulder slumped as she quietly shushed him.

"Officer, I'm reaching into my pocket to take out my wallet." Viper calmly did what he said. *This is bullshit...* He handed his driver's license, insurance information, and registration to the cop, then the police officer walked back to his car.

"Viper, he lyin'!" Troy's eyes were filled with tears, glassy like lakes and the dark irises so rich, he could see his reflection in them. The sight broke his damn heart. His mouth was trembling, and he kept playing with the hem of his T-shirt, balling up the cotton in his hand and squeez-ing it hard as one would a stress ball. "I saw you turn on the signal and I heard it, too! He lyin'! HE LYIN'!" Troy cried his little eyes out.

"Hey, hey, little man… It's all right." He smiled at the little boy, forcing himself to appear more chill than he actually felt. He reached back and rubbed Troy's knee. "He just made a mistake, okay? Everyone makes mistakes. I know I turned on my signal, too, so I'll just take the ticket then dispute it in court. It's fine."

"Troy fears the police, Viper, because of something that happened last year. Too long of a story to get into right now." Majesty swallowed, then closed her eyes, shaking her head in disbelief. After they'd waited for what seemed like an eternity, another police car pulled up right behind the first.

"Shit." Majesty gasped, now looking as worried as her son.

"It's cool. It's all right," he reassured, though inside, he knew damn well it wasn't. He quickly grabbed his phone from the dashboard and hit record. Without having to be asked, Majesty quickly snatched it out of his hand and placed it in her purse just so, out of sight.

The officer returned to the driver's side window, a smug expression on his face.

"Well, well, well. Mr. Martinez, you've got quite the record. Colorful!" He chuckled, as if amused. "A Latin King from Miami. Big, bad boy, huh? You think you're tough, don't you?" Viper stared at the man, whose face started to turn red. His voice rose in pitch and his eyes got this crazy look in them. "I can't stand gangs. You're like rats! Infesting good cities and neighborhoods, ruining them with your drugs, ghetto behavior and crime."

"Officer, I already did my time. I'm not going to discuss or answer *any* questions regarding my past criminal record. I'm not on probation or parole, I pay taxes, and I know my rights. Furthermore, none of this has anything to do with a turn signal."

The officer rested his hand on his hip, then looked in the back of the car, regarding the child as if he were some animal at a petting farm. He could hear Troy softly sobbing. The man then focused on Majesty for a while, and finally back on him.

"You'll answer whatever the hell question I tell you to answer. Who are these people in the car with you?" the cop asked.

"They're here of their own free will, so what does that matter?"

"Did you not hear what the hell I said? I'm asking the questions," the officer stated sternly. "Now who are these people in your car?"

"My girlfriend and my son."

The officer looked back at Troy.

"Your son? Doesn't look like he could be your son. Where you headed to?"

"Disney World."

"I saw you have a few vehicles registered in your name. A lot of cars, and you live in Boca Raton, huh?"

"Yeah." Viper let out a loud sigh.

"How long have you lived there?" The cop looked him

up and down. "Oh, and uh, what do you do for a living?"

"We're not going to do this… play this game. I am not driving those cars right now. I'm driving *this* one. Any other cars I have are my right to own, as is my business. They're legally mine. I paid for them. My house and the neighborhood I live in, the work I do, the food I ate last night and this morning, the last time I took a nap and all this other mess that you're bringing up have nothin' to do with a damn turn signal, sir, that you and I *both* know I used." He glared at the cop, hating him more and more with each moment.

There was a time in my life when I would give in to my urges and do something bad in situations like these. Something very bad.

"Are you accusing me of lying? I don't appreciate being called a liar, Mr. Martinez."

"Can you *please* just write my ticket, or whatever it is you're going to do, so we can be on our way?"

"I don't like your attitude, Mr. Martinez! I don't know who you think you're talking to. Get out of the car. NOW."

Viper's jaw tightened, and his body wanted to act in a way his mind knew better than to entertain. The other officer came to stand next to the first cop, shoulder to shoulder. He studied both of their badges, memorized their names, then raised one hand.

"I'm getting out of the car."

He moved slow and easy, opening the door with his other hand. All he could hear was the sounds of cars driving past, and Troy crying. His sadness for Troy turned to pure loathing for the officers. An emotion that made his muscles jump and his fingers twitch. As soon as he placed both feet on the ground, one of the officers grabbed him by his shirt and slammed him against the side of the vehicle. He stood there, staring at Majesty through the window. Quiet tears streamed down her cheeks as they handcuffed him, then shoved him, hit him and roughed him up, patting him down and kicking his ankles farther apart. He smiled and winked at her.

For he'd been through this countless times.

Sometimes it had been warranted, but most of the time it was not.

There was no weed, open flasks, or drugs in the car. Besides, he would never put Majesty and Troy in a position like that. The only thing of an alarming nature in that vehicle was the sheer love he felt for the two people sitting within it. The cops went on to rattle off various questions that were none of their fucking business, all while grilling him about how he could possibly afford to live where he lived without doing something illegal. They didn't believe he could be who he was, and not only live, but thrive. After the rough and hostile searching of his body, they removed the handcuffs they'd put on him; he could feel the sting of where the skin was rubbed raw. He was then told to get back in his car, and not move a muscle.

"Mr. Martinez, I'm giving you a ticket for an illegal lane change in a construction zone on the highway, not keeping a safe distance, as well as no use of a turn signal," the cop spat, clearly irritated that he hadn't found anything incriminating on him. "Sit tight."

Both officers walked away, their walkie talkies buzzing, and talked for a while.

Majesty's chest was rising and falling, but her tears had stopped. She simply looked straight ahead, her complexion red, her soul screaming for him.

"I'm not crying because I'm sad. I'm cryin' because I'm mad!" Her lower lip trembled, then she bowed her head.

"It's cool, baby." He lay back in the seat. "This is just how it is. This is what's going on in this country. What I've seen my entire life. I saw my father, my friends, my step-father, one time even my mother get done this way." He shrugged. "They try to provoke you so you can do something that will get you arrested. They wanted me to start trying to fight back so they could charge me with something else that would land me in jail. I knew not to fall for it, but I wasn't going to let them punk me, either. Sad that I'm used to it now."

"We say our lives matter, and they retort with, 'Blue Lives Matter,' and 'White Lives Matter,' but swear up and down they ain't racist. We say, 'Stop profiling me because I'm Black or Brown;' they say, 'Comply, do as you're told, and nothing bad will happen.' But bad things happen in those cases, too, and they *still* blame us. They blame a victim because he's Black, but the White people are told they're just passionate or loyalists, while we get told we're ghetto and hoodlums. They want to keep us in our place, to have us remember who's on top. I deal with the same shit at my job. It's politics over and over again. Been dealin' with this shit since 'We Shall Overcome,' Martin

Luther King Jr., but we ain't overcome, Viper. We still marchin' but haven't gotten anywhere. Just going in circles, sometimes going in reverse, and ending up exactly where we started. We get called looters, they get called patriots! I'm sick of this shit, Viper! I'm tired!" He reached over and rubbed her back. As they waited, he looked back in the mirror at Troy. The boy had stopped crying. In fact, he looked detached. Numb.

"Troy. Mr. T!" Viper called out with a smile.

Troy looked up, those big, sleepy eyes of his focused on the rearview mirror as they eyed one another. Looking *through* him.

"It's okay. I'm okay."

"Viper, Troy saw a family friend get shot by a cop. She had called the police because there was a fight going on where we lived. It was in the middle of the street. I got Troy in the apartment; he'd been out playing in the front with a couple other little kids while I watched from the patio. The police came and Sheryl, our family friend, came out to talk to them, to get them to stop, and a cop thought she had a gun and shot her dead. It was her phone... She was going to show them the video she took of how the fight started so they could arrest the right person." Majesty wiped a tear from her face.

"My baby saw all of that. It happened so fast. For the longest, when he'd see a police officer, he'd start crying right away. They got the whole 'Black Lives Matter' organization for us, but they pick 'nd choose who's important. Her case didn't even make it even to the evening news. Black women get ignored more times than not. We're invisible. Cop came up to Troy's school to talk to the kids about stranger danger, and Troy was in there cryin'… I had to come get him."

Viper's gaze drifted to the little one again. He had his head down, and was fiddling around on his iPad. Yet, he could tell he'd heard everything his mother had shared.

"Mr. T., look at me." Troy did as told. "The best way for us to deal with what just happened is to still have fun, okay?" The boy nodded but appeared to be just going through the motions. "Some people want to ruin a good time. We won't let 'em. We won't let that cop ruin our trip, will we, Troy?"

"No. We won't let him ruin it." His voice cracked as he spoke.

"Keep your head up. We're going to Disney World. The best place on Earth." Viper laughed. "We're staying at an amazing hotel! Our room is on the 20th floor, and it's a suite, and you'll have your own bed and your own bathroom, too."

"I get my own hotel room?" The boy perked up.

"We share the kitchen, and there's a living room and two bedrooms. One of them is all yours and it has a television and everything. We'll be able to see each other if we keep our doors open inside the suite, but yeah, it's your own room and there's a pool in the hotel, too. You can swim all night when we leave the park."

"I get to go swimming?!" He smiled big now, lighting up. Even Majesty managed to smile at Troy's reaction.

"Yeah, you can swim in the indoor pool. You can eat all you want at the buffet, too, and play all kinds of fun games, see amazing shows, Star Wars, all that stuff."

"Mama don't like rollercoasters, though. She won't ride them with me and some of them you have to have an adult with you. Will you ride them with me, Viper?"

"Hell, yeah! Your mama is a scaredy cat about heights, but you and me are like the A Team, Mr. T!" Majesty shook her head and laughed. "And you can ride what you want Troy, as long as your short ass meets the height requirements, okay?" He grinned.

"Yes!" Troy was giggling hard now.

Soon, the officer was back with the ticket, his license and paperwork. Viper took the items and waited for the cop to finish his spiel about him staying out of trouble and walk off. None of them moved or said a word for the longest. Majesty was calmer now, though clearly still unnerved. She pulled out his phone, hit SAVE, then handed it back to him.

"I got the whole thing on video. I even had my phone going too in case they asked to take yours. They brought up your record, Viper, and the one guy let it slip that they hadn't pulled you over for the damn turn signal, then tried to clean it up and backtrack. This is racial discrimination. We're fighting this… Do you hear me? We're going to court, Viper." She tightened her seatbelt around her frame.

"Aye, Majesty, it ain't that serious, baby." He sighed as he took his phone, then placed it on the dashboard and turned the GPS back on.

"What? Are you crazy? Of course it is!"

"Majesty, we're in *their* world. That's why in part men like me created our *own* world. To survive the shit they do to us. Yes, I'm angry, but since this has happened so much to me, it's expected at this point. Because of who I am, this is what they do… They don't want a guy like me to have shit. Do you know how many times in my life people have assumed I'm illegal, or are shocked that I was born here? I've had people ask me why I don't have an accent, and sometimes when I'm mistaken for White, they say racist shit to me about other people. It's crazy." He reached for his seatbelt and put it on. "According to them, I'm supposed to suffer and see myself as inferior."

He pulled away from the curb and merged into traffic. "I'm supposed to grovel, beg and plead. But I refuse. I'd rather die. I knew my rights, Majesty, and I knew if they tried to arrest me or search my car without probable cause, I would fight that, and need proof to show what really happened." *Not that that even matters much in today's world. You can have a full, clear video of a murder, and the courts will still take the murderer's side if he has a badge.*

"Well," Majesty said after a brief silence, "I hear what you're saying, but that still doesn't make it okay to sweep under the rug. That's what officers like that are banking on. For you to keep quiet and just be glad they didn't do you worse than they did. They're making our lives hard, so we need to do the same to them, until something changes. Sittin' back and doing nothing isn't an option."

He shot her a look, then took her hand in his.

"Who said I was going to do nothing?"

And then he headed on to Disney World, bypassing the pitstop, wishing nothing more than to put a smile on Troy's face as soon as possible…

CHAPTER TWENTY
Take the Money and Run

*T*HIS SHIT IS *elementary…*

Why should anyone be applauded for doing what they're supposed to do, when they're supposed to do it? You don't applaud a bird for flying, a frog for jumping, or a lion for roaring. So why thank a man for being a fucking man?

Bitch ass behavior is like the new standard. If you can rise higher than fuck-boy status, somehow you deserve a fuckin' trophy. We're not handing out participation, attendance, and 'good try' awards. EARN THAT SHIT, OR QUIT BITCHING.

So many thoughts ran through his mind. He had a billion plans, but it felt like he only had an hour to implement them all.

A glint of metal crossed his vision.

The clicking sounds of loading a gun always turned him on.

Viper spent the better half of the morning cleaning his guns and then placing them away in the hidden compartment of his closet. Then, his monthly routine was interrupted by a visitor—the man who had brought him into the world. His father.

Dad smelled of oil and transmission fluid. His fingernails were caked with grime and his hands marred with the wear and tear of hard labor. He'd been working at his shop all morning, so Viper was surprised to see the man who rarely came to visit him in Boca Raton.

"Do you want something else to drink?" Viper offered while walking past him to the kitchen.

"No, I'm fine."

Viper grabbed himself a bottle of water and joined the older man in the living room. The sound of barking erupted, breaking the tranquility of the television playing old sports at a low volume. Dad's dark eyes hooded, and a sheen of sweat covered his brow. He stared listlessly at the television. Viper sat across from him.

"You've done well for yourself. I see you added some new art. Nice new furniture, too."

"Mmmm hmmm." Viper lit a cigar, then handed it to his father to smoke. "What's going on?"

"Your mother has been causing me problems."

"What kind of problems? I wasn't aware you two were even speaking."

"We don't. Well, barely. I borrowed some money from her about five years ago. She offered it. I hadn't asked. Needed it to pay off an old debt."

"I gave you money when I got out. You said you needed that for debts, too. What's goin' on with the money?"

"The shop was in the red the first few years. I did a lot

of favors for people, too, and it cost me too much. Shouldn't have been so nice." Dad shrugged. "Bad business move."

"You know better than to take anything from Mamá. She'd always want something in return."

"Well, she got something. So did I. We messed around."

Viper scratched the side of his face, knowing his mother had been married to his stepfather for over twenty years, and Dad was also re-married.

"And you thought that was all right?" Viper drank some of his water, then set the bottle down.

"At the time, yes. I guess so… I don't know, Dominic. It was an arrangement, okay? You wouldn't understand."

"I'm not a little kid. I know how this works. I understand. It's you who didn't understand." They were quiet for a bit.

"You don't understand our relationship is what I'm saying. We still have a connection. Your mother will always be mine. Right now though, she's going crazy about this money. I need your help. She's angry with me."

"What do you want me to do about her? I have nothing to do with this. If you owe her money, just pay her back." Viper reached for a toothpick tin he kept on the crystal coffee table. He removed one and rolled it back and forth between his lips.

"She only wants it because her husband isn't working."

"Doesn't matter why. Just pay it back."

Swirls of smoke eddied from Dad's cigar.

"She stopped sleeping with me."

"So what? You say that like you two are a happily married couple but she's keeping the cookies from you. You're not entitled to another man's wife."

"That's not it. We had a mutual agreement."

"Y'all are divorced, man. I feel like this is a movie. This is wild. Nuts. The cherry on top is that you're both married to other people, but you act like that doesn't matter right now. If Ricky finds out about this, Dad, there's going to be a problem. My stepfather doesn't play that shit, and then I'll have to step in before someone gets shot."

Dad shrugged. "First of all, she's not happy with him. Hasn't been for years. Second, Ricky's cock is broken, she says. He can't get it up because of all the fucking medicine he's on, and the diabetes. He knows she fucks around. They just don't discuss it, and he used to mess around on her, too." None of this surprised Viper, but he was dismayed all the same. "Like I said, your mother is mine. Always will be, regardless of whether she has my last name or not anymore."

"I'm not trying to hear all of this." Disgusted, Viper waved his father off. "You two can do whatever you want to do, but then when everything explodes, you want me to come and bail you out. I just need to know what exactly you want me to do about this Maury Povich, Jerry Springer type shit you two have going on? There's no way you would've admitted this to me unless you just had to. So, what gives?"

"I don't have the money to give to your mother. Can you give it to me, please? I can pay you back over time."

Viper ran a hand along his jaw.

"I just shelled out a bunch of money for my business and some other shit I needed to take care of, so how much are we talkin' here, Dad?"

"Four thousand."

"Is that including interest?"

"Yes."

Viper nodded. "All right. I'll take care of it."

"Thank you, Dominic. Thank you so much."

The silence took over for a while.

"You said you just spent a bunch of money. On what? What did you buy? Another car? A boat? I'd like to go fishing with you soon, like we used to."

A lump formed in Viper's throat. He hadn't gone fishing with his father since he was a child, and in that time it was him and Diego. Those were some of the best memories he'd ever had. He still savored them, and could almost smell the sea water and feel the fresh air and breeze all over again.

"Yeah, maybe someday. I bought that SUV not too long ago that I told you about. I also put down a down payment for a place to train the dogs that's away from my house, and I'm going to put in a pool here at home. Renovations, things like that." He could see the disappointment in his father's eyes. Reconstructions, a pool, and a local business spot meant he was planning on staying in Boca Raton. No one understood completely why he'd moved away. They all hoped it was a phase, or that he'd change his mind and move back to Little Havana. But he'd meant what he'd said. He'd had to go.

"Nah, I didn't buy a boat, Dad. I bought a ring."

His father shot him a curious look. "I wondered when you were going to settle down."

"Remember a long time ago when I had that car towed to you? The Dodge Charger?"

"Oh, yeah. I remember. It belonged to her?"

"Yes. We weren't together then though, but I was trying to get with her. Getting her car fixed for her was one of my ways of trying to get close so she'd let me take her out."

His father smiled approvingly.

"I'd like to talk you out of ever getting married, Dominic. Because ya know, on one hand, it hasn't worked out for me, but on the other hand, every man needs a woman. We weren't meant to be alone. It's tricky."

"I don't think I'll have a problem." He stretched.

"Hard for me to imagine you, my son, Viper, only having one lady." Dad pointed at him, his eyes dancing. "So, you really want to settle down, huh? Women love you, and not just any women but *beautiful* women! You could have your pick. Jesus, do you turn heads!"

"I turn heads sometimes for the wrong reasons."

"Youth, I tell ya… You and Diego got so much attention. Pussy pirates. I was so proud of my boys."

Viper grinned at the crazy man, then they both laughed.

"Dad, I thought about all of that, but I'll take quality over quantity any day. I've run through enough pussy in my life that I could be a track star." Dad burst out laughing. "So, I know what's out there. I've gotten it out of my system. I don't mind only having one woman." He shrugged. "Some guys say they don't want the same pussy every day. Then, to me, they're not making love right. It's never the same. It changes each time because you're growing together, you know. You're a different man, and she's a different woman every single day." He paused, then continued, "Loyalty, chemistry, trust and connection are *never* overrated. To meet someone solid nowadays is so damn rare, Dad."

"It is, son… It is."

"She checks all of my boxes. I'm going to cash in while I have the chance." Viper fell back against the couch and closed his eyes as he massaged his forehead. "Her name is Majesty, by the way. She's amazing."

"Yeah?" He could hear the smile in his father's tone.

"Yeah. Fucking gorgeous, too. She's got a smart mouth though, slick tongue. She can say some malicious shit, and so can I, so we've bumped heads a few times. But I can handle her." He chuckled. "Clever. Funny."

"Does she have any kids?"

"Yeah. One child, a son. I love him, too. Good kid."

"Is the boy's father in the picture?"

He opened his eyes. "He died a long time ago. Murdered in Miami."

Dad placed his cigar in the ashtray.

"Is she Nation? Latin Queen?"

"Nah. Not in the organization…" He resumed twirling the toothpick in his mouth. "Black chick, and not Afro-Latina. She's African American." Dad nodded in understanding. "She's baaaad, Dad. Level ten. Wifey material and playa approved."

"You sound blown away by her. I'm glad you're happy. I'd like to meet her soon."

"You will. The Queens like her, except my ex, Shauna, of course. Marie absolutely loves her. Mamá talked to her on the phone. She liked her. You know Mamá is hard to please. So, anyway, do you want me to give you the money so you can front like you're doing it, or me?"

"I still want sex from your mother, so let me do it."

"Didn't we just go over why this is a bad idea? Something is wrong with you, man." Dad threw up his hands and tossed out a lazy laugh, then shrugged. "If that's your motivation, then I'm not giving you the money."

"Oh, come on, Viper. I'm just trying to be honest with you! Would you rather I bullshit you, huh?"

"Both of you are dead wrong for this shit. I actually suspected something a long time ago because Mamá was bringing you up a lot in conversation with me and years before that, your name never crossed her lips."

"Well, it didn't happen often, and she hasn't slept with me in three years. Closer to four. She felt guilty."

"Well, I'm glad *one* of you did. You two were toxic as fuck." Viper huffed. "I love you, you know that, but you're crazy. I'm not giving you anything unless you promise me that you'll leave her alone."

"You can't tell me to leave your mother alone! Who do you think you—"

"Don't do this shit, try to turn it around, make it some power struggle between father and son. I'm not the moral police, but you're wrong." Dad sucked his teeth, crossed his arms, and looked away. "You're playing with fire, toying with each other's emotions. The only reason why Mamá hasn't told your wife is because then Ricky would know, too. If he dies, what do you think she's going to do? Sing like a bird because she wants to hurt you. You both like hurting each other, and it's messed up. Diego and I grew up surrounded by a bunch of bullshit because you two couldn't get your stuff together. Now you have the boldness to sit here, on my couch, in my home, and try to tell me to stay out of this shit? Ha! Man, father or not, straight up, this is some bullshit and you know it. Don't tell me not to tell you to leave her alone. I have the right."

"It's none of your business."

"You *made* it my business! You think I wanna hear about this backwards shit? I don't! You dragged me into this because you're sitting there, and I'm sitting *here*. I'm not the one askin' for money so I can screw my ex-wife while I'm still married and living with another woman, now am I?"

"All right, all right!" Dad raised his hand in surrender. "I won't do it. I won't ask her for sex. I'm being selfish, I guess. I dunno, but she was mine first, you know? I feel like she will always be mine... But yes, I know you're right. I love Veronica, too. Just differently, Dominic. It's possible to love two women, you know." He grimaced at his father. The man talked more bullshit sometimes than anyone else he knew. "Your mother and I had something incredible, but we wanted to kill each other every other day. I never stopped loving her. It was difficult. It is *still* difficult, after all these years. Then, when we…" His Adam's apple bobbed up and down as he got emotional. "When we lost our son, your brother, Diego, we got close again. I don't understand how I can hate and love someone so much, all at the same time."

Viper excused himself and grabbed his phone from the kitchen.

"I was going to write you a check, but they all say, 'Dr. Dogology.' I want to keep all business expenses separate."

"Ayyye! That's the name of your dog training services now?"

"Yeah. Majesty helped me come up with it. I said I wanted something catchier than 'Dog Training Academy.'"

"That's great, Viper. Funny, too!"

"I'm going to send the money to your CashApp. Then, you send it to Mamá, okay?"

"Yes, yes."

Viper typed the information in, then hit 'Send.'

They talked for a while longer, then he walked the man to the door.

"Like I said, I will pay you back."

"You're my father. I don't want your money. Mamá needs her cash, so just make sure she gets it."

His father nodded, then leaned in and kissed his cheek.

"Dad, I do have a question for you though, since you're here."

"Yes, what is it?"

"Remember that crazy friend of yours who lives in Orlando? The one you met in jail that one time?"

"Maceo… Yes. We still talk from time to time. In fact, I saw him last year. What about him?"

"I had a little problem out that way not too long ago. And based on what you told me about him, I think he might be the man for the job."

"What kind of problem?"

"Harassment. It traumatized my girlfriend's son. I don't like that."

"I don't like that, either."

"I tried to play it their way, deal with it in court, but of course, my side wasn't considered, and I was forced to pay the ticket. The money didn't mean shit to me. It's the principle. You don't get to make a little boy and the woman I love cry, and not pay for that. Walk away like you didn't do shit." His eyes narrowed. The darkness swelled within him, and his forked tongue longed to take a swipe at a motherfucker. The fangs were coming out, and he wanted nothing more than to taste fresh blood. "You think Maceo could help me out?" He smirked.

"Viper, what are you cooking up?" His father gave him a suspicious look, mixed with a hint of mischief.

"I'm cooking some red and blue soup, *papà*, but I have to let it sit and cool. Revenge, as they say, is a dish best served cold. But don't worry, I'll add some heat. I wouldn't be a true Latin King if I didn't bring some of that *caliente* fire…"

CHAPTER TWENTY-ONE

Twinkle in Your Father's Eye

"GRANDPA, MY REPORT card came out last week. I got a B in my English, and the rest were all A's!" Troy exclaimed, his eyes big and smile as wide as the sun that shone down on them in the park. He jumped up and down in front of the man. "Can I have some money? Five dollars for each A, and four dollars for the B. Deal?" Daddy laughed and picked him up, then swung him around. *The fake doting father… What a crock of crap.*

"That sounds like a deal to me, Troy!"

It doesn't matter what comes out of his mouth. It's a lie.

Majesty moved leisurely back and forth on the swing, her lips pursed and her heart beating hard with anxiety. Daddy had called her out of the blue, and she'd accidentally answered his call while browsing her social media.

Damn iPhone... He'd said he was about twenty minutes away and wanted to stop by, and she'd had no excuse to offer to avoid that visit. After being caught off guard, she'd settled into the realization that all the running she'd been doing from the man needed to come to an end, anyway. So, she'd agreed to meet him at the park since she'd been on her way out the door.

The man had to be up to something. Daddy was *always* up to something. The very sight of him bothered her because she resembled him so much. No matter how much she wished it weren't true, they had the same eyes and hair. Daddy looked like Billy Dee Williams with his smooth, wrinkle-free chocolate skin, wavy salt and pepper hair, and a suaveness fit for a charismatic king. Yet, he acted more like the sneaky, diabolic lizard creature, Randall Boggs, from the Monster's Inc. movie.

"Troy, go on over there on that slide and let me see how you go down it!"

"Okay, Grandpa. Watch dis!" Troy ran in the direction of the slide.

Daddy waved to Troy like he was watching some parade, then inched close to Majesty. *Here comes the Greatest Bullshit Show on Earth! Step right up, ladies 'nd gents! Be prepared to be amazed at all the lies one mothafucka can tell in a single bound! It's a bird... It's a train... It's Suuuuuper Liar!*

She held onto the chains and kept on swinging, pretending every now and again that he wasn't even there. All he did was stare at her with puppy dog eyes.

"Daddy, what do you want?"

He had the nerve to look shocked, even throwing up

his arms in consternation.

"Majesty, what in the world would make you think that I want something? Can't a father come see his daughter and only grandson? It's not like I haven't been trying to already." He chuckled, looking about as if he had an invisible audience to back him up. A car drove slowly past. The sounds of an old classic, 'Brandy' by Looking Glass, drifted from the red Honda.

"You either want something, come to dig for information, or are gearing up to ask for something later down the line. This is how you make little deposits so when you drop the bomb, it doesn't seem so out of left field."

Her father's smile faded. She stopped swinging and got to her feet.

"I missed you, Majesty. I haven't seen you in forever. Thank God for Facetime, and Allison sending me photos. And she's not even my daughter; she just feels sorry for me, or I wouldn't even know what Troy looked like! I wanted to see my grandson. It's not fair how you've been doing me. There are no ulterior motives. Now, you can believe whatever you want."

"Thank you, I will… Troy, be careful!" she called out as he abandoned the slide and worked his magic on the monkey bars, showing off, acting like some gymnast for all to see. Last time he'd done a flip, he'd ended up with a bump on his head that didn't heal for several days. His friend had drawn a smiley face on it, and they'd named it 'Freddy.'

"I know I wasn't the best father. I've admitted that before, Majesty. What do you expect me to do? I've been trying. He began to count off his fingers. "I call you all the time... you don't return my calls. I've written you messages on your social media. I get no response or the comment is deleted, and now, you've blocked me. I text you, same thing. You didn't block me on your phone because you know I call to speak to Troy, or I'm sure that line of communication would be cut off, too. What can I do to make this right? I can't go back in time, Majesty, but I can move forward."

She looked down at the dirt and pebbles, the tired grass, and the sneaker imprints along the ground. When she looked back up, Daddy was still standing before her, tears in his eyes. He placed his hand on her shoulder.

"I don't want nothing from you, baby. But I do want to tell you what a great mother you are, and how proud I am of you. I heard you were almost finished with college, that you work a million jobs to make ends meet, and you bought a nice house for yourself and my grandson. Your mother and I made a lot of mistakes, but you weren't one of them. I'd do it all over again if I was guaranteed that I could make *you* again."

She blinked a couple of times, then searched for Troy on the playground. She soon spotted him on a seesaw, jerking it up and down and laughing, pretending there was someone on the other side with him. She couldn't help but smile.

What a silly child. My sweet, beautiful, silly child.

Troy had her father's smile. Damn him.

"Daddy, I've been standing here listenin' to your sales pitch: Your generic tryna-pull-my-emotional-strings-byrustlin'-up-some-tears speech with the shaky voice 'nd all." The man huffed and rolled his eyes. "And I've decided, for Troy's sake, I'm going to try to deal with you. But I can't make any promises." Daddy nodded and sighed. "You're like one of those commercials that goes, 'I won a structured settlement, it's my money, and I need cash now!' You ain't J.G. Wentworth. You think just because *now* you feel like being a father, that you *can* be one. I'm grown now. It doesn't work that way."

"I know what this is about, and I know why you're angry, Majesty. I shouldn't have taken my issues I had with your mother out on you. She made things difficult for me when I left, and instead of fighting harder for you, I ran off."

"Yup, and now you blame her for everything, too, when some of it wasn't even her fault. On top of that, you made a whole 'nother family… Troy! Please don't climb up the slide backwards!"

They were quiet for a spell. Daddy put his hands on his hips.

"Well… Majesty, you look good, honey."

"Thank you." He did as well, but she refused to compliment him.

"How have you been?"

"I've been fine. Just fine." She kicked a pebble around. The awkward silence went from a few seconds to what felt like an eternity. "Troy loves you a lot. That's why we're here at the park. I answered the phone by accident. Guess it was your lucky day."

Daddy stood a bit straighter, smiling big at Troy yet

visibly choked up. He had religiously sent Troy presents over the past three years. To his credit, he'd been consistent. He'd started out of the blue, just like this strange visit. He'd call Troy regularly, in fact. Yet, when he'd ask that Troy pass the phone to her, she'd refuse to engage in conversation. At times, she couldn't really understand why she was being so stubborn. *I guess I wanted him to hurt, just like he hurt me...*

"I do want to say one thing. I appreciate you for trying to help with Troy, Daddy. It's hard raising a child... tryna keep him not only well taken care of, but safe and happy. I couldn't imagine missing out on his life. I couldn't imagine having a child, and then forgetting they even exist." She swiped her knuckle along her eye, the tears stinging now.

"I've been trying to make things right. You told me a long time ago you didn't want anything to do with me after that blow up we had years ago, so I waited for a while. I shouldn't have done that. I should've just called you and apologized. I had much on my mind at the time, including a lot of guilt, and I took it out on you."

In the heat of an argument several years ago, Daddy had told her to stop bringing up old shit, that she was just like her mama, living in the past, and that she'd made mistakes too, such as getting pregnant by a thug who'd ended up dead. Then, to drive the knife in deeper, he'd added that her child was a bastard like so many other Black children in the world. So basically, she'd become another statistic. His words had hurt her to her core—reached in all the way and tore her heart out.

"I tried to treat Troy well, make you see that I was for

real about making amends, but you're obstinate. You didn't budge."

"I don't have to jump when you say jump."

"I know that but look how long it has been. I decided to just drive over here... 'cause I needed to see you. Majesty, why did you never call me back? Text me back? I understood your resistance initially, but why did it take so long? I just have to know."

"I didn't trust you. I had my defenses up. I *still* don't trust you. That wasn't the only time you'd hit below the belt. You didn't come to my high school graduation, either. All because you were mad at Mama because of the child support thing from years ago. I was the one to punish in your eyes. I didn't believe you loved me anymore after that. You just weren't there. I used to call you when I was a teenager, and rarely got a call back. My sister and brother had their fathers who'd come around, but not mine... Not mine." The breeze caught her hair and whipped it about. She wished it would cover her eyes for she didn't want him to look into them.

She didn't want this man to see her at her weakest.

He ran his hand absently over his pants and cleared his throat.

"Fathers, mothers, sisters, brothers... We ain't perfect, Majesty."

"No, we're not. Funny though, I never asked for perfection. I just asked you to acknowledge my existence."

"All we can do is our best. I didn't do my best, and life is short. I'm sorry about any pain I caused you, and I know I caused a lot. I have plenty of excuses, some of which I think are legitimate and should be taken into account, but that doesn't make it any less hurtful to you, and if you're willing to talk to me now on account of Troy, then hey," he smiled sadly, "I'll take it. Come here and give me a hug."

She hesitated for a moment, then walked to him and closed her eyes as he wrapped his arms around her and squeezed. She hadn't felt his embrace in so long, it nearly shocked her system. She began to shake and fight tears. She struggled between wanting to hug him tighter and letting go all together. She decided to simply hug him back. Stay present in the moment.

The afternoon wore on. Daddy chased Troy around, huffing and puffing. She tried to keep from laughing as the kid gave him a run for his money. The old man was out of breath.

"Daddy, I have to take Troy home now. We'll call you this weekend."

"Do you promise?" Her heart beat a little faster when he looked at her like some poor soul in a need of a snuggle. She didn't care how he made her feel, and how he was making her hope. Hope that finally, she might have the father she'd once longed for.

"Yes, I promise." Troy threw himself in his grandfather's arms, then the man put a twenty-dollar bill in his hand.

"Good job in school, young man. Keep it up!"

"Twenty dollars! I'm going to use this to buy a dog, Grandpa!"

"A dog? I think it might cost more than that to get a

dog, Troy." He laughed. "But you could put it towards one, I suppose, as long as your mama says it's all right."

"Nuh uh. I got a connection, Grandpa. A hookup. Mama's boyfriend, Viper; he can get me a dog."

"Mama's boyfriend, huh? What does this man do for work?" Daddy crossed his arms over his chest, his expression sharp and attentive.

"He trains dogs. Bad dogs. He trains 'em at his house, and Mama said he teaches classes on dog training, too, and now he bought a building to train 'em at. But he gotta train and hire um, what's it called, Mama? Taffy?"

"Staff, Troy." She huffed, aggravated that once again, her child was spilling all of her tea to the lowest bidder.

"Yeah, staff. He got a bunch of dogs, Grandpa, and he plays his music real loud. It shakes the whole street… like an earthquake. Sometimes the police come, but when they leave, he got it turned back up again. Mama used to be mad at him. She hated him. Now they call each other 'baby'." *Oh, Lord.* Majesty could feel her face flushing with heat as Troy told all her damn business! "…And he helps me with my math homework sometimes, too. He's good with numbers. And then the cop slammed him against the car. He had a bruise on his arm when we went to Disney World, but it was hard to tell 'cause of all of his tattoos…

"He got a tattoo of a big ol' scary skull and a naked lady, and a crown like the one on a king. And a lion… He slapped Mama on the booty in the kitchen one time when he didn't think I was awake… His friends talk Spanish, too, and I found out that *culo* means ass in Spanish, Grandpa… He was doin' wheelies down the street on his motorcycle… His friend came over one day when I was playin' with his dogs, and the guy had a black eye. Said he got into a fight with some La Raza members… Viper is cool, Grandpa!"

And on and on it went. Daddy thankfully let Troy rattle on without asking her for more details, though it was obvious by his facial expression he was a bit concerned by what the boy was telling him. Daddy walked them to their car. She got in and made sure her son put his seatbelt on. How eager she was to head home, run a bath, and relax.

"Bye, daddy." The man leaned in the driver's side window, kissed her forehead, then stood back.

"Bye, baby. I'll talk to you soon."

She nodded, then started the car.

"Bye, grandpa!" Troy yelled as they pulled away. The short two-minute drive would be over before they knew it. Troy talked non-stop the whole way, and before she could even get in her driveway, her phone rang. It was her sister, Allison.

"Hey, Allison. What's up?"

"Something's wrong with Mama, Majesty."

Her chest felt suddenly heavy. Mama was rarely sick, and she was consistent. Consistently rude. If there was any deviation from the norm, that was definite cause for concern.

"What do you mean something is wrong with Mama?"

"She's acting funny. I just left her house, and she practically rushed me out the door. It's like she was trying to hide something, and I could tell she'd been crying. Her eyes were red and puffy."

"Maybe that damn dog died."

"No, Beijing was there and very much still alive, despite looking like something that had been thrown up."

"Okay, I'll call her."

"All right. Love you."

"Love you too, Allison. I'll call you back in a bit." She ended the call, parked in her driveway, and got Troy into the house. When she called her mother, it went straight to voicemail. She tried again a few minutes later, and then a third time—same thing.

Shit… Mama usually answers her phone, and the few times she doesn't, she calls right back. It never goes straight to voicemail, either. Her phone has to be turned off… "Troy!" she called to him from down the hall. He'd gone into his room, probably to play with his iPad.

"Yes, Mama?"

"Put ya shoes back on, baby. We gotta go to Miami. I need to check on your grandma…"

CHAPTER TWENTY-TWO

Great Balls of Fire

*F*LORIDA IS ONE *of the sunniest places on Earth, yet the people who live here are some of the shadiest people of all…*

Some are shady because that's all they know, others because they desire to be that way.

Some are born crazy. Others become that way over time due to trauma. Either way, it's good to know at least one that is sly, skilled, and insane, and willing to school the younger generations. My father knows of many people like this from all walks of life. Though he was never incarcerated for lengthy periods of time, he didn't tolerate disrespect, and would often suffer the consequences of his hair-trigger temper by spending a little time in the joint. He became responsible for the deaths of two men, one of whom he'd killed in self-defense. He's been in countless fights and has had to engage in altercations at his car shop when people failed to pay and attempted to drive off with their vehicle fully repaired.

Nowadays, Dad has my three-hundred-and-thirty-pound cousin,

Dalian, an OG Latin King with a neck circumference of forty-nine centimeters working part time at the shop to help with these matters, or he would surely go to prison, especially after suffering a couple attempted robberies that resulted in him having to pull out his gun and fire. He's calmed down in his old age. Still, his associations are what they are and his passion for life is very much intact. Unlike my father, I'm not quick to respond. I'm not reactionary, so most people don't know what I'm thinking, or what my next move is going to be. I prefer it that way. Natural camouflage. That's why I can do my dirt in plain sight…

Viper caught his reflection in the glow of the truck's side-mirror. Flames shot out of the house four doors down, as if some imperceptible demon was squeezing a dragon's throat with its bare hands, forcing it to vomit flames until the whole place was engulfed in Nature's fireworks. An ungodly heat spread like chicken pox, and he could feel his temperature rising. He looked back at the house and smiled…

It was two in the morning, and Officer Pinkerton's house was wedged between the Devil's ass cheeks as he farted. Out shot the sweltering demon of fire, bleeding motherfuckin' hellholes as he tumbled from the force of pushed gas and heated intensity. Window shutters fell to the ground in fiery bursts of orange, yellow, and reds. The house had been empty, Viper had made certain of that and timed things just right. He would have preferred that Pinkerton had been home as it would have been the icing on the cake, but the possibility of him being there alone was slim to none, so Viper had settled for the next best thing: The Pinkerton family's two-day trip to Tennessee.

They might as well have been in a galaxy far, far away. While here in Orlando, the motherfucker wielded his vocational racist antics like a sword, but he'd made the mistake of believing Viper was the sort to let the violation slide.

Viper slipped a toothpick in his mouth and twirled it, satisfied with himself. *I did well… That's some good ass work.* He'd doused the entire fucking house under the guise of a yard worker, without ever needing to enter the house and disable the alarm system. He'd even sprayed the yard with fake pesticide and had his white 'Bug and Weed Killer' truck parked out front. Blended right in, like drops of rain in a pool. It had taken time, meticulous preparation, and patience. Viper had all of that in spades.

After digging deep into Pinkerton's private life, he'd discovered a treasure trove of instances of racial harassment, and the man had never gotten so much as a slap on the wrist. His superiors didn't give a shit, nor did the courts. This motherfucker had free reign. But then, Viper had stumbled upon a jewel of a tidbit that had sparked his interest. He'd also found out how much the man hated fire. Once, when called to assist with a blazing building, he'd freaked out and had frozen on the scene. A further investigation revealed that Pinkerton had been in a fire as a child. How fitting. *You give someone I love nightmares; I give you some, too. It's either this or a gunshot to the head.*

Viper had arranged a special meeting after making a few calls to his LK Brothers in Orlando, had them follow Pinkerton, then get an idea of the man's comings and goings. The motherfucker didn't know who he was fucking with. One did not mess with a Latin King Warlord and go on with business as usual. This was why many of the police officers coming to his home about the noise ordinance issue knew to leave well enough alone. They didn't want to be involved with him unless they just had to. Some of the Latin Kings were known to put out hits on any case witnesses or law enforcement that forgot their place. This was one of the reasons they were hated so much: LKs showed no fear. If they were going down, you were coming with them. *Amor de Rey…*

But every and now again, there was someone like Pinkerton, who tested the waters and ended up drowned.

That was when his father's lunatic old cellmate had come into play. Maceo was a career arsonist. He'd only spent time in jail once, during his stint with his father, but not because his work was sloppy. The problem had been his ex-wife ratting him out to get full custody of their daughter. Maceo was often hired by people wishing to get insurance money for their burned down properties. His was a lucrative business he clearly enjoyed. On top of that, the irony of it all was beautiful. The motherfucker was also an ex-firefighter and had tips on how to do the deed and hide one's tracks like one wouldn't even believe. This information couldn't be found on Google or in a YouTube DIY video. It was the type of intel that stayed 'in house.'

Viper had paid him to get the supplies, and to extend his knowledge and assistance in the matter. Now, he was able to sit here and enjoy the bonfire from afar. He'd carried out the deed on his own, followed the instructions to the letter, and even had his father let him borrow an old pickup truck.

Popping a salty peanut in his mouth, he sat back and continued to enjoy the show.

The scars Pinkerton had created would be slow to heal. Troy had experienced a nightmare in the hotel room the first night in Disney World. After a long day of fun, and they'd retired to bed, he'd heard the child's faint whimpering as he'd quietly made love to his mother in the adjoining room at three in the morning. Viper had gotten out of the bed and tossed on his boxer shorts to check on things. When he'd opened the door that separated them and discovered the child balled up in a fetal position crying his eyes out, that had been the final straw. Majesty had slipped in Troy's hotel bed and cradled her child close to her chest. She'd rocked with him and hugged him tight, keeping him in her arms for the rest of the night, even after Troy had fallen fast asleep.

The boy would forever be affected by that traffic stop and had confessed that he had cried in the car on the way to Disney World because he'd been convinced Viper was going to be shot and killed by Officer Pinkerton. No ifs, ands, or buts about it. Troy's trauma ran deep. What Viper didn't divulge to Majesty was that this son of a bitch had squeezed his nuts so hard during the search, his name should've been Christmas nutcracker. His testicles ached for hours afterwards. That had been the pathetic officer's last-ditch effort to provoke Viper to punch or kick to defend himself, to make it appear as if he were fighting and resisting arrest. None of that would have shown up on camera since Pinkerton had cleverly kept it discreet. Who would believe the word of a high-ranking gang banger over that of a seasoned cop with an impeccable record? Viper was no fool. He was a member of one of the most prolific gangs in Southern Florida, certainly the largest. Added onto that was his lengthy criminal history.

If he'd given in to his urges to strike, it would have resulted in him being thrown in prison, and who knew when he'd get out again? His freedom would be gone. His woman, gone. His dog training business, gone. Everything he loved and worked so hard for… gone.

So, he'd forced himself to remain quiet and not give the bastard the satisfaction of knowing the pain he was in. He'd forced himself to think about what was at stake, and how, if he'd just made it through that, his life would not change for the worse. His wrists had remained sore long after the handcuffs were removed, and on top of it all, his wallet had been rifled through and most of his cash stolen after he'd refused to let them search his vehicle, no doubt hoping to find an illegal substance.

Oh yes, that son of a bitch had been desperate for an arrest, and had no issue hiding behind his badge and stealing from people he felt didn't deserve to breathe the same air as he, let alone have a nice car, a beautiful girlfriend, and money to go on a weekend family trip to Disney World anytime he damn well pleased.

You steal from me, I take from you…

And Viper wasn't talking about the money…

Troy had had his serenity and excitement snatched away from him that fateful morning. His woman's peace had been robbed at racism-point, causing her to be distraught both for her own sake and for the sake of her child and lover. Their happiness had been temporarily jilted, tricked into slinking away to allow room for a hideous force to enter and pilfer the simple pleasures of life. Viper glanced at the house burning the fuck down, mad as hell as he replayed the events in his mind that had led him there.

People in the neighborhood exited their homes, moving like sleepy zombies clad in their pajamas and robes. They stood in their doorways or on the sidewalk, holding their phones up as they pointed at the billowing black smoke and glorious flames.

He turned on the ignition. The engine of the old beat-up truck vibrated, then purred. He lit a celebratory Cuban cigar and drove off, slow and easy, like a well-timed thrust in Majesty's tight, wet pussy. The flames dancing in his rear-view mirror looked beautiful with their wide, red hips and upward flowing hair. Shifting in his seat, he snuck a glance at the red rosary hanging from the truck, like the one in the bedroom the night Dad had left.

The gunmetal body of Jesus on the cross caught the glow of the blaze as he rode on past, a flicker of passing light moving across the nails in the Messiah's hands and feet. Fire trucks approached, the sirens blaring. They sounded like broken cries, oozing from the automatons that arrived to put out the infernos of pain… But they were too late. That pain had spun into a mighty wrath, and that wrath erupted into controlled madness. Nothing was salvageable, just like when God had destroyed the world with the flood. This time, there was fire. Two tragic sheep, two ravenous lions, and two guileful serpents loaded upon Noah's ark. The Viper and his shadow counted as a pair…

He turned up the speakers to drown out the sound of the alarms, all crying for a lost cause. He got back on the highway, and as he passed where he'd been pulled over that morning to be dishonored by Officer Kenneth Pinkerton, in the opposite direction going back to Boca Raton, he waved. Masego's 'Navajo' serenaded him on his journey. The snake had left the protective cover of the garden of Eden, and now he'd returned, his belly full and his needs satisfied…

CHAPTER TWENTY-THREE

Diamond in the Rough

M AMA SAT ON the back patio of her beautiful home
in Miami. Her thinning dyed reddish-brown hair,
dry with gray roots, was pulled back in a small ponytail.
There was no wig atop her head, no sparkly jewelry or
$50.00 lipstick smeared across her lips. No plunging
neckline blouse, no diamond bracelets, and no fancy jazz
music playing from the speakers while her housekeeper
cleaned her place to spic and span.

"Troy, go on inside, fix yourself a snack and watch TV
in the living room."

"But I wanna—"

"Now."

Majesty didn't take her eyes off the woman, who sat
with a cigarette in hand. Troy disappeared through the
sliding door, closing it behind him.

"Mama, what's going on? Allison said you've been
acting funny. I'd have to say in the five minutes I've been
here, I agree. For the past couple of days, I've tried to get

in touch with you, but you didn't respond and when you finally did, I only got one-word responses. I tried to get over here a few days ago, like I told you. Drove straight down, no hesitation. You weren't home, or you claimed you weren't. Now I'm back, and I want answers."

"I'm fine." Mama crushed the cigarette into the ashtray on the glass table in front of her and sighed. "Allison is just overreacting because I had a rough night the evening she'd come over. I just haven't been sleeping well. Old age is trying to take hold." Mama shrugged and kept her eye on the swimming pool. It was a tranquil day with a mild breeze.

Mama had bags under her eyes, but this looked less like exhaustion and more like a woman fighting her own demons. She usually wouldn't be caught dead without a face full of makeup, even if it were only delivery people showing up at the door. Yet here she was, with only a pair of small gold earrings and not a mascara-laden eyelash or blush in sight.

"You wasted your time coming all this way, Majesty. I'm fine," she repeated. "Take Troy home. He has school in the morning."

Majesty looked past the patio door. Troy was at the kitchen counter, pouring himself a glass of orange juice. Crossing her arms, Majesty studied her mother. The woman was rocking her leg back and forth and tapping the chair arm.

"Mama, you're not fine, but all right." She huffed. "You don't want to talk. Okay. I can't make you talk to me, so I guess I'll leave. I just wish—"

"Oh, before you go, I wanted you to know that I'm going on a trip to Belize soon!" Mama perked up, though something about it seemed forced, unauthentic. "I saw this amazing bracelet when I was out purchasing my outfits for the trip, and I thought you'd love it. I know you can't really afford these sorts of things right now, but every woman should have nice jewelry and even if you do become a human resources director, that probably wouldn't bring in enough money, either. You know, after you pay for daycare, school loans, Troy's extracurricular activities, food, insurance, rent, and all of that jazz."

Majesty bit her tongue. It took all her resolve to not give Mama a piece of her mind for her cutting words, but something about the woman triggered her empathy. She looked so pitiful. Mama got up from her seat and entered the house, Majesty close behind her.

"I'll be right back. Going to go get it!" Mama exclaimed with a big smile on her face before disappearing up the winding staircase. Majesty joined Troy in the big glossy white kitchen and wrapped her arm around him.

"Grandma actin' funny," he said before jamming a handful of sesame crackers in his mouth, then chasing it with the juice.

"I know…" She kissed the top of his head and rubbed on his shoulder.

"Why is she acting like that, Mama?"

"Because she doesn't handle her emotions well, baby. Some people have a hard time admitting when something is wrong, especially if that something is them."

Her mother soon returned, this time with her eyeglasses on. That damn dog of her's peeked around the corner, then hobbled off.

"Majesty, look at this diamond bracelet, honey. It's so you! I bought a few of them, actually. Had to share."

The damn thing sparkled like the fourth of July.

"Oh, wow, Mama. You didn't have to buy this for me."

"Of course I did. I want you and Allison to always have the best." The woman smiled proudly as she clasped it around Majesty's wrist. Although Mama liked to give her, Allison, and Michael gifts, it still seemed like something was off. Then, alarm bells rang when Mama proceeded to give Troy a barrage of hugs and kisses, a pitiful demonstration of grandmotherly love that was definitely not her style. Sure, she did show affection most times, but not like this.

"So Troy, you can take those crackers with you. I don't eat them anymore. Watching my figure so I can get into my new bathing suit."

Majesty gave her mother a kiss and a hug and thanked her again for the bracelet. Troy waited for her to bag up a bunch of food and expensive treats from Trader Joe's and Whole Foods that she claimed would increase her waistline if left in the house. The three then made their way towards the front door, Mama practically itching to get them out of there. Just like she'd done to Allison.

"Oh, Mama, before I go, I need to use the bathroom. It's a long drive home."

Mama looked a bit perturbed, then quickly fixed her face, as if suddenly realizing she was looking like a loon.

"Oh, uh, yes, of course."

Troy started to talk about the science project he was working on when Majesty made her way down the hall into the powder room, which smelled of bleach and other cleaning agents. As she relieved herself, she looked around. The fancy bathroom was decorated with black and white posters of London. She'd seen it all before. A sleek medicine cabinet hung above the sink and a plush black and white rug covered the tile floor. Her gaze drifted to the towel rack. Typically, there'd be two towels, but she only saw one.

She washed her hands, then made her way back to the hallway.

"And the toy poodle was bad, and chewing up stuff, so Viper taught it how to stop," Troy was rattling on to his grandmother.

Mama turned to her, darkness in her eyes.

"My grandson tells me you're seeing some man who is big, tall, and has a bunch of tattoos, one of which is a damn cross on the middle of his forehead! Majesty! What is wrong with you?!" She raised her arms in exasperation. "You're beautiful! You have a nice home now, you work; surely you can find you a decent man who doesn't look like a walking billboard covered in graffiti! And he's a dog trainer of all things?! I mean, I suppose I should be happy he's not another damn drug dealer, but there's no way that income is stable or lucrative. Oh, my God…"

"Mama, you don't know what you're talking about, and I don't have time for this."

"You come over here and ask what is wrong with *me*,

Majesty? No, ma'am! What the hell is wrong with you?!" She shook a finger at her. "You are addicted to thugs! It's always—"

"But Grandmama, Viper isn't a thug. He's nice to me!"

Mama tossed on a fake smile as she looked down at Troy.

"Oh honey, you don't know any better… You're just a child. Your mother definitely knows better than to do this though!"

"Come on, Troy. Let's go before things get ugly."

"Oh? Ugly like your repeated need to be with men who are incapable of getting normal jobs due to choosing a life of crime, no doubt? Troy told me he speaks fluent Spanish, and so that means he's probably Cuban or Puerto Rican, right?"

"He's Cuban, Grandma."

"Hmph. He probably just wants citizenship, then."

"Mama, you really are a miserable person, aren't you?"

"Well, misery must love company then, Majesty," The woman chortled, amused with herself. "Because you're here, at my home, uninvited. So, if the shoe fits, wear it. I'm going to finish my point, since you want to take pot shots at me. Troy said he looks like a White man with a good tan, so I'm leaning on him being one of those uppity Cubans who think they're White and believe they are better than us. I'm right, aren't I?"

"If he thought he was better than us, then why would he and I be dating? You know what? You're right. I shouldn't have come over here. Bye, Mama." Majesty waved the insane woman off. "Oh, and put your dusty wig back on… Maybe it has magical powers that make you more tolerable. If you lost it, I'm sure any ol' dirty rag the maid left behind will do." Majesty stormed past her, Troy's wrist in her grip as she walked out the door and down the front steps. Mama slammed and locked the door behind them. After she got Troy in the car and ensured he had his seatbelt on, she backed out the long driveway, and merged onto the street.

"I promise, Mama, I wasn't tellin' yo' business like you say I do. Grandmama asked me about it. See, she asked me if you had a boyfriend, and I didn't want to lie. I like Viper. What's citizenship?"

"It's when someone is a citizen of this country. People can't just come here and live without special papers, Troy. Grandma was being racist and trying to imply that Viper came to this country illegally. Viper is as American as you and me. It's not your fault, baby. I don't blame you for what my mother said."

"Why was she so mean today?"

"Baby, your grandmother has some issues, and I stopped trying to figure her out years ago. I am telling you to do the same, or your brain will explode. It saved me a lot of unnecessary stress." She laughed mirthlessly. "I love my mother though, Troy, so that's why I drove us here to check on her. She has some good qualities, but a lot of that is overshadowed when she gets like this."

"She's nice. Sometimes. She gives us a lot of presents."

"Yeah, well, I'd rather she be dirt poor and give me love, than gifts and constant judgment and disapproval." The words slipped out before she could even think about them. Her heart twisted in the cage of her being.

The two were quiet for a while as she headed back home, exhausted.

"I didn't tell her we saw Grandpa. I know Grandmama don't like him."

"Yeah. I'm sure she would've had something to say about that, too. The whole mess about Viper was enough drama for one day. Look, your grandfather and I have problems, too, but at least he came to me as a man and admitted he wasn't perfect and wanted to work on things. I'm not perfect, either, and I was wrong to keep avoiding him so long, so I'm going to try, just like I told him, to see if we can move forward. It won't be easy, but because of my love for you," she smiled at her son through the rear-view mirror, and he was smiling back, munching on something from the bag that Mama had given him, "I'm going to put my best foot forward. Okay, baby?"

"Okay, Mama. I love Grandpa. I love Grandmama, too. She just… I don't know. Weird."

Majesty burst out laughing, then quickly stopped, not wishing to encourage the behavior. Soon they arrived home, and she was surprised to see Viper sitting on her porch, with Sarge at his side. Before she could even get the car in park, Troy had leaped out and raced up to them.

"Sarge!!!" Troy wrapped his arms around the dog, as if it were his long-lost best friend.

Viper stood, his light slouchy blue jeans and light gray cotton hoodie covering his head, and the zipper down exposing his chest, making him look hella sexy.

"What are you doing here, huh?" She approached him

with Troy's goodies he'd abandoned in the back of the car, then gave him a kiss. Viper wrapped his arms around her, pulling her in for another.

"I just wanted to see you."

"I need to give you a key." She gave him another kiss, then opened her front door.

"Sarge, wait right here," Viper ordered.

"Awww!" Troy pouted.

"All right, all right." Majesty huffed. "He can come in. I'll just take Benadryl."

"Yeaaah!"

They all entered the house, and Sarge was looking around in a way that made her laugh. She locked the door and as she turned around, Viper caught her wrist.

"Whoa, whoa, whoa! You cheatin' on me? Whose ass do I need to kick?" he teased. "Who gave you the bling?"

"Oh." She laughed. "My mother. It's her way of telling us kids she loves us, while simultaneously browbeating us." She huffed as she worked her sneakers off. "Troy, are you hungry?" She called out as the boy started to play with Sarge in the living room.

"No, Mama!" he said between giggles.

"I think I need the clasp adjusted. It's a bit too tight. Or my ass is probably just getting big. Probably the latter." She chuckled. Marie had struck again. The woman kept cooking for Viper, and he kept giving her the damn food! She was officially addicted to Cuban food. There was simply no way around it.

"Here, I'll adjust it for you," he offered, removing it from her wrist. She walked into the kitchen, ready to pour them a glass of wine. Viper followed with a strange look on his face.

"What?"

"This is nice, but uh, it's not real."

"Huh? My mother doesn't buy or wear fake jewelry, Viper. Of course it's real!" She grabbed two glasses from the cabinet.

"Baby, I know real diamonds. There are some good fakes out there, but this is just mediocre at best. From a distance, it looks real, but when you look closely, you can see it's glass. This shit is fake, and I should know, baby. I did a lot of hustling back in the day." Viper shot a quick glance at Troy, then lowered his voice. "When I was a teenager, my crew used to sell shit like this all the time. We'd pretend it was hot, like we got it from a real jewelry store, like the shit was real and they were getting a deal. We targeted tourists, baby. This is straight up fake."

She couldn't believe her damn ears.

"You have to be kidding me!"

He shook his head.

"Nah, Mami, I'm serious. It's nice, though. You can still wear it. Many won't be able to tell." Troy kept popping his head up, trying to eavesdrop no doubt.

"Boy, what are you looking at?" She put her hand on her hip.

"Nothin', Mama!"

"In there trying to dip in on grown folk's business!"

He tittered as though he found her comment funny.

"I don't have a problem with fake jewelry, Viper. Over eighty percent of my collection is fake, and I don't give a shit. What I have a problem with is *frauds*." …And Mama is a whole scammer. "Why in the hell would she do something like this?" And then, it hit her. "Oh my God!"

"Baby, what's wrong?"

"I can't believe I didn't see this sooner! That explains it all!" She put her hand up to her mouth. "I have to call my sister."

Brushing past him, she snatched up her purse and removed her cellphone.

"Allison! You won't believe this!"

"Believe what? Mama said something atrocious, didn't she? If that's the case, I *definitely* believe it," the woman stated dryly.

"Allison, it's not that. I think Mr. Gerald and Mama broke up."

"What?! I doubt it, Majesty. She'd tell us, wouldn't she? Why do you think that?"

"Mama is looking and acting crazy. That's clue one. Of course, she was acting all snooty tonight, per usual, but it was extra, like way over the top. There was only one towel in the guest bathroom, too."

"Why is that a big deal?"

"You know there is usually one for her and one for him. He likes to have his own! Remember she told us that a few years ago? Oh, and check this out. Her refrigerator has hardly any food in it. It's always stuffed."

"Yes, I did notice it looked a bit bare. I just figured she hadn't had time to go to the store, or her grocery delivery hadn't arrived yet."

"And here's something else. The maid who's usually

there all the time wasn't at the house. The pool wasn't clean, either, and you know how crazy Mama acts about that damn pool. She's also clearly depressed. Bags under her eyes. She didn't have her makeup on, and not a wig was in sight. That damn dog wasn't on her lap, and now…" She looked at Viper, who stood close by with his big ass, muscular arms crossed. She wanted to run into them for shelter but stayed put. "And now, she gave me a fake ass tennis bracelet, tryna pass it off as real! She's clearly concerned about her cashflow but wants to keep up appearances."

"How do you know it's fake?"

"Girl, my boyfriend knows a fake diamond from a million miles away! She is cold busted!"

"Oh my God! She gave me one, too. Is there a way we can find out if he's gone for sure since Mama clearly won't tell us the truth?"

"Yes. I need you to call Michael but make him promise not to tell Mama that we suspect anything. Call him and ask if he can ask his friend down there at the courthouse if he can check if there've been any filings for a separation or divorce."

"Okay, yes! Yes, I will."

"All right, then after you speak with him, call me back."

"Okay."

Majesty ended the call, her chest heaving. Her emotions were all over the place, feeling both anger and sympathy for her mother. Then, she spotted Troy again. His head popped up like some groundhog's and disappeared again, out of sight.

"Troy! That's the fourth time I've caught you spying on me. What are you doing?"

Troy got up, with Sarge on his heels, and came to stand beside Viper. The man took his hand.

What's going on here?

"While you wait to hear back from Allison, can I ask you something?" he asked.

"Yeah sure, honey," She took a deep breath and rubbed her head. *I can't wait to take a hot shower and get my ass in the bed...*

"This isn't how I planned this."

"Planned what?" She shifted her gaze between the two of them.

"I asked your son, last week, if I could ask you to marry me."

Troy's head dropped, all shy like, but she could see he was smiling.

"This can't be real!" She pointed at her child, truly shocked. *Troy can't keep a secret to save his life.*

"It's true, Mama. It was that day he took me out for ice cream. He lied and said it was because of my good grades on my report card." The little boy chuckled. Heat spread from her body to her face. She gripped the edge of the counter to steady herself. Viper pulled out a gold box from his pocket.

"Viper..." She could hardly get his name to roll off her tongue.

He opened the box and showed her a diamond so big and bright, it was practically blinding.

"Look at that, Mama! That's real! That's a real diamond, not a fake one!" Troy pointed at the ring as if he were some jewelry expert with a keen eye. "And Viper said he wouldn't have to get me no dog, 'cause all his dogs would be my dogs, too, if you say yes. He said, if you want, we can all move into his house and there would be room for all of us! He said he wants to spend his whole life with you. I said he could."

They all burst out laughing.

"Well, thank you, Troy, for giving me away without my permission!" She chortled.

"Come here." Viper took her hand, then dropped down on one knee. "I wasn't expecting you to have a blow out with your mother today, so things got kinda screwed up, but since I'm here, and Troy knew I was going to ask today, I won't let him down. I want to know if you'll marry me, baby? *¿te casarías conmigo mi amor?*"

She bent down to Viper's level, close to the cool ground where the snake lay and waited. Then, she placed her hands along his face and kissed him. Like the frog in the princess stories, she imagined that from her love, he'd change… But in truth, she didn't want that at all. Like Marie had said, *'Accept him as he is…'* Viper was what he was, and she didn't care who didn't like it. Love was love, and if the man on bended knee before her was good for her and her child, nobody else mattered. *Amor dey Rey…*

"Troy approves. I approve. Yes, I will marry you, baby."

Viper grabbed her and kissed her hard as Troy cheered and Sarge pranced around, barking every now and again from all the ruckus. After sliding the gorgeous ring on her finger, Viper stood up. He kissed her again with such passion, her soul left her body. Then, he seized Troy and picked him up, swinging him high in the air, making the kid giggle and scream. After things settled, and her son went back to playing with Sarge in the living room, she poured those forgotten glasses of wine.

"Viper… I'm so happy. Y'all got me!" She took a sip. "I had no idea! Troy is so bad with keeping secrets that he has amazed me with this one."

Viper curved his lips faintly. "I know that you and your mother's relationship isn't exactly the best."

"That's an understatement, but yes." She shrugged.

"You know my mother and I bump heads sometimes, too, but she and I actually get along really well, so I am not actually familiar with what you're going through. But despite all that has happened between you two, I am sure you love her very much."

"I do…"

"And I know you want her to be proud of you, although you pretend you don't care about her opinion."

Majesty couldn't look him in the eye. She gripped the side of the kitchen island and nodded, trying to catch her breath… trying to process the deception and sadness of it all. It wasn't the bracelet being fake that upset her, but what her gesture represented—basically how fake Mama had been all her life. It was reprehensible. Painful. Tragic.

"I know I'm probably not the type of man your mother would want you with, but I was hoping to meet her soon." She looked up at him. "I'm Cuban American, obviously, but my culture is important to me. It's not exactly like American culture." She nodded in understanding. "Where I come from, Majesty, mothers are revered. It's important to try and… what's the word? Protect them. To try to fix what's broken if we can. If it can't be resolved, then there's nothing you can do. But in our case, you, me, and Troy are family now. We were family before I proposed. Even if you'd turned my marriage proposal down, as far as I'm concerned, that's still my son." He pointed towards the living room where Troy was rubbing Sarge's belly and watching television. "I fell in love with you fast. And that's not my style, Majesty. I had no control over it though. It just happened, and I'm not sorry about it. I'm grateful."

She swallowed and sniffed, wiping away quiet tears.

"If your mother doesn't accept me, so what? Won't be the first time someone has judged me without knowing me, but I still want to meet her. I think, from what you've told me, she really does love you, and she does want you to be happy. She's just… broken."

"She is…" Majesty grabbed a tissue to dab at her nose. "Viper, my mother, has been awful at times. I don't care if she meets you or not, quite honestly. All she is going to do is talk down to you, try to belittle you, but knowing you, you'll get into a heated argument with her because I know you well, and culture or not, you won't take her mess, and it'll be a disaster."

He mulled her words.

"Okay." He held up his hands. "Just listen to me. Hear me out. I'm not tryna compare her to my dogs, okay? You know, nothing disrespectful like that, but people like her remind me of them. The hard cases. The ones people gave up on. The dogs people want to put down. I know how to work with broken animals… because I'm broken, too. The only difference is, I know who and what I am, and I'm okay with it. Your mother, on the other hand, is uncomfortable with being broken. That's why she wraps herself in lies and make-believe, hopeful that no one will see her fractures and cracks. She gives you the hardest time of all because you're her mirror; not the fun house mirror, but the real one with the 3X zoom. She fights with you the most because you're braver than she is, and you see her flaws… *all* of them. That's what mirrors do. Reflect the truth. You live your truth while she hides from it. Of course, she has problems with you, baby. She named you Majesty because for a moment at least, she saw you were royalty, possessing the best parts of her… But now, you're her 'mirror-mirror on the wall.' And damn you for not lying to her about who's the fairest of them all…"

She wrapped her arms around him and squeezed, tears trailing down her face. He rubbed her back, giving her the love she so needed at that moment in time…

CHAPTER TWENTY-FOUR

The Graduate, The Mother Hen, and the Snake...

"SHE GAVE WHAT she came to give, and it's givin' what she got, baby! Yaaassss! The new graduate is up in this bitch! My girl got a *whole* master's degree in Human Resources, baby! She ain't come to play-play! It's the Black Girl Magic, for me." Destiny exclaimed, snapping her fingers adorned with long, stiletto aquarium nails, and causing an uproar in laughter. The woman with the bright red lipstick and pretty eyes beamed, then wrapped her arms around Majesty.

Clad in her dark purple satin cap and gown, her heels sinking into her living room carpet, Majesty relished the moment. The house was packed with guests, and the living room couch was covered with presents and cards. It seemed like all her friends and most of her close family members had attended her special day. She caught up on the local Miami gossip, and loved on them hard. Her elation soared through her and the only time she recalled being any happier was the day she gave birth to Troy. Filled to the brim with excitement.

"What time is the hall open?" Trina questioned, smacking on her gum.

"Girl, it's open now," Joy replied before Majesty got a chance. "Gina ain't coming," she added, rolling her eyes. Gina was a friend from back in the day who'd always acted a bit iffy. Her girlfriends that mattered were there, surrounding her, all looking gorgeous and giving their full support. The love was palpable. A few haters stayed home... and she was grateful.

"So, what's the plan now, Maj?" Destiny questioned.

"We are about to roll out. This was a pitstop. Remember I said just follow me home to get these wine bottles, so that's what we're doing." She pointed to the kitchen where Viper was chatting away with a bunch of her cousins, uncles, and aunts. Mama was outside waiting in her white BMW, hardly speaking to anyone, as usual. Moments later, she and her friends loaded up a few boxes of liquor and wine into several car trunks. Some of the vehicles were already full of balloons.

"The cake is in the refrigerator," Viper stated as he closed the trunk on Trina's car and walked around it. "I'll go get it."

"Is Troy riding with Betty or Daddy?" Majesty asked, wanting to be sure who her child would be terrorizing for the twenty-minute trip down to the party hall for her graduation dinner.

"Your father. He's in the car with him right now. He said he was taking him over."

"Okay. We'll meet y'all down there. I need to put some more stuff in Viper's truck." Trina nodded and started up her car, waiting to merge with the rest of the vehicles heading to the party spot.

Majesty walked back into her now empty house. Viper grabbed a large empty cardboard box from all the mess in the living room.

"We can take this for people who show up late and have presents for you at the hall. That way, things aren't spread out and it'll be easier to get everything when it's time to roll out."

"That's a good idea."

He walked out the front door while she made her way back into the kitchen. Opening the refrigerator, she spotted the grand cake her sister had gotten her. A large sheet cake with elaborate flowers, decadent vanilla frosting over a marble cake with her name written in purple on top along with 'Congratulations' and a graduation cap. She and Allison had grown especially close over the past few years, and she savored her closeness with her little sister. They'd always been like this, but it seemed as Allison matured and got away from their mother's at times toxic influence, she began to realize that Mama wasn't the prototype of perfection she pretended to be. She closed the refrigerator door and toed off her heels.

"Ahhh... Damn, my feet hurt."

The straps of the heels had been digging into her skin,

leaving them red and sore. On her way to the bedroom, she heard the faint sound of children playing outside, and the freezer clonking as it made a new batch of ice. She turned on some music and disrobed, then plucked her gray and cream bodycon dress that hugged her in all the right places from the closet, laying it on the bed. Doja Cat's, 'Like That' was playing and she swayed to the beat, feeling the vibe. She closed her eyes, a big smile on her face, snapping her fingers, falling into the groove. Proud. On cloud nine…

"Stop!" Her body was swept in the air so fast, it felt as if she were flying. Her man was lifting her with one damn arm, a big, slick grin on his handsome face. She was relieved when she felt his other arm wrap around her waist, adding support and subtracting from her anxiety. That anxiety soared right back up though when the bastard laughed and spun her around like some damn frisbee.

"Nooo! Viper, stop! STOP!" She laughed and screamed at the same time.

When he lowered her to the floor, she was dizzy, but he held her steady as he pressed his soft lips to hers.

She slapped his shoulder in irritation.

"You play too much." She shouldered past him and began searching for a comfortable pair of low heels. The sexy mama ones she'd planned to wear wouldn't do in her current state.

"Shit, don't get mad at me," he chided, as if truly offended by her response. "I thought there was a party goin' on in here. You've got the music on loud." He stepped back, stroking his jaw and sporting a lascivious grin as she placed a pair of slides on the floor. "And you're butt ass naked."

Their gazes hooked. He looked like he had a dozen and one reasons to ravish her body right then and there. She glanced down at his crotch, where his pants were tented. He smirked when he noticed *she'd* noticed, proud pervert that he was. It was over. And she knew it.

"We have to go, Viper. I'm going to freshen up and change clothes. People are waiting on—"

He shut her up with a kiss. Urgent, needy tongues flickered and danced, and so did their bodies. Viper outstretched her arm, and moved his hips to the beat, as if hearing salsa music. She wasn't quite sure how to move, so she followed his lead into the next song in rotation: 'Rules,' by Doja Cat. His hard cock pressed against her stomach. The motherfucker wanted to drop low, and go *in*.

"Sing the song to me, baby... The hook." he mouthed in between hot kisses along the crook of her neck, then stared intensely into her eyes, waiting. Demanding.

His eyes narrowed to slits, and when the light hit them, they reminded her of a snake's. Glossy and sinister...

"Play wit' my pussy, but don't play wit' my emotions..." she whispered the lyrics as he cupped her pussy. She shuddered when he dragged his lips across her breasts, rendering the nipples wet and hard.

"Boy, stop." She struggled, but the attempt was weak. "People are waiting."

"I'm waiting, too." He pushed her against the wall. "I wanna graduate with honors… I'll show you some magna cum laude… Let me put on a magnum, and cum loudly…"

She giggled at his silliness.

"Come on, Viper. People are hungry…"

But he kept on masturbating her and kissing her all over.

"Aren't you hungry, too? Wanna taste me? Don't you want your king's dick in your fucking mouth, baby?"

His words turned her on so much. It was a done deal.

"Yes…"

Her pussy throbbed with need and moisture collected between her trembling thighs.

"That's what I thought. You love suckin' my dick, and I love eatin' your pussy. I wanna eat you up and swallow you, baby. Mmmmm… It's time to fuck."

Viper went right back to her tits, sucking and licking them, driving her crazy. He knew all of her weak spots and exploited the hell out of them, making her weak at the knees. With her nipple in his mouth, he undid his shirt buttons. His tongue flicked back and forth and all around while he flung his shirt to the side. He stood back and quickly removed his dress pants and boxer briefs, exposing a throbbing, deliciously menacing hard-on.

She whimpered and sighed, both elated and frightened at his roughness. He tossed her dress off the bed and positioned her how he wanted her. Hovering over her on his knees, he grabbed the back of her head and fed his long, fat dick to her, inch by inch. Wrapping her hands around the thick base, she greedily slurped and sucked his nature, the rigid, veiny flesh calling her name. She slipped one hand away to stroke his abs, watching his lips part and his eyes hood as he fucked her mouth, harder and harder.

"That's it, baby... Suck it... Fuck, you give good ass top! Open wider..."

She did as he asked and he pushed more of himself in her mouth until she could take no more. She could feel her perfectly done mascara going to ruin as trickles of sweat raced down her cheeks. She sucked harder, almost orgasming from the sounds of his groans and the way his dick felt along her tongue. She stroked his soft, black pubic hair, then his balls.

Soon, though, he pulled his dick out of her mouth and slammed her on her back, then burrowed between her thighs, her legs over his shoulders. All she could see when she looked down was black hair, muscles, and tattoos.

"Shit! Oh shit!" She snatched a fistful of sheet as the man terrorized her pussy, sucking and licking in a frantic then slow rhythm, over and over. "Eat my pussy, baby! Fuck, that feels good! ... This is inconsiderate... Oh, God! People are... People are waiting... peep-pull... People are wait...ing on uuuussss! SHIIIIIIT!" She came hard, her back arching as she lost all sense of time for a moment, damn near forgot her own name. He kept going, shaking his head back and forth as he gripped her around the waist, dining on her with enthusiasm and vitality, as if his very existence depended on getting her off. She came again, then again, then fell against the sheets, exhausted...

Some time later, she heard him open the drawer where

she kept condoms for when he'd spend the night. She listlessly looked at him as he sheathed himself, seeing two of him, her head still spinning. He made her so high. Viper fucked her and made her crazy. He made her hallucinate, his loving so good… inebriated from his addictive kisses and damn good dick, each and every damn time.

"Get your sexy ass over here." He slipped a pillow under her behind and thrust his dick in her pussy, without preamble. With his wind-knocking stroke, her soul collapsed. But then his soul picked her back up…

"God!" She clawed at his chest and stared up at his placid expression while he tore her in two. He fucked her ruthlessly until he was balls deep. She'd never gotten completely used to his size, even after all the times they'd made love. But he did it so well, she couldn't give it up. She didn't care that she customarily couldn't walk straight for a few hours after he'd turned her inside out. The impairment was worth it. "Dominic! Shit!"

The bed groaned beneath them as he gave it to her, showering her with delicate kisses all over her breasts and neck. Masego's and Don Toliver's, 'Mystery Lady' started to play, and he slowed to the beat. Torturing her. He slipped one hand beneath her head and his tongue in her mouth. They kissed leisurely while his hips and tongue moved to the beat of the music. With closed eyes, she fell into his dream, escaping the nightmare of her past. His love was her 'good morning,' his lust her 'good night.'

He clasped their hands together and she burst free, her orgasm firm and strong, flowing and lazy like the rivers and lakes she was used to, and the oceans, too…

His pace increased, their bodies soaked in sweat and their limbs sliding against one another like twisted Georgia Candler oak tree branches covered in Spanish moss. He was wound around the golden apple tree in the Garden of Eden, warning her that her beloved was an unworthy abomination, and he was *her* true King… *Amor de Rey*…

"…Ahhhh… Ahhh…" And he came, his body spasming as he filled the condom with liquescent warmth. His hand squeezing hers, he buried his face in the crook of her neck while she lay content. Happy. Free. Her lover's muscles locked and released, and his heavy groans and sighs poured from his mouth in uncontrollable, raw, wild ways…

His were no quiet whispers or subtle hisses. He came with all that he had in him, and the way he held her as he spent the very last drop, the way he slowly kissed her face while his body kept trembling said it all.

> *The Viper had shed his skin…*
> *An old soul with a new heart.*
> *He was here.*
> *He was hers…*
> *Forever.*

THE AROMA IN the house reminded Viper of the smell of the hotels in Disney World. He noted how clean everything was. Sparkling. He'd dressed well in a loose white shirt, buttoned halfway down, and matching white pants and loafers. Although he'd made no effort to hide his tattoos that proved his associations, he had taken extra care to get a good shave and haircut. And of course, his favorite cologne, Tom Ford's, 'Fucking Fabulous.' He could hear Troy and his cousins playing, as well as Majesty and her sister laughing in a room on the second floor of his soon to be mother-in-law's Miami house. They'd left to give him and the lady of the house some time alone, per his request. Jazz music played throughout the house, and across from him, the Queen had arrived.

Dressed in a flowy pale-yellow dress and a short black pixie cut wig atop her head, the stately woman took her throne upon a gold and silver couch, a glass of iced tea in one hand and a long, skinny cigarette in the other. She'd offered him nothing to drink, eat, or smoke. She'd offered nothing, but a look of total disdain.

They stared at each other, then he let his gaze drift to the décor, noting the art and mirrors hanging in the palace of a house. Nice, but overdone. The entire place was dripping with female dynamism. Devoid of male energy, and full of estrogen. He could not detect any balance.

"Majesty let me know that you wished to speak to me. Two weeks ago, at Majesty's party, you and I didn't have a chance to talk much." She crossed her long legs.

"You decided that. I had attempted to speak to you at the graduation party, like I had with her father, brother, and sister. I spoke with them at length…but you walked away."

The woman glared at him, then shrugged. Unbothered.

"Okay." She rolled her eyes, as if bored. "Since I see you don't need to be handled with kid gloves, I will say I don't like you, Dominic. You're not good enough for my daughter. You may have, I don't know, put your old ways behind you, and although my child is a hard worker, she needs to start being a hard receiver. I am tired of her struggling. I am tired of Black women struggling, period. She deserves someone who has good income, is financially and mentally steady. You know she has a child, my grandson, and from what she tells me, you're good with Troy, but that isn't enough. I do not want my daughter dating, and definitely not marrying, someone who is in a gang, has spent time in prison and is uneducated. This isn't a racial issue. It's a character issue." She took a taste of her tea, then set it down on a cork coaster along the long glass table that separated them.

He leaned forward and ran his hand along his jaw. Thinking.

"Mrs. Gerald, with me, what you see is what you get. I don't pretend to be someone other than who I am. I presented myself to Majesty, Troy, and now to you in a way that is authentic." *Something you know nothing about.* "So, although, in a perfect world, my fiancée's parents would like and embrace me into the family, I have had enough disappointments in my life to be happy when things go better than expected, yet not distracted when they don't go my way. I've endured too many storms to be worried about one single drop of rain. Now, here's how it is. Number one, I'm not going to apologize for being a Latin King. I'm not going to apologize for being Cuban, either."

"I don't want an apology, and you being Cuban, as I stated, is not my concern."

"You say it's not a race thing, but to me, the fact that you even brought it up shows that that isn't true. Now, here's the thing," he cured an itch on the side of his eye and continued, "I'm marrying your daughter. You can either be there, or you can choose not to. Majesty and I love each other, and I'm not giving her up for nobody. I respect you. I respect your right to do what you want, say what you want, and tell me how you feel. It doesn't bother me in the least. The only thing that would bother me is if you take your feelings about me out on Majesty." He shrugged, then flopped back against the couch. "It's really just that simple."

The older woman sipped a little more of her drink, then took a drag from her cigarette, which she set down in a white owl-shaped ashtray. She cocked her head to the side and studied him for a long while before speaking.

"My request is also simple. You'll never be accepted into this family. I want you to stay away from my daughter."

"And I've told you, respectfully, that I don't give a shit what you want."

They stared daggers at one another.

"My grandson is impressionable. He doesn't need someone with your background influencing him! He has already had a father that was just like you! It's not fair that you—"

"Yeah, and his mother was impressionable at one time, too. And yet, you fought, yelled, screamed, and made all kinds of unpleasantness around her as she was growing up."

"You weren't there, you have no right to speak about what went on in my household and try to judge me as a mother."

"And you weren't there during my childhood, or when I was in prison, or anytime during my past or present, and yet you sit there and judge me as a man like you know my whole life story." She snatched her cigarette from the ashtray and took a puff. "Yeah… I can play the same game you can, only better. As if you were mother of the year."

"I'm a damn good mother, and you don't have children of your own to say a damn thing about me, boy."

"Damn good mother? You told Majesty she wasn't going to be anything."

"I never said that to her! Did Majesty tell you that?"

"You said it. I could see it in her eyes when she told me about it. She wasn't making that shit up. Majesty isn't a big liar, like some people who lie about diamonds that are actually no better than some crap from a bubblegum machine…" The woman's nostrils flared. "You told her that she would amount to nothing even before she got pregnant, so don't sit there and act like you're all about the fuckin' kids. Like Troy's safety and happiness are your main priority. Like you got an A+ in child rearing. And who the hell are *you* to judge *me*," he pointed to himself, "or Majesty, when you have three baby fathers and a reputation as one of the biggest gold diggers in Miami in the '90s? Fuck outta here." He snarled. "And Majesty will tell you, I don't even have a problem with gold diggers and whores; I knock nobody's hustle. But what you're not going to do is sit here and turn your nose up at me when your house is made of glass, just like the rest of ours."

Not once did he raise his voice or let her take him off his center. There was no need for yelling and carrying on. The woman was out of order. She could do this the easy way or the hard way, and he knew how to handle broken people who tried to break others. You beat them at their own fucked-up game.

"How dare you come into my home and speak to me this way?!" Her voice shook.

"You don't respect people who let you walk all over them, Mrs. Gerald." He licked his lips and shrugged. "I knew when I walked in the door what I needed to do if you decided to come at me like this. Majesty didn't have to tell me a thing about you for me to see what and who you really are. Just like most if not all of what you said about me is true, the same applies to what I said about you. I *am* a gangbanger. I didn't graduate from college. I have a history of violence against fellow men. I have stolen things. I have hurt people. I have robbed. I have killed. You, Mrs. Gerald, have destroyed. You have deceived. You have alienated. You have broken hearts. You have cheated. You have fucked your way to the top, using the beauty you once had and your gift of gab, and faking class, to reach men of means. You can't treat me how you treat your kids, talk to me how you to talk to them and expect it to fly. To think that shit is going to roll. I'm not Majesty. I don't know you. I didn't come out

363

of you. I don't give a fuck." He shrugged. "I don't care if you like me. Yeah, it would be nice, but I won't lose a wink of sleep over it. The show must go on."

"I want you outta my house, and out of my daughter's life. You're trash! Why can't you just leave my daughter alone, huh? Money? You want me to pay you off or something?" He laughed and shook his head. The woman was unbelievable. "I'm sure you can get someone else, Mr. Martinez! Despite you using your body as some human etch-a-sketch, I can see under all of that... art... that you're actually a nice-looking man. Get another woman! Geesh! It's not that hard! Yes, Majesty will hurt for a short time, but she'll be okay eventually. She's strong."

"She is. But are you? You're fighting awfully hard for something you have no say in."

The woman leaned forward. Her eyes turned to slits as she pointed her finger at him, menace in her expression.

"I would be wrong to not fight for my daughter and grandson. I don't want you for my daughter, and neither does God. And yes, motherfucker, I'm strong as they come!"

"Strong people don't usually have to announce their strength. They just show and prove. You're really something." He laughed, and she seemed at that moment as if she wanted to choke the life out of him. "I never tested to see just how true your words are... you know, Majesty's strength levels. I don't have to bend Majesty in all sorts of crazy ways, break her down, hurt her, to feel powerful." He smirked. "Unlike her mother, who needs others to suffer to feel mighty. As far as moving on to another lady, well, I don't want another woman, Mrs. Gerald."

"You may not want another woman, but she *needs* a different man."

"Let me paint a picture for you." He grinned and raised his hands in the air. "Picture it. There's a bunch of cereal in the breakfast aisle, right? Rows and rows of boxes. Ya got Cheerios, Frosted Flakes, Fruit Loops… those are Troy's favorite, the classics. You've also got hot cereal like oatmeal, and all these new ones poppin' up like Oreo, and coffee flavored, shit like that, right? And lo and behold… in the midst of all of this is your daughter. Majesty Rings, something like that. She's the only box that looks the way she does, and boy does she taste good. She's expensive though, and there aren't any coupons, Bogo, store specials, nothing like that, but you know you're getting your money's worth if you grab her while she's there.

"She won't be on that shelf long. She's most wanted, and one of the last boxes of her type, not just the store, but the entire country. So, you see, your daughter is the only flavor and brand that calls to me. She's top shelf. I've had many types of cereal, Mrs. Gerald, but Majesty Rings are bar none the best. To top all that, she's got a prize inside, one that's just for me…"

He winked and chuckled. Majesty's mother grimaced and sucked her teeth. "I've got my spoon and bowl ready. I was *born* ready for your daughter, Mrs. Gerald. So, I did what any man in my position would do. I put on a bib and brought her home, and I must say, Trix are for kids, but I don't play games. I know that I'm Troy-tested but apparently not his-grandmother-approved. The only approval I need, though, is Majesty's, and she's greeeee- aaaaaat! Little Tony the Tiger for ya! She's magically delicious, too." He cackled.

"You're crude. Rude. Disgusting."

"I don't know what you're talking about." He laughed all the harder. "I'm just giving you an analogy about why I won't walk away from your daughter. You know what's crude, rude, and disgusting? The fact that if I did what you asked, you don't care how that would affect her and Troy. It's all about you. What you want. You're broken. We're alike. You hate me because I'm you, only I don't lie about my ugliness. I embrace it."

The woman's chest rose and fell, and she looked like she was about to have a fit.

"I've got a business. As you know, I train dogs. I train people, in my own way, too. And what you're not going to do is mindfuck me, like you do everyone else, and hurt Majesty anymore. This ain't about you. It was never about you. This is about your eldest child who has fallen in love with someone who can do all of the things for her that you claim I can't. You have no damn idea what's in my bank account. You don't know how much money I make, or anything about my mental health. You don't know my beliefs, and you don't know what I do for your daughter and how she feels about me, down to her bones—because you never asked. You looked at me, heard something or other about my past, and you ran with it."

Her eyes narrowed on him, obviously sickened by his words. "Only God can judge me, and speaking of God, don't tell me what God thinks of Majesty and me."

"I know the God I serve wouldn't approve of you."

"You honestly think that when we both die," he wagged his finger between the two of them, "God is going to look at you, with all of your fancy clothes, and say, 'You've been amazing, in spite of the way you treated your children, friends, and family, and all the sleeping around you did, and the lying, manipulating and hurt you've caused, but *THIS* motherfucker,' talking about me of course, 'is going *straight* to hell because even though he told the truth, and he treats his girl, his mother and father well, and loves his fiancée's son, and helps animals, he's *still* Cuban, has tattoos, and used to gang-bang.'"

The woman's face turned a deep shade. She picked up her cigarette once again and smoked.

"This isn't going anywhere. I'm no longer sure why you're here, Dominic. Majesty told me that you wanted to meet me, introduce yourself, and have a civil conversation, but all you've done is devalue, argue, and try to convince me that I should accept what's going on. I don't accept it."

"I never tried to get you to accept what's going on. I told you that if you didn't accept it, then that was on you, that it wouldn't stop anything. I'm speaking candidly. If you do right, shit won't go left." He shrugged. "That's all there is to it. You can either be treated like a queen from me, because that's exactly what I'd do for the mother of my wife-to-be, or you can lose all communication with Majesty. Because we both know she'll choose happiness over deceit. *The viper over the mother hen...* She's at her wits end with you. You don't have the right to talk about anyone's marriages, either. When she asked you about your own marriage, you looked her dead in the face and lied."

The woman swallowed, and her eyes bucked. She clutched her blouse.

"What are you talking about? I didn't lie. My husband is away on business."

"Your husband fucking left you. Stop the bullshit. Majesty knows. Allison knows. Michael knows. You've been pretending to be someone you're not since before Majesty was even a glint in her father's eye. You can't con a retired con-artist. The very first time Majesty even said anything to me about you, just a few short words, I had your number. There's nothin' original about you. Faking the funk has been going on since Adam and Eve were in the Garden of Eden. You can fool the gullible, but you can't fool the King."

Her face turned ashen now, as if she were about to pass out, and she visibly trembled.

"How long has she known?"

"She just found out for sure last night, but she's suspected it for weeks. Majesty is smart. You raised a very intelligent woman, so you really shouldn't be surprised." She turned away and gave a half nod. They sat quietly until Majesty entered the room. After surveying the situation, she turned and walked back up the steps, without so much as a word.

The older woman sighed, then got to her feet. She picked up her iced tea and took a dainty taste, her baby finger extended.

"It's apparent you'll be marrying my daughter against my wishes."

"Yup."

She casually nodded and continued to drink while the ice clinked and clanked in the glass.

"I do appreciate how you stand up for my daughter." And that was all she said before leaving the living room.

He ran his hand along the side of his neck, closed his eyes, then yawned.

You train people how to treat you. What you accept or not accept shows someone what you're willing to accept them doing to you. Humans aren't so different from dogs. There are always those who wish to follow, be a part of the group. We want to eat well. We want to fuck and mate. We want to have fun, play, and run around. We want to be held and loved. We want to belong to something greater than us. But there can be only one leader. One alpha. A gold and black Viper leads the pack...

CHAPTER TWENTY-FIVE

Passing the Collection Plate

HE COULDN'T RECALL the last time he'd been to church.

His *abuela* was Roman Catholic, as was most of his family, but this was different from what he recalled as a child. Much different.

Viper looked around, hands on knees. Today, he'd dressed in all black slacks, shirt, and Givenchy dress shoes, along with a large diamond crucifix around his neck. He and Mr. Earl sat in the second pew of the place of worship, his head bowed while Reverend Miller cradled his bright red Bible and spoke of duplicity and disobedience.

"Genesis 3:1 says, 'Now the serpent was craftier than any other beast of the field that the Lord God had made. He said to the woman, "Did God actually say, 'You shall not eat of any tree in the garden?'"

Sweat gathered at Viper's temple. It was hot inside the sanctuary, yet he was at peace. Just like when he'd entered Mr. Earl's home the day prior. Just yesterday, the old man had been trying to get his mail into the house, and as he'd ridden past him on his motorcycle, he'd paused to help him gather his letters and packages. The older man had invited him inside where he'd immediately caught the distinct aroma of sautéing beans and onions, cornbread, and that 'old people' scent that transcended time. There was comfort in that, reminding him of his *abuela*, gone so long ago...

What began as a common courtesy ended up with the two of them talking at a long dining room table adorned with a white lace runner, and surrounded by gaudy gilded frame art, mostly of a White Jesus and his disciples. Mr. Earl asked if he was religious. Viper said, 'Sometimes.' And that was the honest answer. He believed in God. He believed what his *abuela* had taught him as a child when she'd take him, Diego, and his cousins to her church, but he was not convinced that everything occurred in the manner it was written. Regardless, he respected the older man's views, but what he really clung to was this old man's love for a woman who no longer walked the Earth. He still had faith in what he could not see or hear.

Mr. Earl believed his wife, Arnette, was still in that house. Perhaps she was. He'd met her once. She'd brought him a delicious homemade pie, and then, just like that, she was gone.

Now here Viper sat, in a church. The minister went on, and he listened to the gifted orator with the silver tongue speak, even as he slipped his phone from his pocket to read the new text from Jaguar…

I need to speak to you privately. There's something we need to discuss…

Jag had been out and back in Miami for two weeks. In that time, Viper had greeted the man with cigars, coffee, and alcohol. As the others had done, he'd placed money in his palm and embraced him. He attended a huge party in Jag's honor and made no moves to engage in heavy discussions. But the time had come for deeper interaction. A High Crown King meeting.

Viper placed the phone back in his pocket as the church members kept on humming and encouraging the minister to continue speaking with head nods, utterances of understanding, and affirmation. Black churches intrigued him. He'd been to two in the last year, for funerals of his homeboys. Yes, though not the norm, there were Black Latin Kings as well, and some of them had passed on, just like most gangsters in the world.

"We may eat of the fruit of the trees in the garden, but God said, 'You shall not eat of the fruit of the tree that is in the midst of the garden, neither shall you touch it, lest you die.' But the serpent said to the woman, 'You will not surely die. For God knows that when you eat of it your eyes will be opened, and you will be like God, knowing good and evil…'"

He looked over at Mr. Earl, who was nodding in agreement, his eyes closed as he rocked back and forth to a song only he could hear. Dark brown, heavily veined hands clenched one another as he prayed. Yesterday, they'd been surrounded by ghosts. In that old man's house, while sitting at the dining room table with the dim lights, and the paintings of the Savior, he'd said to him while they drank beer, "My son used to come with me to church. He grown. Moved on now. Doin' his own thang... don't come no more. I go by myself."

Viper had taken a sip of ice-cold beer from his bottle. All was quiet around them, with only the rattle of an old icebox in the garage interrupting their conversation. And in that moment of silence, he'd said, "I'll go with you."

So this morning he drove to the old man's house in his Bugatti, and Mr. Earl's eyes lit up like headlights. He helped him inside, and they rode in style to that over-packed church full of Black and brown faces, surrounded by so many crowns: kinky curls, ebony braids, silky black, red, and blond tresses, oversized hats adorned with feathers and fruit, and shiny twists. The place was alive with the flavor of heaven and the warnings of hell. Viper could feel strange yet soothing vibrations throughout his entire body as the choir sang about better days to come, and how God would never turn their back on them. The organ player, the pianist, the guitar players, and drummers were covered in the blood of Christ as their talented fingers helped usher the soulful melodies from the mouths of faithful women and men draped in thick robes. All for promises of eternal life and walking streets paved in gold. Back and forth the choir swayed, a series of bodies in sync. The place was on fire with spirits. A fast seduction of epic, poignant proportions. Swaying... Swaying... Swaying...

And he sat there, remembering the rosary swinging back and forth in that little room while he was cowered in the corner, full of fear and regret. Soaked to the bone from the rain and told by his big brother to be a man, to never cry. Jesus was his big brother, too. Perhaps, God had been waving that rosary to get his attention? Maybe it had been a visit from the Father, the Son, and the Holy Spirit? Maybe God himself had been trying to hypnotize him before it was too late…

"…So, when the woman saw that the tree was good for food, and that it was a delight to the eyes, and that the tree was to be desired to make one wise, she took of its fruit and ate, and she also gave some to her husband who was with her, and he ate…"

Golden apples. Where was Adam? Hiding in the darkness of the bush, while I was coiled on the branch, trying to talk her out of it. This can't be true…

His mind began to torture him with the dream he couldn't let go. It had felt so real. An Eve of his own, with the face of the woman he loved. The Viper and his Majesty. *Then, the human man, a mere mortal, who hadn't earned her love or her keep, stole her away…*

He was dragged out of his deliberations by an uproar of applause, so he joined in the clapping. When service was over, and Mr. Earl had introduced him to several people, during which time he had to shake hands and hug people he didn't know much to his dismay, they finally left.

"How are you and that young lady gettin' along?" Mr. Earl asked after a bout of silence during the ride back.

"That pretty girl with the nice boy that lives 'cross from you." The man had a gleam in his eyes.

"We're getting married."

That earned a smile from Mr. Earl.

"That's fine… That's good. That's a beautiful thing."

"Majesty told me that you tried to encourage her to go out with me."

"Mmm hmm." He looked out the passenger window. "I did."

"Why'd you do that?"

The man took a while to respond, as if gathering his thoughts. "'Cause I don't believe God put a man like you 'round a woman like that for no reason. I seen how you looked at her. I know she's a pretty lady, but you looked at her like there was more to it than that. I saw how ya handled her boy… How you'd play ball with him in the yard. How ya'd sit on the porch wit' him, drinking water 'nd such, talking and reading. I then seen you bring those dogs over for him to play with in his yard, too. And you even let him walk one every now and again… Then slide him some bread."

"You're observant." Viper wasn't surprised.

"Naw. I'm just bored and nosey." They both burst out laughing. "You two remind me of my wife and me. I was unsophisticated. Too dark. I'd already been married once before and had a son. Didn't make enough money. Her parents didn't like me."

"Hmm, you must've been a fly on the wall at her mother's house the other day." Viper chuckled.

"I take it you didn't get a standing ovation from her?"

"Not at all. After a confrontation and words were exchanged, I got shown the door."

Mr. Earl shook his head, as if that were a true pity.

"What about your folks? Do they like 'er?"

"My mother's only concern is that Majesty doesn't know how to cook Cuban food, and she wants me to give her grandchildren and hopes we will take care of that. Both issues are quite serious to her, and my father's worried that I will end up just like him." He shrugged. "But yeah, they like her."

"Well, good cookin' can be taught. She's got a grandson comin' through marriage which is sometimes better than blood, and *you* decide who you become and whose footsteps to follow. You ain't said nothin' that can't be addressed." Viper couldn't agree more. "I seen you got someone diggin' 'round in your backyard."

"Yes, I'm putting in a pool."

"That's nice. Are you and Majesty planning to move away after the wedding?" Even though the old man was smiling, there was something in his tone that let Viper know he didn't want that.

"No. Actually, we worked out a plan where she and Troy will move into my house, since it's the bigger of the two, and I'm going to pay off her property, since she has a rent to own contract, and then we're going to rent it to a friend of mine. Marie. She'll stay there with her daughter and run her catering business out of it. She's like a second mother to me."

"That's nice! Sounds like y'all got it all planned."

He pulled into Mr. Earl's driveway and helped the man

out of the car. Holding onto his arm, he noticed the man seemed short of breath as they made their way towards his front porch.

"Are you okay?"

"Oh, just tired." He smiled wistfully. They entered the house and the alarm went off. Viper followed him inside to the kitchen after he'd punched in the code, to make sure he was truly okay. Viper washed his hands, opened a cabinet, and pulled out two glasses. Then, he grabbed a fistful of ice from the freezer and poured them both glasses of water. Mr. Earl sat at that kitchen table, looking aimlessly towards the window. Outside was a big lemon tree.

"Arnette planted that lemon tree." He smacked his lips then drank some water. "You like lemons?"

"Who doesn't like lemons?" Viper grinned.

"She'd take the lemons off, bring 'em in the house, wash 'em, and there would be fresh lemons in the tea, on the baked chicken and fish, lemonade, lemon pie, lemon cake, lemon puddin', and lemon in the water for weeks on end. And I loved it." His tone held so much nostalgia. "Dominic, get that thang outta there for me." He waved towards a drawer by the sink. "It's a tin box."

Viper got to his feet and opened the drawer. Inside was an old Bible, a gun, and a tin box. He placed the box before Mr. Earl, then sat back down. The old man opened it and removed a pipe and some tobacco.

"People are like lemons," he finally said after getting situated. The room began to fill with smoke. "See, you got some that get picked too early, forced to serve up themselves too fast, and it ruins they whole life 'cause see, the person pickin' 'em did it before they was ripe. A boy forced to be a man, a girl forced to be a grown woman, way too soon. Then, you got some folks who wait too late to pick 'em, baby 'em, coddle 'em, and the lemon can't make it on their own, 'cause they been hangin' on that tree all that time, wasting their life away, surrounded by all those other lemons who don't make 'em stand up on their own. Some lemons are sweeter than others, while others are just bitter, and ain't no way to make 'em taste good. You offer sugar or a good recipe, and they say, naw'll." His nose wrinkled as he shook his head. "They're happy bein' miserable.

"Some lemons are bruised but make the best lemonade if just given the chance, but something about lemons, that people don't understand, is they were all created with purpose. Them lemons got Vitamin C, 'specially in the skin we discard. That skin can be turned into zest... Zest for life. They don't understand that they're not just lemons, they're doctors too, out here curing all sorts of ailments. People call cars that don't work right 'lemons.' But that ain't fair, 'cause lemons are bright and cheery. They give zing to a dull dinner, and they've been used since the dawn of time for medicinal purposes..." The man took a puff of his pipe, then crossed his legs like he was the host of Masterpiece Theater. "I done lost my damn train of thought..." He sat there for a bit, working his brain.

"You were talking about the lemons having zing. You were using lemons as a metaphor for me, trying to teach me some sort of lesson, right?"

"Shiiiiid! I ain't tryna teach you no lesson."

"Oh, really? Well, damn… I was enjoying it. I was into it. I was waiting for the whole, 'Son, life is like a tree of lemons… You never know what you're going to pick.'"

"Sorry to let you down, but I was looking at that tree," he pointed to the window, "and thought of my Arnette. Not only did she plant it, but we had got into it 'bout me not picking up my clothes in the laundry room. She said she married a lemon of a husband, then took it back 'cause she said actually lemons is good, and I didn't deserve such a nice title. Then she flipped it around again and said, no, actually lemons can be bad, so she gave it back to me and I had to sit and hear the same silly shit I'm tellin' you right now."

Viper burst out laughing, and Mr. Earl was changing colors as he succumbed to mirth, too. After they'd settled down, he drew serious.

"When y'all tying the knot?"

"Next year. Haven't set an exact date, but it'll be in the summer."

"Can I come? I'd sure like to be invited. If ya don't mind."

Viper took a sip of his water and leaned forward.

"If you can't come, nobody can come."

His face split with an exultant beam. They continued to talk for a while, during which a pair of binoculars lying on the counter caught Viper's eyes. *I wonder if he's a bird watcher? I doubt it, but he's definitely the curious kind. I bet Mr. Earl sees all sorts of things that happen around here… all kinds of shit.*

The afternoon wore on in friendly interaction, and Viper didn't mind that his plans for the day had gone out the window.

"Did I ever tell you the story about this big, beautiful Asian woman I used to sock it to before I met Arnette?"

"Nah." Viper smirked, then shook his head. "I would've remembered that."

"Boy, get up and grab us some beers!" Viper hopped up, excited to hear the sordid details of a sailor who'd traveled all over the world. "And grab that bag of pretzels on the counter, too. It's story time. I know it's the day of the Sabbath, Lord forgive me, but Viper, this lady, Li Xiu Ying, could suck the skin off a cucumber wit' her bare mouth and wrap that monkey 'round some sausage so tight, she'd have you givin' her all yo money. So much so, she should've changed her name to Ching Ching!"

MAMA SUCKED HER teeth as she sauntered along the sidewalk in flat gold sandals, her purple maxi-dress blowing in the slight breeze. Atop her head was a lavender turban, and on her ears large gold earrings. She'd painted her nails a pale pink, and smelled like expensive perfume and disappointment.

"How long?" Majesty asked, walking at her side.

"Four and a half months."

"When will the divorce be final?"

"He just filed. It was a separation at first. I'm not

sure."

They took a few more steps in silence.

"Do you have a good attorney?"

"Of course. That pickle-headed motherfucker is going to pay me my got damn money, and I'm not signing a damn thing until this is ironed out and settled." Mama pursed her lips, venom, rage, and sadness emanating from her. Funny how the real person emerged when she was vexed. "Left me for a twenty-four-year-old child. The bitch didn't know him for more than a month, Majesty. All she saw were dollar signs. For the record, his penis stays soft half the time, and he doesn't want any children."

"Mama, I didn't really need to know that."

"Well, it's important because he didn't have any of his own during his first two marriages."

"Didn't want any children?"

"Right. She told him she wants to have his kids and allegedly he agreed to it." Mama rolled her eyes. "She'll find out... His old, rotten ass will trade her in for a younger model in a few years, too, and if she *does* happen to fall pregnant by an old man with arthritis like him, the child will cry when it rains because their knees hurt!"

Majesty swallowed a laugh and kept on walking.

"Mama, I know you're upset, and you have every right to be, but trust me, he did you a favor. If Mr. Gerald could do something like this to you without a second thought, he's proven he isn't worth your time."

Mama's lower lip twitched. In truth, the woman didn't care about the man's integrity. She just wanted to have a rich husband, even if it meant being in a loveless marriage.

She hung her hat on that status, which allowed her to rub elbows with some local elite. Mama's identity was wrapped around other people and however she presented herself to be, and nobody really knew the real person beneath the façade.

"I'm not going to waiver in my lifestyle, I tell you that. I've been a bit more frugal, if you will, with the money while this is being straightened out, but I should keep the same standard of living I had before he left. I was that bastard's backbone for practically all his business ventures. It was my idea to change his emblem from that stupid siren to a sailboat! I'm the one who hired people for his Toronto office! I'm the one…" And on and on she went.

"Mama, who are you?"

The woman stopped walking, appearing genuinely confused by the question.

"What are you talking about, Majesty?" She placed her hand on her hip.

"I'm asking who are you as a woman, Mama? If I were to remove the glitz, the money, the makeup, who are you underneath it all? Who is the real Josephine?"

"The same woman you've known your entire life."

"But see, that's just the thing. You gave birth to me, and I still don't know who you are outside of your exes, including my own father, and outside of you striving for financial security."

"That's not true, Majesty."

"It *is* true. I ask you your favorite color, and you joke and say, 'money green.' I ask you where your dream vacation is, and you say, 'Sugar Daddy Island.'" Mama averted her gaze. "I know what you like to do only in the context of social climbing and financial stability. I don't know who you are on the inside. Where it counts." Majesty waited for her mother to protest. Deny. Deflect. Lash out. Move the goal line and not fight fair.

But much to her surprise, the woman started blinking back tears.

In that single, solitary moment, Majesty pushed her anger and resentment aside and embraced the woman who'd given her life with all the strength she could muster.

"Don't feel sorry for me," Mama uttered, the heat from her breath brushing her shoulder.

Mama hugged her back loosely at first, then tighter, and squeezed.

And she cried. And cried.

Majesty swallowed past a lump in her throat. She wasn't used to dealing with this side of her mother. Only twice she'd seen her cry, once when her own mother had died, but Majesty didn't know her maternal grandmother to feel any sort of way about the death as a young girl. Another time, she'd never disclosed the reason but Majesty had noticed the swollen, red eyes and sad demeanor. Still, she'd never witnessed the pure, raw emotion from Mama, who proudly wore her strong Black woman disguise.

When Majesty released her, she began to cry, too. Mama's tear-streaked face looked so pitiful. She almost jumped when the woman took hold of her hand, a gesture she rarely made. They began to walk together. Step by step.

"I wish I had brought my cigarettes." Mama smiled weakly. "What would you like to know, baby?"

Majesty slid her hand into her capri jeans pocket and pondered the question. *She won't answer me truthfully. Right now, she may want to, but she won't… It'll break her. I think how Viper spoke to her got to her, too. She's been acting peculiar ever since. On top of it, she asked me how he was doing today. Odd.*

"What are you thinking about?" Mama's naturally sultry voice broke into her thoughts.

"How you want to be real with me. Maybe. But you can't. Asking you a question that goes beyond surface level may not get me anything other than frustration."

"You might be right. You might be wrong. You don't know me, remember?" They paused walking, and Mama had a strange look in her eyes. Broken. Sad. It gave her chills, reminding her a little of the way Viper had been one evening when they were lying together naked on the couch, and he related a prison tale about a friend of his being branded with a hot piece of steel against his will. Yeah… that was the same damn look.

"I'll start from the top." Mama cleared her throat as they began to walk again. "I was born in Miami, Florida, as you know. My mother was verbally and physically abusive. That's not something I discussed with you."

"Why not? Shame?"

"No. I just wanted to forget about it. Not discussing it meant, on some level, that it never really happened. My Daddy didn't want me. He had enough children, he said. I was the middle child of seven. The three after me were from my mother's second husband. Two different fathers.

Five girls. Two boys." She stopped to pick up a little weed that was pretending to be a white flower, then twirled it in her hand as they resumed their jaunt. "I watched my mother struggle to get money. She resented all the mouths she had to feed, as if it were somehow our fault." She let out a broken laugh, drowning in a well of sadness. "I left her home in the eighth grade to go live with my grandmother, Tabitha."

"You told me a little about Tabitha."

"Yes. That was my mother's mother. Things had gotten too bad to stay with Mama. She was a loose cannon and wouldn't stop hitting us, especially me and my two oldest sisters. While living with my grandmother, I found out some things that a girl my age shouldn't have been thinking about. She would always tell me how pretty I was... that I was prettier than my sisters, and I could use this to my advantage. She acted like she loved me. Maybe she thought she did." Mama shrugged. "Men who were way too old to mess with a girl my age would pay my grandmother to spend a little time with me." Majesty's heart dropped in her gut. "At first, I was confused... shocked.

"It was never sex, let me make that clear... but I had to let 'em kiss me. Hold me. Touch 'em. That's when I first learned the art of leaving my own body, you know? I could do these things and be okay... I told myself it was okay because technically, I was still a virgin. I justified it in my mind. Somehow, I made it work. The years passed, and I took over the reins of my own destiny. It was finally me who was in control. No one was going to get paid off

385

the work I put in, and the time I spent doing it, except for me. I would never let anyone use me again. No one wanted me around unless it was to use me in some way, Majesty."

"Did you ever talk to your mother about what was going on at your grandmother's house?"

Mama shook her head. "No. My mother was no better. It would've been like tellin' Satan what one of his awful demons had done. Useless. She didn't want me anyway except to help watch the younger children, clean, and be her punching bag because of her own poor choices. My grandmother never saw herself as a pimp, but she was. Yes, she kept a roof over my head, made sure I finished high school, let me wear pretty dresses and I didn't want for anything, but I found out later she'd done the same thing to my mother and her sister."

"What about your father? I know you said he didn't want children, but were you still in communication with him?"

"Now, that's an interesting story." Mama plucked a few of the little petals off the weed. "I found out when I was seventeen that my father had died. His eldest son told me that man wasn't my dad though, and rather, it was a man named Samuel. He said my mama had cheated, and that's why the man I thought was my father didn't want anything to do with me. Long story short, I found out this Samuel guy had moved to New Jersey from Florida and hadn't been here in years. I don't remember how I got his number, but I did, and he talked to me on the phone.

"We decided to exchange pictures. So, I sent him a

photo of me, and he sent me one of him. Splitting image."
Mama smiled proudly. "I looked just like him, Majesty.
Mama had to have known. Maybe that's why she hated
me. She treated me the worst outta everyone. I never
confirmed it, but I believe her first husband left her over
me. Anyway, Samuel was a very nice man. Godly. Polite.
He didn't know I existed, but he said he'd known my
mother around the time I was conceived, and they had
had a short relationship back then. He'd admitted he had a
girlfriend at the time of their encounter, but they'd been
on again, off again, so he had his fling with my mama
during that off cycle. So, we talked some more, and he
made plans to come visit me."

"How'd the visit go?"

Mama plucked the rest of the petals off that poor little
limp stem, then tossed it aside.

"We met one time, Majesty, and I will never forget
how complete I felt. Like I had finally found some peace.
And my missing piece of the puzzle. He told his family
about me, upfront about the whole thing. He had no
other children but was married. He told me what college
he'd attended, all sorts of things. We agreed that we could
move forward and build a father-daughter relationship. I
was planning to visit him three months later. He was
going to introduce me to his wife, his brothers and sisters,
his mother, the whole nine, and we were going to talk
about me moving to Jersey and going to school. But it
never happened…"

"Why not? He got cold feet?"

An expression of total devastation came over Mama's

face.

"Someone shot him. Gunned him down in front of the barbershop he owned. Somebody shot 'nd killed my daddy." At that moment, Majesty saw her son in her mother's eyes, and the vision broke her down, snatched and ripped at her core. "I had tasted love, Majesty. I had tasted what it felt like for someone to be excited that I existed. Not so they could get something out of me, but so I could get the love I deserved. And it was yanked away just as fast as I'd been served." The woman snapped her fingers. "It was such a cruel thing. Made me question God's existence. I didn't have a relationship with my mother. Now, both of my fathers were dead. My brothers and sisters and I didn't always have the best communication and relationships, and on top of it, I had no money. I couldn't go back and live with Grandma; she was senile and about to be put in a home. So now, here I was, an orphan as far as I was concerned. I was homeless."

"What did you do to get out of this jam?"

"I fell back on what my grandmother taught me. My looks got me what I needed, and I became focused on using them to get ahead. It worked. When you add fucking to the mix, true blue dirty, grimy sex, that's where the money is… That's where your soul is lost. And after a while, I was numb. I met your father a couple years into it and thought he would be my ticket to a normal life. He wasn't. He was just as fucked up as me. I tried over and over again, meeting different men that couldn't give me what I needed in one way, or another. I was determined not to be broke. Not to struggle. I wanted to find a man like my daddy… my *real* daddy. But God must've broken the mold. Deep down, I didn't really think I deserved someone like my father though, Majesty. I deserved filth. Disillusionment.

"Married dicks and no calls back the next day. I deserved cum stains on my shirts. Stacks of money flung all over my hotel room. The stench of cheap spilled wine and a frantic wife callin' me in the middle of the night asking for the whereabouts of her husband. I deserved threesomes with church women while their minister husbands fucked me too or sat back and watched their lesbian wives eat my snatch. I deserved men that wanted to be pegged and walked on with my 6-inch heels, all over their damn body until they bled.

"So, that's who I am, Majesty. A numb woman who has spent years trying to survive by spreadin' her legs and spreadin' lies. I knew you were the child who would eventually figure it all out." Majesty grabbed her mother's hand and squeezed it. Mama reached up to cradle her cheek with the other hand and smiled. The sun beamed on her beautiful face and hopefully, warmed her cold heart. "After a while, I never cared about being loved by anyone anymore, honey. I figured love is overrated. Being taken care of is where it's at. Tina Turner was right, baby. 'What's love got to do with it?' It hurts. Tears you apart. I loved my daddy. I loved your father. They're the only two men I loved, actually, and both of 'em broke my heart. One died on me; the other was simply a turnip I couldn't get blood from. Yeah, Majesty… take it from me. Love is a fairytale, baby. It's too damn expensive. Loving someone cost me too damn much. And no matter how much money I have, honey, even if I had all the jewels, gold and diamonds in the world, it became crystal clear that I just couldn't afford it…"

CHAPTER TWENTY-SIX

The Viper and the Jaguar Met in the Jungle...

*T*HEY SAY THE *best things in life are free.*

But really, there is always a price for everything. It may not be money. It could be the time you put in something. The love you gave. The lust you reciprocated. The respect that was given. The expectation that you'll show gratitude.

Doesn't matter. You're going to pay something for everything you need. And you're going to pay for every damn thing you do...

Marie stood in the kitchen making coffee. The sound of a spoon being stirred in a cup reminded Viper of a scene from the movie, 'Get Out.' The taste of liquor coated his tongue. He'd just had a dash of tequila in his café con leche, while wolfing down his *desayuno*, a plate of Tostada Cubana, diced potatoes, scrambled eggs, and half of a *preparade*. It was early in the day, and the sky was overcast. The sounds of guitar instrumentals played on low volume, while several televisions were on in his house, tuned to various sports channels.

He retrieved his phone from his jeans pocket and typed a text message to Majesty.

Mi reina, good morning. I'm training a difficult dog today here at the house. I know you're at work, but in case you call me on your break and I don't answer, that's why. I can't have any interruptions at the moment. When I'm finished with his session, I'll give you a call.

He slipped his phone in its place, then reached for a red, silver, and gold rosary his grandmother used to cherish. She'd had many of them, but this one his mother had allowed him to have. The one his *abuela* had worn the most. Several others had been buried with her. He recalled looking at her body in the casket, and a part of him had wished to climb inside it with her. Her death had crushed him so.

Setting aside these dark thoughts, he wrapped the holy beads around his wrist tying them like a bracelet, then heard the doorbell ring. Marie walked out of his kitchen, her red heels clicking on the floor as she made her way to his front door. He heard her greet his guest, then the voices of several men. Viper made his way to the foyer.

"*Buenos días*, Reye Víbora."

"Good morning to you too, King Jaguar."

The two greeted each other, embracing and bumping fists, then settled in the living room. Jaguar had two other Kings with him. All three men were dripping in gold and name-brand shirts, snapbacks, and shoes.

"Sit, sit." He gestured to the oversized leather couch and presented them with his special box with the best cigars in his collection. As soon as he lifted the lid, a heavenly scent escaped. Viper only smoked on special occasions. He was happy to offer these to his exceptional guests. His brothers. His *Reyes*.

While they engaged in small talk, Marie brought in cups of her strong, delicious coffee. Jag sat in the middle, boxed between the other two who barely spoke.

"I'm going to get right down to business," Jag said after polishing off his coffee and depositing the empty cup on the table. Like a bee, Marie buzzed into the room to pick up the crockery, then made a hasty retreat. Jag removed his Nike cap, allowing his dark brown waves to fall free over his shoulders. He rested his cigar on the ashtray. "I appreciate you holding things down while I was away, Viper."

"Mmm hmm." Viper lit his own cigar.

"Now that I'm out and see how things are going here, there's going to be some changes."

"Such as?" Viper casually blew the smoke out the side of his mouth.

"I want to put King Torque in your place."

"King Torque?" Viper took another drag of his cigar and rested it in another ashtray, one shaped like a gold serpent. "You request for me to quit my position?"

"No. This isn't a demotion, Viper. It's a restructuring." Jag snapped his fingers, and one of the men beside him put something in his hand. "Oh, and here's a gift I forgot to give you." He handed the item to Viper – a lighter featuring a snake inside a skull head, only the snake was dead, with X's for eyes. Viper laughed and tossed it on the couch behind him. "Also, we have another issue. I found out you've been… how shall I say it?" Jag waved his hand about. "Talking shit behind my back regarding Wild. I know he was your homeboy, but you've got to stop taking shit so personally, Viper. I liked Wild, too. He was a liability, though. You and I both know that. Let's talk about this right now because—"

"It's no secret, and I'm not taking it personal. I don't talk behind people's backs. There's right, right now, later, and wrong. King Blood made it clear how we're supposed to handle these sorts of situations. I didn't talk shit at all behind your back, Jag. I wrote you a letter. Told you on the phone. Told you to your face. I can write that shit in the sand, have a plane scribe it in the clouds or tattoo it on your face next, if you want."

One of the guys sitting next to him chuckled, then stopped when Jag shot him a look.

"Do you have a problem with me, Viper? I feel like we have a problem." Jag smiled in an unnerving way, his dark gaze tapering as he pushed his lightweight gold and black jacket open, exposing his heat.

"Yeah, we've got a problem, man." Viper grinned, showing all his teeth. "Jag, the problem is actually *you*."

"How so?"

"You're like a time bomb, blasting everything away. You're not a critical thinker. You jump, then look. You come in here after I was doing your work on the streets for years, damn good work too, and instead of thanking me, you try to demote me and insult my intelligence by telling me it's something else. You've got brothas running around Miami, some of them catching cases on account of you. If you're going to kill a mothafucka, it better be over disrespect, disobedience, or disregard, not because you want to try and set someone up, a bruised ego, or make it seem like we're down. That was sloppy work on your part."

"Sloppy work? Viper… you don't talk. And then when you do, you say the wrong shit." Jag chuckled and shook his head, as if he were truly amused.

"I talk. I just don't talk to *you*. You have the fucking audacity to tell me not to get bent out of shape about this. You want to replace me with someone weaker who will be your 'yes man.' Everyone can see what's going on here, and you'd have to be stupid to think I didn't see this writing on the wall. I knew you were going to come to me with this shit, and that's fine, but just admit the reasoning."

"Awww, you feel picked on, Viper?" Jag mocked.

"You're threatened by me." He was met with more chuckling on Jag's part. "But you must go through the proper channels to do that, man. You can't just stroll into a man's house and tell him he's out. In the Nation, you're only one step above me in the ranks. That's it. In real life, in the streets where it counts, you're ten steps below. You'd need to be on your motherfuckin' tippy toes at the top of Willis Tower to be even *close* to on my level, motherfucker." Jag's smile faded. "Don't nobody respect you, man… ho ass fuck-face." Viper looked down at the asshole. "They just fear your repercussions. Respect is stronger than fear. Respect gets you things done for years to come, not just for right now. No one important will be spittin' on my grave, but they'll dance all over yours like they're Michael Jackson 2.0. I don't even answer to you unless I *want* to. I can go over your head, and you hate that shit."

"Viper, you've always been a cocky son of a bitch. People think because you're chill, you don't keep shit going, but I've been onto you since we were kids, nigga! I know how you move! This is why you have no control over these motherfuckers! They're running wild. Wild… King Wild." He grinned. "His death is on your shoulders. You should've kept your ass in Little Havana instead of showin' off, moving out here, forgetting your roots. You weren't there to babysit, and it all went to hell. You deserve to not only be removed from your post, but also flipped, nigga. You're devious and—"

"You don't run me, mothafucka! I'M THE MUSCLE, NOT YOU! I'M THE MOTHERFUCKIN' BRAINS, TOO! I figured it all out, mothafucka! You kill anyone who gets into your fucking way, 'cause you're weak! And I know why you're here. To plan my funeral."

"Finally. Something we both agree on."

"But you aren't my God, and you damn sure aren't the honorable King Blood. You're beneath me, mothafucka!" Marie raced into the room, trying to calm him down, but he shooed her away. "I know you got out of prison early because you're a damn snitch!"

Jagger put his hand on his gun. His eyes shined rays of death.

"You're a fuckin' liar, Viper."

"Oh, really? You told the Feds about Wild and the guys under him, so that you could get a lighter sentence. There's no way you'd be out right now without cutting a deal! You must think we're stupid! They went and grabbed his ass, and then you got freaked out because you realized Wild had a bunch of dirt on you, and if he ever found out it was you that ratted him out, if *he* didn't get you, someone else would on his behalf! That's why you wouldn't listen to me when I told you to just leave him alone. You already knew what was up! You killed Wild because he knew too much, and he was loyal to me. On top of that, you're pissed because you found out I contacted The Council about the Reyes who were up for disciplinary action after you sent them to take his ass out, and they got handled accordingly because they didn't run that shit past me first! You're a fuckin' snitch, bitch! A coward!" The two Kings beside him stood up... Their nostrils flared as they exposed their guns. "You're not even good enough to lick my Pit Bull's balls! Look at you; you couldn't even come here by yourself. You had to bring protection. Are you a dick in need of a condom, motherfucker? When it comes to me, you've got a gangsta mouth with police hands, and you better call them. 911, what's your fuckin' emergency?! IT'S VIPER, MOTHER-FUCKER!"

In a flash, the men in front of him pulled their guns and aimed them at him. Viper smoked a little more of his cigar before getting to his feet. and Jaguar and his boys followed suit. He rounded the table. Approached slowly, with a smile. Standing so close to the mad man, their noses practically touched, he looked into his eyes.

Viper grinned as his heart beat the shit out of his chest. He kept his hand on the trigger of his gun as his father, cousin, and several Latin Kings emerged from various rooms. All of them were strapped. Jag looked around; fear etched on his face like a tattoo.

"They all know, man… The jig is up. The Council knows what you did too, now. You can kill me, Jag, but these mothafuckas will be waiting for you. You will never be safe, man. Then, they'll go after your family. Allow me to let everyone in on a little something extra…" Viper walked backwards, his arm still raised, putting space between him and Jaguar once again. "Jag tried to get me on Little Havana soil for this meeting. I refused. He knew if I'd accepted, I wouldn't shoot him. I'm from the old code where we promised the King elders we wouldn't spend our brothers' blood on that land. Jag was right about one thing though. I am definitely a devious motha-fucka. I've been planning this for a long ass time."

"Planning what?!" Jag screamed, the veins in his neck twisting and bulging.

"This motherfucker right here," he raised a shaky hand at his nemesis, anger coursing through his veins, "killed my brother Diego!"

Several men's eyes went wide.

Keeping his gun aimed, Viper bent down to pull out one of the coffee table drawers. From inside he picked a piece of yellowed notebook paper, which he shook to unfold.

"Marie. Come here, baby."

The woman stepped over with her gun on her hip and her diamond accented reading glasses on. She stood beside him and read the letter, which was written in Spanish...

To my little king, my little brother, my best friend, Dominic.

I must tell you that it's dangerous here, Viper. I will not make it. I've done too much. Seen too much. The worst of it happened now. Jaguar and I have been beefing and he threatened my life. He meant it. He wants to do something I don't agree with. Something that will get us all in a lot of trouble. I won't go into what that is because if I tell you, it could make you a target. I don't want that for you. You're in good standing. Just know that I spoke out against him.

You know what happens when you speak out against Jaguar. You end up missing or dead. We are no longer friends like when we were little, running around having fun. Jaguar has changed, Dominic. He's not the same person. I don't know what happened, but something must've caused him to be this way. Do not trust him. Ever. He has turned many of our brothers, who were my friends, against me. He has labeled me a snitch. The kiss of death. He is pretending to care for me and be my brother, as though we squashed the beef and he's over it, but it is all an act. He is giving me money and weed in front of others always, to make it appear like we are close and we're fine. We are not fine. I'm leaving this letter in our special place. I told you last night that I love you. You thought that was strange because I never say that. You know I do, though. You're not just my little brother, you're the only person in this world that I trust. My best friend.

If I die soon, Jaguar did it.
You know what to do.

Diego 'King Dominoes' Martinez

Marie neatly folded the letter, then slid it in between her cleavage. Viper glared at Jag, his jaw tightening as pain and the desire for violent pleasure emerged. The room was so quiet, one could almost hear a newly formed thought growing in the back of one's mind. Jag's complexion turned ashen, ghostly, and a sheen of sweat covered his face.

"…. Ladies and gentlemen, my brother Diego, was killed exactly two days after this letter was written."

"I didn't kill Diego. Diego had enemies!" he yelled, looking frantic and terrified.

Viper shook his head. "We all have enemies. It was you. You broke code. Killed my brother in cold blood on sacred ground, all because he refused to do your bidding. Then, during all this time, you've had at least eight kings killed for what you called disobedience, a liability, or disorderly behavior in the Nation. How interesting that some of those kings were prospects to rise in the ranks, maybe even bump you out of the way. You're not second in command because of talent, ingenuity, intelligence, or strength. You're second in command because you knocked off your competition. So, of course then you'd come to my door today to remove the last one standing, after you tried to use me for all of your dirty work. What you weren't banking on was that I'd beat you to the punch. Revelation 2:2…'I know your works, your toil and your patient endurance, and how you cannot bear with those who are evil, but have tested those who call themselves apostles and are not, and found them to be false.' Thanks to Mr. Earl, for acquainting me with such fitting scripture. There's a Judas in my midst, but I don't have the patience of Jesus…"

Without warning or hesitation, Viper raised his arm and riddled Jag's body with bullets. BAM! BAM BAM BAM! BAM! He started with one to each hand, forcing him to drop his gun. He then went for the feet, and the final one to the head.

The two kings beside him stepped back as Jag dropped to the floor. The clean shot to the middle of his forehead, still smoking. Leisurely reaching for his cigar, he took a final draw, then extinguished it.

"Thank you, King Cross and King Ace, for your service this morning. I'm sure it was difficult that for quite some time, you had to get close to Jag and befriend him, earn his trust, and at the same time, endure his abuse." Both men nodded as they picked up the heavy weight of the fallen, shamed king, and dragged his ass towards a back room for the next phase of his dethroning. The two young men had been friends of Wild, who'd given them a place to stay and showed them the ropes. They'd been pissed when he'd been murdered in jail. Viper had let the little cat out the bag, at just the right time, about who had sent out the orders for the hit.

When they'd shown up for the apartment clean-up of the botched robbery and spoke with them, Viper had recognized in them the perfect candidates to stand in as

Jag's lackeys. He'd needed a couple younger Kings with high hopes and aspirations to get next to the bastard, and their lust for revenge was all the fuel they needed. Regardless of his motives, he'd spoken the truth, while Jag had spouted nothing but lies.

Viper had asked them to appear as though they hated him. They needed to put on airs in order to earn Jag's trust faster. "Remember now, cut him up the way you were taught. Then, we'll put him in the swimming pool soil that the contractors dug up in my yard." There was a large gaping hole in the backyard now, and several tall piles of dirt. "He'll be hauled away tomorrow with the rest of the garbage."

They nodded in understanding. Marie tucked her hair behind one ear as she observed the two men prepare to follow his orders.

"I'll put on another pot of coffee, then clean up the floor." She patted his shoulder as she walked past, humming a pretty tune.

Viper stared down at the blood that had seeped from the fucker's body onto his floor. Jag's cigar was still smoldering in the ashtray. Then, when his gaze met his father's tears were running down the man's face. He'd just told him about Diego's letter the previous evening, which his brother had left for him all those years ago in the back of their closet. The two would go inside that closet and talk when the world became too loud and ugly.

Viper hadn't told a soul up until that point who'd stolen his brother's life. He knew he had to be very careful about how he went about this, and he could trust no one until he was sure of things. So many times he'd wanted to put his parents out of their misery when they'd bring up Diego's death, wondering how nobody had ever been charged for their son's murder. Jag even had the audacity to attend the funeral, and pretend to be sick with grief, hugging on his mother like some third son she'd never birthed.

Diego had taught Viper well. He'd given him countless lessons on silence. How important it was to be true to code. To follow traditional King rules, and to never let the left hand know what the right one was doing.

His father walked over and wrapped his arms around him. Viper returned the gesture, tuning out the sound of the saws and electric drills. None of this would bring Diego back. King Wild. King Fiend. King Decree, and countless others that Jag had merked purely for the sake of his own injured pride.

Still, he'd done this in their honor. Vengeance was served. The Viper was resting easy in the Garden of Eden, and now, the sun had finally set.

Amor de Rey.

CHAPTER TWENTY-SEVEN

Power to the Kings, Glory to the Queens

*W*HEN A GANGSTER *gets married, it's not just him celebrating. It's the entire world, or at least, that's what it feels like. We're amazed to be alive, to be feeling such exhilaration. To take another breath when we didn't believe we had any left.*

Viper was surrounded by his family, friends, and brothers, all dressed in black tuxedos with red ties and vests. Red was a compromise. Majesty had forbidden him to go with yellow or gold. "No gang colors!" This had resulted in an argument and angry make-up sex. He was still salty about it, but he'd opted to let it go.

This was one of the many pitfalls of falling in love with someone as stubborn as he. He'd grown up Roman Catholic, but rarely attended church. Majesty was a non-denominational Christian but went at least once a month for self-care and to promote prayer and belief in her son. They were merging cultures, religious beliefs, and families.

That in itself was a beautiful undertaking.

The Loft At Congress was where they'd decided to tie the knot. Neutral ground. It was a beautiful place with flowing white drapery, twenty-two-foot-high ceilings, state-of-the-art lighting, and the design was an effortless blend of East coast edge and southern Florida feel. They were having a formal ceremony and dinner affair, and exactly one hundred and eighty-six people had RSVP'd. Viper was certain more would show up that had not confirmed, so he'd prepared the caterers for that eventuality.

He looked around and noticed the minister speaking with one of the photographers. A priest had been out of the question. Most attendees, including Majesty, weren't Catholic and additionally, the wedding was being held outside the church. They'd found a minister they both liked, recommended by Majesty's father who'd proclaimed he'd also received spiritual counseling from the man, and from then on, everything was in motion.

"*Felicidades.*" King Virgo approached, AKA 'Serious Puerto Rican,' his bright blue eyes striking against dark tan skin. His features were the source of wonder and a few jokes in their circle. Virgo hugged him, patting his back and showering him with love, as he offered his congratulations.

"Thank you and thank you for attending."

"I wouldn't miss this for anything, Viper. We're all happy for you." They fist-bumped, then Virgo made his way back to his table which had been set with beautifully printed schedules and candles all aglow.

The place was full, with everyone dressed in their best jewels and attire. A mixture of classic perfumes and heat created a comforting aroma he'd often smelled at other weddings, children's birthday parties, and yes, even funerals. Mamá was sitting in front with her husband, wearing a beautiful dark red dress and blazer. Her hair was impeccable, not a strand out of place. She'd just spoken to Majesty's mother, who was dressed better than anyone in there, possibly even the bride. Viper snickered at the thought. Mamá had confided that she didn't care for Majesty's mother based on first impressions, but promised to not cause a scene. He could see she'd already been crying happy tears, and the ceremony hadn't even begun.

His stomach began to knot and twist as the singers and musicians started setting up, as well as the DJ for the reception. *This is real… This shit is real. She's going to be my wife. This is forever. I can't believe the woman of my dreams moved right across from me. She fell into my lap. All I had to do was literally walk across the street and claim my blessing. Damn.*

He glanced at his watch, and when he looked back up, his cousins were surrounding him, fussing over him. He laughed as they smothered him with affection, throwing barbs in Spanish about being attached to a ball and chain, officially off the market. They'd done the same at his bachelor party the previous weekend. A wild night at an upscale strip club where he watched gorgeous naked women undulate their bodies, and went home a bit tipsy to make love to his fiancée, wanting nothing more than to feel her skin against his.

"She's here!" Marie squealed. She was talking to

someone else, but Viper's ears perked up. Ten brides-maids, dressed in unbelievably tight red gowns and heels, walked by, disappearing into a room on the other side of the venue. Of the friends he'd met, he really liked the ones his woman hung out with. Some of them were kind of wild, but they had their shit together. Majesty kept the company of women who loved her, encouraged her, and were in her league. This, he really cherished about her. He smirked when he spotted some of his brothers practically breaking their necks to catch a glimpse of the ladies who'd raced past, their make-up and hair on point, showing cleavage and leg.

Dad gave him a wave as he grinned proudly, dressed in his tuxedo, and looking the part. He and his wife sat down not too far from Mamá and on the other series of pews, Mr. Earl was sitting with Majesty's mother and father, just as they'd agreed upon. The old timer was sporting a dated brown sports coat and pants that were a wee bit too short, but he still looked great, and Viper was thrilled he was there to rejoice with them. He'd had a mild stroke a few months earlier, so he and Majesty had kept a close eye on him, finally convincing him to allow them to hire someone else to mow his lawn and help clean his house once a week. He loved Mr. Earl, and he'd begun to call him family, too.

"We're going to begin the ceremony now. Please re-main seated. Thank you," the hostess announced. Then, she repeated the same thing in Spanish.

Everyone drew quiet, except for Majesty's Aunt Peaches, who kept blowing her nose and snorting. Both their parents were escorted out. Then, the violinist and the accompanying musicians began to play an instrumental version of 'Stay with Me,' by Sam Smith. The minister, and the hostess who was also an interpreter, approached. Reverend Appleton, with his long gold and white robe, stood beside Viper holding onto a black Bible. They shook hands and waited while his mother was walked down the aisle by King Pedro, and Majesty's mother was escorted by Troy who was also dressed in a black tuxedo and red tie. One of the youngest kings, a fifteen-year-old, approached the two mothers and went down on bended knee. With one hand behind his back, head bowed, he offered each a golden rose with black stems. Majesty wasn't aware of this little plan; Viper figured she'd see it in the tape later after their honeymoon, but by then, he'd be safe. He curved his lips as he surveyed the beautiful scene.

Moments later, a little Cuban girl dressed in a frilly white dress, King Brick's six-year-old daughter, approached holding a gold crown on a pillow. People ahhhed, oohhhed, and giggled as her cheeks plumped and she exposed a snaggle-toothed smile. Viper bent down, and she placed the crown on his head, then he sent her on her way with a hug and a kiss.

The ensemble started a new song, and a vocalist stepped to the microphone to sing, 'Here Comes the Sun,' by The Beatles. As the song began, ten bridesmaids emerged, with the maid of honor, Majesty's sister Allison, leading the pack. All were escorted by a Latin King brother. Honorable men who still followed the code. His best man was Pedro, who'd done a one-eighty and turned his life around. He was working a real job, as well as being trained to work with the dogs eventually, too.

I miss you, Diego. You are my best man in spirit...

One by one they came, arm in arm, looking absolutely beautiful and handsome. Once everyone was lined up, the kings surrounded him and placed gold and black rose petals at his feet. This was met with abrupt pockets of applause, dog barking noises, lion roars, and a few shouting, 'Amor de Rey!' A little Cuban boy, one of the Latin Queen's seven-year-old son, walked over with a white pillow that had a crown for a king and queen embroidered on it, and in the center sat a symbolic golden wedding band.

"Come stand by me, little guy," Viper urged, patting the little boy's back.

MAJOR's, 'Why I Love You' was now being performed by the male singer, who paused when the host took the microphone.

"The bride is coming. Everyone, please stand." She repeated the same words in Spanish. Everyone got to their feet. The back of the room seemed a million miles away. Viper felt hot and flushed all of a sudden, dizzy with excitement and flooding with love. He wasn't afraid to confront other killers. He wasn't afraid of spending time in prison. He wasn't afraid of hardly anything. But the thought of never having a love like this hurt him to his core. He began to shake, feeling anxious and overwhelmed. He closed his eyes when tears threatened to pour. Then, he felt the strong hand of the minister on his back.

"I've got a handkerchief if you need it," the reverend said soothingly. "I know it's a lot. The woman God made for you is coming, and you two will be joined as one. It's all right to feel like this. Stop hiding your face…"

Viper slowly lifted his head, opened his eyes, and let the tears fall. There, in the back of the room, was his father holding Majesty's left arm, and her father holding the right. Troy stood behind her, helping another woman hold her train. And at that sight, he lost it…

The sobbing echoed in his soul. His own tears were destroying him, one by one, as he folded within himself and screamed with joy. He soon heard others crying but didn't dare look. Now Pedro was crying, too, and he only knew that because the man yelled out, "Viper, man, stop… You got everyone in here messed up, including me! You killin' us, man!"

This was met with a wave of laughter. Viper stood straight again and pressed his hand against his mouth, in awe as Majesty was practically floating towards him, dressed in ivory and holding a bouquet of beautiful dark red roses. Her dress was form-fitting but not too tight, with a slit on the side. A jewel hung across her forehead in the shape of a gold and diamond crucifix, just like the tattoo he had. His jaw tightened painfully hard as he bit down on it, then looked up at the ceiling, trying to stop the endless trail of tears that refused to stop pouring. He shook his grandmother's rosary; he'd once again worn around his wrist, to simply feel the weight of it.

The minister asked who was giving her away, and her father stepped forward, saying, "We do," while glancing at

Majesty's mother, who nodded in agreement.

Viper stepped down from the dais and shook hands with Majesty's father. The two then embraced. With tears in his eyes, he said, "Take good care of my baby, Dominic."

"I will."

The three of them took their seats, leaving Majesty beside him. The emotion in her bright eyes made his gut clench. Her skin was flawless. Her dark hair was pulled away from her face, and long strands flowed down her back in lustrous spirals. Gorgeous, glossy lips called to him, and diamonds sparkled in her ears. She blinked several times, working hard to stop her tears. He was entranced, unable to turn away.

"Dominic... Mr. Martinez, can we start now? Can you give me some eye contact? We've been waiting three weeks for you to stop ogling your bride," the minister teased, triggering an outburst of laughter from their guests.

"Yes... yes." He caught his nose between his thumb and pointer finger, heating with embarrassment as another tear fell from his eye. "I'm sorry."

"No need to be sorry. You've been blessed... Now, let's begin. Everyone, please be seated..."

For a moment, he forgot anyone else was in that room but her.

"Husbands, love your wives, even as Christ also loved the church..." the minister began, reading the scriptures. He then commanded them to hold hands and face one another. The guests were instructed to bow their heads in prayer, and when it was over, he nodded at Viper.

"Go ahead, Dominic. Begin…"

He took a deep breath.

"Majesty, I remember the first time I saw you. It wasn't when you came to my home to complain." This caused an expected roar of laughter. "But it happened when you were moving into your home. I was in my kitchen, surrounded by friends, at a place in my life where I was confused and hurting. I wanted something else, and I was making those steps, but something was still missing. I had felt that way months before you arrived. I was looking at my friends with their girlfriends and wives, and for the first time, I felt envious.

"So, that day, I looked out of my kitchen window and saw a beautiful woman with a smile that rivaled the rays of the sun. There was a moving truck in your driveway. I was secluded… like Adam in the Garden of Eden. I had thought about my grandmother often that day, and my brother, too. I was having a party, but these people I'd loved weren't there. Though I missed them, I was seeking a different type of companionship. Not someone to complete me, but someone to show me how to complete myself. I didn't know how… God answered my mother's prayers. He'd packed you and your child up and brought you to me."

He could hear the sobbing again.

"Weeks and months passed as we got to know one another. I will never forget our first date, and when that date was over, after we danced on your porch and laughed, I knew you were the one. I could feel it. I'd never had that connection with anyone before. I'm not going to lie, it worried me. It happened so fast, but I refused to run away. In fact, I had to keep moving forward. Towards you. I had to have you."

He took a deep breath, then continued, "From that day forward, you've been there for me, through ups and downs. You watched me grow, and never made me feel badly for simply being me. You watched me remove barriers, so you could get closer to me. You watched me... you watched me fall in love with your son, now *our* son, Troy, and you said that made you love me even more. I promised him many times, and I am promising you too, that I will be a good father to him. He deserves nothing less." He dried his eyes while she cried quietly.

"I've watched you work your fingers to the bone to take care of others, your child, and make things better for all involved. I've observed you being so tired from work and school, you literally fell asleep on your feet, and once in mid-sentence while speaking to me on the phone. I've watched you get the promotion you so deserved, starting a new job as a Marketing Director. Your vocational dreams have come true, and you are a blessing to so many people. I've watched you make miracles out of monstrosities, and I've watched you love and care for people who didn't deserve to even be in your presence. You've taught me so much. I'm a work in progress, but... I look up to you. You're my greatest love. The best thing I've ever done in this lifetime is follow my heart when it comes to you.

He smiled at her. "Thank you, for trusting me. Thank you for coming over to my home, my garden, and seeing my beauty, *while* appreciating the beast. You're my Eve. I love you. My friends love you. The Kings and Queens love you, my blood family loves you. *Te quiero más que las palabras pueden decir. Encontré mi corazón. Vive en ti.*" The room erupted in cheers.

Allison handed Majesty another tissue. She dabbed at her eyes, then took a piece of paper from her sister, unfolded it, and began to read.

"Dominic, I thank God for loud music and broken ordinances. It gave me an excuse to march over to your house but when you opened that door…. Bay-*be!*" The room erupted in laughter. He grinned. "I looked up and saw this tall, ridiculously handsome man whom I wanted to remain angry with, but it was hard to do that when I was drowning in a pair of gorgeous hazel eyes… until you slammed the door in my face, that is." The ruckus resumed, with catcalls and whistles galore.

"That was rude of me. I'm sorry…"

"No, you're not!" He shrugged, agreeing with her. Everyone was having a great time with their banter. "Anyway, that was the day my life changed forever. As time wore on, I noticed you seemed to have a crush on me, and then, Mr. Earl…" They both looked out into the crowd at the man, who smiled and waved. "Mr. Earl said something that made me realize that there was nothing wrong with wanting to get to know you better, too. Before long, I couldn't resist anymore, and we became insepara-ble. You've been wonderful to my son, who lost his biological father in an untimely death."

She paused, working hard to contain her emotion.

"You... you've stepped into those shoes, and you didn't have to, and what's so amazing, Dominic, is that you did it so well, as if you'd been practicing for years. Troy, I know, has confided in you about things he didn't feel comfortable sharing with me. He has asked you things that only another man could truly address. He feels comfortable with you. Safe. He loves you. I love you.

"So, as I stand here in front of our family and friends, I want you to know that you're everything I want and need in a spouse. No, things have not always been easy for me, or for you, but in each other, we've found peace." Her voice quaked, and she sniffed back tears. "You understand me. You get me. I don't have to explain who I am to you because you just know. I found out early on that you and I have a lot in common. Despite being from different backgrounds, we share many of the same likes, have similar beliefs and goals in life. We've grown together, we've been good influences on one another, and I know you in ways that many don't. Dominic, you often keep your feelings guarded, but with me, I've seen you bloom like a rose. You are vulnerable with me. Truthful. Loving. I love you so much, Dominic. I fell in love with you, and there's no turning back. You are the one for me, and I'm so grateful for you. I promise to be here for you, just like you are here for me. I promise to continue to be a good mother to Troy, and to any other children we may have together from our union. I promise to be faithful, and I promise to be the person you can turn to. In your darkest hour, you are not alone. I will be there, shining a light on you, and our love."

Emotion pulsed in every corner of the room while Majesty folded up the paper and handed it back to Allison.

The vows began, and things progressed. Viper responded to the questions, going through the motions, but in his heart, he was already married. He'd already recited his vows to this beautiful woman before him. Soon, they exchanged rings, and the minister said, "Dominic Martinez, you may kiss your bride!"

Before he could grab her and show her what he needed right then and there, the woman cradled his face in her palms and dragged him down to her height to kiss him. The crowd cheered as Majesty took over the reins. Not one to be outdone, he picked her up off her feet, causing cheers and laughter, then wrapped his hand around her neck and kissed the life out of her...

When he set her back down on the floor, she reached up and wiped a bit of her lipstick from his mouth, her eyes glossed over, and a proud smile lined on her face.

"I present to you, Mr. and Mrs. Martinez!"

The two of them jumped down the step, hand in hand, as the brothers chanted, "Power to King Viper! Glory to Queen Majesty!" Gold and black confetti floated in the air and Majesty's face balled up tighter than a baby's fist holding a rattle!

"Viper! I told you no gold and black. You got these men in here throwin' up gang signs and all this mess, and I saw those black and gold rose petals by your shoes, too." He laughed, not realizing she'd seen Pedro do his thing. But then he kissed her hand and gave her his trademark smile and she instantly softened.

"You knew what I was… You know what I am." He kissed her hand once again, then started to let go but she held on and gave him a peck.

"I know. It still won't stop me from wanting my way." She winked.

"You should've never stepped on my side of the garden if you didn't want the fruit. I'm not Adam… I'm the Viper." He ran his hand along her shoulder, wanting her so damn bad, his dick throbbed with need. "You were made for me."

"Yes. I wouldn't have it any other way. You bastard." They both burst out laughing.

"Black and gold is what we are, Majesty… You and me. Don't resist. My beautiful Black Queen is by my side, and her Gold King has her front and back. Always. It's us against the world, baby!"

SAAAAALUTE! Amor de Rey!

SANTORINI, GREECE WAS one of the most beautiful places Majesty had ever seen.

She rolled on the white and blue sheets, which felt so cool against her skin. Bags of goodies were against the wall from the late afternoon shopping, and she was giddy with excitement. Viper was talking in Spanish to his mother on the phone in the adjoining room. They'd only been there one day for their seven-night honeymoon at the Anastasis Apartments, so they were still a little jetlagged. However, they didn't let that stop them from going out and looking around before the sun set. They had dinner plans but before they proceeded, she'd called Troy and checked in. He was staying with her sister, having a great time.

Viper returned and pulled his shirt off, tossing it on an accent chair, then proceeded to go brush his teeth. Putting the television on mute, Majesty closed her eyes and took it all in. There'd been so much going on, so many things that still needed doing. Such as getting the rest of her things moved over to Viper's house. There wasn't a lot left, but she wanted Marie to begin moving in there, as per their agreement. Viper's business was booming, and he'd had to work late up until the last second before they'd left to ensure that he felt comfortable leaving his staff alone with the dogs under his care. She had a lot of learning to do regarding her new position at a big company that specialized in manufacturing sports equipment; the nice salary came with a large learning curve. Viper made enough money and she didn't have to work, but she wanted to—something her mother still couldn't under-stand but seemed to be learning to respect.

She took a deep exhale, forcing herself to just relax and enjoy the moment. When she opened her eyes, Viper was standing in front of her, butt ass naked. She rose from the bed, leaning on her elbows.

"Viper, as soon as the plane landed, you tried to jump on me. We were both exhausted, so I said we're going to have an amazing, wonderful time this evening. I've got candles, black lingerie, my little bullet like you to use on me and—"

"No, I don't want to hear it. I'm not waiting any longer. We can do all of that, but I want some pussy right now."

"Viper, come on! Stop being a baby!" She laughed. "It's not like I was saving it for my wedding night. You're being silly."

"I don't care that we've been fucking this entire time. I don't want to wait until tonight to get my first honeymoon sex session. You told me you were tired, so I left you alone, but then I saw you shopping and having all the energy in the world this afternoon. Spending up our money." He laughed. "So now, you're about to give me what's mine. Open up for business…"

"I hate how my body wants you, but I want to sock you with my fist!"

Looking thoroughly amused, he lay on top of her, then stretched her arms up above her head and clasped their hands together, intertwining their fingers. He lavished her with needy kisses and grinded his groin against hers, forcing her sundress up her body. She sighed with want as he removed her panties and cast them aside.

"Shit…"

He wasted no time tasting her love. She moved in rhythm with the twists and turns of his tongue, cursing him and loving him at the same time.

"Cum in my mouth, Queen. Let me taste that fucking honey…"

Viper worked his long, fat tongue against her clit, then up and down until she shattered. She screamed and shook, losing her mind.

Before she came down from the high, he crawled up her body and slid the sundress off her trembling form, not giving a damn that she was weak and unable to focus. He wanted to have her… and have her he would. Gripping her hips, he yanked her towards the bottom of the bed, then draped her legs over his shoulder. She watched listlessly as he gripped his big, long dick and plunged it deep inside of her.

"OH, GOD!"

A deep growl escaped his lips when he slammed into her, fucking her ruthlessly… as if he wanted to meld his body to her's by sheer effort. He paused to kiss her ankle, then started up again, pounding the hell out of her pussy.

"You're mine, baby. This is *my* pussy! You like this dick, don't you? You love it, love how I beat up your pussy, don't you, baby?"

"Yes! Fuck me, Viper! Fuck me with that big dick!"

He moved faster, balls deep, and pivoted his body in just the right way to hit her zones and drive her crazy. Soon, she was hit with another orgasm.

Both drenched in sweat, they kissed languorously, then he turned her over on her stomach and rammed into her so hard, she had to hold the sheets and bite into the pillow for leverage. She loved every nasty thrust, every painfully pleasurable plunge, every tender kiss. After a while, he turned her on her side, opening her legs like a pair of scissors. He fucked her in an upward motion, so deep, damn near touching her heart. The way he looked into her eyes let her know he'd meant what he'd said: She belonged to him, but in the most beautiful of ways. He slowed down, making love to her nice and slow now, gently stroking her cheek, kissing her lips, fingering her hair out of her face.

Then he rolled her onto her back and claimed her again, the ruthlessness of his thrusts rendering her speechless. She gasped for air as she clung to him. Long white nails digging into his shoulders. He kissed her passionately, with all of his being, and lavished her face and neck with pecks. But through it all he never slowed. His hips moved from left to right, back and forth, as if he were dancing, gliding with precision inside her flowing river. His lips parted and his Adam's apple bobbed. She knew that look, that feeling. He was near...

Cradling her head, he groaned against her lips as he filled her with warm cum, his body spasming violently.

They lay down nestled against each other, as one, his dick still inside her, twitching every now and again. His body was so heavy yet comforting against hers. His rapid breathing decelerated. After a while, he kissed her on the cheek and went to the restroom while she waited, feeling lazy and in love. Feeling things she'd never imagined possible. When he came back, he was drying off his hands, then went to the luggage rack to get himself a pair of boxers and some nice pants. She enjoyed watching him dress, loving the way his gold and diamond wedding band looked against his skin, and especially, her tattooed name that was now right over his heart, with a queen's crown above it.

"I'm starting to get hungry. Dinner reservation you made is at six, right, baby?" he asked, breaking the silence as he buttoned up a black shirt.

"Yes. The restaurant is called Misteli." He nodded,

then sat on the edge of the bed and put on his socks. "This doesn't even seem real, does it, Viper? It's like we're in paradise."

"I was thinking the same thing. I always wanted to come to Greece. I'm glad you suggested it for our honeymoon." He turned around and kissed her forehead, then reached for his watch. He started to put it on but then paused, his gaze roving up and down her body, paying special attention to her hips, pussy, and breasts.

"What? I have a few minutes before I need to start getting ready."

"I suggest you get ready *now*, or we'll miss dinner."

"Look, just because I've been late a few times for our dates in the past doesn't mean—"

"No, you don't understand. Majesty, you have no idea how much you turn me on. Put on some damn clothes or we'll never leave here tonight. Real talk." He walked out of the room, and she knew the sex-crazed man was dead serious. Giggling, she headed to the bathroom to clean up. A tap sounded on the door.

"Yes, baby?" she called out, the sink water on full blast as she washed her face.

"This feels like paradise to us because it is. You're my everything, Majesty. There's nothing you need that I won't make sure you have, nothing you want that I won't turn the world inside out to provide for you. There's only one thing I can't ever do… and that's give you up."

With that, he walked away…

EPILOGUE

Three and a half years later...

TROY CLUTCHED THE video game controller, his headset on, and his eyes focused on the large computer in his room.

"Yes, Mama, yes! I'll do it right after this! I promise! BOOM! I got you!" he cheered. Viper looked on through his open office door, where he sat going over some invoices. He watched his wife look around Troy's room that was in desperate need of a cleanup. "And I need you to walk the dogs. Poor Belleza had that surgery, and you know she can't walk as fast but likes being outside."

"I'll walk the dogs, Mama, I promise. Just give me a minute... HA! Yo, Eric, watch out! They're right behind you!"

He'd been holed up in there for a while, talking to his friends on that headset and glaring at the big, oversized computer screen that, as Majesty put it, showed nothing but him blowing up things, and plenty of blood and guts.

Suddenly, Majesty's face turned sullen. He knew what the issue was. She'd been rather emotional about it lately. Troy wasn't a baby anymore. He'd just turned 13, and his voice had begun to drop. He was much taller, too. The baby face he'd had when he'd met him was gone, and his biggest concerns were his grades, video games, and some girl named Makayla Ackerson.

Soon after the wedding, Viper had asked Troy for permission to legally adopt him. Troy had been ecstatic about that, jumping into his arms with joy. Then, during the adoption process, Majesty had told him how the boy's name had actually been her mother's suggestion since the woman had expressed a desire to name her grandson. Majesty had obliged to make her happy, but then only through a recent discussion with her mother did she discover that Troy had been his mother-in-law's biological father's name. The man she'd found. The one person she'd adored yet lost far too soon. And now that her relationship with her mother had opened up more, she appreciated the love Mama always showered on Troy. Because that, if little else, had *always* been real.

MAJESTY EXITED HIS room, closing the door behind her as the boy continued to yell and rave, probably not even noticing she'd walked away.

"Come here," he called out to her. She paused for a moment, then entered his office from the hall. He put down his pen and held her in his arms. "What do you want to do this weekend?"

"I haven't even thought that far. Maybe we can go on a staycation. Tampa?"

"You got it. We'll do it."

Suddenly, her cellphone binged with a text message notification.

"Oh, it's Mama. She wants me to call her right now and confirm."

"Confirm what?"

"Believe it or not, she wants all of us to come over for dinner in a couple of weeks! She's got a new chef, and she wants us to meet her new boyfriend." She laughed and rolled her eyes.

"What's wrong with that?"

"Oh, nothing. This one doesn't have much money though, and he's twenty years younger than her. She is just using him for sex. Ugh! Just the thought of it makes my skin crawl." Viper burst out laughing. "Now that Mama has all of that money from the divorce and said she's never getting married again, she's been running through men like water, getting her freak on. She had the nerve to say that she's keeping this one though, talkin' about he's packing. Gross!"

Viper shrugged. "Life is short. Let her live."

"Yeah, but it's not your mother, so it's easy for you to say that."

"Hey, my parents aren't much better! They're still married to other people while messin' around with each other. I just know it. You act like I've got 'Leave it to Beaver' going on over here. My parents are Bonnie and Clyde, only they make it a habit to rob each other instead."

Majesty broke into fits of giggles.

"That's a whooooole drama! Just messy! Your mother doesn't even seem like the type to do that! I still don't believe it. Maybe your father is lying."

"He's not. Trust me on this. My father, see, *ese es punto.* He even—" Just then, the baby monitor went off. "Look who's awake from his afternoon nap." Smiling, he got up and moved around her to go to their eight-month-old son's room. "I'll get him."

"No, I can do it. You were working," she offered.

"Go call your mother back, baby. Besides, I need a break and want to see my little man." He kissed her, then made his way to Zyair's room. He was immediately met with big hazel eyes so huge, they looked as if they belonged on a stuffed animal, and two tiny tan hands clutching the bars of his crib. Viper picked up the infant and took him over to the changing table. He pulled out a new diaper, a packet of wipes, and got everything together. Zyair looked up at him, his adorable face beaming.

"What are you smiling about, huh? Have you smelled this? You should be ashamed of yourself," he quipped. "You're lucky you're so cute." He finished cleaning and changing him, then held him to his chest. Soft black curls brushed against his chin as he cradled the baby's head. Just then, rap music started blasting from Troy's room, the dogs were barking outside in the backyard, and Majesty's faint laughter could be heard while she spoke to her mother on the phone…

He stroked Zyair's back, then kissed his crown.

A lot of shit has happened. Some bad, some great. I spent years plotting revenge on someone. That hatred in my heart led me to find love. A love like I've never known. Majesty is my angel.

Our union has helped others, too. Like, I was able to get a woman I cherish, Marie, into a much nicer home, Majesty's old house. And now, she's got a small business doing catering out of there. The perk is that Majesty, Troy, and I get fresh Cuban lunches and dinners free of charge. Majesty has never learned to cook the Cuban food exactly right. My mother brings it up, but that's okay. She makes delicious coffee, and my mother loves Majesty to death, despite her gossiping to other family members about my wife's cooking.

Pedro is back in prison. I hate that for him; he'd been doing so well. When he gets out though, I'm still going to give him a chance. I told him he has a job waiting for him. I've been trying to mentor him, explain that being a King doesn't have to mean he has to do the things he used to do, just to prove himself down for the cause. We must evolve. Mr. Earl had another stroke, but he's okay now. Majesty and I hired a nurse to come and stay with him a few hours each day, and he goes to the clubhouse and plays cards, too. He still talks about Arnette sometimes as if she's still alive. I love that... He had a marriage that I dream of. I want to be able to celebrate fifty years and counting with Majesty one day, too.

I don't judge my parents. I just don't want that drama they have, and Majesty doesn't want what her parents had, either. Her mother is rich after taking her ex-husband to the cleaners, but according to Majesty, still somewhat unhappy. Her father has had some recent health issues, a situation which has brought on guilt and depression. He feels like he wasted too much time. My mother won't divorce my stepfather; she says it would be cruel. But he can't make her happy, either. My father is actually thrilled with this crazy arrangement, but of course, he isn't the average man. He chuckled at the thought.

Business is going so well for me, I had to temporarily stop accepting new clients. Quality over quantity. I've been featured in a few magazines, too, and an Animal Rights group interviewed me, claiming I've saved over fifty dogs from death.

But best of all, I'm now a father of two. Majesty had my baby. It was a situation where neither of us were certain how we'd feel about having a child. We talked about it before we got married. I wanted children and so did she, but we were concerned about so many things, like, making the time, and I had my own fears... I didn't want any child of mine, to ever feel the terror and sadness I'd felt when my parents parted ways, although I was just as miserable when they were together. I had to handle that. Deal with it.

We never said never, so we just went with the flow. Then, it got to the point where I wanted a baby for sure. I couldn't fight it anymore. I made it crystal clear and told her straight out: "I want you to have my baby." I wanted to experience the process of my wife being pregnant and giving birth to my child, and so much more. Troy had been asking for a baby brother or sister, anyway, so after thinking it over, Majesty felt the same way I did, and so, we started trying.

It didn't take long. And now, here's my son. I have two now. My little prince, Zyair Diego Martinez, the newest member of our family. He looks like a mixture of Majesty and me. My eyes, her nose and mouth, and my ears. Our fingers are even shaped the same way. He's flawless. Majesty and I would like to have another child, too, but we'll probably wait a year or so. Three children seem like a good number for us. I know my mother would be happy. She loves having grandchildren. She loves Troy, treats him like her blood, and spoils Zyair rotten…

He walked out of the room with the baby and made his way down the steps into the kitchen. After placing the baby on a mat they kept in there, he grabbed a bottle of breast milk from the refrigerator. He picked up Zyair, who began to get antsy upon seeing the bottle.

"I know, I know, here it is." He sat down at the kitchen table, feeding him while Sarge snored in his dog bed, and he let his mind drift.

Yeah, I know what you're wondering… The answer is yes, I'm still a Latin King. The culture was taught to me at an early age; it's a way of life. Of thinking. Of following what's in your heart. It's true what they say: 'Once a Latin King, always a Latin King.' I'm active and high ranking, and I navigate both worlds well. Of course, things happen, shit that I keep away from my family. That's not their world, and it's my job to ensure it stays that way.

Majesty's not stupid though. She knows what I am and what I'm capable of. She's seen both the darkness and light in me, from the moment she spotted me in the garden, high up in the tree. She looked up at me, we locked eyes… and we both knew our fate. Regardless, she is aware she and the children come first in my life, regardless of my affiliations.

I was born this way. An O.G. once told me, gangsters are born and seldom made. Now, I'm an O.G. My father is ruthless, and so is my mother. But they know how to give and protect. Even through their craziness and dysfunction, they also showed me and Diego how to love.

I'm a husband and lover. I'm a father to two princes. I'm a son. I'm a best friend, and brother. If you hurt someone I love, then I am an enemy.

I'M A MOTHERFUCKING KING.
This is my castle. The Viper lives with, protects and
worships his queen, the Majesty.
Almighty Latin King and Queen Nation!

Amor de Rey for Life!

~The End~

MUSIC DIRECTORY
The Viper and his Majesty

1. Sylvan Lacue – Clam Chowda
2. Hector – Shooter
3. Trick Daddy feat. Lil Jon & Twista – Let's Go
4. Mellow Man – Mentirosa
5. N.O.R.E. Ft. Daddy Yankee, Nina Sky, Gemstar, and Big Mato – Oye Mi Canto
6. DMX – We Right Here
7. 50 Cent – I Get Money
8. N.O.R.E – Mas Maiz
9. Norega – I Love My Life
10. Delinquent Habits – Tres Deliquentes
11. Cypress Hill – Insane in the Membrane
12. Santana – Tales of Kilimanjaro
13. Kid Frost – La Raza
14. George Clinton – Atomic Dog
15. Doja Cat- Juicy
16. Bryson Tiller – Exchange
17. Rusherking – Ademas De Mi
18. Johnny Gibbs – Love is Blue
19. Stwo – Neither Do I
20. Mokenstef – He's Mine
21. Tony Toni Tone – Anniversary
22. Queen Naija, featuring Ari Lennox – Set Him Up
23. Cardi B and Bruno Mars – Please Me
24. Maluma – 11 PM

25. PJ Morton – Say So
26. Dvsn – Between Us (featuring Snoh Aalegra)
27. Luther Vandross – 'Don't You Know That – (chopped and screwed version)
28. Kwaye – Runaway
29. KAMAUU, (featuring Adeline & Masego) – Mango
30. Nasty C and Ari Lennox – Black and White
31. Free National- Beauty & Essex (feat. Daniel Caesar & Unknown Mortal Orchestra)
32. Lucky Daye – Access Denied
33. Q – Garage Rooftop
34. Jhené Aiko – Chilombo Medley
35. Fat Larry's Band – Act Like You Know
36. D'Angelo – Spanish Joint
37. Luis Fonsi -Despacito (featuring Daddy Yankee)
38. Machine Gun Kelly featuring blackbear – My Ex's Best Friend
39. Looking Glass – Brandy
40. Masego – Navajo
41. Doja Cat – Like That
42. Doja Cat – Rules
43. Masego's and Don Toliver – Mystery Lady
44. Sam Smith – Stay with Me (Instrumental version)
45. The Beatles – Here Comes the Sun
46. MAJOR – Why I Love You

ABOUT THE AUTHOR

USA Today bestselling author Tiana Laveen writes resilient yet loving heroines and the alpha heroes that fall for them in unlikely happy-ever-afters. An author of over 60 novels to date, Tiana creates characters from all walks of life that leap straight from the pages into your heart.

Married with two children, she enjoys a fulfilling life that includes writing books, drawing, and spending quality time with loved ones.

If you wish to communicate with Tiana Laveen and stay

up-to-date with her releases, please follow her on social media platforms as well as visit her website.

Tiana Laveen website

www.tianalaveen.com